THE SOJOURNERS

The Crockett Chronicles Book 2

JENNIFER LYNN CARY

Praise for the Crockett Chronicles

"This book is so good! If you like Christian Historical Fiction, you will love this book. It hooked me on the first page and I couldn't put it down." —Ann Ferri

"I thoroughly enjoyed the book! A big fan of Christian Historical Fiction, this one was absolutely great! Looking forward to the rest of the series!" —Amazon Customer

"I was drawn in by the idea that this series chronicles the descendants of Davy Crockett written with the fictional imagination of a direct descendant. The time period and a glimpse of the Huguenots made for an interesting story. I am excited to read more." —Jennifer Berry

"Exciting and grabs your attention from the first page! You find yourself there! A must read!" —Nova Forrest

"Excellent story of the Crockets. I could not put it down. The characters touched my heart." —Mary Rima

Also by Jennifer Lynn Cary

Available now:

The Patriarch: The Crockett Chronicles: Book 1

The Sojourners: The Crockett Chronicles: Book 2

Coming soon:

Tales of the Hob Nob Annex (May 2020)

Relentless Heart (July 2020)

Wedding Bell Blues (September 2020)

Relentless Joy (November 2020)

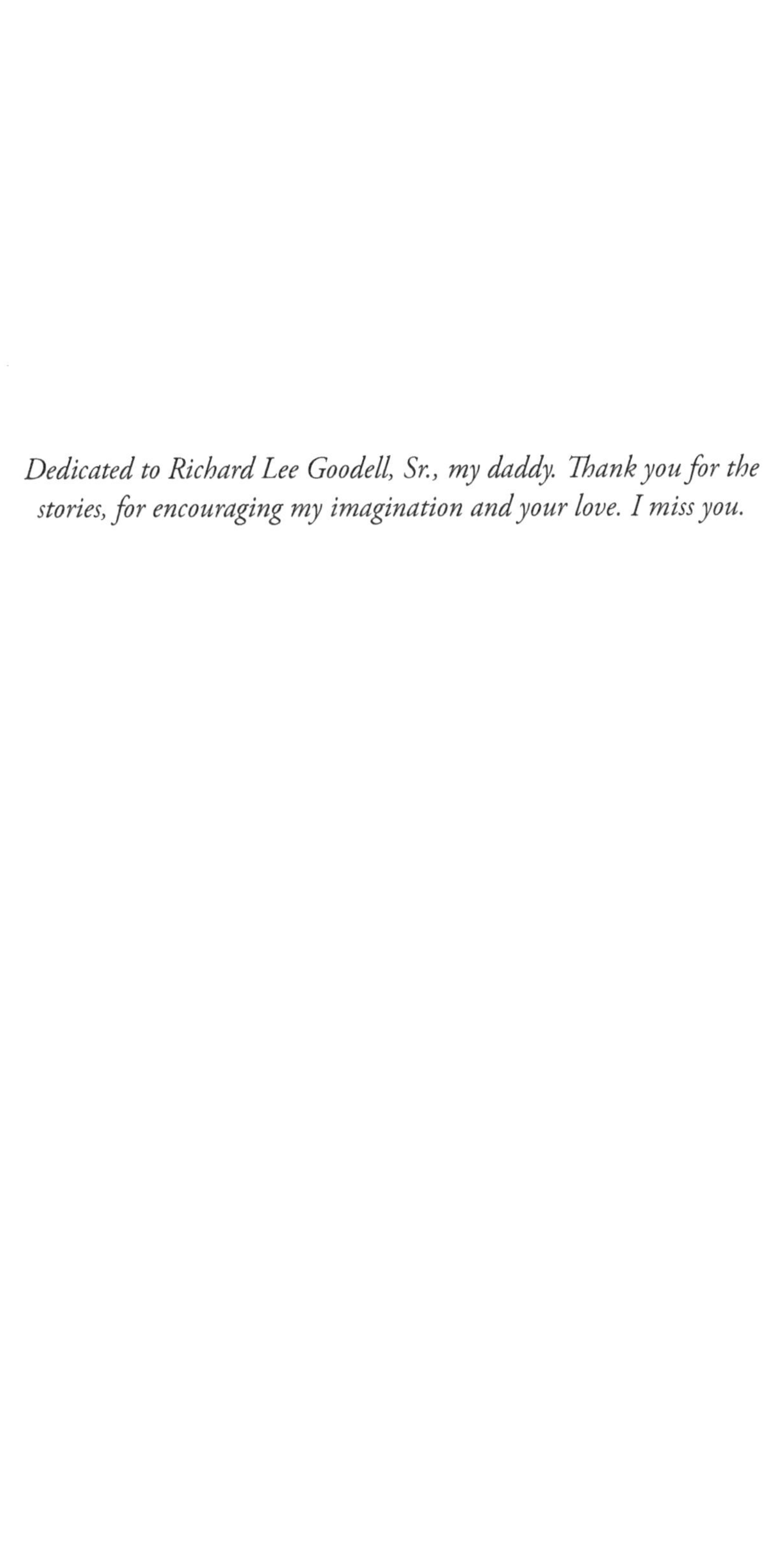

Dedicated to Richard Lee Goodell, Sr., my daddy. Thank you for the stories, for encouraging my imagination and your love. I miss you.

Trust in the Lord with all your heart, And do not lean on your own understanding. In all your ways acknowledge Him, And He will make your paths straight. Do not be wise in your own eyes; Fear the Lord and turn away from evil. It will be healing to your body, And refreshment to your bones.

— PROVERBS 3:5–8

Chapter One

County Donegal, Ireland ~ 1698

She was gone.

Joseph teetered on the brink of insanity. Could someone feel numbness and anguish at the same time? He didn't trust his mind.

Joseph could feel Father's arms. Mama softly cried. Others, heard above the rush of the wind, sniffed in dignified grief. Then everyone grew quiet. The Reverend Fontaine spoke.

He was trapped in the now, filled with all its agony, as they laid his wife to rest.

Kathleen.

Mama wept.

The wind, as it cried through the trees was the answering call to the empty wails of his heart.

"It is time, son." Father's hand rested on Joseph's back. The coffin bearing his life rested at the bottom of the grave. Yet, for him, there was no rest.

He picked up a handful of dirt. Panic inched its way to his soul. Kathleen loved being with people. Now she lay alone.

The reverend's words filtered through. Kathleen was not in

the grave. She lived with her Savior. What they buried today was an empty shell left behind by her faithful spirit.

Deep inside Joseph, the words rang true. Kathleen, free of earthly cares and woes, no longer knew pain. Rather it was his own soul sliding off faith's edge.

He unclenched his fist, letting the dirt slip through trembling fingers onto the coffin. A simple task, yet it rent Kathleen from his grasp.

He could not let her go.

Too late, he grabbed at the dirt. His hand, like his heart, remained empty. He watched the lightest of the particles drift from his fingertips to the pine box below.

Release her. Cling to Me. The voice cajoled, invoking the image of a heavenly hand reaching down to him.

The same hand that snatched Kathleen away.

"No."

He fled the cemetery.

⚜

"I ache for him, Antoine." A salty tear pooled at the corner of Louise's lips. "I understand he is a grown man, but he is still my son. My child. I want to take away his pain." She dabbed at her eyes.

"*Je sais, ma petite,* I know." Her husband drew her close. "He will need time."

Louise walked with the love of her life to their home. Others followed.

Antoine glanced over his shoulder at the entourage following them back to Edenmore, their estate. "We will have much company today." Family and friends, both young and old, gathered to pay their respects.

The manor came into view. Louise sighed. They had landed on English shores with only what they could carry. So much had happened over the past quarter century.

Antoine guided her through the door of their home—the home where her children had been raised.

"Josephine, we are arrived." Louise removed her cloak, tying on her apron before slipping upstairs to the nursery.

Josephine LeSeure, more family than servant, had remained behind this day to care for Louise's new grandson. Wee Joseph slumbered in Josephine's arms, unaware that his mother also now rested.

Louise stroked her grandson's feathery hair. He favored Joseph at that age. "How I would love to coddle you, ma petite, but I have work to do."

Leaving the babe to Josephine's care, Louise returned downstairs to examine the sideboard. *Oui*, there were enough savory oatcakes and black tea for those wanting refreshment before leaving.

By sunset, most of the callers were gone. That is, except for Sarah Stewart. As far as Louise was concerned, she might as well be one of her brood. As Louise watched the girl help her daughters put the house to rights, she was struck by how the freckle-faced tomboy who could outrun the boys bloomed into a willowy and spirited young woman.

While the guests departed, Louise noted the lass slipped upstairs, presumably to check on Wee Joseph. Now that all the visitors were gone, Sarah sat in the nursery rocking the baby, cooing in his ear.

"*Merci*, Sarah. I thank you for all your help today." Louise leaned over the young woman's shoulder, looking on her grandson again for the hundredth time.

"I'm glad to help. He's so…small." Sarah turned a misty glance at Louise, and then back to Wee Joseph. "I need to be telling ye something."

Louise waited. Sarah's profile showed her fine bone structure and classic features. All were enhanced by delicate freckles and rogue tendrils of russet-tinged hair. Oui, she had grown into a beauty.

Sarah continued to focus on the baby. "Kathleen and me, we had a talk about a week ago. Back then I told her it was stuff and nonsense, but now I'm thinking she might have known something like this could be." She rocked slower as she spoke.

"About what did you speak, dear heart?"

"We'd been going through all the wee things she made, and our talk turned to whether the babe was to be a boy or girl. She turned to me and she says, 'Oh, I know tis a boy.' 'Oh, ye do,' says I, and she says, 'Aye, he'll be a fine, strapping boy and we'll name him after his father.'"

Sarah's voice grew taut. "Then she says to me, 'Sarah, if something should go wrong…' I stopped her and said nothing would go wrong, but she held up a hand. 'If something goes wrong, please tell me you will care for me men. Both of them. Promise me. Joseph won't be knowing what to do, and this babe will be needing ye.' 'You're talking foolishness,' says I, but she says, 'Promise me, and I'll be talking no more foolishness.'" Sarah's voice softened to barely a whisper. "I told her 'Aye, I promise,' and we spoke of it no more."

Continuing to rock, she took a slow breath before turning to meet Louise's gaze. "Now I have a promise to keep." Tears ran down her cheeks, glistening in the firelight.

A glimmer of hope flickered in the darkness of Louise's grief. Perhaps in the flurry of Sarah's words was the answer to her prayers for Joseph.

Bending, she kissed the top of Sarah's head. "Never in all my days have I known a more loving person than you, Sarah Stewart."

◈

The wind pushed Robert Crockett along, hurrying him like some dilly-dallying child. In many ways, Robert saw himself that way and didn't like it. Here he was, at twenty years of age, still running errands for his mother.

Of course, he would have done it without her asking, if only he'd thought of it first.

Lights peeked through the cracks of the Stray Dog, gleaming slashes against the dark. A *shebeen*, though barely a pub and little more than a stall, it had hosted many a celebration. The Stray Dog was a handy place for the men of the area to share their news, give advice, and drown their sorrows. The host, a discreet little man with a pleasant grin and a mildly shady repute, went by the name of Cullen O'Keefe. With a heart as big as his girth, he served Catholics and Protestants alike. Most turned a deaf ear to the rumors concerning Cullen's past and considered the Stray Dog an oasis of truce.

Another time, Robert would have heard Cullen call out a hearty greeting and ask, "What'll it be, lad?"

Tonight, though, he just gave Robert the briefest of nods and motioned with a quick shake of his balding head to a back table.

Robert followed the direction, finding what he'd expected. Ignoring the chatter and the sour smell, he made his way through the less than half-filled room to his brother.

Joseph's hands were buried under his dark mane. The golden bottle of whiskey at his elbow emptied. His brother made little sounds, more like a child's cry than drunken snoring.

Robert pulled up a crate and sat, wondering if he should wake him or let Joseph sleep it off. Apparently, the liquor had failed to alleviate his suffering. Even in his stupor, Joseph reeked of devastation.

A noisy entrance across the room drew Robert's attention. A swirl of auburn hair stormed in. "What in the world is Sarah doing here?"

Most of the regular patrons held their tongues in respect for the lass, but one drunken lout pushed up from his bench by the hearth and staggered toward her.

"Aye, an' looky what the wind's blown in, laddies. Come on o'er here an' give us a kiss, lass."

"Twill be the back of my fist ye'll be kissing, Christopher Dougherty, or maybe ye should be thinking more about the hands ye should be kissing if your sainted wife finds out how yer talking to me."

Sarah's retort only added fuel to Christopher's fire, but all he could do was stutter and sputter.

Robert sprang to Sarah's side, beating some of his neighbors to her defense. He overheard Christopher muttering something about a tren targer as Robert steered Sarah toward Joseph's table. There were many things he could think of to call Sarah at this moment, but that wasn't one of them.

"What are ye doing here?" He grabbed her elbow and whispered in her ear. "This here's no place for the likes of you."

"I can handle meself, Robert Crockett." Sarah hissed back. "I've come to find Joseph and take him home."

"Then we're of the same mind." He led her to the table Joseph held down with his head.

"Well, what are ye waiting for? Ye take one side. I'll take the other, and we'll *oxtercog* him out of here. "

Robert sighed, and with Sarah's help, struggled to haul Joseph to his feet.

Sarah gritted her teeth and glanced at Robert. "Maybe tis a blessing we both came looking."

Robert merely grunted.

Out cold, Joseph gave no resistance or help at all. His arms slid to his sides as gravity pulled his body toward the floor.

Finally, with Cullen's assistance, Robert flung one of Joseph's arms around his neck and Sarah did the same.

Joseph's head lolled from side to side as they maneuvered three abreast around tables and benches.

Cullen held open the door. The wind threatened to tear the plank off its hinges.

Robert stumbled out with his load into the nearly starless night, dragging Sarah along on Joseph's other side. The door shut tight behind them, and at once the world became black.

Howling winds made it too difficult to talk. That didn't stop Robert from berating himself with every step for not thinking to bring a wagon. Drunk like this, Joseph was as heavy as an ox. He surely must be a strain on Sarah, although she never complained. Perhaps the wind kept her complaints at bay.

What was she doing here in the first place?

Robert knew why he was here. He was the dutiful son, responsible now that Gabriel studied in Glasgow and Joseph no longer resided at home. That left James as the only other brother at home, yet he wasn't there either. How did that big brother get elected the family messenger? One by one, Robert's brothers, all grown men, made their way into the world and left him behind. He could feel the familiar resentment begin to rise.

But he had no time to dwell on it. The faint outline of the two-room stone cottage Joseph built for his bride came into view. Robert needed to get the three of them inside.

After he fumbled with the door until the latch gave, he shoved it open with his shoulder. They stumbled in, struggling to get Joseph the last few yards to the bedroom. Despite Robert's best efforts to be gentle, Joseph dropped with a thud on the bed.

Sarah turned her back and lit a lamp while Robert undressed his brother.

He drew a handmade quilt over Joseph's intoxicated form. "I'll fetch something to get this fire started. You'll stay with him?" Robert knew the answer even as he spoke.

"Aye, I'll be keeping watch." Sarah brought the lamp closer to the bedside.

He paused at the door, observing as she pulled a three-legged stool next to Joseph. With a shake of his head, he left.

Silence filled the room. Sarah, fists opening and closing at her side, viewed the sleeping figure of her childhood friend. Joseph had always been her favorite of the Crockett brothers. "Aye, and ye still are, Joseph." He didn't stir, so she braved more whispers. "I always could tell ye my secrets. And since ye are asleep, I'll tell ye one more." Her gaze traveled to the doorway and back. "I've kept every letter ye sent me while ye were away to school."

She had memorized each one from reading them a thousand times over.

"Oh, Joseph, why my cousin? Why Kathleen? I loved her like a sister. Never will ye know how ye killed me inside."

Sarah had silently watched while Joseph and Kathleen married and began a family, dying a thousand deaths it seemed. And now? Now she had this promise to keep.

This would be so much harder than she thought.

She squeezed her eyes shut, took a deep breath, and slowly counted to ten. It was an old trick she used to handle her temper, one she should have remembered back at the Stray Dog. Only this time, it wasn't her temper that was out of control.

Slowly she let out her breath and glanced about the room. Spotting a bucket, she set it on the floor beside the bed.

Just in case.

And because sitting still only made things worse.

Lamplight carved shadows over Joseph's face, making him look older that his twenty-two years. His beard showed coarse on his hollowed cheeks. A sable-colored forelock tumbled across his brow. The sight tore at her heart.

He stirred and mumbled.

She leaned forward and brushed damp curls from his face.

Raising his arms, he pulled her to him, his azure eyes glassy. "Kathleen."

Her soul ached at his touch.

"I'm not Kathleen, Joseph."

Instantly his eyes focused, his face flushed. As if she had burned him, he jerked his hands from her. "Oh, God." A sob choked his voice, followed by the heartbreak of another. And another.

Unsure of what to do, she moved to the edge of the bed and held Kathleen's husband.

She was still consoling him when Robert brought in the peat.

After giving her a sympathetic nod, the younger brother went to the hearth. Moments later, the earthy smoke of the fire seeped into the room. She could hear him brush his hands over his breeches before taking a seat in the front room.

When at last Joseph's grief had spent itself, she eased him back to the pillows. Restless sleep claimed him.

She wiped his face once more and drew the coverlet over him. Then she moved into the front room with Robert and eased herself into the rocking chair Joseph had made for Kathleen.

"What happened?" Robert leaned back with his eyes closed. "I thought he was out for the night."

"Nothing. He just thought me Kathleen 'til he saw the truth of it." And it broke his poor heart. "He's out for the night now, I'm thinking."

"Aye." Robert sighed. "Still, twill be a long night."

She nodded, sure his prophetic words were understated.

"So why were you at the Stray Dog?" He almost sounded uninterested, but not quite.

Sarah had asked herself that question more than once. "I overheard Ann Wallace carrying on about how Joseph had run off. I didn't want yer mother to worry."

In truth, Sarah hadn't wanted to worry.

"She wasn't worried. She sent me." Now a touch of irritation crept into his voice.

"Oh." Well, she wasn't about to explain about the promise she'd made to Kathleen. Robert would never *ken*.

And he might tell Joseph.

She leaned back in the rocker and closed her eyes.

"Twill be a long night."

THE PEACHY-PINK FINGERS OF DAWN PULLED THE SUN UP over the eastern horizon as Sarah cracked opened her eyes. She rubbed her sore neck and gazed about the room.

Robert still slept in his chair, looking remarkably like his brother, only without the etched pain.

She noticed his blanket before realizing that she too was covered. He must have put a quilt over her and taken one for himself while she dozed.

She stretched and stood. Wrapping the coverlet about her, Sarah walked over to stir the fire and start the water for tea. That done, she tiptoed outside, breathing in the crisp morning air.

This was her favorite time of day. Most days she reveled in the newness. Today her heart was sore.

Robert came out and joined her.

She suddenly wished she'd taken time to rebraid her hair. Loose as it was, it must be as wild as a lion's mane. "What say we let him get all the sleep he can? I'll fix us something to eat." She needed to do something, anything.

"Aye." He stared at the horizon.

She went back inside, poured them each a cup of tea, bringing his to him. "The *brochan* will be ready in two shakes of a lamb's tail." She retraced her steps.

After making her hair more presentable, she prepared the porridge. Then she folded the borrowed blankets and put them away while it cooked.

Kathleen always kept a tidy home.

When the porridge was ready, she called to Robert but received no answer. The only sign he had been there was the empty cup resting on the sill.

"Now how am I to keep a watch on Joseph here and still go to take care of Wee Joseph?" She brought in the cup.

Her hope that Robert would stay with his brother while she went for the baby was postponed for the time being. She wasn't too concerned, though. What with his grandmother and Josephine, not to mention his three new aunts—Lucy, Mary Frances, and Sarah Beth—that little one would receive a lot of attention.

The sound of blankets being thrashed brought her to see to her ward. Joseph sat on the edge of the bed, elbows posted on knees, his hands clutching his head.

She averted her eyes from those long legs.

"Morning, Joseph." That was too happy. *Don't sound so happy.*

He minutely turned his head to the side, peering at her from the corner of his eye. "What are you doing here?"

She winced. "I'm here to help."

"Not s'loud, woman. Where're my pants?" He waved off her explanation. "Just point."

Obediently, she indicated where Robert had tossed them, then left the room.

A minute later Joseph stood in the doorway, needing the support of the doorpost.

"Sit and I'll dip ye up some brochan." She held up a ladleful.

One look, however, and he retreated to the bedroom.

She could hear the bucket being used. Perhaps porridge hadn't been the best idea.

Soon he staggered back, this time making it as far as the front door. He stood on the threshold, leaning against the post.

She brought him a cuppa.

He took the tea, tried a sip or two. "Thanks."

She waved her hand. "'Tis nothing." The awkward silence became unbearable as she rocked back and forth onto her toes. "I'll be in the kitchen." So it was a cowardly retreat. After last night, what might he be thinking?

The porridge pot bubbled, so she stirred and moved it away from the flame before gathering up the things to be washed. All the while she kept an ear out for Joseph.

However, after an extended quiet, she peered around the door.

She was now alone at the cottage. Oh, that man. Sarah plopped in the rocker. Just like his brother. There one minute and gone the next. Not even a thank you for sleeping in a chair all night or keeping watch. Nothing. Why did those Crockett men have to always be going somewhere?

She rocked harder. She should have just let the ungrateful oaf suffer. Except, God help her, it hurt to see someone suffer. Especially when she cared for that someone very much.

A tear dripped off the end of her nose as she pulled the rocker to a halt. She swiped it away. She would not cry. It had been foolish to think she might ease the man's pain.

However, there was Wee Joseph to think about. No matter what, she wouldn't—couldn't—go back on her promise to his mother.

God, what should I do?

Sarah listened but heard no answer. Pulling her shattered pride and feelings together, she rose. Who knew better how to handle Joseph than his mother? She would speak to Mistress Crockett.

For Wee Joseph's sake.

Chapter Two

Louise heard the carriage. It was a bit premature in the day to be receiving. After all that the family had been through, it was poor taste to be arriving at this early hour. She peeked between the lace curtains of the nursery window, and recognized Sarah's parents.

Josephine would show Thomas and Margaret Stewart to the parlor.

Louise frowned and hurried downstairs. They wouldn't be here without reason.

The Stewarts and Crocketts had been neighbors for more than twenty years. As the children grew, it was a sure thing that if you could not find one of your own, it was because he or she enjoyed the company of the other family.

All this being said, it was still out of the ordinary.

"Meg, Thomas, is something amiss?" Louise hurried into the room, straight to her friends. "Please sit, will you not?" She indicated the brocade sofa, taking a chair for herself.

"Nothing is wrong…" Thomas began.

"At least we're not believing so." Meg's glance darted toward the stairs. "We've come to retrieve Sarah. Perhaps she stayed last night? Is she up yet?"

"I am sorry, but Sarah did not spend the night here." Upon seeing the worried expressions of her friends, she paused. "At least, I do not believe so. It is possible she is in with one of the girls. Let me check. *Excusez-moi.*" She left, closing the parlor door behind her.

Halfway up the steps, she heard her name.

"Mistress Crockett, might I speak with ye?"

Louise discovered the missing girl at the foot of the stairs.

"Sarah. I am so glad to find you. Your parents are in the parlor. They are worried for you."

"I dinnae want them to worry. I just need to speak with ye, if ye have the time."

"For you, sweet girl, oui, I have time. But first, we must let them know you are safe." She brought Sarah back into the parlor.

Meg rushed to her daughter. Thomas put his arms around them both, guiding them toward the front door. "We're sorry to have inconvenienced ye, Louise," he said over his shoulder. "We'll be going now, and we thank ye."

"No, Da." Sarah pulled to a stop. "I need to speak with the Mistress. Tis important."

Thomas moved closer to whisper in his youngest daughter's ear, though Louise could still hear. "We've some important matters to discuss, Sarah. I think you'd best be coming along." He took hold of her elbow and again tried to steer her to the door.

Sarah could be quite stubborn, a trait come by honestly from her father.

"*Pardonnez-moi,* but I believe I hear the baby. Would you like to speak here in the parlor while I see to him?" The baby made a lovely excuse.

Meg smiled in return, sitting back on the sofa. "Aye, thank ye, Louise."

Louise winked at Meg and headed for the stairs.

MAMA PATTED THE CUSHION NEXT TO HER.

Sarah scrutinized her father and then her mother. Finally, she sat.

Before Sarah could stop her, Mama took hold of her hand. "We know this has been a difficult time for ye, daughter. Ye and Kathleen were as close as sisters. But we're worried. We had a visitor last night and then, when ye didn't come home, we want to get to the bottom of this." Mama's face lacked her usual smile.

"What visitor?"

Da's finger shook in the air. "Never ye mind that. Where were ye last night, Sarah?"

She should have known her father would be upset. But she had not done anything wrong, so she told the truth.

"I was standing watch over Joseph."

"Alone?" Mama gasped.

"No, Robert was with me."

"You spent the night alone with two men?" Now Da's voice held a dangerous growl.

"Aye, one was heartsick and drunk stupid. The other worried sick over his brother. Neither had eyes for me, I can tell ye that much. Twas Joseph and Robert for goodness sake." Her blood temperature dangerously rose.

"And what made ye think that any daughter of mine would be *allowed* to be passing the night with two grown men, no matter what condition they were in?"

"I was keeping a promise."

"What promise?" Her parents spoke simultaneously, Da's voice gruff, but her Mama's tone gentle.

"I made a promise to Kathleen, God rest her soul, a week ago. She asked me to care for Joseph and the babe should anything happen to her." Sarah eyed her skirt, smoothing the wrinkles and objections away. "I agreed to it thinking she was nervous about the baby coming so soon. But, now, I've made it and I must keep it."

Her parents glanced at each other.

She knew she pushed. But she must keep it, whatever it took.

"I'm sure Kathleen did not foresee ye sleeping in her home in order to keep that promise." Da paused, shoving his hand through his gray hair, a color he swore was Sarah's doing. It was a sure sign he'd made his decision. "Ye will be coming home each night before dark, after doing what it is you need to be doing to keep yer word. Are we clear on that?"

"Aye, Da." Sarah focused on the floor. Obedience came much easier, having won the argument.

"And ye will keep Bridget with you."

Her head snapped up. The housekeeper's daughter playing her shadow? "Da."

"And, no daughter o' mine will be traipsin' through the likes of the Stray Dog for all the neighbors to see."

"How did you…Aye, Da." Sometimes it was better to just accept one's victories and let sleeping stray dogs lie. She bit her lip to keep back the smile. Besides, it wouldn't be that difficult to get rid of Bridget should she get in the way.

"Now that all this is settled, let's be going home before we end up wearin' out Louise's hospitality."

"Da, I told ye, I need to be speaking with the mistress. I canna be going now."

Da wavered, his expression softening.

She stood on tiptoe and kissed his cheek. He really was a dear when he wanted to be.

"Then come soon. And, remember, ye'll be spendin' tonight and each night at home. I'll have no more gossip out there about me daughter."

"Aye, Da." Sarah hugged them both. Closing the door after them, she leaned against the post to think.

She would never want Kathleen's memory besmirched, nor

her parents or Joseph dishonored by mean-spirited gossip. Still, she couldn't go back on her word. With a sigh of resignation, Sarah headed back into the parlor.

Mistress Crockett came down the stairs. "Is everything now agreeable, ma petite?"

Sarah nodded.

"And you wanted to speak with me?"

"Aye, if ye have the time." She hoped Joseph's mother could read the growing urgency in her eyes. If she didn't get this talked out soon, it might explode inside her.

"Let us sit in here and you can speak to me." Mistress Crockett motioned toward the settee. "One thing, though…"

"Aye, Mistress?" What now?

"There will be no more of the 'mistress' talk. You are a grown woman. We have known each other too long, and have been too close, for you to address me as 'mistress.' You may call me Louise."

"*Och*, but that wouldn't be fitting. I don't think I could bring myself to do that."

"Well, then, why not Tanté Louise. It would be nice to have someone refer to me as tanté. I cannot think of anyone I would rather hear call me that than you, Sarah. Are we agreed?" The mistress took Sarah's hand and gave a gentle squeeze.

"Aye, Mist…I mean Tanté Louise." Sarah took a deep breath, then plunged ahead. "Tanté, I've been thinking about my promise to Kathleen. I mean to keep it, only the problem is I'm not sure how. I hadn't thought taking care of a friend would cause so much trouble. Of course, if I had thought about it instead of just doing it, I might have realized the implications, and thought of another plan." She gave a rueful smile. "I don't want to be casting aspersions on those I love, or Joseph, or Kathleen's memory, but I *will* keep this promise." She paused and searched the Mistress's face. "So, how do I do that, Tanté Louise? What should I do?"

"Sarah, ma petite, I do not know how to answer. Shall we pray about this?"

"Right now?"

"Can you think of a better time? Here, let me take your hands."

She let Tanté Louise take her hand and listened.

"Dear Father, thank You for the loving and loyal heart of this sweet child. I pray that You would fill her with Your wisdom and discernment to guide and direct her along the path You have for her. May Your love pour through her generous heart and onto those she serves so selflessly. Lord, she is unsure of what You would have her to do to keep her promise. We ask that You show us where to start and be her guide as she continues her course. And, Lord, may she be blessed as she blesses those around her. Help her to do as You would do. In Jesus's Holy Name we pray, amen."

Sarah echoed the *amen*. She sat enveloped in the quiet. The person Tanté Louise described in her prayer seemed nothing like anyone Sarah knew. Given her feelings for Joseph, it would be hard to say she was working from a purely generous position.

As Tanté Louise continued to sit with closed eyes, Sarah began to worry. What was on her mind? Would she ask about Joseph? Would Sarah then have to tell her about the whiskey, and how she and Robert had found him at the Stray Dog?

When she finally raised her head, Tanté Louise smiled and patted Sarah's hand. "Dear heart, please know we would love for you to spend time with our wee one. You may come and rock him and play with him here at the house anytime until Joseph is ready to bring him home. And as for Joseph—"

Sarah knew what was coming. She wasn't needed. Joseph didn't need anything but his family's help. Her muscles tensed for the blow.

"If you make sure he eats and has clean clothes, you will be doing an enormous service. You can send laundry here to the house. I will see that it gets done with the rest of the clothes of the family. You may need to visit our larder, too, as I am sure food will start running low before Joseph thinks a thing about it."

Tanté Louise sighed. "I wish I knew how I could get him to take his meals here with us, but I know him. He will want his privacy. The most help you can be to my son is to listen. He is a tough one to get to talk, that one, but you have been a friend for as long as any of us can remember." She gave Sarah's hand a little squeeze. "If he will talk with anyone, it will be with you. Just listen. That will be better than giving advice and will help the most."

The ideas brought hope, and a starting place. "Thank you, Tanté, thank you. I'm thinking we have a plan, now."

"*Bon.* I noticed Wee Joseph waking when I was upstairs. Would you like to hold him?"

"Oh, aye. That I would." She wrapped her arms around the older woman and gave her a peck on the cheek. The mistress, rather Tanté Louise straightened her back, but then a smile lit her face as she patted Sarah's arm.

"Let us go see that sweet grandson of mine." Tanté Louise led the way up the stairs.

Walking behind her, Sarah could hear the softly whispered prayer, "Lord, let the words of my mouth be the words of Your heart."

❧

ROBERT FELT HIS BROTHER'S PRESENCE BEFORE HE HEARD or saw anything. There was something about Joseph that you could feel his presence, not that he was loud. If anything he was staid. But one knew when he was there.

Joseph stood at the barn's entrance.

"I already looked in on the sheep, so I thought I'd see if there was anything else I could do." Robert returned to the task at hand. An old harness had captured his attention. He'd soon have it repaired.

"Thanks." Short and curt.

"If you'd rather I wasn't here…" The hangover most likely limited Joseph's words, but if he wanted to be alone, Robert could give his brother some room.

"No, stay. I'm not much in the way of talking. But you can stay." Joseph stood in the doorway, staring into space.

"I'm surprised you're up already." Robert rehung the harness. "I was sure the whiskey had you out until noon."

"The sleep was fine. The dreams I could have done without."

"Aye." Robert knew better than to say he understood. He didn't. He knew he didn't, and God willing, he never would. "How is the wee one this morning?"

"I haven't been over to the house. I probably should. I just don't know if I can."

So low were the words, Robert wondered if he'd really heard.

JOSEPH BLINDLY REACHED OUT FOR ANYTHING THAT MIGHT busy his hands. His confession was barely more than a thought. But once spoken aloud, he wished the floor would open up and swallow him. He was a father now, the only parent his son had. It was his duty to go to see him.

That's what haunted him. It was all he felt for the baby right now. Duty. If he tried to feel more, would he hate the little life that had cost his wife hers? Would he love him too much, and then lose him like he had Kathleen? He kicked at the straw. With very little effort he could go mad and tear the place apart. An acid more powerful that any sense of duty boiled and bubbled within him, ready to pour out on those around. If he didn't keep it locked down.

More for Kathleen's sake than anything else, he made himself leave Robert and the barn and begin walking to his parents' home. He steeled himself to handle the onslaught of pity he knew awaited. There would be those with advice and those with questions. But the worst would be the eyes full of pity.

He lumbered along, working to clear his mind. *Do not think. Do not look about. Just go.*

Joseph's desire to feel nothing fought against what lay locked inside. He couldn't imagine living without Kathleen, which meant his own death must be eminent. If only it would come quickly, maybe then he could find peace.

Put one foot in front of the other. That's all he had to do. Keep one foot in front of the other. He became so focused on this exercise he nearly walked past his destination. Coming in through the front, he hoped fewer people would see him. However, the parlor was empty and what sounds there were, muffled and quiet, came from the back by the kitchen. He mounted the stairs to the old nursery and pushed opened the door.

The vision captured his breath. He ran his hand over his eyes. Sarah sat in the rocker holding his tiny son, singing, while Mother gazed on, stroking the downy fluff on his little head. Sunshine streamed through the window, casting halos around all three.

The only thing missing is Kathleen.

The unbidden thought pierced his heart faster, deeper than any dagger.

Both Sarah and his mother glanced up.

He refused to be seen as pathetic.

With a hand on the doorknob, Joseph raised his other—half in salute, half to ward off their onslaught of compassion—and then left.

He was down the stairs and out the door in an instant, hoping Sarah hadn't caught sight of him.

She had.

He knew she would follow.

She did.

Faster. Move faster.

It didn't matter. Soon Sarah paced beside him, matching him stride for stride. She remained wordless, keeping up the tempo.

They traveled for several miles, over meadows filled with spring daffodils and past sheep and lambs munching on sweet grasses. Not that he noticed much, but Joseph had lived in the Laggan his whole life. He knew this district of land in any season.

Never once did they speak.

After the first mile or so, Joseph knew where his feet took him. It brought understanding. There was a destination.

They arrived at a wild spot on a bluff overlooking Lough Swilly. Several large boulders loomed near the edge, and an ancient Celtic cross stood sentry.

Joseph moved to the brink and stared at the raging waters, made swift and deep from melting snow. "What are you doing?" The silence had lasted so long, the shock of his own voice startled him.

"What do you mean?"

"What are you doing here? Why did you come with me? Why are you with me, right now?" His voice remained quiet, in spite of his pulled-taut emotions. He couldn't look at Sarah, so he focused on the waters below.

"I thought ye might want some company." Her voice quivered.

"Why?" Joseph resisted the urge to seize her by the shoulders.

She remained mute.

He grabbed a rock and heaved it into the river. "Why are you here?"

"Joseph, yer me friend and I yers. Isn't that enough?"

Her words caught him off guard. He strode to her, face to face, staring deep into her soul.

She never flinched but stood as still as the surrounding boulders.

A steadfastness he found within her threw him a lifeline. He clutched it with everything he had left and leaned against an outcropping.

Sarah blinked and exhaled, taking a seat on a lower ledge.

He'd scared her. He'd scared himself.

She gave a timid smile and let her legs dangle.

"I don't know what to say, Sarah."

"Then dunna say anything. I dinnea know of a law that says we must talk. We can just be watching the river awhile." She scooted over making room for him.

He sighed, letting tension flow away. He dropped next to her. Leaning forward, it was as if they floated over the wild waters below. At that moment, Sarah became his safety net. He could think his thoughts, feel his pain in silence, and believe she would not let him go too far.

One more look confirmed. No pity stared back. He wasn't sure what it was he saw, but knew it wasn't pity.

It was safe, then. He was safe. They had been friends too long for him to hide his tears, so he let them fall. The river carried them away.

It was the release he needed.

Chapter Three

The house appeared peaceful as James and the other two riders approached.

They had been on the road since he'd delivered the hurriedly scribbled note from his father recalling Gabriel home. None had taken time to rest. Now that their destination was in sight, James breathed easier, his aching backside happy to get of his horse from the round trip.

He spotted a flutter of movement at an upstairs window, and heard a cry of recognition from the house, before the doors flew wide.

Open arms rushed to embrace James's big brother, not him. Of course.

"It's Gabriel." Lucy called out, but Sarah Beth reached him first. She grabbed hold of Gabriel's boot. James thought she would pull the poor man from his saddle.

Gabriel dismounted and hoisted her high. He whirled her around, before greeting his other two sisters. Finally, he turned to his mother, hugging her. "How is he?"

She shook her head and gave him a peck on the cheek before linking her arm in his, leading him to the house.

"Hey, what about us?" James hoped the smile on his face

showed he wasn't really offended. But then, in truth, he was. A little.

"I missed you, James. I'm glad you're back safe." Mary Frances tugged at his sleeve.

"And that's why you're my favorite, little one." James laughed and hugged his next to youngest sister. "Hey, big brother, you've forgotten your manners."

"You are right." Gabriel motioned to the third rider. "Ian, my apologies. Mother, this is Ian MacKenzie, my friend of whom I have written you. Ian, this—" he opened his arms wide — "is my family. The female part, at least."

His mother moved to the stranger, who had dismounted. "Sir, please forgive my rude manners. We have been longing for the return of Gabriel, and so much has happened that I have neglected to be a good hostess. Please forgive me and join us in the house for some refreshment."

James smiled at the proper English blended with the thoroughly French accent. Such music, his mother's voice.

Ian took his mother's proffered hands, bowing over them. "Tis nothing to forgive, and I would be honored to take refreshment with you."

"Bon. Let us go inside where we may sit and speak." Mother linked up between James and Gabriel, leading the way.

James's spotted his sisters, over his shoulder, chattering all at once, and nearly dragging Ian along in their attempts at making him feel welcome. A servant gathered the men's belongings and cared for the horses.

"I am thrilled you are home, son. Now all of my children are here. James, you made good time. I am thankful for your safe trip." His mother squeezed his hands. Then Lucy left to make tea.

"Was there any warning there might be a problem?" Gabriel chose to remain standing. "Kathleen always seemed so healthy."

"No, nothing like this was expected. Everything was normal until after Wee Joseph was delivered, and then the bleeding refused to stop. The little one is fine. Perfectly beautiful and fine, except for being motherless."

"In this house? I've no doubt he has more mothers than any child in all County Donegal." James winked and knuckled Mary Frances's chin. "And none better I might add."

"It is true, he receives much female attention. Widow O'Connor, from over Porthall way, is his wet nurse. She and her Wee Samuel are staying in the room off the nursery."

"Didn't she lose her husband to the fever last winter?" Gabriel asked.

"Oui." Mother's voice dropped to just above a whisper. "I desire to help her, but she is a proud woman. By caring for Wee Joseph, she does not feel she is taking charity. I do not know what we would have done without her. It is difficult on her, living in our home. I believe she harbors a fear of us, because we are not Catholic. Perhaps she worries we might cast a spell on her little one." Mother shook her head. "But I believe she is starting to trust us. She certainly loves Wee Joseph."

"May we see him?" James asked. Gabriel added his request.

"I think it should be all right." Mother stood. "Sarah is with him now."

"Sarah is here?" Gabriel asked, voicing James's thought. What was that all about?

"Oui, she comes daily to look after the baby. She also makes sure Joseph eats."

James caught the knowing glance Gabriel sent him, but neither made a comment.

"You may come too, Ian." James said. "You might as well get used to it. You are one of the family now and will have to speak up to get a word in edgewise."

"I must remember that." Ian smiled, and followed the family up the stairs.

The door opened to Widow O'Connor playing a game on the floor with her toddler while Sarah rocked the baby, crooning a soft lullaby. James couldn't help but think that, to see this, none would guess the pain that brought about this moment.

Sarah must have heard the door. She turned, and with great effusion, hopped up from the rocker to embrace both James and Gabriel with her free right arm.

"Gabriel, Jamie, when did you return?" She whispered.

"Just now. It looks like you are in your element," Gabriel whispered back. "Oh, I would like you to meet my friend, Ian MacKenzie. Ian, may I present one of my dearest childhood friends, Sarah Stewart."

Ian bowed over her free right hand.

James chuckled. "That's a pretty thing to say, especially knowing you usually were chasing her out of your hair. Childhood friend, is it? I thought it was more like childhood pest."

"Oh you." Sarah started at him, but Wee Joseph moved and made a little squeak, capturing her immediate attention. James was saved from a friendly tongue-lashing. "Oh, Joseph Louis." She pronounced Louis in the English way, using his full name. "'Tis nothing but your big uncles here to make a fuss over you. Aye, and that's right. Over here is your Uncle Gabriel. Get a good look at him. No doubt he'll be back off to Scotland before the month is out, so you will have to be committing his face to memory. And here is your Uncle Jamie. He'll be around, but I'd be taking care to watch out for him. He is as ornery as they come."

"I'm cut to the quick." James grabbed his chest and pouted, though he couldn't help smiling. "Jamie" was a childhood nickname that all but Sarah had forgotten. It warmed his heart to hear it on her lips. "Hand him here." He feigned grievance.

Sarah cautiously handed her bundle to his outstretched hands.

He cuddled the baby close. "I'll tell you some secrets, Wee Joseph, about that redheaded crooner what's had her hooks in you. She's got a whale of a temper and—"

"I do not. How dare ye fill that baby's head with such nonsense."

"—she cheats at games—"

"Not true. Not one word of it. Gabriel, won't ye defend my honor?"

"—and she's the one you need to be teaching ye how to run as she can outrun all of the lads here about."

"Well, now, that part would be true. And I'm glad ye remembered." Sarah grinned.

Wee Joseph let out a howl, and Sarah took him back. "Yer probably hungry, little one, but I wouldn't put it past that uncle of yours to have pinched ye just for orneriness."

"You wound me, lass." James grasped at his chest while Mother, Ian, and Gabriel chuckled at the exchange.

"I don't think you will ever get anything past her." Ian grinned.

"I never could." James wanted to bite his tongue at the slip. He glanced about. Only Ian seemed to have heard.

Sarah handed Wee Joseph to Bridget and then joined the group.

James followed as they left the nursery.

Noise sounded from the back of the house as they reentered the parlor. Before James could see to the cause, his father entered.

"Welcome home, Gabriel, James." He clapped them both on the back. "I'm glad you are safely returned. And who is your friend?" He extended his hand.

"Father, may I present, Ian MacKenzie. Ian, this is my father, Antoine Crockett."

"'Tis a pleasure, sir." Ian responded with a handclasp and bowed over his host's hand.

"You are the famous Ian of whom we have heard so much from Gabriel's infrequent letters." Father cleared his throat but couldn't hide his smile. "Welcome to our home."

The tea arrived. Lucy poured.

"Is this your first trip to Ireland, Ian?" Father relaxed in his favorite chair, one leg crossed over the other.

"Aye, that it is."

"Racing through the countryside is not the best way to see the Emerald Isle," Gabriel said.

"True, and there is so much beauty to see." Now they had started his father's favorite topic. James knew what was coming. "Some areas are quite civilized, where others have a wild beauty. Here in the Laggan, it is fairly flat. We have good farming areas due to Lough Swilly and the River Foyle. But a short trip north of here you'll find the Dooish Mountains. Farming there is next to impossible."

"I noticed the difference in the area as we came through." Ian leaned forward. "When we go back, I'd like to spend a wee bit o' time in Londonderry. As tis, we dinnae disembark the ship until we got near to Johnstown. I'm thinking this part of Ireland must be quite similar to the Highlands. I look forward to seeing more of her afore going back."

"We'll see to it you do, sir."

"Father, I understood the Reverend Fontaine was here for the service. Was he able to stay on a bit?" Gabriel would want to see the man, James knew.

"No, son, he headed back. It was only by Providence that he was even here at the right time. He asked of you, though, and your studies. Do you yet know if you will be able to have a parish near here?"

"I had hoped to discuss that with him." Gabriel paused before continuing. "It looks like Glasgow is where I am needed, but I would dearly love to be closer to home."

"You know we will be praying about this."

"Especially Mother." James winked at Gabriel.

"Now, do not tease. She misses having all her chicks at home." Father put an arm about her shoulder and kissed her cheek.

"I am not the only one who misses Gabriel. I have caught

your father looking at his map of Scotland with a faraway look about his eyes." Mother tipped her chin, trying to look stern and then laughed. "But, for now, you are home and I am grateful to have all my sons again close. I will send word to Robert and Joseph that we are having a family dinner tonight. Then I will truly be grateful."

James smiled at his mother's hopeful expression but would Joseph come?

Chapter Four

I reland for Ireland. Do ye think twill work?" Michael O'Toole seemed to enjoy and fear the idea, all at the same time. He continued to scrunch his well-worn cap between his work-worn fingers.

"Can you think of a better solution? This is the reason Albert and I brought our families out of France." A thick French accent might still color his speech, but Antoine loved his new land. And it wasn't enough to hope and pray for peace. They could do something about it, maybe here and now, in this room, peace could start. He searched the faces of the five other men seated around the table. It had been a trying two weeks, but he knew he had to get back to what he and Albert had longed to do. This was the reason he called the meeting." But he mustn't get ahead of himself. Best to explain. "Why is it we always must be defined as Protestant or Catholic? Huguenot or Presbyterian or Anglican? Why not children of God—United *Irish* children of God? When will we learn to forgive as Christ forgives and leave retributions for the past in His very capable hands?"

"I stand with you, my friend," Albert de Grillet responded in his thick, French accent. There was brotherhood in his longtime friend's voice, and he knew this dream was not just his own. He peered around the room at the other men, waiting to see who else might respond.

"There is much bad blood between the Protestants and the Catholics. I do not know if tis possible. You weren't here to know the terrors of forty-one. I were only a lad, but well I still remember the fear as the stories from Ulster spread like wildfire. Portadown, they got the worst of it. Me grandmother knew Elizabeth Price. Five children she had, all torn from her and thrown off the bridge to drown. Then the hallions hung her to make her confess and when she finally said all they wanted to hear, they held her feet to the fire 'til her soles were fried poundies. She was one of the few to live through the nightmare, and she told me grandmother she wished she hadn't. More than two thousand people massacred, thrown from bridges and bashed in the head if they tried to swim free. Tis a lot to forgive." Thomas Stewart slammed the table with his meaty fist, his gray hair falling in his eyes.

"Aye. But then let's not be forgetting the punishment already handed down on the Catholics, many of whom had nothing to do with the uprising. Cromwell, the divil take 'im, more than repaid for forty-one. What he did in Drogheda in forty-nine more than made things even, what with killing priests and burning defenseless families alive, and in church, mind ye. Me poor father, may he rest in peace, claimed to have heard the screams of the mothers for their babies five years after as he walked by the ruins of that church. And I've no doubt tis true." Paddy Flanagan's blue eyes pulsed with intensity as his leathery face pinked with emotion.

"Aye." Michael O'Toole added, his dark head bobbing in agreement. "And then in Wexford, just because they didn't submit quick enough to suit him, Bloody Cromwell killed off twenty thousand of the citizenry."

Antoine could feel things going from bad to worse as Paddy and Thomas each tried to top the other with religious atrocities.

"Well, let's not be forgetting what dear ol' James II did just ten years ago at Derry, starving out the good Protestants 'til they were even eating their mice. The Reverend Marshall told tale of a man there that was so fat, he was afraid to go into the street for fear of being someone's dinner."

"Aye, but the Protestant troops were winning against the Jacobite forces at Newtownbutler at that very same time. And there's been far more Catholic children starving than Protestant children over the last fifty years."

"Now, let us think a moment. I did not ask you all here for a history lesson." Antoine feared the men were near to blows. "This reminiscing and keeping score is why Ireland is in such pain. France lost her greatness all because she would not accept the Protestants. And I believe Ireland will be torn apart if we Protestants and Catholics will not all work together for a common good. Can we do that? Can we start here?"

Albert chimed in. "I chose you, Michael O'Toole and Paddy Flanagan, because I believe you to be honest, true men who will listen and do what is right. We need leaders here from both communities who are willing to do that—do what is right, even when there is heated excitement to go along with the crowd. If our leaders, on both sides, can set the example, maybe the fighting will end."

"That's all fine an' good, but what about the soldiers? You know they look for reasons to separate us an' then destroy our lands an' homes. They know that if we can't pay our rents, they can throw us out. And if they can time it just right, they can starve us out. More than once I've seen potatoes be all that's standing between families and starvation. All because the banshees didn't burn under the ground when they set the fields aflame." Antoine knew from the start Flanagan would be a hard sell. Though a good man, he had reasons not to trust another protestant.

"What would ye be thinking we need to do to make this work, Crockett?" Thomas Stewart leaned back in his chair, arms crossed over his chest.

"The first thing I see is we have to set an example. We help those in need, no matter their faith. If we find that someone needs help, and they won't respond because we are of different faiths, we can help through each other. For instance, suppose I knew of someone with a need for some assistance, but they did not trust taking help from a Protestant. I could tell Albert and he could help, or even take what I have to give in my place. They would not have to know the help was from me." Antoine and Albert had actually been doing this for many years but hoped to see this plan of help more widely used.

"Aye, that sounds reasonable." Michael O'Toole nodded his shaggy head.

"Aye, but what else have ye in mind?" Paddy warily glanced from Antoine to Albert.

"We can set an example by not showing favoritism in our dealings. Be fair to all, no matter the faith."

Choruses of offense, disclaiming any favoritism, quickly spread around the room as the men jumped to their feet.

"I did not say any of you *did* show favoritism." Antoine raised his voice above the din and, finally the men sat. "I only am pointing out that we need to be very open about 'no favoritism,' so we are setting an example with the hope the practice will spread. If our communities see this is the way of business—the way Christ would have done things—then perhaps they will join us. When we work together, we get to better know each other.

"Which brings me to another issue. It is with a united front that we, as Irishmen, can stand against the onslaughts of England. I am not looking for a fight with them, but neither do I see a reason for Ireland to be slaves for England. The only way to stand together is to trust one another. And the only way to trust one another is to treat and love each other as Christ would do." Antoine paused before standing and placing his hand, palm down on the table before him. "Who is with me?"

Albert stood, adding his hand to his friend's. He and

Antoine searched the face of each man seated at the table. Thomas Stewart and Michael O'Toole both rose at the same time and placed their hands on the table as well. The eyes of those standing now moved to the last two men. Paddy Flanagan stared hard at the hands on the table and, as if coming to a final conclusion, rose and very deliberately slapped his weathered hand alongside the others.

That left only Cameron McHugh, who had not spoken a word since the meeting began. Cameron, a quiet man who seemed to tower over the rest of the population, was not a man to be cajoled or bullied into a decision. Nor would he be shamed into something just because everyone else was doing it, though, the fact he looked not at the others might lead a stranger to believe that was the case. In truth, the reason Antoine chose Cameron McHugh was that he never made a decision without first taking it to prayer.

Paddy Flanagan chewed at the corner of his lip, undoubtedly ready to say something caustic that would unravel all Antoine and Albert had accomplished, when, with a scraping sound, Cameron McHugh raised his great hulk from his chair. "Twill be much harder to live this plan out there than it was to speak of it in here. But tis what my Savior would have done, and I can do no less. Tis not the caring for the poor ones, nor the fairness in business that gives me pause. Tis the knowing that our solidarity will cause pain, and perhaps danger. Not everyone will like this. There'll be those who choose to fight. Even we Protestants have our own divisions. Stewart, you know the Anglicans will not be as excited to accept this as the Presbyterians and Huguenots. But Jesus said to take up His cross, and so—" placing his hand on the table—"that I do."

Silence hung in the air until, suddenly, a cheer went up. Then the men began to hug and slap backs as if ready to start an adventure.

Antoine raised his hands, calling for their attention. "My friends, my partners in this endeavor: This plan has been on my heart for so long. I have no doubt that it was placed there by God to show us how to live together in His love. Now that we have pledged ourselves to His plan, let us join together in prayer for His leading and guidance."

The men quieted as one and bowed heads. The three Catholic believers quietly crossed themselves as Antoine began to pray for them all. "Holy Father, we thank Thee for joining our hearts as one with Yours. You are the God of all and the One Who will lead and guide us for Thy Name's sake. Show us Thy heart, Father. Help us to love as You love. Let us see with Thine eyes, that we may lift Christ in all we do and say. We need Thy strength, Lord, and Your protection for our families and communities. We need Your wisdom and discernment to accomplish this task Your way. Lord, we ask that You cover us with Thy wings, as we abide in Your Almighty shadow. Open our ears to Thy voice that we may follow Thee, our Shepherd, wherever You lead. And may all the glory and honor in this endeavor be Thine, now and always. Amen."

A chorus of "amen" murmured around the table as Albert, Michael, and Paddy again made the sign of the cross. This moment was sacred, all six men stood still with heads bowed. Antoine realized life had just changed. He had yet to know how, but for himself, he knew there would be no turning back.

Not now.

Not ever.

Chapter Five

I'm here with the bairn, Widow O'Connor. Why don't ye take a wee stretch of the legs whilst I keep an eye on yer Samuel for ye? If ye've the mind, that is."

Shannon, feeling the sun's rays caress her face with invitation, nearly missed Miss Stewart's unexpected offer. She suspected the young woman had noticed her staring out at the waiting world. Twas a fine spring day. What with the noon meal completed and both children fed, bathed, and put down for a nap, the offer sorely tempted. Never had a day appeared so glorious.

"Tis kind of ye, Miss, but I'll not be leaving ye alone with the lads." Pride steeled her back, keeping her from glancing out the window one more time.

"I'm not alone. Aye, there's Bridget, my ever-vigilant shadow —thanks to me father—and this house is never without someone coming by to see about Wee Joseph." Sarah gently squeezed Shannon's shoulder. "Ye must be longing to go. I can hear the sunshine calling to ye."

The words made Shannon smile and nod. A kind suggestion. It had been several days since she'd been outside the house. In truth, she couldn't even remember when she had last been alone.

"Aye, I thank ye for yer offer. Tis the green what's calling to me." She nodded her thanks once more, grabbed her shawl from the foot of her bed, and wrapped it loosely about her. "I won't be but a whipstitch."

"Take yer time." Sarah smiled.

Watching to see that her Samuel slept, curled up with the rag doll she'd made, Shannon slipped out, treading lightly down the stairs. Not yet through the backdoor, though, she glanced over her shoulder. Might some harm come to Samuel while she was gone? Then she remembered the kindnesses shown her over the past few weeks. She put her imagination to rest.

The Crocketts were more than kind. They allowed her to attend Mass at the rock whenever she wanted. At first, she'd thought to steal away, but they apparently knew all about the Mass Rocks and the need to keep the locations secret. The de Grillets even went with her to the clandestine service, in full knowledge that to be caught worshipping as a Catholic could mean prison. Or worse.

Shannon dinnae ken. The two families seemed so close. More than just close. Like family?

True, both came from France, but the Crocketts were Huguenots. Protestants. The de Grillets were Catholic. It made no sense.

All the kindness and understanding the Crocketts extended to Shannon felt foreign. Her mind warned *beware*. But daily experience revealed another side to this family.

Shannon remained lost in thought, wandering to a nearby brook through fields dotted with sweet cicely and meadow fescues. Seating herself on the bank, she slipped off her shoes and oft-mended stockings to dangle her toes in the water. She lifted them, letting tiny rivulets roll down her feet before dunking them once more. Freedom misted over her with each droplet splashed.

So much happened this past year. As a rule, she managed to

force the past from her mind. Except at night when she snuggled down with her Samuel. Then she prayed exhaustion would keep her from thinking. But now unbidden memories flooded. Surprisingly, many were of happy times.

Sean's rakish smile and twinkling eyes danced in her mind, bringing back the good times they'd enjoyed before his illness and premature death stole her exuberance for life. She lay back, putting her arms beneath her head. This had been their spot where they talked and dreamt of their future. She knew every gold fleck in his hazel eyes. And that nose of his, turned up at the tip, wrinkling when he laughed. Ah, that laugh. Robust and from his heart. Shannon heard the promise of it in her Samuel's sweet giggle. Sitting up, she fanned her feet, watching water beads fly, a rare giggle of her own erupting in the joy of the moment.

So lost in her thoughts, the quiet footsteps from behind made her jump. Shannon hadn't heard the other person until he was nearly upon her. Turning, she saw Master Mackenzie, the family's guest. He smiled and tipped his hat before continuing as if to pass her by.

"G'day to ye, Widow O'Connor. Don't mind me, I'm just out to take a gleek at the land."

"G'day to ye, sir." The heat rose in her cheeks, while watching him continue on his way. A handsome man with a gentleman's bearing. She noticed him more than she wanted to admit. He had hazel eyes.

Like her Sean.

A shiver rolled down her spine.

Maybe that was it. Master Mackenzie's eyes resembled Sean's. Shannon picked up a sock and began fitting it over her toes.

Other than their eyes, though, the two men appeared nothing alike. Where Sean was shorter with a muscular frame, Ian Mackenzie was tall and leanly built. Sean was darker in complexion where Ian was fairer, with honey-blond hair and the remnants of soft freckles across the bridge of his nose. They were two different men, but both very handsome, each in his own way.

But why had she taken note of Master Ian Mackenzie?

More important, why was she so bothered?

Shannon threw her other sock against the tree with disgust. She had no time for men. Yet she couldn't deny it. Like it or not, she still lived. Convincing herself it was merely an observation, she fetched her sock. She didn't need to dwell on Master Ian Mackenzie or any other man. For now.

SARAH LAID THE SLEEPING WEE JOSEPH IN THE CRADLE just as Samuel opened his eyes. She expected him to cry when he didn't see his mother. But the little one surprised her by holding out his arms. He snuggled into her with a hug before leaning over, wanting down. Sarah joined Samuel on the floor and began a game of peek-a-boo. Over and over she hid her face. The toddler giggled just as hard, maybe even harder, each time she pulled her hands away. A lovely sound. Sweet, innocent, musical. She laughed right along.

While her fingers covered her face, she heard the nursery door creak. Thinking it was Bridget returning with clean nappies, she didn't even look up. "Just put them in the top drawer of his chest, Bridget."

"Put what in the top drawer?"

James leaned in the doorway.

Turning back, she felt his gaze while the toddler continued to delight in their game.

The most outgoing brother of the group, James had friends everywhere. Thinking back, though, Sarah couldn't recall any women friends. She had wondered about this in the past, and again did so when the thought briefly crossed her mind. Funny, kind, and good with babies from what she could tell, Jamie appeared to dote on Wee Joseph. Maybe she should introduce him to one of her friends.

"He's taught ye well." James laughed, walking over to where they played on the floor.

"Samuel enjoys the game, and that's for sure. We've been at it for more than half an hour. He's giggling as much now as when we started."

"Move over and let me try."

James sat down and Samuel scurried straight into Sarah's lap.

"Well, we know what he thinks about ye." She chuckled.

"Aye, he is a little flirt. He has an eye for the ladies, I'm thinking," James chuckled, too, and stretched out on the floor.

"He's a sweet bairn with a brain to know to stay away from the likes of ye."

"That's a bit harsh, don't you think?" His brogue deepened as he teased. "What'ere 'ave I done to ye to deserve such ill treatment?" He flashed her a look of wide-eyed innocence.

"Ye mean aside from tormenting me, calling me names, pulling me hair…"

"Now wait a blessed minute. That was when I was a calloused youth with no understanding of the fairer sex."

"Oh, do ye mean yesterday?"

"Aye." He winked. "Today I am mature and responsible."

"I see. And can ye tell me this, Jamie lad? How am I to know ye've made this miraculous change?"

As if right on cue, Wee Joseph woke, letting out a cry.

"I'll show you." He jumped up, "Come to your favorite uncle, little man. Tell me what's ailing you. Ah, there, there."

At once, James's eyes bulged.

Sarah grinned, knowing the cause, and pointed to a small chest next to the cradle.

"The clean nappies are over there, and the rags for cleaning him are in the drawer beneath the pitcher and basin."

Already James held the baby aloft at arms' length, "But, but—"

"Oh, aye." She laughed. "I can see how ye have matured and become responsible." Sarah reached for the baby, but James resisted.

"Now, hold on. It can't be all that hard. I've worked around farm animals all my life. I should be able to change a soiled nappy." Turning to his nephew, he continued. "Let's show this Miss High-an'-Mighty that we men are quite capable too." Laying one of the rags down on the chest before placing Wee Joseph on top of it, he unbundled the baby until he'd removed the soiled garment. James glanced around, gingerly holding the offending cloth between his thumb and forefinger.

Sarah snickered but took pity on him. She disposed of the dirty diaper, while James wet a rag in the basin and cleaned the little bottom.

Finally, he placed a fresh linen napkin under Wee Joseph and smiled at the sweet face. A tiny fountain sprang up, playfully spraying the front of his shirt.

"Wha—? You little imp. I'm supposed to be your favorite uncle. Why didn't you save that trick for Sarah?"

It happened so quickly, Sarah couldn't keep from laughing. "Little boys will do that. Even at this innocent age, one canna trust a male."

James, wiping off the front of his shirt with another clean rag, joined in the laughter.

Sarah pushed James out of the way before deftly removing the wet diaper and replacing it with a fresh one. "Now if ye'll hold the bairn, I'll clean up the rest for ye."

"That I can do." James took Wee Joseph to the rocker.

"Aye and now, little man. We need to come to some kind of understanding if I'm to be your favorite uncle. There'll be no more antics like we've had today. Are you clear with that?"

Sarah smiled to herself while listening to the one-sided exchange.

"And, for good measure, we'll let Sarah handle the nappy changing from now on." Wee Joseph made a cooing sound. "Aye, that's right. So, we're in agreement."

Aye, he would make a wonderful father one day. "I think he's taken to ye, Jamie." Sarah leaned over his shoulder.

"And why shouldn't he? I tell ye, I'm his favorite."

"I just wish…" She paused, unsure whether she should finish her statement.

"Ye wish what, Sarah?" He didn't bother to look up. "What do ye wish?"

"I wish Joseph would spend this kind of time with his son. I'm not even sure he's ever held him."

The rocker stopped. This time James swiveled to look Sarah square in the eye. Avoiding his gaze, she turned her attention back to Samuel. She sat on the floor, resuming their peek-a-boo game.

"Ye mean to tell me he doesn't ever come see this wee one? Has he gone daft?"

"No, I don't know, for sure." Sarah continued playing with the toddler while choosing her words. "I believe he might be afraid."

"Afraid? Afraid of what? Wee Joseph couldn't hurt a soul."

"Aye. But what if Joseph thinks the babe killed his mother?" She wanted to take the words back as soon as they were out of her mouth.

With Wee Joseph asleep, James quietly placed him in his cradle before facing Sarah.

"That's daft. Completely, ridiculously daft." James's vehement whisper continued. "Kathleen died because she bled to death."

"Giving birth to Wee Joseph," Sarah said. "It's possible, isn't it? That Joseph sees this bairn as what took his wife away from him?"

"No." James shook his head. "No, that cannot be. Can it?"

"Can you think of another reason for him to not come be

with his own flesh and blood?" Sarah quickly glanced toward the door before locking gazes with James. "I think he blames Wee Joseph for Kathleen's death."

Chapter Six

"Father, do ye have a moment?" Gabriel leaned in the doorway of Antione's study.

Antoine smiled, delighted. "Of course, come in, son." He had missed this wonderful son of his. Antoine was again taken with how this strong, young man seemed to have inherited his black hair and blue eyes from his father but his bent for life from his mother. Gabriel and Louise's personalities were so similar, it had made for a close relationship.

However, Antoine had been the one Gabriel turned to when he first heard the call to ministry. The two men spent hours discussing what it would mean to Gabriel's future. Antoine thrilled at Gabriel's decision to pursue the ministry but was cautious in case it was only out of a moment of excitable passion. He wanted Gabriel to be sure he understood the depth of surrender such a calling demanded.

After much soul-searching and prayer, it became obvious to both men that Gabriel had indeed been called. Antoine also had concerns as to whether Gabriel might become so full of knowledge, he would lose sight of the simplicity of the gospel message. He'd met enough learned men who could talk all about the facts of God but had long forgotten about the love of God. He didn't want Gabriel to become one of them.

However, a moment in Gabriel's company and it was obvious there was something special about him. Antoine knew that special something was an intimate, daily fellowship with Jesus. And, since both men experienced that special relationship, they never tired of talking together about God's wonderful love.

Therefore, it was no surprise that Gabriel would stop by the study to talk. Antoine would have been disappointed if he hadn't.

"Father, I'd love to know what I can do to help Joseph. It seemed like he wasn't there at dinner last night. He was the last to arrive and the first to leave with hardly a word throughout. He's always been quiet, but not that quiet." Worry lines appeared between Gabriel's brows. "Isn't there anything I can do?"

Antoine started to shake his head when he thought of something. "Gabriel, do you recall studying any of the Reverend Richard Baxter's work?"

"The name is familiar. I cannot place him. Is he someone ye know?"

"I met him briefly when your Uncle Albert and I were in England searching for Aunt Mimi's sister. In fact, he was the one who gave us the tip to look where we did. His influence opened many doors and provided the means for us to bring Momo home. We talked then and after corresponded for a quite a while. He died about seven years ago, which is why you probably don't remember him."

"Aye, but what has he to do with Joseph?"

"Richard lost his wife about ten years before his own death. He married late in life. She was somewhat younger than he, but they were very much in love and close partners in his ministry. In fact, Richard lost four people very close to him in a matter of six months. The last to go was Margaret. It seemed to be the final straw. He was inconsolable. By this time, he was already an author with over ninety published works. He shared that returning to writing was the best way he found to deal with his grief."

"Aye, but Joseph isn't much of an author."

"That is not what I was getting at, son. It is *what* Richard wrote that I'm hoping you can help me find. I believe there might be some help for Joseph in Richard's words. Let's begin our search for the piece, and we can also be praying the Lord will show us the right time for sharing it with Joseph."

"What is the title?"

"It is a volume called, *The Breviate*. It covers the history of Richard's life with Margaret and how God brought him through this time of grief. I thought I might have a copy, but perhaps I'd only borrowed it. I never thought to ask the Reverend Fontaine while he was here. Anyway, should you happen to come across it, let me know. We can take it from there."

"I'll begin looking right away, but what can I do in the meantime?" Gabriel bit the corner of his lower lip, while puckers deepened between his eyebrows.

Antoine recognized this not-too-satisfied look and understood his son wanted to do something—and do it now. Antoine smiled. This trait came straight from the boy's father.

"What is it that you want to do, son?"

"I don't know." Gabriel paced the room, fingers sifting through his hair. "Something that would help him to be more like his old self. Something that would help him not hurt as much." He shrugged.

"Son, Joseph will never be exactly the same. He is a man. He has married and become a father. That in itself changes one. Now he has lost his wife." He could see Gabriel needed an illustration. "Do you remember when you fell off that outcrop of rocks over by Lifford when you were ten?"

"Aye."

"Do you remember what your forearm looked like when we finally got to you?"

"Aye, it was covered with blood and dirt. It was a proper mess."

"I do not mean to simplify things, but in many ways, Joseph has had a bad fall. He's been bloodied. What does your forearm look like now?"

"It looks like my forearm."

"Look at it closer, son. See it as it is."

Gabriel shoved up his sleeve and examined his right forearm, turning it different angles. Antoine saw the light in his son's eyes.

"Aye, I understand. My arm works just fine, still the scars are there. It doesn't look like it would have if I had grown up without the accident. Do you think Joseph will heal so he can live with the scars?"

"That is my prayer. The memories will always be there, but in time he will be able to start living instead of existing. And he will remember the real reason for joy. But right now, we can help him by being there, listening, and praying. God hears and answers before we know to ask." Antoine smiled. "He is the only One your mother and I trust with our children."

Gabriel returned the smile.

"I'll start searching for *The Breviate* right away, Father." Gabriel started for the door but turned back. "Father…thanks." The smile he flashed was equally matched with one of Antoine's own.

❧

James rounded the corner of the cottage in time to see Joseph coming in from the fields. His brother walked without purpose, shoulders sagging, eyes following the ground. Sympathy mellowed the righteous indignation that propelled James to confrontation. Perhaps he should feel his way a bit instead of charging in with words flying. He raised a hand of salute. "Joseph."

Joseph raised his head. The hint of a smile played at his

mouth, and his hand rose part way in a half-hearted wave. He pointed toward the barn.

James nodded and turned in that direction.

The brothers met at the door.

"Joseph, I—" James began, but when he got a closer look at Joseph's eyes, he changed what he was about to say. "Want to go fishing? I hear the salmon are running. Besides I haven't been able to spend any time with you since I returned."

"Sure. I need to feed the ewes first. You want to grab the gear?"

"Aye. I can do that." James chose a pair of poles and a net before leaning against the doorjamb. He watched in silence as Joseph plopped the hay down in clumps to the new mother sheep.

"So, let's have at it."

"What are ye talking about?" James glanced to where his brother worked at the outside haymow door.

"I've never known you to beat about the bush on something, so let's have at it." Joseph tossed another clump, still not looking at James.

James paused while he set the fishing gear against the barn wall. Exhaling slowly, he walked out to where he could get a better view into the loft. "When are ye going to spend time with your son?"

The silence pressed in, weighing heavy like the stones that formed the new barn.

"I asked you to speak your mind. Now I should speak mine." Joseph forked another load of hay and tossed it to a pen below. "I don't know if I can. Every time I see him, I am cut to the core."

Blood drained from James's face. "Then it's true. Ye believe the wee bairn killed his mother?"

"What?" Joseph stared at him, his eyes wide, as though he had been punched in the stomach and couldn't get his breath.

"That's what you think of me? That I cannot bear to look on my son because I think him a murderer?"

"If that's not the truth of it, what is?" James all but glared at Joseph, seeing the anguish, but refusing to be touched by it. Any sympathy he might have had evaporated like the morning dew. He knew anger now controlled, but he didn't care. "What other reason could there be for a father refusing to hold or even see his newborn son?"

The pitchfork clattered to the wooden floor. Joseph dove out of the haymow onto his brother.

The first blow stunned James. The second hit him square in the mouth, the taste of blood rousing him. He began to fight back, landing as many blows as he took. They rolled against one pen, then another, pounding at each other.

"Stop it. Stop it now."

Someone wrenched Joseph out of his reach. Baby brother Robert held Joseph, arms locked behind.

"Don't say that." Joseph, breathing hard, struggled and seethed. "Never say it. He's but a baby. I'll tear you apart."

"Now you want to sound like a parent?" James scrambled to his feet. "But where've you been when he needs you? Nowhere." He leaned forward, hands on his thighs, chest heaving.

"You're letting Sarah and Mother raise your son."

Robert stood eyes wide and mouth open, still holding Joseph.

"Away with you. Don't be letting me ever hear you say that again." Joseph wrenched free, grabbed James by his shirtfront, and hurled him against the barn door.

James landed with a thud, the wooden door cracking. He struggled to balance himself before drawing to his full height. If it was a fight he wanted—"Fine, I'll go. I'll go right back to the nursery and hold that wee bairn what's needing a father to care for him."

Joseph's eyes blazed. With a strangled cry, he threw himself at James again. James sidestepped out of reach. Robert grabbed Joseph from behind.

"Let go. Let me go." Joseph raged.

Robert pointed toward Edenmore with his head. "Go get Father."

James wanted to rebel, but the deep draughts of oxygen he panted not only filled his lungs but cleared his mind. He stared only a moment before sprinting for the house.

❧

Rage coursed through Joseph. It was raw and overpowering and white hot, incinerating all thought but the need to break free. He buried himself beneath the weight of it, sagging within the force that confined.

And then he felt it, a release. He was lowered to the ground. It was all he needed.

Joseph jumped to his feet and grabbing item after item, scythes, harnesses, pitchforks, flinging, throwing, creating his own whirlwind of chaos.

Barn animals ran past and out into the open pasture area. At one point he thought he saw Robert duck something flying about as he ran for the safety of openness.

But Joseph didn't need safety. Safety was the last thing he wanted.

Chaos ruled Joseph's heart, mind, and soul as debris flew about him, splintering the fragile peace that had allowed some semblance of sanity. Loud animal-like grunts echoed in his mind.

He stopped to breathe. The whirlwind ceased. Heavy panting replaced the grunting noise. Realization dawned. The grunting sounds came from him.

A shockwave charged through Joseph's system, nailing him into the whitewashed stone corner of his barn. Scanning his surroundings, nothing resembled the well-ordered barn he knew so well. He inspected at his hands. The brass bowl of large betty lamp lay in his calloused palm, round, cool and smooth.

With slow deliberation, he poured out the oil, hearing it splatter at his feet. Though he knew the toes of his boots were now drenched, his eyes riveted to the lamp. His hand slid down one chain to the wick pick. He cut his finger on the sharp point. Joseph felt pain.

Real and tangible, the pain entered his finger, creeping up his arm and moving straight to his chest. Now each heartbeat pounded harder and harder until he thought his heart would punch a hole in his upper body from the inside out. Breathing grew more difficult as the pain sent wave after wave of attacks. He fell to his knees.

No escape was allowed him. Truth burst in his brain like grape shot from a cannon—his wife was dead.

And he killed her.

He ran from this truth the moment Kathleen's lifeblood drained from her.

She wanted a family right away. Something to bring them closer together. All Kathleen ever did was pour out love to him.

And you killed her.

She shouldn't have been the one to die. Their baby needed his mother much more than he needed a father—especially a father who couldn't even handle looking at his own son.

"Joseph?" A familiar voice broke through.

Joseph's gaze slowly rose to meet his father's before looking back to his hands.

"What do you have there, son?"

"A lamp."

"I see. What happened to your finger?" His father's voice soothed, slowly closing the gap between them.

"I don't know." Joseph's voice sounded faraway, child-like, even to his own ears. Focusing a moment on his finger, he watched the blood drip into the dirt and oil smeared over the normally clean floor. "Maybe I should cut it free. Cut myself free. Maybe I should burn this all to the ground."

"Why would you want to do that?" His father was closer than he was a moment ago.

If only he were a small child, able to crawl into those secure arms where everything was safe.

"It's all my fault."

"What is, son?"

This time he focused on his father, silently daring him to turn away. "I killed her."

Father's arms enveloped him. Still he resisted, rigid with guilt.

"Son, you loved Kathleen. She knew that. She loved you. You were united in marriage. A baby is a natural result of that love. You didn't kill her, Joseph. You loved her."

His heart was falling but his father remained to catch him. The secure arms held him safely once more. If only he could believe.

"I'm sorry, I'm sorry…" The words and remorse poured from him. "Oh, Kathleen, I'm so sorry."

"She knows, Joseph. She knows."

The arms held tighter. The torrent broke through the dam of Joseph's resistance and flooded him. "I'm so sorry, so sorry."

"I know, I know." Father reassured.

"Why? Father I don't understand."

"I don't have any answers, son."

Those were not the words he needed. Pulling back from his father, he listened harder, hearing his own breathing, shallow and gulping. He took a deep breath, forcing himself to slowly exhale. "What do I do?"

"Trust."

"Who, what? What is there to trust?"

Laying his hand on Joseph's shoulder, his father answered. "Trust God."

"No." There was no need to think about it. That option fled with Kathleen's life.

The father-arms again encircled firm. "Then trust your family. We love you. We are here for you. Trust yourself to care for Wee Joseph."

Joseph allowed himself to be pulled to his feet. "I don't know if I can. Trust myself, I mean."

"Then trust us until you can. We fiercely love you and Wee Joseph. Do you think for one minute your mother or I would let any harm come to our son or grandson?"

A knot of fear settled deep in his gut, but he saw truth in his father's eyes. He would only fail if it were beyond his power to succeed. He closed his eyes for strength and slowly nodded his head.

Chapter Seven

Louise paced before her bedroom window. Since Antoine had left with James she'd been pacing. Pacing and praying. She wanted to go too. James said only Antoine was needed, though. So, she stayed and prayed and paced, keeping watch for her men.

Time crept while she strode back and forth. Yet only this morning she'd thought how it had flashed past ever since Wee Joseph's birth. One look at him and she could see just how fast he grew.

Already three weeks old, she daily noticed changes in her first grandson. She loved to sit in the old nursery and rock him in the early morning as the sun cast golden rays on his soft hair. He would grasp her little finger and stare at her with such complete trust, locking her adoring gaze with his bright sapphire-blue stare. He looked like his father, so serious it brought a smile to her face.

And still she paced.

And prayed.

Often when she prayed, she received a peace flooding her very soul, giving her the surety that God was in control. She could rest in that. But peace wasn't as easily forthcoming this time.

She continued her prayers. "Father, please give Antoine the wisdom he needs. Fill his mouth with Your words. Open Joseph's heart to know Your compassion. Protect them all, Father. Please bring them safely home, especially Joseph." His safety seemed especially critical. In fact, when her mind strayed to other areas, she continued to feel the nudge to cover her men with prayer for safety.

Finally, peace returned followed by the sound of male voices drifting in from outside. She spotted James and Robert from the window and hurried downstairs to greet them.

Breathless, she met them at the door. "Is everything all right?"

The brothers exchanged a look before Robert answered. "Joseph is with Father. Everything is under control, I think."

James, uncharacteristically quiet, simply nodded.

Relief poured out with a sigh. She pulled each son to her and hugged them in turn. "Tell me what happened."

The brothers stared at the floor. She'd seen that look before. Back when two naughty boys got caught swiping one of Josephine's apple pies. Louise again felt concern rise. This was more than a childhood prank.

"Robert… James… Tell me what happened." Would she ever stop feeling like a parent to them?

"I'm not sure what happened, Mother. I arrived in time to see James and Joseph scuffling a bit." Robert rubbed his knuckle against his cheek. A dead giveaway, that. Even as a boy, if Robert began rubbing his cheek, something wasn't right.

She sighed. "James? How did this start?" She couldn't let this go. Her hands went to her hips, her feet stubbornly planted in place as she stared up at her silent son. Hadn't she prayed for their safety? She would understand what happened. And he would explain. Now.

"I just went to see him. Nothing of importance." James

scuffed his shoe against the floorboards as if he were ten years old.

"Well something must have been important in order for two grown men to come to blows. Now start talking." She stared.

He ran his fingers though his hair and squeezed his eyes shut before taking a deep breath and letting it whoosh out. "I saw Wee Joseph and Sarah. I just thought I'd look in…my first nephew and all."

She cleared her throat.

James glanced at her before continuing. "She mentioned that Joseph never goes to see the baby. We talked about the possible reasons." He paused again, and stared at his boots.

She motioned with her hand to get on with it.

Bit by bit, James's poured out the story.

She needed air. Even Robert turned a serious face toward his brother. When he opened his mouth as if to say something, she firmly motioned him quiet. Inwardly she wanted to throttle James but remained silent, praying for divine guidance.

James's eyes revealed true pain, but she wasn't sure whether it stemmed from guilt or from her assumption he had caused the problem.

Lord, give me the words. She took a deep breath, stared him square in the face, and plunged.

"Do you still think Joseph blames his son for Kathleen's death?"

James winced. With head bent low and voice soft, he whispered. "No, not now I don't."

She stood on tiptoe and gently stroked his cheek before lifting his chin to look into his eyes. She didn't have to reach so high the last time she did this.

"Jamie, he sees his wife when he looks at his son. In time that will be a comfort, but right now it is painful. He has come in to see Wee Joseph. It is usually when no one else is around, and he only looks. I've heard him in the hall and caught him watching. For now, that is all he can do. But the time will come when he will be able to hold his baby boy."

"How do you know, Mother? How do you know that he won't just go off one day, leave and never look back? If the pain is so great, what keeps him here?" James pleaded for an answer, his eyes moist with his need to know for sure.

She cupped her hand to his cheek. "I know." She stated it with calm assurance. "I *know*." And she knew that she did. The peace God had begun to pour out while she prayed now flooded her entire being.

James gazed into her eyes; he craved her guarantee.

Louise remembered back to when she had held James as a baby, just like Wee Joseph. He, too, had held her gaze with complete trust.

A smile flickered to her lips. She patted the now manly cheek of this impetuously passionate son, all the while gazing as deeply into his eyes as possible. She spoke the words he needed to hear.

"*I know.*"

JOSEPH TREKKED BACK TO THE HOUSE WITH HIS FATHER. A mixture of anticipation, embarrassment, and dread churned in his stomach. He knew he'd gone too far. He needed to stay strong, for his son. The sooner he got over this guilt and fear, the sooner life would have some semblance of order.

His mother greeted him at the door with a brief hug, almost like she wasn't sure if it were the right thing to do or not. Wonderful. Now everyone would be concerned about doing the wrong thing, maybe causing him to do something stupid again. Did she breathe? Then the door opened wider.

James stepped into his line of sight. He resembled a kicked puppy as he chewed his bottom lip.

"I'm sorry."

They both said the words at the exact same moment. Joseph pulled James to him and then they were in each other's arms, both repeating, "I'm sorry, I'm sorry." The rest of the family huddled around them.

Joseph pulled back. "I'm going to do it. I am going to hold my son." He spoke as much to himself as anyone.

"Would you like someone…" Mother put her hand on his arm, but Father shook his head.

"No. Thank you, Mother, but no. I need to do this myself." Joseph leaned over and kissed her gently on the cheek before ascending the stairs.

❦

WITH SAMUEL BACK TO SLEEP, SARAH GAVE HER FULL FOCUS to Wee Joseph. Oh, how she loved caring for this sweet baby. He was as good-natured as any. She longed to be his mother. She even caught herself envying Shannon the ability to nurse him because that was something she couldn't provide. She loved him as if he were her own and, in her mind, Kathleen had given him to her. "Ah, Wee Joseph, I am tightly wrapped 'round that baby finger of yers."

Now fed and changed, he alertly lay in her arms, his tiny fist tightly clamped about her right pinky. She whispered endearments to him as he cooed back.

She felt another presence though she never heard the door. She couldn't say how long the person stood there, and probably never would have paid attention if not for Wee Joseph's eyes darting up and over her shoulder.

Without looking up, she spoke in the singsong voice she used when speaking with the baby. "I just now got 'im to meself, Jamie. Aye, that I did. And I'm not ready to be handing him over to ye yet. No, I'm not."

"I'm not James."

Joseph's voice startled her. She jumped to her feet.

Wee Joseph whimpered at the sudden movement, drawing her attention back to him.

"Here, I'll take him." He reached for his son.

She pulled the baby closer. "Are ye sure?" She stammered, confusion and concern dancing all about her brain.

"Aye, Sarah, I'm sure. May I hold my son?" His arms were still outstretched.

She reluctantly put Wee Joseph into his father's arms.

"Make sure ye got yer arm under his head now. And put yer hand here…"

"I've held babies before, Sarah. I've got three younger sisters, not to mention Robert.

"Aye, yer right, I know, but he's so little an'…"

"He's my son, Sarah," His tone was firm. "I can do this. You're not his mother, Sarah. You're not Kathleen."

Her world tumbled about her. She returned his pointed gaze. If he wanted a battle, he would get one.

"Yer right, I'm not Kathleen. I'm Sarah, yer friend. And I've been the one tending yer son. I've been the one to rock him and hold him and wash him and change him. I may not be Kathleen, but I'm as close to a mother as he's got. And don't you forget it."

"I'm not contesting that, Sarah. I just want some time alone with him. Please."

Wee Joseph started to cry.

Joseph expertly cuddled the baby, closing her out.

She watched, helpless to do anything but stand. Seeing the two of them together, not needing her, proved more painful than she could bear. Without another word, she slipped from the room, shutting the door on her way.

JOSEPH TURNED IN TIME TO SEE THE DOOR CLOSE AFTER Sarah.

"Seems I'm off to a brilliant start, son. Aye, sir, I'm your father and you are my son. You probably don't recognize me. But we've been needing to talk for a while, and it looks like the time is here."

Gaze locked with his son's, protective love for the miracle in his arms overtook Joseph. His mind flooded with all he would need to do to keep this sweet innocent from harm. Now that the moment he had feared was here, he found he had no words, only wonderment.

Fear evaporated. Instead he found love, perfect love. Overwhelming, fierce, protective love growing stronger as the gaze grew longer. Never before had he known anything so powerful. It shocked and thrilled him to his core. "This is my son." No longer a word, but a relationship. He was a father holding his son. The words weighed profound.

He sat and rocked away time, unaware of its passing. Wee Joseph gently cooed and gazed, seemingly content to let time pass by them, as well. So this was fatherhood.

"Let me tell you about your mother. A lovely lass with raven hair down to her waist and eyes the color of robins' eggs."

Joseph closed his eyes, Kathleen's smiling face danced before him. He let the wave of grief wash over again. There had to be an end to it. There had to be.

"And she glowed more lovely each day she carried you, son. There was nothing she wanted more than to hold you in her arms." That wasn't exactly true. There was one other thing she longed for but could never have no matter how they both tried. Again, guilt assailed him, but he focused on his son.

"Your mother used to sit and rock you, while she still carried you, and would sing you lullabies. She said it made you kick in time to her singing." That memory made him smile. Maybe if he could focus on the good things. And there were good things.

"I know, I will tell you the story of how we met. It was a warm July evening…"

Chapter Eight

The brisk walk to the cottage helped Sarah work out the anger threatening to overwhelm her. With each step she picked up speed while her mind spun out defensive accusations. The beauty of the countryside—the wildflowers, neat hedgerows, pastures dotted white with sheep—all blurred by angry tears until she burst through the cottage door and slammed it shut.

Why did he throw Kathleen back in her face?

She was his wife.

Couldn't he see that she and Wee Joseph were bonded together like any mother and son?

But he is Wee Joseph's father.

How many times did she have to lose?

What exactly have you lost? Was it ever yours to lose?

She gazed around the small, neat cottage. It was hers, yet not hers. She became acutely aware she had been so diligent in her duty, she'd lost sight of an important fact. The family she cared for as her own did not really belong to her.

"But I love him."

Which one?

A long pause allowed her time to sit in the hand-carved

rocker and ponder that one. She finally answered back. "I love them both, Father. I love them so much it hurts."

Her statement, though whispered, resounded in her heart like an echo. Sarah realized she felt more hurt than anger.

Why are you hurt?

That took some thought. Through her tears, Sarah realized the hurt stemmed not from what Joseph said or did, but from the letdown of reality. He hadn't reacted the way she had imagined he would. Ever since she began to care for Wee Joseph, she had secretly dreamed of the day Joseph would come to the nursery and see how well she saw to his son. As time went on, she understood he avoided the nursery. She had prayed that one day he would come in. She would help him hold his son. He would be grateful and love her for her attentiveness. Their eyes would meet over the baby's head and he would know, as she already did, they were meant to be a family.

Only that didn't happen.

What *had* happened proved he didn't need her.

She wasn't needed.

The thought slapped her in the face. For so long he hadn't even been able to enter his son's room, and yet when he finally came, he made it clear he didn't need her at all.

Some dreams die painful deaths.

You lose him every time you allow yourself to get close to him. He never cared for you. He never sees the real you. He doesn't appreciate all you've done. He will never see you or love you the way you want him to. This new voice called to her aching soul, threatening to drown out the gentle guiding whisper, feeding the self-pity beginning to take hold.

But the tender whisper continued to speak to her, though self-pitying loudly taunted. A corner of her heart heard the gentle request. *Release them into My care, Sarah. Trust Me. Hold on to Me.*

"Father, hold me." She cried out with the last of her

strength. "I feel so lost. I don't know what to do. Hold me close. I surrender… it all."

And though nothing in the outside world changed at that moment, the peace that flooded her aching heart stilled the cloying self-pity and held her in a comforting embrace. In the smallest of whispers, she voiced her gratitude, leaning her cheek against the back of the rocker, almost feeling the reassuring arms of her Heavenly Father as He gently comforted her.

Shannon decided she could get used to this alone time. She could even imagine sometimes taking Samuel with her and basking in the joy of seeing him toddle among the spring mayweeds, and purple toadflax. He might spy a bird or butterfly and try to capture it in his baby hands. The thought made her desperately wish for Sean to share in Samuel's growing up. Her heart ached for about the hundredth time that day.

She stood, stretched and shook tiny floral remnants from her apron. The act returned her to the responsible present. Off in the distance the large house rose vigilant over the land. It marked the spot where now her world lived. Her ears couldn't hear Samuel's voice, but her heart surely knew his unmistakable summon.

Joy of anticipation filled her. She suddenly felt younger— much closer to her true age of nineteen. Being off by herself had done her a world of good, and she started back toward the house feeling more like her old self.

Out of nowhere, Shannon heard her name. Alain-Robert de Grillet waved a hand and called to her. She stopped, letting him catch up, all the while puzzled as to his greeting.

Though she had met Alain-Robert, Albert and Mimi's eldest, in passing, he was more stranger than acquaintance.

"Hold up, Widow O'Connor." Alain-Robert, slightly out of breath, pulled alongside Shannon.

"G'day to ye, Master Alain-Robert." Not sure which he preferred, she went with the English pronunciation rather than the more musical French.

"Good day to you, Widow O'Connor." His slight French accent still soft in his speech.

He fell silent. His eyes seemed to light everywhere but her face. Shannon waited patiently, then figured it must be her turn to say something. "'Tis a lovely day, aye?"

"Oh, ouí, it is, that it is."

He again became silent. She hadn't a clue why he had called to her. Finally, her desire to return to Samuel overtook her curiosity.

"If there's nothin' more, I've a need to be back at th' house." She hated being blunt, but she had a place to be.

"Oh, a… no. I— I just…" He stammered, turning beet red, then stammered all the more. With flaming cheeks and downcast eyes, he eventually managed to get out, "No… I saw you walking and just thought to join you. That is all."

"Ye know the way, I'm sure." She started off at a steady pace toward Edenmore.

The rest of the walk proved silent. Alain-Robert was either the strangest or shyest man she'd ever met.

Ten minutes returned them to where Shannon had left but an hour before. As much for superstition's sake as for propriety, she made sure to return through the back door. Twouldn't do to enter by way of another door when she'd left this way. And she was merely the wet nurse.

Shannon turned to the man to express gratitude for his company—silent though it was. He halted at the bottom of the steps. "Master Alain-Robert, I thank—"

A thud pounded her back and launched her off the three back steps. She landed in a heap on the grass. A twinge in her ankle sent a wave of pain through her system. Shannon gasped for breath, stunned. At her side, Alain-Robert helped her to sit up. The burn in her lungs rewarded her first taste of air. As breath came easier, she became aware of the silence. All eyes focused on her.

It was at that moment she recognized Master James, sitting on his bottom in the doorway, an expression of horror on his face. She knew what happened. His habit of throwing open the door and tearing out of the house without looking about him just landed her on her backside on the lawn. This time it also found James on his backside as well.

With both men looking so stricken and concerned, an irrepressible urge to giggle bubbled, making its way up to the top of her head, followed closely by another and another, faster and faster, until she laughed uncontrollably, tears streaming down her face.

Both men gazed from her to each other and back in stunned silence. Then James's face broke into a smile. He roared out loud with her, his eyes brimming. The more Master James laughed, the harder Shannon laughed. Her sides desperately ached, yet she couldn't stop.

Alain-Robert stood to his full height, again staring at his two laughing companions as if they had grown extra heads. With a shrug, he turned and walked away.

"Alain-Robert. Hey," Master James called out between giggles. "Come back. Alain-Robert."

But he never turned around.

The sight of the dejected shoulders headed down the path sobered her.

Master James stood, quickly giving himself a dusting swipe, and then held out his hand to her.

She took it and tried to stand. "Oh!"

"What seems to be the matter?" His eyes grew large and his eyebrows looked about to jump to his crown.

"Tis me ankle. I think it's wrenched."

"Hold on to me." He scooped her up. "I'll get you inside where my mother and sisters can help you."

Surprised at the ease that placed her in his arms, Shannon

felt as if she weighed as little as Samuel. She rested her head near his shoulder and closed her eyes. The scent of his clothes was pleasant. And the feel of his shaven cheek made her head start to spin, reviving thoughts she had long believed silenced.

No longer comfortable, heat rose in her cheeks. "Put me down."

He ignored her.

"Put me down!"

He peered at her as if she had transformed into someone entirely different.

She nodded to him, calmly adding "please."

"As you will." He let her down to a standing position.

With as much dignity as she could muster, she hopped, protecting her injured foot, to the nearest piece of furniture. The mistress entered the room just as she sat.

"Mother, the Widow has wrenched her ankle." Master James pointed out the obvious.

Shannon waved. "Tis nothin' really."

"It is *somethin'*, Mother. She cannot put weight on it."

"All right, James." The mistress patted his arm and knelt in front of Shannon. "Allow me to see."

Shannon started to pull back, but the mistress held firm. Always before, Mistress Crockett respectfully called Shannon "Widow O'Connor." But now, as she reached out to offer assistance, that changed.

"Shannon, please allow me to help you. I will make sure nothing is broken and assist you with wrapping it. James can fetch some water from the well, and then you can soak it to keep down the swelling."

Becoming more uncomfortable by the second, Shannon folded her hands in her lap to keep them still. "Samuel is upstairs. I need to be able to tend to Wee Joseph and my son."

"That is not a problem. We will get you upstairs. Then I will tend your ankle. James, it appears the Widow needs your assistance. Please carry her upstairs while I fetch bandages." The mistress stood and swept out of the room—too quickly to hear Shannon's protest or see the look of glee on James's face.

"Being the obedient son that I am, I best be starting up the stairs with you."

"Oh, no, ye don't."

"Aye, but ye h'aird me sainted mither." Master James began to pour on the blarney, grinning all the more as he picked her up in his arms. "I'm to get ye up the stairs, m'lady. Ye might be of a mind to hold on else we could be havin' another catastrophe."

Shannon squeaked at the thought of falling down the steps with him. She held tight, even holding her breath and keeping her eyes closed the whole way. At the top she exhaled and heard him chuckle. A part of her wanted to thump him on his chest— his strong, broad chest—but propriety won out. When they reached the nursery door, he handily opened it, and maneuvered her into the room.

Master Joseph glanced up from the rocker. Wee Joseph slept in his arms. He motioned them to be quiet. But Samuel sensed his mother's presence and awoke from his nap.

"Mama."

"I'm here, darlin' boy."

Master James placed her on the side of the bed where Samuel lay. The toddler snuggled into his mother's lap, every once in a while peeking out at Master James with a shy smile. The big man began to play peek-a-boo. Samuel giggled.

What is going on? Did Samuel know Master James? He seemed to have a way with children. Samuel, normally a reticent child, held back from new people. *Had he worked some kind of magic on her son?* The boy enjoyed himself, even to the point of reaching out to the man. And wonder of wonders, Master James plucked him up out of her arms.

"Don't be looking at me like I've cast a spell on the boy." He responded as if he read her mind. "He's wise enough to recognize a friend when he sees him."

"Oh, he is, is he? Maybe I should be tellin' of some of his other antics. Ye wouldn't be callin' him all that wise."

"And this from his own mother."

"Aye, but tis a mother's duty to know her child. I know he's an innocent, trustin' one, an' bright for his age too. But, goin' to ye, like that, is not what I'd call wise."

"So Widow O'Connor, what would ye be calling it?"

Just then the mistress arrived in the room with the bandages followed by the daughter, Sarah Beth, who carried a bucket.

"Let me get your ankle wrapped, and then we can have you soak it in the bucket. I have more rags so we can change the wrap in a while to a dry one. Then you will need to prop your leg to keep down the swelling." Louise knelt. "How did this happen? Did you fall off the steps?"

Shannon glanced at James and shook her head. The mistress watched their expressions. "Well, do you want to tell me, son?"

"Not really." He laughed, trying to make it more of a cough behind his hand.

"Perhaps I shouldn't know?"

"Oh, no. Tis not like that…" Shannon didn't need the mistress to think she had done something improper.

"No, Mother, the Widow is protecting me." He chuckled. "I knocked her off the back steps."

"James, you what? Are you sure you are all right, Shannon? How did you…?"

"I was looking out the window and saw that Sarah—" He paused. A strange look cross his face before he continued, "Ah, Sarah left the house. She looked a mite angry and I thought I'd try to catch her, only…"

"You didn't look and …" The mistress cocked an eyebrow.

"An' I was at the door." Shannon added.

"We had a sudden meeting of the minds, you might say." Master James gave his trademark grin.

"Well, I won't say 'you know better' although I know you

do." Though the mistress scolded, laughter showed plain as day in her eyes.

Master Joseph laid Wee Joseph in his cradle and joined the group, putting an arm around his little sister. "Did I hear ye say Sarah left?"

"Aye, and I'm thinking she was heading for your cottage. Since Mother has things under control here, I can run down and see what the problem is."

"No need. I already know. I'd better go."

Shannon watched this exchange. There was more to this than met the eye. Well, it was none of her business.

"I want to speak with her. I'll go." Master James's voice rose. When everyone turned and stared, his face reddened.

"Fine, you can go, with my blessing. Just don't wake the baby."

"Fine, then, I'll go."

"Then, be gone and the rest of you can be quiet before you wake my grandson." The mistress put a finger to her lips.

James nodded to the group in general and left.

Shannon felt like he took a piece of her with him.

OCCASIONALLY WHEN JAMES CAME BY THE COTTAGE, Sarah's lilting soprano could be heard on the breeze. However, today all was silent, and he nearly turned to retrace his steps. But some niggling thought persisted, telling him she really was inside. He quietly pushed open the door and entered. He found her, asleep in the rocker.

She lay turned, her right cheek resting against the back of the chair. Her legs were drawn up into the seat. Sunlight streamed in through the west window, making her auburn curls glow as if on fire. In spite of the tear streaks lining her cheeks, a glow of peace radiated from her face.

James feared he might destroy something sacred should he

wake her.

He wasn't conscious of how long he stood watching her sleep, whether two minutes or two hours. There was a naturalness, a belonging that James couldn't explain. It awakened in him a longing to *do* something, though he wasn't sure what. Unable to bring himself to arouse her from whatever had brought about such holy beauty, he quietly retrieved a quilt off the bed. As tenderly as he knew how, James draped it across Sarah before leaving, feeling more confused than ever.

❧

SARAH AWOKE WITH A START. THE CRIMSON SUN DIPPED behind the glowing hilltops.

She was at Joseph's cottage.

With a sense of urgency, she hopped up and nearly tripped over a blanket laid about her. Where did that come from?

Her father would suffer no compromise about her being home each evening. She cast one last look about the place. Joseph had not been home to eat.

But who put the blanket about her? The realization left her with a mixture of embarrassment, disappointment and confusion.

Why hadn't he come home? Or had he and seen her asleep? Would he think she was not doing a good enough job? Did he add the blanket?

It was the same old trap.

"Stop, foolish woman," she addressed the plaguing questions. "The cover was a gift of the Father. Thank ye, Father. And Joseph probably decided to eat with his family. Thank ye, Father, for our families. I'll not be looking for troubles of my own making." She folded the blanket, her decision made. Taking one last look about, she headed for her home, feeling more thankful than she had in a long time for the loving family that awaited her there.

Chapter Nine

Louise smiled welcome to the men as they arrived, directing them to her husband's study. Four months had passed since the last official meeting. Louise knew Antoine was eager to discuss the progress of their plan.

Albert arrived first, pulling up seconds before Thomas Stewart. Louise, returning from showing the men to the study, heard the next knock, but found her eldest, Lucy, already at the door, opening it to Cameron McHugh, the big man with the gentle heart.

"Aye, wee one, an' how is the bonniest lass in the Laggan?"

Lucy blushed. "I believe you would have said that to whoever of my sisters answered the door, Master McHugh."

"Aye, but you, me lass, are the one to open it. That makes you the bonniest." He winked.

Louise laughed and escorted him to the study. This time, she arrived as Lucy greeted both Michael O'Toole and Paddy Flanagan, who had come together.

"Monsieur O'Toole, Monsieur Flanagan, welcome."

"Top o' the mornin' to ye, Mistress Crockett, an' to ye, Miss Lucy." Monsieur O'Toole removed his cap and elbowed his friend to do the same. Monsieur Flanagan tucked his cap under his arm, nodded, and, with an uncomfortable-looking half smile, kept his eyes lowered. The men followed Louise to the study.

ANTOINE CLAPPED THE MEN ON THE SHOULDER AND SHOOK their hands. They joined the others, and after exchanges were made, they sat at the table where only months earlier they had made their solemn agreement. It was hard to miss how they all now turned to him, awaiting the next move.

"Gentlemen." Antoine stood before the group. "I thought we could share some successes, needs, and perhaps encourage one another today."

"Aye." Paddy uncomfortably glanced about. "I see an awful lot of need, but I've not seen much success. I don't know if there is enough encouragement to make me think this'll work. Mind ye, I'm not givin' up, but I'm not seeing the changes I'd hoped for after last time."

"If nothin' else, I'd say tis worse." Michael O'Toole's voice sounded raspier today.

"In what way?" Albert asked.

"We've not made a secret about comin' here, and now people I've called friends me whole life are startin' to treat me like I'm diseased."

"We knew this wouldn't be easy. I, for one, think it will get even worse before it gets better. But I see no other course before me." Thomas spoke more to himself than the group.

"What could be worse than me life-long neighbors behavin' as if I've the plague?" Paddy's fist came down on the table with a loud smack. The room stilled.

Thomas broke the silence. "The Combers are back." In his position as Laird, he was often privy to information.

"I thought rounding them up was the one thing the English got right." Cameron leaned in at the table.

"Are ye sure?" Michael O'Toole's gaze jumped from person to person.

"Aye, I am sure. They were overheard at a shebeen. Nothing one might legally use, but enough to know they're back. If it were found out they'd been overheard, someone might not wake on the morrow."

"What's this to do with us?" Paddy Flanagan obviously already knew the answer. Antoine wondered if he were planning to separate himself from the rest.

The silence deafened. But rather than say more, Antoine said, "Let's pray."

⚜

"WIDOW O'CONNOR, I'M THINKING WE SHOULD HAVE AN outing today." Sarah had been cooing over the wiggling form of Wee Joseph when the idea popped in her head. He giggled at the faces she made at him.

"You and Wee Joseph will have a wonderful time, I'm sure." Shannon wiped a damp cloth over Samuel's dirty face without meeting Sarah's eyes.

"Aye we will, won't we little one. Aye, we will." Her head nodded over his, while small fists grabbed at her tresses. "And so will Samuel and so will Widow O'Connor, won't they?" She tickled his tummy.

"Oh, but me and Samuel, we canna be goin'."

"And why not?" Sarah continued to smile and coo over Wee Joseph as she spoke with the widow.

"But… I'm workin' here." A frown creased her brow.

"But your duties are with Wee Joseph, and he'll be on the picnic so, there you are." Sarah blew a loud buzz on the baby's stomach before looking up to add, "You must come. And we want you to. Please?"

Sarah knew the widow had taken few trips away from the house since the excursion resulting in her twisted ankle. Physically, she was good as new. However, she avoided James.

"But what about the mistress? How will she be takin' to me goin' gallivantin' 'round with the babe?"

"Tanté Louise will be fine about us taking an outing. The boys need to be outside in the fresh air, and we need the relaxation. Perhaps we might ask if she'd like to join us."

"Ye do the askin' then. I'll make the babes ready."

Sarah caught a touch of a smile lifting the corners of the young woman's lips just before she headed for the stairs. Tanté was in the parlor with her needlework. "Tanté Louise, what would you say to a picnic today? The weather is too lovely to stay cooped in the house."

Tanté put down her hoop and patted the seat beside her. "I'd say, lovely idea. And I'm sure it is yours. I'm guessing you and the widow want to take the babies. I believe that should be fine as long as you stay on our property. Don't stray far from the house."

"But you are coming as well. Please, come with us."

"No, I cannot today. Antoine has company in the study. I need to stay close. But you girls go and take the babies with you. They will enjoy getting out of the house. Assure Widow O'Connor you have my blessing." Louise added a wink as she patted Sarah's hand.

"Did I hear someone mention a picnic?"

Sarah turned to see James, with Joseph Louis standing close behind. Joseph's handsome features were still too distracting. Even now his sapphire eyes twinkled.

"Sarah and the Widow O'Connor are taking the boys for a picnic. Since I am unable to attend, why don't the two of you go in my stead? It would make feeding you men so much easier." Tanté smiled as she gave James's cheek a pat and a pinch.

Sarah's heart skipped a beat. *Say no. Say no.*

"Why, we'd love to go, wouldn't we, Joseph?"

Joseph eyed the group, the first small smile Sarah had seen in a long time curving his lips.

"If that is all right with you. And the Widow, of course. It is all right, isn't it, Sarah?" James taunted with his most charming smile.

"Of course it is." Tanté didn't give her the time to protest. Instead she gently squeezed Sarah's shoulder. "And I will feel better knowing you have two strong men with you."

"Right, we're strong and here to protect you." James flexed his right arm, then his left.

"James, who will be protecting us from you?" Sarah couldn't resist, the retort flying from her brain through her mouth before common sense could quell it.

"Mother, will you allow her speak so of your darlin' boys? Joseph, I believe our reputation has been sullied."

"No, I believe *your* reputation has been sullied. I'm hungry. What are we having for lunch?"

With a laugh, Tanté led the trio to the larder where she helped them put together the picnic necessities.

Even though she laughed at the banter, Sarah's heart fluttered at the thought of being so close to Joseph. Could she bear it? The idea terrified and tantalized her all at the same time.

❧

Joseph followed as Sarah led the little group to a quiet field dotted with a few remaining columbine and delicate yellow flag irises scattered here and there. He lugged the picnic supplies, she carried Wee Joseph, and James bore young Samuel on his broad shoulders. Shannon, hauling a large patch quilt, tramped close by, seeming to not want Samuel too far from her. The ever-present Bridget brought up the rear, her arms full of last-minute items.

"This is the place." Sarah stopped.

Joseph set down the basket.

"Here, you take him, and I'll set the meal." She handed the baby to him.

Shannon brought over the large quilt and began spreading it out. Bridget set down her supplies to help.

Joseph watched over Wee Joseph's head as Sarah, organized and in charge, moved the basket to the quilt and helped Shannon open the packages of food and supplies. He felt hungrier just watching as she lay out garden-fresh carrots, cooled steamed potatoes, and a dozen of Josephine's wonderful lamb pies. There was goat cheese, a delicious brown bread, and salted butter, plus several skins, some with wine and others with water. As delicious as the food appeared, the one setting it all out caught his gaze. Sarah appeared more beautiful now than he could ever remember. Her face glowed when she was excited. Her eyes flashed when she became angry. But at ordinary times like this, when she didn't know she was being watched, she was most beautiful.

A door in his heart cracked open a bit. He slammed it shut. He could never again go down that road.

"Don't just stand there gawking. Sit and eat." Sarah stood, hands on her hips. "Here, I'll take Wee Joseph."

"Let him play here on the blanket." Joseph put the baby on his belly. Wee Joseph promptly rolled over, grabbing at his feet with his fat, little fists. In less than a minute, he successfully connected with one and began to suck on his toes. Joseph watched the small triumph and quietly chuckled.

Stretching out on the grass, it dawned on him how very long it had been since he'd felt this much contentment. Joseph closed his eyes, hearing a yellow wagtail in the trees on the other side of the grazing sheep, singing thanks for his dinner.

"Looks like there's enough blue to make a cat a pair of pants."

Joseph opened his eyes and smiled at Sarah's observance,

glancing toward the western mountain peaks. The summer sky glowed azure between. A good sign for a good day.

"Aye, maybe even two pair." They were only talking about the weather. The subject was safe, but they were talking for a change.

Sarah returned his smile, leaning back against a nearby hawthorn tree and stretching out her long legs.

Joseph rolled to his side, propping his head on his fist. His mind recalled those legs that once outran every boy in the Laggan, legs now prudently hidden by lady-like coverings. He turned his gaze away. It wouldn't do to let his mind wander any further.

James sat Samuel on the quilt, but the toddler promptly popped back up.

"Samuel darlin', come here to your ma." Shannon held open her arms. Samuel turned as if to obey and then, with a giggle, wobbled off down the grassy hill. James snatched him by his white gown. Samuel, arms flapping and little feet flailing in the air, laughed all the harder.

"I think your mother called you, young man. You need to see her." James chuckled, handing the scamp to Shannon. She sat with her son. Laying him across her lap, she tickled his stomach and tousled his hair. Samuel's giggles filled the air.

"If I stretch out and put my head on your lap, would you do that to me?" James sounded so innocent, but an ornery gleam twinkled in his eyes.

Joseph couldn't believe James would be so bold. He shook his head. But then, this was James. No one could predict what might next come out of his mouth.

"Not even if all the crown jewels were laid at me feet." Shannon's expression danced with friendly mirth.

Joseph had to give the Widow credit. She wasn't easily riled.

"A fellow has to take a chance now and then, you ken, don't you, Widow O'Connor?" James had charm to spare.

"Oh, I ken perfectly."

"We all do, Jamie." Sarah sweetly smiled. "Actually, I might consider letting ye put yer head on my lap."

Joseph's fingers twined tightly around the grass under his hand. Had he heard her correctly?

After a lengthy pause, Sarah scrunched her nose. "It would make it so much easier to wring yer silly neck, ye goose."

Joseph laughed along with the rest, feeling a strange sense of lightness and relief.

The women kept watch over the children while they ate. Samuel inhaled a huge portion of a lamb pie with little help while Wee Joseph lay on Sarah's lap contently cooing.

Joseph could not remember the last time he'd known such fun. This is the way it should be. No one should hurt. And he wouldn't let those he loved hurt, if he could help it. The thought seemed to pull all his other thoughts together. If God wouldn't protect the ones he loved, then he would do it himself.

"Shannon O'Connor, I thought you'd have more sense than to be spending time with these Crockett laddies." The voice came out of nowhere, startling the group into silence.

Joseph sat, recognizing the speaker.

"Christopher Dougherty, this is a private party. You best be moving along." James slowly rose to his full height. Joseph joined him and, shoulder-to-shoulder, they stared down the little man with the big mouth.

"Tis all right, boys. I'm talkin' with the lady, here. Shannon, ye be knowin' better'n to be in the company of these heathens." Dougherty's speech slurred.

"And you've got room to talk." Sarah's ire sounded.

Joseph cut her off with a look.

She held Wee Joseph closer.

"Excuse me, Master James, Master Joseph." Shannon drew Samuel close to her side. "Christopher Dougherty, tis a might early to have been drinkin' so much that you'd be talkin' this stupid. I know yer wife would be preferrin' ye spend a bit more time at yer own business and less time drinkin' and runnin' your mouth. Now, if you'll be movin' on, we can continue to enjoy our meal." She picked up Samuel and quickly moved to stand by Sarah and Bridget.

Dougherty paused to look at his dirty fingernails.

Joseph could feel it in his bones, the inebriated fool was scouting for trouble.

Christopher took a step toward Shannon, arms outstretched toward Samuel.

That was all Joseph needed. He and James grabbed the drunk, pinning him to the ground. Nose to nose, Joseph smelled the soured whiskey breath. It turned his stomach. Still he spoke with deadly calm. "You heard the lady. You need to be moving along. You are on Crockett land. We won't take kindly to you again being on it." Low and slow he asked, "Do you understand?"

Christopher Dougherty's bloodshot eyes widened to near sobriety. Slowly, he nodded his head.

"Good." Joseph stood.

James offered Dougherty a hand, but Christopher slapped it away, standing on his own. He took time to brush off his clothes before stumbling away. After a short distance, he turned. "Be mindful. Combs can be used for more'n one thing." Then he turned on his heel running as if chased by a banshee.

Joseph observed Shannon's reaction.

She turned to check on Samuel.

It had been a clear threat. A vine of fear crept up his spine. Quickly, he pulled James aside, knowing Sarah would try to overhear and not wanting her to.

"I've not heard of the Combers before in this area." Joseph kept his voice low.

"I thought they'd been banished."

Joseph brushed the hair back from his forehead. "We'll be needing to get the women and babes back to the house. I'll let father know what was said.

James rested his arm over Joseph's shoulder. "If anyone has heard anything, he'll know."

The merriment of a few minutes prior evaporated into an air of awkward tension.

Joseph attempted to break the strain. "I do believe the wee ones are looking ready to return. Shall we pack up and get them home for a nap?" The women mutely nodded. It cut him to know they were alarmed. Here on Crockett property where they should feel safe, they'd been frightened by a big mouthed drunk.

James grabbed the large basket, picking up the remnants of the picnic. The rest followed his example. Soon they were packed.

This time, Shannon and Sarah carried the children, Bridget held the quilt, and the men carried the baskets and leftovers. They walked five abreast with the women on the inside. The men, rigid, as if on a military maneuver, surrounded them on the outside. Even the wind and the birds seemed to go into hiding, leaving a stillness in the air that swallowed all other sounds, including their footsteps—the entire way home.

As they came in sight of the house, Shannon stopped and pulled the now-sleeping Samuel closer. "No more. I will live in fear no more."

Joseph caught her gaze.

She straightened her stance. "We were havin' a good time. It has been so very long since I have let meself enjoy life like today. And then with one brief moment of stupidity from that inebriated lout, we're all skulking home in broad daylight like terrified children. Well, no more. I will not be bullied or told with whom I may spend my time. I will not be threatened into hiding. Miss Sarah?"

"Aye?"

"Samuel and I thank ye for the idea of this merry noontime. Gentlemen?"

Joseph and James answered in unison.

"I thank ye for yer company and help. And now, I've babes

to attend so I will be headin' for the nursery and wishin' you all g'day."

And as he watched her walk boldly to the house, Joseph couldn't help but wonder.

Why wasn't he as brave as the Widow Shannon O'Connor?

Chapter Ten

"Cullen, a jug of your finest." Kevin O'Rourke stood as his companions coarsely snickered at the word *finest*. This was far from their first drink of the day, and Cullen O'Keefe was beginning to tire of their presence. But to placate all, he did nothing but hope they would get bored with drinking in his shebeen and move on. In the very near future.

Cullen heard the door open behind him but took no outward note. Instead, he brought a smile and bottle of whiskey to the table.

"Christopher Dougherty, ye look like yer in need of a drink. Join us." O'Rourke waved his hand. Cullen turned to see Dougherty, appearing as if he had no need to catch up to what Kevin and his company had already imbibed. There was a stagger to his walk, but Cullen couldn't read the strange expression on his face. With clothes rumpled and dirty, and breath potent enough to send the stench halfway across the room, he knew something had happened.

"Aye, I think I will do just that, laddies." Christopher pulled up a stool. "Ye'll never guess who I just saw."

"Out with it, man."

"All right, I'll tell ye. The Widow O'Connor, it twas. She

were out with that Crockett clan and had her wee bairn along, she did. I says to her, 'Widow O'Connor, why do ye bring yer babe, Sean O'Connor's only son, God rest his soul, out amongst the heathen? Ere ye in need o' help gettin' away from the wicked brood?' And she says, to me face, mind ye, she says, 'Christopher Dougherty, black-hearted mither that I am, I've sold me wee precious babe to these heathens, I have. I had no choice an' now must suffer the infernal fires o' hell. Pray fer me soul, Christopher,' she says, 'n' me wee Samuel too.'"

"I dinnae believe such—ye bin listening to the banshees sing again, Dougherty? Shannon O'Connor selling Sean's son to the Crocketts? I'll not have a word of it."

Dougherty stood. He started to put his hands to his hips but swayed so hard he grabbed the table for support. "Ye can believe it or not, but tis true, I tell ye. And when I tries to take back her son and release the poor tortured soul from their filthy grasp, the whole houseful attacked me, they did. I could have fought off six or seven, but they called all the household—I had twenty-five o' them Frenchies keepin' me from protectin' Sean O'Connor's own."

"Aye, twenty-five, ye say?" Kevin winked at the others at the table and pulled Christopher back to his stool.

"I'd have liked to have seen that, I would."

Though Cullen could hear O'Rourke and his companions scoff, it seemed to have no effect on Dougherty.

"Those Frenchies haven't seen the last o' Christopher Dougherty, I can tell ye that."

"Right ye are. To Christopher Dougherty, lord protector of widows n' children. A toast." All at the table, and a few at surrounding tables, raised their tankards, grinning at the ludicrous concept. Dougherty, though, took it all quite seriously.

"As I fought me way free o' the heathens, I reminded 'm, I did, that combs can be used for more 'an just sheep." The merriment immediately quieted as those seated with him began to nervously look about.

"Perhaps ye shouldna be so free with yer talk, Christopher, me boy," Kevin clapped what might have been a friendly arm around Dougherty's shoulder, pulling him close.

It appeared more like a warning. A quick scan of the place and Cullen surmised most all had let the allusion pass. All, except for the men at O'Rourke's table, and the quiet young man in the corner whose eyes briefly rose from the whiskey he'd been nursing for the last hour.

The cogs in Cullen O'Keefe's brain were already spinning. Some kind of trouble lay ready to roll into the Laggan. He wasn't sure exactly what kind of trouble, but the burn in his round gut said the wheels of change were now in motion.

"Sarah, are you so soon back?"

Louise glanced up from her needlework when she heard Sarah rummaging by the door. She hadn't expected to see any of the picnickers for an hour or more. Then they had trekked in with the little ones. The women had taken them straight upstairs. Now Sarah was back down.

"We'd had enough and decided to put the bairns to bed." Sarah called from the foyer.

"Well, then, come sit and tell me all about it."

Sarah peeked around the corner. "Let me put these things away and I'll be right in." She returned a few minutes later.

Louise patted the seat next to her. She could sense something wasn't quite right. "Where did you go?"

"Not far, just by that little stream next to the copse of elm to the west." Sarah sighed as she slumped into the seat, her long legs extended as she bounced her heels off the floor.

"You look unhappy. Did something happen?"

"Oh, Christopher Dougherty just made a fool of himself. He stumbled onto our picnic and began to make trouble. Joseph and James took care of it. But they decided we had to come home. Somehow, I keep thinking we've made a big deal of nothing. Or I'm hoping that is the case."

"In what way?" If she could just keep her talking, Louise might learn what got into her sons. As soon as they walked in, they tore past her down the hallway, knocked at Antoine's study, and closed the door.

"Christopher said something, trying to get back at them for knocking him to the ground. At least, I am fairly sure that's all it is."

"They knocked Christopher Dougherty to the ground? Whatever for?" She set her needlework down to give Sarah her full attention.

"He was drunk and made a grab for little Samuel. Joseph and James pinned him down while they told him to leave and to never again bother the Widow. You should have seen his eyes, Tanté. I'm sure he was just blathering, idiot that he is, but he seemed to know more than he was saying."

"What did he say?" She watched Sarah's heels bounce faster. Sarah's discomfort must have something to do with Dougherty's words.

"It was something about combs, and how they can be used for more than one thing." Sarah turned to her. "He can't really be serious. Can he?"

"I'm sure he's not." Though she reassured, her own mind began to roam with the awful possibilities.

"Why do people behave so hateful, Tanté?" The question cut to the very heart of their conversation. Sarah's eyes had an added sheen with tears ready to spill.

She put her arm around the young woman, who curled up like a child, putting her head on Louise's lap. As she stroked a renegade copper coil from the softly freckled forehead, an idea bloomed. "Have I ever told you the story of how I met Antoine?"

"No." Sarah turned, gazing up at her. "How did you meet?"

"Well, let's see. It turned out the king of France had nothing better to do than play matchmaker."

Sarah's eyes grew.

Louise smiled at the memory. "It's true. I was visiting Versailles with my tanté. Antoine was assigned as my escort." She sobered. "Sadly, while there I made two enemies. I struggled for years trying to understand what I had done wrong. Finally, the Lord showed me it wasn't me. It was who they perceived me to be."

Sarah eyebrows rose.

She patted her hand. "One enemy saw me as a threat to her position, even though I did not want her position and had never thought to attain it. I did not even understand that other women wanted such positions." She shook her head as the memory of her encounter with the Marquise de Montespan, Louis XIV's mistress at the time, flooded her thoughts. The Marquise had explained, quite clearly, she would not tolerate anyone coming between her and the king. Not satisfied with Louise's assurance, the Marquise began plotting to have her killed. The memory still brought a shiver.

"The other enemy was jealous, plain and simple. Since I had spent much of my adult life as my tanté Marie's companion, this trip to Versailles was a holiday for me. I was not used to servants doing my bidding. I made friends with the young woman assigned as my lady-in-waiting. She was very sweet. Her twin, though identical in looks, was the exact opposite in nature. Thoroughly jealous, she perceived me to be a spoiled, rich, social climber."

"I cannot imagine anyone thinking that about you. What happened?"

"Poor Momo found herself drawn into the Marquise's plan to kill me. Only God intervened. The king remanded the Marquise back to Paris and Momo ran away."

"Momo? I've heard that name before. Wasn't that the name of Mistress de Grillet's sister?" Understanding seemed to light the young woman's eyes and she sat up. "You mean Mistress de Grillet's sister tried to kill you?"

Louise nodded.

"But isn't she buried over in the cemetery?"

"Oui, dear heart, she is. Mimi loved her twin and missed her terribly. When we all left France, Albert and Antoine made lengthy searches for her. They finally found Momo in a very poor section of London, ill and pregnant. By then, we had all settled here in Donegal, so they brought her home. Mimi and I nursed her as best we could. But she was so sick and the baby so weak, they both died before the night was through. God was gracious to all of us, though, giving us a few weeks before her labor started. Mimi was reunited with her sister and, before she died, Momo and I put the past behind. She asked for, and I gave her, my forgiveness."

"I don't know if I could do that, Tanté." Sarah stared at the ceiling. "That is a lot to forgive. What if she had killed you? You wouldn't be here, nor Joseph, nor…"

Louise was not surprised by Sarah's feelings for her son. "But she did not kill me, dear heart. And she could not have, unless God allowed it. That is the same for what Christopher Dougherty spewed. Unless God allows it, it is only empty words. Our Lord has well protected us thus far, and He will continue. Things have not always been easy, but we have always been in His hand."

"Now you sound like my mother."

"I take that as a compliment. She is one of my dearest friends and quite wise." Louise smiled and patted Sarah's hand. "It could be Christopher will stir up trouble. Or maybe nothing will come of his words. Still, whatever the outcome, 'Be anxious for nothing, but in everything by prayer and supplication with thanksgiving, let your requests be made known to God. And the peace of God, which surpasses all comprehension, shall guard your hearts and your minds in Christ Jesus.' It is the best plan I know."

And with that, she stood, kissed Sarah on both cheeks and left the girl to ponder.

⸙

The latch sounded as it securely snapped into place.

Antoine, engrossed in his thoughts, searching for a reference among his library, jumped at the metallic thud, scattering papers over his desk and floor. He peered up to see Joseph and James's concerned expressions.

"The Combers are back." All three spoke in unison.

"You know?" Both young men approached the desk as though magnetically drawn.

"Thomas heard through his contact. I did not tell the rest of the group today, but this time, I think they may be receiving help from the English. Thomas would not have been told that. It is only a hunch on my part."

Disbelief showed in his sons' faces. "I thought the English had rid us of that scourge. Now you think they are in league?"

Joseph mutely shook his head.

"The last thing England wants is a united Ireland. The easiest way they've had to keep us apart is with our differences. Religious differences. But when we stand firm together as believers in Christ, we become fearsome to those in authority." Antoine could see his sons grasped the implication.

"So, they use the Combers to punish anyone who forgets his place."

"Yes, Joseph. It seems word of our meetings has made someone in high places nervous. Now he wants to make us nervous. Enough to stop us."

Antoine remembered the stunned looks when Thomas shared his news at the meeting. Even now, the name *Combers* sent shivers up Antoine's spine. He had seen the aftermath of their work more than once. Terrifying, especially for the women, children, and elderly. The Combers left scars inside and out.

He had no fears for himself. As a soldier, he had fought many battles. But now he was a husband and father. This would be a different type of battle—more reminiscent of when he, Louise, and newborn Gabriel escaped from France. Instead of running, though, here he would stand. Stand and fight, if need be.

The expression on Joseph's face mirrored his own thoughts. And no wonder. Joseph, though younger than James, understood life as a father. "My sons, let's take this before the Lord. We don't know the depth or width of this fight, but He does and will guide us."

James shook his head. "Father, there are times for prayers and times for action. We need to take action, now."

"You're right, James. We do need to take action. However, never think of praying as standing idle. We have no concrete knowledge other than a slip of the tongue here and there. We need something more. Until then, I will pray. I will ask for the insight and guidance needed to keep us safe and allow us to be witnesses to those without faith. I will keep my eyes and ears open to His leading."

Joseph remained quiet throughout the exchange. James always had been the more vocal of the two, but this was especially quiet, even for Joseph.

"We can go roust Christopher Dougherty, see what he does know." James paced as he threw out ideas. "We could make him tell where he got his information."

"I've raised you better than that, son. No, you will leave Dougherty alone."

"But—"

"No buts. Our help is not in our own might. Remember Who is in control. We will follow what He has to say."

Joseph's gaze met his. "What if He remains silent. Would we simply lay down our weapons and allow the Combers victory?" Though softly spoken, Joseph's words were filled with emotion.

"No, son. We will not allow the Combers to do as they wish.

But our hope is in God, and that is where we begin. Let us pray, now."

Antoine realized they bowed their heads out of respect but did not know if it was out of respect for their father, or their God.

Oh, Abba, let it be for You.

Chapter Eleven

I'm going to look in on my son." Joseph nodded toward the stairs.

"I think I'll join you." James grinned, taking the steps two at a time, and making a beeline for the room at the top of the steps.

Joseph gave a quiet laugh and shook his head. Did the Widow return James's interest?

In the nursery, the little one lay cozy in Shannon's arms while she rocked him, humming a lullaby. Joseph watched little eyes valiantly trying to remain open, but finally succumbing to sleep.

Shannon whispered to them in cadence with her song. "I think I left Samuel's toy in the basket with the food. If you can take Wee Joseph, I will run downstairs and fetch it."

"I'll go." James to the rescue.

"Sh-h-h." Shannon and Joseph corrected at the same time.

"I'll go." This time James whispered and left.

"Oh, Master Joseph, I noticed something when I was changin' the babe. Let me show ye."

Both heads were bent over the baby while Shannon lifted the

skirt of his gown to reveal a couple insect bites on Wee Joseph's chubby little calves. Joseph heard the door open, expecting James to bring the beloved toy to Shannon, but he heard no one enter.

Looking over his shoulder, he saw Sarah's fleeting form heading down the hall. A nice view. The front view was nicer though. He couldn't believe the thought flitted through his mind. But the impression lingered as he watched over his shoulder.

"She's in love with ye, y'know."

"Who?"

Shannon nodded toward the open door.

"Sarah? I don't think so."

Shannon took on a patronizing look. "Men. Unless we women write it out in blood, ye never seem to catch a clue. Aye, Miss Sarah's in love with ye, and I'm supposin' she has been for a long time."

"Are you sure?" He followed her. "What has she said?"

The Widow wagged her finger at him. "Master Joseph, ye sound like an old gossip, ye do. A woman understands these things about another woman. And this woman says Miss Sarah's in love with ye."

Joseph shook his head. "No, she's just a good friend."

"I'm sure she is, but… if ye don't mind my askin', what are yer feelings for her?"

He didn't want to answer that question. He knew he should say he still loved his wife. And that was true. He knew he had deep feelings for Sarah too.

Deep feelings? That was mildly put. He had loved her his whole life. Not being able to be together had been his first great heartache. Today they had friendship and sharing. But love? Could he ever admit that?

"I don't know." The sound of his voice made him feel the lie. Catching Shannon's gaze, he lied again. "I don't know."

"If I may be so free, perhaps ye should be figurin' that out. If yer in love with her, she needs to know. And if yer not, to be fair, she needs to know that too."

"The Widow's right." James voice startled Joseph. "You need to decide how you feel and tell her."

"You don't know what you're talking about."

Shannon placed her gentle hand on his arm. "Speak what's in yer heart, Master Joseph. Speak what's in yer heart."

Joseph sadly shook his head. He'd placed such a lock over his heart, it would be dangerous to let any of the feelings out.

A danger he could ill afford.

DURING THE SUPPER HOUR, MOST OF THE MEN WHO frequented The Stray Dog returned home. Some would come again after eating for a drink or two before going home to bed. But for now, only one or two customers remained. Cullen O'Keefe decided he could leave his wife to care for their needs while he ran a brief errand.

If he hurried, he could be back in less than half an hour and no one would be the wiser. The longer summer days meant twilight came later, but with care, he wouldn't be seen.

Sticking close to tree-lined areas, Cullen made his way to the two-story house and circled around to the back. Little there afforded a shield, so he hoped someone would quickly answer his knock.

"No need help now. Return on morrow." The old woman with the thick French accent tried to close the door.

Collin stuck his foot in the way. "I need to be speakin' with the master o' the house, if ye please." Cullen pulled his hat from his head and anxiously kneaded it in his hands.

"Too late. *Le* morrow."

"It canna wait, mum. Please, tell the master tis O'Keefe here. He'll ken." He hoped the urgency in his voice convinced her.

"Wait."

She began to close the door, but he kept his foot in the path.

"Please, might I wait inside?"

She inspected him up and down and turned her nose up. "No. You wait here. I get Monsieur."

"I'll wait here, but hurry." Cullen rubbed the back of his neck, looking for a more shadowed position. He brought important news but dare not stay away from the shebeen long. And he didn't dare get caught between there and here. The more he worried, the more his lips puckered in and out.

"O'Keefe. Get in here." Master Crockett, napkin in hand, held the door for him, glanced cautiously about and closed the door securely. "You've heard something. Out with it, man."

"Beggin' yer pardon, sir, fer botherin' ye like this, but ye said to bring any news I might learn."

Antoine nodded, motioning to continue.

"I don't have anythin' for sure, but I did hear Kevin O'Rourke hushin' Christopher Dougherty for speakin' freely of the Combers. O'Rourke made like it was some joke, but I could see his concern about the mention. I've been listenin' for more, but today were the first anyone even spoke of the cursed lot. As for now, I'd keep a watch on Christopher Dougherty an' Kevin O'Rourke. I'm thinkin' O'Rourke is up to his eyeballs in this, but Dougherty may know more an' is stupid enough to slip an' say somethin'."

"Thank you, O'Keefe. You're a good man and I don't want to cause you any trouble." He took out two gold pieces.

"No thank ye, sir. I hate those Combers worse'n ye. I remember them from afore. But I do need to get back to me misses." He replaced his hat and shook hands with Master Crockett.

The master opened the door. "I will be praying your help does not cause you trouble. Again, thank you, O'Keefe."

Cullen tipped his soiled hat and hurried off in hopes of learning more. And in hopes of not getting caught.

ANTOINE RETURNED TO THE DINNER TABLE. "James, Joseph, Robert, come with me. Excuse us, my love." He caught Louise's hand and squeezed. Her nod said she understood. He motioned for his sons to follow and headed to the office without looking back.

"Close the door."

"Father, what have you learned? Who was that at the door?" All three spoke at once.

Antoine raised his hand. "That was O'Keefe. He has nothing more substantial than what we already know, except another name to watch. He suggests we keep an eye on Christopher Dougherty and Kevin O'Rourke. He thinks O'Rourke is the one who knows the most, is most likely involved. But he believes Dougherty may be key, knowing more than he thinks and might be willing to talk."

"Then let's go talk with him now." James appeared like Antoine felt—ready to drag Dougherty back to thoroughly question him.

"Son, as I told you before, you are not to go near him. As stupid as you may think he is, Dougherty isn't so daft as to let you push him around without causing trouble."

"So, what do you want us to do?" Robert returned Antoine's gaze. "What is your plan?"

"This needs to come from our committee. It will be a show of strength and solidarity. Plus, Dougherty will feel more like cooperating if he sees others of his faith in the group."

Antoine heard James's quiet snort but continued. "I want you to beware. Remain cautious. Keep a sidearm close at all times. Do not go anywhere without another. Make sure someone is with the women anytime they leave the house. We do not know in what way the Combers may attack, but for sure, we have more strength in numbers."

Antoine watched as his sons nodded and left, knowing they were not satisfied. Especially James. He could feel in his heart something big was just under the surface, ready to erupt. His gut told him James could end up in the middle. His gut was rarely wrong.

❧

James left the study and took to the stairs. He found Shannon on the floor playing with Samuel. She wore her sandy brown hair pulled back with a ribbon, the curled ends dangling over her shoulder. Her laugh lilted like music.

He drank in the scene. This is what he needed. Just watching the Widow O'Connor's gentle ways soothed his spirit, made him forget the ugliness of the world outside these walls.

So enchanted was he in the picture framed by the nursery doorway, James missed Joseph's question. "I'm sorry, what did you say?" He hadn't even heard his brother follow him up the stairs.

"I said I want to stop at the Stewarts' on the way to the cottage. Care to come along?" James caught a look of determination on Joseph's face.

Remembering his father's words, he sighed. "Aye."

Robert, who followed behind Joseph, declined, saying he thought he should stay home. James and Joseph headed downstairs and out the front door.

They walked in silence for most of the way. It ate at James, this silence. His own mind whirled, not knowing what to do in his own case, and his heart floundered in a quandary. Maybe he could learn something. Then again, maybe not. This was Joseph, after all, who kept everything locked inside. Curiosity had the better of him. He wanted Sarah to be happy. For a long time, he'd hoped she could find her happiness with him. But, somehow, images of Shannon O'Connor flooded back far more than thoughts of Sarah these days. "What do you plan to say?"

"I haven't thought it all out. I'm hoping the right words will come when we can actually talk."

"So why am I here? You don't want me to chaperone, do you? You could always wait for the morning."

"Father is serious. I prefer to do things his way. He has a way of being right. Besides you can help me keep watch over the cottage and my barn tonight. And, I need to do this before I lose my nerve."

James gave Joseph a friendly punch in the shoulder. "Then I will see you safely to the Stewarts' and await you at your cottage. You really don't need me, and I've got some thinking to do myself." James could feel Joseph's grin more than see it in the dwindling light.

"I guess you do. However, don't leave just yet. If we both go, no one can accuse me of calling on the lass."

"Isn't that what you're doing?" The crunch of broken seashells lining the drive to the Stewarts' tower house echoed from under their boots.

"I don't know." Joseph walked up to the door.

James chuckled. "Do you plan to be honest with her?"

"What do you mean?"

"You're obviously not being honest with me or the Widow. I wonder if you're even being honest with yourself." James winked at Joseph, hoping to soften his words.

Joseph said no more but stepped up to the front door.

Bridget swiftly answered his knock. "Might we speak with Miss Sarah?"

"Aye, sir." The practiced curtsey made her cap bob. "Will you not come in?" Bridget held the door wider, allowing the men entrance before closing it with trained silence. She led James and Joseph to the parlor before notifying Sarah's parents. The Crocketts had often been guests at Balleylawn. James knew the parlor by heart.

"Joseph and James." Meg Stewart sounded surprised as she floated into the room. "I understand you've come to see Sarah?"

James and Joseph briefly bowed. Looking to his brother, James remained silent. This was Joseph's plan. He would have to be the one to answer. Joseph seemed to get the message.

"Aye, Mistress Stewart. Might we speak with her?"

"Of course. Please be seated. I will get her. Might I get you some tea?"

Joseph declined and James shook his head. Mistress Stewart smiled before floating back out to find her daughter.

Joseph nervously rocked on the balls of his feet. It was hard not to laugh. Joseph rarely displayed signs of nervousness. This younger brother of his had always seemed so solid and sure. He never made a mistake nor did anything out of line. And he usually had a well thought out plan before he did a thing.

Well, that was until Kathleen died.

He seemed almost back to normal. Maybe a little more serious, but considering what he'd been through, that was natural. James put his arm over Joseph's shoulder and gave him a brotherly wink.

Joseph smiled and nodded.

"Is everything all right with Wee Joseph?" Concern filled Sarah's voice as she nearly ran into the room.

"He's fine, peacefully dreaming." Joseph motioned to a chair.

Sarah took the seat, her graceful fingers folded together in her lap, her green eyes wide.

"I think I'll wait outside." James pointed to the door and left his brother to figure things out.

SARAH CAUGHT JOSEPH'S GAZE AND GLANCED AWAY. HE remained standing. "Why are you here, Joseph?" She couldn't look at him and keep her voice normal, but smoothing her skirt seemed to help. Only a short while ago he stood with Shannon, their heads bent close over Wee Joseph. Just like a family. She blinked back the threatening tear.

"I wanted to speak with you about something." He paced. It must be important.

"Is the cottage satisfactory?" Again, she glanced up, but still couldn't hold his gaze. Instead, she watched his feet walk back and forth over her mother's imported carpet.

"Fine, fine. I spend so little time there now. You probably don't need to keep going. What with Wee Joseph with my parents and my eating most meals with them, you needn't work so hard at the cottage."

"Oh." Her heart dropped. Again, she was no longer needed. "I don't mind, really." This time she caught and held his gaze. *Please don't take the cottage from me too.*

"Sarah," He coughed and stared at the floor. "I… um… you love Wee Joseph, don't you?"

"Like my own." Would he take him away from her as well?

"I've been thinking. We've been friends for a long time, right?"

Sarah nodded. Where was this going?

"The Widow needs to be able to have a life of her own. Wee Joseph needs a mother." Joseph paced harder now. Was he about to tell her he planned to marry Shannon? How many times must her heart break? She would leave this place. She couldn't stay here any longer. Where could she go?

Joseph dropped to one knee and took her hand.

"I was thinking we should get married."

All air sucked from her chest. Did she gasp out loud? Those words, those were the words she had longed to hear.

She blinked. "What did you say?"

"I just asked you to marry me. You would be able to be a full-time mother to Wee Joseph. You and…"

And then she heard it, or rather, realized she hadn't heard it. Never once had Joseph said anything about love between them. Nothing had been said of his feelings for her.

He only wanted a substitute for Kathleen.

Sarah rose to her full height and mustered every ounce of

dignity she possessed. "No thank you, Master Crockett. As you have pointed out to me more than once, I am not Kathleen."

She fled the room, closing the door on her hopes and dreams.

Chapter Twelve

Anger oozed from every pore. Sarah began up the stairs feeling embarrassed and hurt. By the time she reached her bedroom, her feelings had expanded into full-blown rage. What made him think he could just use her to replace Kathleen? Did he think so little of her? Did he know her so little to think she'd marry him just to give his son a mother?

She picked up the hand mirror on her dressing table. Her image reflected red-rimmed eyes and a blotchy face. Tears made one ugly. Her hand reacted, the mirror raised for a dramatic throw. Only she stopped, the last drop of common sense hitting its mark. She flopped on her bed. The mirror dropped from her hand a safe distance from the carpeted floor.

"Why, Lord? Why is this so hard? Why can't he love me?"

It has only been six months.

"I know. But he asked me to marry him. Why? How could he do that?"

Isn't that what you want?

"Not without his love. I couldn't bear it without his love."

Love bears all things, Sarah.

"But not this. It is too hard." She sat up and wiped the tears from her cheeks. "I need to leave. I'll visit mother's family in Glasgow."

What will that change?

"I don't know. I DON'T KNOW." She began gathering clothes and travel necessities.

What about your promise?

Sarah froze. The promise. The reason she had spent so much time helping. The reason she had not moved on with her life.

That promise.

"I can't keep it." Her knees buckled beneath her and she slumped in a heap, sobbing. "I can't."

She'd never run from a challenge in her life. But this was no mere challenge. It was everything. "I can't keep it, Lord. Don't ask me. It's too hard. I just can't do it." She waited for the voice inside to argue, but all she heard was *What about your promise?*

⁂

"WHAT WERE YOU THINKING?"

Joseph seldom saw his father this angry. He didn't like feeling as if he were again a small child. "Maybe I wanted to check on something here at the house? I don't know. What do you want me to say? When I finished my business at the Stewarts', James had gone. I chose to come here before going home. More habit than thinking."

"I was explicit. *No one* is to be out after dark. *No one* is to go anywhere alone. That wasn't only for the women, Joseph. Did you even carry a sidearm?"

"It's back at the cottage." His father started to respond, but Joseph cut him off. "Father, I'm sorry. We were together, but he gave me some privacy with what I had to do. I thought he only stepped outside the door. He probably figured to go on to the cottage, thinking I'd catch up. I'm sure he's just fine."

His father, normally a gentle, caring man had also been a soldier. This business with the Combers probably felt like war to him, leaving him to pace the floor, a tiger ready to strike, his fist pounding into his palm. Joseph had never seen his father like this.

"What would you want me to do, Father?"

"It's a little late for that now, do you not think?"

Joseph stared at the floor. He knew he was wrong. His father still worried about him, about the family, about the community. He shouldn't have given him more worry.

As if Antoine read his mind, he waved his hand erasing the words from the air. "Oh, I am sorry. Stay here tonight, and pray James is safe at your cottage. Tomorrow we will look for your brother." Antoine patted Joseph's shoulder as he left the room, shaking his head, though Joseph could have sworn he heard him mumble again, "What *were* you thinking?"

❧

"WHAT WAS I THINKING?" ALAIN-ROBERT MUSED AS HE slipped out the door of The Stray Dog. He walked around back to the stand of elms where, after finding some privacy among the trees, he stopped to relieve himself. He had nursed his tankard of ale as long as he could, avoiding everyone.

Everyone but the host.

One didn't avoid Cullen O'Keefe so much as Cullen O'Keefe blended in. He wasn't what one might call handsome. Neither was he ugly. If anything, he was round. His head was round, his eyes were buggy, his nose, bulbous. His mouth naturally formed a circle when deep in thought, leaving small rosettes of color on his plump cheeks. He had a dirty blond circlet of hair left on his pate surrounding a bald spot at his crown. And, it seemed he had the appearance of being about as tall as he was wide. Cullen O'Keefe was a round little man who tended to roll in and around the conversations at the Stray Dog without anyone taking much notice.

To be that invisible proved to be an art worthy of cultivation.

Enough mind wanderings. He would have to start for home soon.

But he didn't want to go, not yet. A little while longer, and no one at home would notice him. He preferred this easier way. Disappear and no one expected anything of you.

A light from the shebeen gleamed, brightening the night. Someone left the tavern. To wander home, he supposed.

And then it was dark again.

He wanted to go back in but lingered a moment so his eyes could adjust. No need to trip on the way.

As his pupils again became accustomed to the darkness, Alain-Robert de Grillet realized he was not alone. Someone, no, make that two, were ahead of him on the path.

He froze, using the low branches of a large elm for cover. The figures leaned into one another, one supporting the other, their voices indecipherably slurring. Then they stopped, and the one on the left leaned against a tree.

Hearing a thud like a dropped melon, Alain-Robert watched in horror as one figure again struck the other one.

Transfixed, he watched the single dark figure retreat into The Stray Dog. Just as the door opened, light poured out, and the figure turned to survey his handiwork.

Alain-Robert closed his eyes and slid down the side of the elm. Arms wrapped around his legs. He shook uncontrollably. "What do I do? What do I do? I am such a fool. Stupid, stupid, fool." He pounded his head on his trembling fists.

Maybe the man wasn't dead. Maybe he needed help. Alain-Robert sat straight. But if he helped the man, would the attacker know who he was?

The man was probably already dead. But if he wasn't... Alain-Robert's head banged into the tree.

"Ouch."

Terrified at the sound of his own voice, he jumped to his feet and scanned the area once more. There. On the pathway. Who was it? Had he heard?

Alain-Robert recognized the whistle before he saw the face. Even so, just his gait gave the man away. Perhaps he should step out and explain what he'd seen. But should he? *Make up your mind before it's too late.*

And then it was.

The whistler tripped and fell headlong over the injured man. Alain-Robert held his breath, quiet as stone, as the whistler stood, and dusted off his pants. An exclamation echoed in the darkness. The whistler picked up the injured man and carried him to The Stray Dog. He kicked at the plank door and shouted to those inside.

⌘

"Hey, Cullen, open—" The door nearly knocked James over, the last thing he wanted. The man he carried didn't need any more injuries.

"Who ye got there?

"Don't know, Cullen. Help me lay him down on the bar."

"What d'ye do?"

James wasn't sure who called out the question, but he hadn't expected to hear such a sneer. It made him pause a second while setting the man down to see who he carried. The wounded side of his head turned away. At once everyone recognized the battered man.

"Christopher Dougherty."

"Ye killed Christopher Dougherty, ye did." While the words came from his left, the push came from his right.

"No. No, I just found him on the pathway. I brought him here to get him some help."

No one listened.

"Hold on, give me some room. We don't know if he's dead

or alive—let me check." James pushed the crowd back from the body.

One close look told the tale.

"He kilt Christopher Dougherty. James Crockett kilt Christopher Dougherty, he did." Seamus Flaherty led the charge, but Kevin O'Rourke shouted the words. "Ye had words today, and Christopher said the Crocketts threatened his very life. Now look what he's gone and done."

The crowd pressed in.

A line of sweat trickled past his ear to his neck as his pulse picked up speed. James now knew fear—this moment presented real, unadulterated fear.

Glass shattered.

Everyone spun toward the sound. Cullen O'Keefe stood atop a wobbly table, a broken bottle poised like a weapon. "The next one of ye to take another step toward Master James, 'ere, will be findin' his person accommodatin' a few more holes than the Maker first intended. Are we clear on that, lads?"

No one answered. But there was silent assent.

The crowd backed away, and James breathed again. Barely. He turned to Cullen, who seemed to be the only voice of reason. "I didn't kill him. I only found him outside and brought him in."

"Yer shirt's all bloody." Kevin O'Rourke didn't back down easily. Others began mumbling about his bloody shirt.

"I tripped over him—that's how I found him. Besides, you saw me carry him in. I was bound to have some blood on me."

Cullen jumped down, broken bottle still brandished. His patrons parted before him. "Master James, I'm thinkin' it'd be best all 'round if I sent me nephew for the sheriff. Ye can make yerself comfortable behind the bar 'ere 'til he arrives."

James spotted the nephew; a long, lean towhead, out the door before Cullen finished speaking.

No one seemed concerned about this teen running into trouble on the way to get the law. That made James wonder. Did the crowd really think he did it and all was safe out there now? What if one of them did it? Might everyone know who killed Dougherty, but planned to blame him?

There was nothing he could do about it now. Fuming, he found a barrel standing on end behind the counter and made himself comfortable, as directed. It would be a long wait. He continued to keep a serious watch on Kevin O'Rourke, Seamus Flaherty, and their crew.

How did he get into such messes? This was not what he planned.

And then he remembered. Neither was this what his father had planned.

IT FELT VERY STRANGE TO BE SEATED WITH THE FAMILY. Though everyone went out of their way to make her comfortable, Shannon still found it odd to be included in a family gathering. She folded her hands in her lap, adjusted her skirts around her chair, laced her fingers on top of the dining room table, unlaced her fingers and brushed a stray tendril from her forehead only to twiddle her thumbs in her lap again. How she longed for the sanctuary of the nursery.

Part of her worried one of the babies might wake. Another part of her felt so out of place, she wanted to bolt.

Miss Lucy leaned over, patted her hands, and offered a friendly smile. It helped. She gave Lucy's hand a gentle thank you squeeze and watched to see why Master Crockett had called this meeting.

"I hoped to have resolved questions before I called you all together. But, apparently, I need to make sure everyone understands a few things." Master Crockett's voice sounded calm, but firm. She listened. "Rumors fly at the moment. That is all they are, rumors. We have not one shred of evidence. I am looking into it. But the rumors tell us we may again be dealing with the Combers."

Shannon quickly scanned the other faces around her. The Combers rarely bothered Catholics, their focus being the Protestants of the area, so she had never learned to fear their name. One look at the others, though, showed her they had.

Master Crockett spread his hands. "Now, we don't need to get in a panic. We just need to be cautious. I'm expecting each of you to abide by some basic rules. No one goes out after dark. No one." He paused and stared directly at Master Joseph, who gazed at the table.

"And when you do go out in the daytime, you women will be with at least one man. He will be armed. We will not provoke a fight, nor will we stop helping those in need. But we will not be foolhardy. Is this understood by one and all?"

Miss Mary Frances waved her hand in the air. "But what about James? Where is he?"

A strange look passed over the master's face before he assured his daughter he would speak with his son first thing in the morning. God bless Miss Mary Frances for inquiring. Shannon had also wondered but felt awkward about asking.

Once again Master Crockett, standing behind the Mistress, repeated, "Is this understood by all? I need to know I can depend on you."

"Yes, Papa."

"Yes, Father,"

"Oui, my husband." Louise patted his hand as it rested on her shoulder. A sudden jab of envy made Shannon avert her eyes.

Each in turn nodded or spoke their assent. When Master Crockett focused his gaze on her she sat up straighter in her chair, looking him square in the eye. "Aye, Master Crockett."

His smile lingered a moment, and he gave her a nod of approval before moving on to Miss Lucy. That smile, more than anything else, made her feel like a member of the family. Maybe now she really was one of them, she mused.

But what in the world did that mean?

❧

Joseph couldn't sleep. What with the reprimand from his father, the dismal failure of his proposal to Sarah, and the heightened security around the house, he couldn't focus on anything. And, of course, there was his wayward brother who left him to face his father's ire. Was James really in danger?

He'd relit his lamp and tried reading *The Breviate*. That tribute to a dead wife did nothing for the turmoil, in spite of the intentions. Laying aside the book his father loaned him, he finally wandered to the nursery to watch his son sleep.

Apparently, Wee Joseph took after his father. He sat wide-awake on the widow's lap. Grabbing her index fingers, he pulled himself to a wobbly stance, and blew bubbles of spit with delight.

"Yer so strong. Aye, that ye are, young master, that ye are." Shannon cooed back as she rubbed her head in his belly.

An amazing sense of accomplishment filled Joseph, though he couldn't understand why. He hadn't done anything.

But his son had. "Come here, son. Come see your da."

Instead of obeying, Wee Joseph grabbed handfuls of his nurse's hair.

"OW!"

Joseph wanted to laugh, but he managed to control himself, revealing only a smile. "Here, son, none of that. You've got to let go of the lady's hair."

He tried to untangle the baby's fingers from the locks, but Wee Joseph began to wave his tight fists up and down.

"Ow. Help me, please."

This time Joseph couldn't restrain the laugh. He picked up the baby in one arm and worked to release Shannon's fine hair from the tight little fingers. It took nearly a minute, but she was freed.

"Ye can keep the scamp awhile." Standing, she smoothed her hair into place. "He's not ready to settle in for the night." She grabbed a tiny fist and kissed it.

"I can understand that. I'm not ready either." Joseph lifted his son over his head, moving him like a bird in the sky.

"Somethin' on yer mind, Master Joseph?"

"A lot of things are on my mind. Not the least of which is your bad advice." Thinking about it now brought back feelings of confusion, embarrassment, and hurt he'd shoved aside with his father's reproof. He lowered Wee Joseph back to chest level.

"My bad advice? And what bad advice might that be?"

He paused to think. "Perhaps you didn't give me bad advice. But you did steer me in the wrong direction."

"And how would that be, Master Joseph?"

"By telling me you think Miss Sarah is in love with me."

"Aye, but she is."

"No, but she's not."

Shannon stood before him, hands on her hips. "And how do ye know she's not? Did ye ask her?"

Joseph could feel the heat rising up his neck to his face.

"No, well, I didn't ask her that."

"What did you ask her?"

Her eyes bored into him. Then her face registered under-standing.

"Ye didn't. Tell me ye didn't go an' ask the poor girl to marry ye just on my say so."

Joseph nodded his head, keeping his eyes on Wee Joseph.

"At least tell me ye first declared yer love."

This time Joseph shook his head. Shannon could teach his father a thing or two about reprimands.

"I thought ye had more sense in that head o' yers. What woman would say aye to a proposal of marriage without knowin' how her intended feels? What is it what makes men so daft?"

A light of understanding illuminated the whole situation. How could he have been so stupid? Sarah had too much pride to agree to a marriage of convenience. Which is exactly how she must have viewed his plan.

He never said the words she needed to hear.

Could he have said them?

He winced. How could he have hurt her so deeply?

Shannon grew quiet. Taking Wee Joseph from him, she sat back in the rocker. A cloth tossed over her shoulder, she tucked the baby under it, modestly setting him to nurse. "It looks like ye've got some thinking to do, and I've got to get yer son to sleep. If ye'll excuse me…"

Joseph nodded. But he exited the nursery knowing tonight he wouldn't get a wink of sleep.

Chapter Thirteen

A jolt, followed by the sudden sensation of falling, sent a shock through James's tired, cramped body. His head banged the wall just as his three-legged stool crashed to the floor, leaving him sprawled on his backside.

"Crockett, ye've got visitors." The sheriff nudged James's achy shoulder with the metal tip of his boot, giving James a swift understanding of how he'd ended up on the floor. "Up with ye now, and I'll bring ye some breakfast while ye talk." The sheriff was all business, but at least he wasn't cruel. James rubbed his backside. He wasn't exactly gentle, either. Hopefully, he was honest.

James felt he'd wakened from an ugly nightmare but quickly realized he'd only awakened to one. Thank the Lord, the sheriff had gotten him to the cell without incident last night. He may be sore and cold, but he was still alive.

James stood, stretched and dusted his bottom. Dark and dank in the room, the main noise seemed to flow from a constant dripping. Soon treading sounds on the old broken stone steps alerted him to his visitors. "James? Son, how fare you?" He heard his father before he ever saw his concerned face.

"Aye, Father, I'm fine. Feeling stupid, but fine. I should have listened to you. I had this idea that if I could just sit at the Stray Dog awhile, I'd hear something useful. But trouble started before I even got inside."

"O'Keefe came around early this morning and told me what happened."

James almost wished his father would yell or scream or strike him. Anything. He knew he deserved something of that sort.

Instead, the man offered reassurance and hope. "Don't worry. We'll get you out soon enough. You are my son, even if you don't listen well." He gave James's shoulder a gentle squeeze. "I know you would never take the life of another like this. We will prove your innocence. Do not worry, my son."

James wrapped his arms around his father and held him close. He wanted to drink in the confidence, cling to the strength that had taken care of him throughout his childhood. He wanted to hang on forever.

"Father, I didn't do it, I swear."

"You do not have to swear. Never was there a doubt in my mind. You are my son. I know you." Antoine loosened the embrace and stepped back. "I will return for you, I promise. And your mother is praying—you know what that means. So, stay strong. All will be well." He kissed James on each cheek and left.

James had never felt so alone in his life.

CULLEN DIDN'T LOOK THE LEAST BIT SURPRISED TO SEE Crocketts enter his establishment. Glad enough to let his father do the talking, Joseph surveyed the room, looking for clues. It only brought memories of his last visit. Robert told him how Sarah exploded into the room, setting off eruptions in her wake. He could see her in his mind's eye, wreaking havoc and looking beautiful. He shook his head. He didn't have time to daydream about Sarah.

"… and nothing unusual occurred before this? No new person?" His father pressed O'Keefe for any tidbit of information.

"Ye know, Master Crockett, I keeps me eyes on things and brings ye what I learn. I wish I had better news for ye, but I canna think of anything else."

The towhead wiping off tables finished his job and brushed past. "Uncle, what about that stranger what sits in the corner over there. Ye know, he's been here ever' night fer a fortnight, now."

"Who is it, O'Keefe? Do you know him?"

"Aye, I know him and ye do too. But he hasn't none to do with the killin'."

His father grabbed the front of O'Keefe's dirty shirt. "How do you know? Who is he?"

"Now Master Crockett. I do not think he wants anyone to know he comes in here." Cullen's dirty hand crept up to the back of his neck. "He keeps to himself, orders one tankard of ale and sits quiet for hours. Never says a word. He wouldn't know anything to help ye."

Joseph knew his father was losing patience. He could feel it drain from himself.

"Let me decide, Cullen. This is my son we are talking about. We both know he did not kill Dougherty, but he will hang for it if I can't get to the bottom of this. Tell me, who is the stranger?"

Cullen O'Keefe took a deep breath and slowly blew it out. "He's no stranger to ye. Tis yer friend, Master de Grillet's son."

✦

ANTOINE STARED. HE RELEASED THE MAN BEFORE TURNING on his heel and slamming out of the shebeen. A part of him expected Joseph to follow, but he never glanced back. He didn't know what to think. How did he tell his best friend that his only child held a possible clue to help his own son? How did he break Albert's heart?

Determined steps sped him to the one-story stone cottage, a mile down the beaten path. Standing before the door, he realized he had no words. Joseph's hand squeezed his shoulder. He knocked, knowing he was about to change Albert's world.

"Antoine, I just heard." Albert embraced him. "Come in, come in. You, too, Joseph."

They entered and Mimi came to greet them. "Sit. I'll bring tea."

"No, thank you. We must hurry." The words stuck so he cleared his throat. "Albert, I need to speak with you in private."

Albert glanced at Mimi. She smiled, nodded at the men, and left the room.

"I'm sorry to be rude. This is a great shock."

"Antoine, we all know James is innocent. He could never have murdered another in cold blood." Albert placed his hand on Antoine's arm. The touch made Antoine feel like a traitor.

"We just left The Stray Dog. I'd thought to find some clues. O'Keefe told me about a man who sits in the corner, drinking every night. He's done so for more than a fortnight."

Albert's eyes narrow almost imperceptibly. If they had not been friends for over a quarter of a century, Antoine might not have caught it. He took a breath and continued.

"O'Keefe is sure this man has nothing to do with the murder and didn't want to give me his name."

"But you know it." The simple statement held a low growl.

"Yes. I believe you do too."

Though neither man spoke, Antoine heard the silent plea of his friend—don't say it.

"Yes, yes, I'm the silent stranger."

Antoine turned to the voice, coming from the bedroom doorway. Alain-Robert stood, shaking, with wild frightened eyes. He finger-combed his already unruly hair. "Yes, I'm the one who sits night after night in the corner, minding my own business. I don't bother anyone, and no one bothers me."

"Why son? Why do you—"

"Avoid everyone? That's easy, Father. So I don't see the disappointment in your eyes—like I'm seeing now."

"Disappointment? You are my son. I love you."

Alain-Robert stared at the floor, shaking his head. Finally, he met his father's gaze, his whisper nearly inaudible. "I know you love me. More's the pity. If you didn't love me, I would not be such a disappointment to you."

"How? When are you a disappointment?"

"I always disappoint you. I could not finish school. I have no aptitude for numbers or the law. I have not enough faith for the priesthood." He drew a ragged breath. "I have never measured up, even as a child."

Albert grabbed his son's arm. "What do you mean, son? What do you mean?"

Alain-Robert pulled away. "I see it when you look at me. I have always seen it in your face." He stared at the floor. "Ever since that day."

"What day? Tell me."

"You said, 'Take care of your mother.' You were gone and soldiers marched through. We were at the market. One of the redcoats—he took the package from her hands. I tried to get it back, Father, I did. But he shoved me to the side. He touched Mother and I jumped up. I pushed him. But he was so tall. I only came to his thigh.

Alain-Robert raised his head. "But I promised you I would take care of my mother. He shoved me to the ground and put a boot on my chest. 'Tell your brat to stop and I'll leave you alone.' Mother's eyes never showed the fear, though I wet myself in terror. 'Do not bother the soldier, son,' she said, as if he were a guest in her home.

"I failed. I knew then I had failed. I've never been good enough since."

Albert gathered his son into his arms rocking side to side while tightly holding him. "My son, my son. I never knew."

Alain-Robert pulled back, doubt clouding his face.

"Son, you were only four. I didn't expect you to be anything but a four-year-old. You have brought me only joy. Any disappointment you have seen has been in your own mind. I love you. I have worried, because I could not understand what bothered you." Albert pulled him back into the embrace, and Alain-Robert returned the hug. "Oh, son, you do not disappoint me. Never, never do you disappoint me."

Antoine hated to disturb them. He witnessed an answer to years of prayers. But now his own son sat in a filthy, dank cellar of a jail, waiting for help. James's life lay in the balance, and he would disturb whatever it took to free him.

He cleared his throat and Alain-Robert pulled back. "Father, I have information that should clear James." The young man stepped away from his father, looking Antoine in the face. "I stepped out of the shebeen for a moment when I saw the murder. I did not realize who died at first and had no idea James would be blamed until we got word this morning. James told the truth. He only tripped over the body. I saw the murderer's face. Kevin O'Rourke killed Christopher Dougherty."

Gratitude welled and tears ran down Antoine's cheeks "Thank you." He reached out to embrace the young man. "Thank you." He pulled Albert into the embrace. "Thank you."

He still thanked them as he and Joseph raced out the door.

❦

Halfway to town, chills slithered Joseph's spine.

"Father, we've got to get word to the Stewarts and de Grillets. Once James is free and O'Rourke in custody, his gang will be out for blood. No one will be safe, especially if he really is connected to the Combers."

Antoine agreed. "Everyone who has been meeting with me

will be in danger. We need to keep as many of us together in one place as possible. See if the Stewarts can house Cameron McHugh and Paddy Flanagan and their families. We'll have the O'Toole's and de Grillets come with us."

"They may want to stay and defend their own homes." Joseph couldn't see either Michael O'Toole or Albert de Grillet backing down from a fight for their property.

"You will have to reason with them." His father spoke as though he thought it through aloud. "It will be quicker to get the ones with smaller homes to the Stewarts or our place. There is strength in numbers. Our house and the tower house make the most sense, have the most room. Tell them they can bring anything they wish, but immediately get to one of the homes. We can all work together to keep all our families safe."

Joseph turned to leave when his father grabbed his arm. "Son, I'm very proud of you. Be careful."

They briefly embraced before he hurried to warn the neighbors.

◈

"I know your Aunt Gwendolyn would love to have you visit, Sarah, but why right now?" Sarah's mother kept pushing for information—information Sarah didn't want to share.

"Mother, I just want to get away. I have been so busy helping and doing, I thought the time away would be nice." Sarah hoped her explanation pacified, but a look in her mother's eyes told her she needed to be a better liar.

"I could hear you tossing and turning all night last night. And you are looking a might pallid." Her mother brushed a strand of hair from her face. Sarah knew she felt for fever.

Her mother almost believed.

"Fine, I'll speak with your father. Perhaps we could take a trip all together."

Sarah gave a weak smile but inside felt thwarted. She wanted away from her parents, too, before they began prying into things she wanted to bury deep.

"Meg, Sarah, I need you now." Thomas's voice rumbled up the stairs.

Her father stormed into the room, taking charge. "Make room for two families. It will be an extended visit."

"What is it, Thomas?"

Sarah waited for her father's answer; she wanted to know too.

"Christopher Dougherty was murdered last night. They arrested James Crockett but since have learned Kevin O'Rourke did the deed. The Combers are sure to make much of this, and no house will be safe. Since Paddy Flanagan and Michael O'Toole have been working with us, it won't matter whether a body is Catholic or Protestant. The axe is going to fall on us all."

Sarah and her mother flew down the stairs.

Her mother stopped, suddenly grabbing Sarah's hand and turning to her husband, eyes full of fear. "Thomas, who will be coming here?"

"Cameron McHugh and Paddy Flannigan will bring their families. The de Grillets and O'Tooles will go to the Crocketts'. We could house them all, but you know Antoine. He must defend his home. By dividing forces, we can hopefully keep both our houses safe and give protection to the others."

Sarah's stomach felt like lead.

Her father pulled her and her mother close. "We're safe enough here. There are plenty of guards, and the building is secure. I'm more concerned for the Crocketts."

Sarah buried her face in her father's chest. "Me too."

Meg pulled back and tucked a loose tendril behind Sarah's ear. "And just last evening Joseph Louis and James were here."

Sarah tensed at the memory.

"Here? Why wasn't I informed?" Her father dropped the hug, waiting for an answer.

"You were in your study and left word not to be disturbed. They wanted to speak with Sarah."

"What did they want?" He directed the question at Sarah.

"Joseph asked Sarah to marry him."

"Mother!"

Her father's grip on her shoulders increased. "What did you say?"

"No. I said no."

Quickly, he gathered her close again and kissed the top of her head. "Good, that's me good lass. That's what I told him meself."

Something wasn't right. Joseph wouldn't have asked her if her father had said no. Sarah pulled back from her father. "When? When did Joseph ask for my hand?"

"Never ye mind. Ye don't belong with the lad." Thomas reached to embrace her to him.

Sarah pushed his arms away. "No. Father, when did Joseph ask you?"

"Two years ago."

The blood drained from her face. Two years ago? Before Kathleen even arrived in the Laggan. Joseph asked for her, before Kathleen. He wanted her first.

"What have I done?" The room spun and the floor dropped from beneath her feet.

Chapter Fourteen

The house was quiet. Too quiet. The silence unnerved Shannon. More often than not she was trying to get some peace and quiet for the babies, but this unnatural calm prickled the hair on the back of her neck.

Samuel napped and Wee Joseph lay in his bed, enamored with his toes. Not even a bird sang outside the window.

And James wasn't here. What did that matter? He spent time elsewhere too. But this time he's locked up. It wasn't his choice.

Why did she worry about James?

She knew why though admitting it even to herself was difficult. It was his smile she missed. And the way his eyes twinkled when he thought up some devilment with which to torment her. She remembered how strong his arms were as he carried her when she twisted her ankle. And…

No. She shouldn't dwell on those things like a dreamy schoolgirl.

The door creaked open, startling her. Mistress Crockett entered.

"Widow O'Connor, we will be having a large amount of company for the next few days. They should be arriving anytime soon."

"Aye. Is there anything you wish me to do?" Her curiosity was aroused, but she didn't want to pry.

The mistress's smile seemed sad. Shannon longed to comfort the kindhearted woman but, in spite of the kindnesses shown, she knew this was not her place.

"You can pray for James and for all of us. Antoine may be overreacting, but then, maybe he is not. He is a good one for planning." Mistress Crockett sat down on the edge of the bed and patted the area next to her. "Quick, I'll tell you a short story from when I first met Antoine." Now the smile was brighter as Shannon took the seat indicated. "I first met him at Versailles. That evening, I also met Voltaire—it's true. He was a kind, gentle man. My first night at the palace, we were seated next to one another at dinner. Little did I know he was in league with Antoine to learn more about me. I spoke of how I loved to ride horses, being outside, sketching… The next morning, Antoine took me for a lovely ride to a glade where he had arranged a wonderful picnic. After we ate, he produced sketching materials and let me draw to my heart's content. He was so thoughtful. But what had seemed like spontaneous coincidences came from careful listening and planning.

"He is still like that today. I'm sure he's planned for this moment but hoped to never put his plans into action." The mistress took Shannon's hand between her own. "So now, I cover his plans with prayer, asking that God will direct his thoughts and that He will give him wisdom and the flexibility to adjust according to God's plans. Antoine will quickly get James released, I have no doubt, but please keep praying until they are all home."

Shannon nodded, and the mistress let go of her hand, patting it before standing. "Thank you, dear girl. I am so glad you are here with us." She bent and placed a gentle kiss on Shannon's cheek before leaving the room.

Shannon's fingertips traced the planted kiss and wondered again at this family.

❧

"AND YOU WILL SWEAR IN COURT THAT YOU SAW KEVIN O'Rourke kill Christopher Dougherty?"

All eyes in the room focused on Alain-Robert de Grillet. An eternity passed before James, who had been brought up from his cell to hear the proceedings, observed a slight nod and a mouthed, "Aye."

"A little louder, for the record." Master Aaron Murphy, Thomas Stewart's secretary, obviously wanted everything done by the book. With no formal court available, Stewart's decision would serve. But, since the Stewarts and Crocketts were well-known friends, propriety held this needed to be carefully documented.

"Aye." This time with enough volume for all to hear.

"Do you need anything else?" His father was as anxious to wrap this up as he was.

"I'm thinkin' that should be enough. I'll swear out a warrant for Kevin O'Rourke and bring him in."

"What about protection for our families?" James had worried over this for hours.

Murphy turned his back to sign the release papers, and Thomas explained. "Your father and I have figured this all out. In fact, Crockett, de Grillet, you both are still welcome to bring your families—"

"No, we have made our plans. We will stay at Edenmore." There'd be no changing his father's mind. "If that is all, we'll be going." Father nodded toward the door, leading the way where he held the door for James.

Stepping out he breathed deep. Fresh air had never smelled so good. Thomas Stewart followed them, climbed aboard his horse and waved as he left.

The four men walked in silence for several minutes—the older friends together up ahead, the young men together behind.

James inhaled another deep breath of freedom. "I don't think I thanked you back there."

Alain-Robert gave him a sideways glance with a slow half smile. "No need. I should have said something right away." He softly coughed before looking James full in the face. "I am sorry." And then he turned his head back to the road again.

Realization slapped James full force. Alain-Robert could have kept him from spending a horrible night in that miserable cell. The little coward had only to speak up. With every step his anger rose. Why didn't he tell what he knew before this?

James well remembered the damp cold, the moldy smell, the constant sound of dripping. *Drip, drip, drop.* Each step home resonated with imagined water droplets plopping on the road instead of his footfalls. Before long, he wanted to take a swing at the mouse walking so nonchalantly next to him.

At least he could shout out in rage. Yet he bit his tongue and placed one foot in front of the other. *Drip, drip, drop.* He wouldn't take bets on how long his control would last.

❦

"Bridget, you've got to help me." Sarah lay on her bed, where someone had placed her, a damp rag clenched in her hand. Her father's admission still rang in her ears. She had to get to Joseph. She had to tell him she loved him.

"Miss Sarah, ye need to lie still, lass. Yer father an' mother are worried sick over ye." Bridget took the damp rag from Sarah, rewet it and tried to put it back on Sarah's forehead.

"Oh, Bridget. Please. I'll give you whatever you want. Name it." Sarah pushed her way off her bed and opened her armoire. "Would you like any of my dresses? You choose. It is yours." Leaving the closet door open, she ran to her dressing table. "Jewelry? Would you like jewelry?" Sarah rummaged through a drawer. "I think I have some money in here. You can have it. You can have it all. Just please, please help me."

"Miss Sarah. I dinnae fash yer clothes nor yer jewels nor yer money. I'm just doin' me job."

Sarah rushed to the girl and grabbed her hands. "Your job is to help me, correct? Please, Bridget, I'll do anything. I implore you by all that's holy…" Sarah sank on the bed in a sob.

What if something happened to Joseph? Or Wee Joseph because she wasn't there to protect him? She'd broken her promise and heaven removed its blessing.

Bridget placed her hand on Sarah's shoulder.

Sarah raised her head to meet the girl's gaze.

"What would ye have me to do, Miss Sarah?"

"What if I put you girls in the nursery, the O'Tooles in your room, and Albert and Mimi in James and Robert's room? Your brothers can sleep on the floor downstairs, and Alain-Robert can join them. I doubt if the men will be doing a lot of sleeping, or they will at least be sleeping in shifts." Although she appeared to be explaining things to her daughters, in reality, Louise was thinking things through out loud. A habit she'd developed that appeared in times of stress.

"I want to keep the study clear, so the men have a place to talk in private. And, our bedroom can be used for those needing rest during the day after an all-night vigil. Meals can be served in the parlor when wanted. And, the dining room can be used for giving aid to those in need. Does that sound like it will work?"

"Yes, Mama. We can start moving our things now." Lucy immediately jumped up. Sarah Beth followed her sister, but Mary Francis held back. Shy and sensitive, Louise pulled her middle daughter close and gave her a hug.

"Are you sure James is all right?" Mary Frances's face turned up, her eyes wide with fear for her big brother.

"Ouí, dear heart, I am sure. Your father will be bringing him home anytime now."

Mary Frances returned her hug before racing up the stairs to help her sisters. For years Louise had only mothered sons—four strong, handsome sons who had grown into four strong handsome men. But then the Lord blessed her with three lovely daughters, just now beginning to bloom. As much as she wanted to alleviate their fears, she also wanted to wrap them in a strong hedge of protection. *Ouí, your father and I will protect you.*

She found Josephine making an inventory of the larder. Seeing the old woman busy gave Louise strength. They had named Joseph for her. She joined her friend, nay second mother. Together, they made plans for feeding such a large group.

"We have plenty of mutton stored, so meat will not be a problem." Josephine spoke in her native French.

"Bon, but are there enough vegetables in reserve? How does the garden look? If this situation lasts for any real length of time, we may—"

The sudden knock made Louise jump. "I'll be right back." She left to answer the door. It was starting.

Michael O'Toole and son, Liam, stood on her steps looking like refugees. How old was the boy now, twelve, thirteen? Mary O'Toole stayed in the carriage, her face pinched and unhappy.

"Come in, come in. Mistress O'Toole, you don't have to sit out there. Come in, everyone." Louise smiled to ease the tension.

"We can take your things upstairs and get you settled." She continued explaining all the way up the steps. "I hope you do not mind. I've put you all in my daughters' room. They are in the nursery with the Widow." She opened the bedroom door for them. "Your son is welcome to be here with you or with my sons downstairs. I'll leave it to you. I am just very glad to have all of you here." More smiles. "If you would like to rest, I can call you for dinner. Master O'Toole, I am sure you will want to talk with my husband when he returns. I will let you know when he arrives—or more likely you will hear the noise of James coming home." Her laugh was a tad strained, she knew, but no one mentioned it.

Louise left them and returned to help Josephine, who really did not need her help. But before they had even started again, she heard the front door open and Mary Frances's voice. "James. You're home."

And there he stood.

Yet her heart knew as much uncertainty as it did relief.

❦

"James is home." His sisters all spoke at once, scurrying for the stairs. Shannon found her feet had a mind of their own carrying her right along with the happy greeters. She caught sight of a dark scowl that melted away as he swung Mary Frances in the air and planted a kiss atop her head.

Then he glanced up, and their gazes met. A shock ran through her system. Shannon had never felt so shy in her life, nor had she ever seen his smile so broad. He managed to get close enough for her to choke out, "I'm glad yer home."

His hand brushed hers for the briefest of eternities, and he replied, "Me too."

Then his family whisked him away into another room.

She was left behind. She returned to the nursery, her domain, her sense of security. It may be located in the Crocketts' home, but she had some control of her life, and Samuel's, inside this room.

"Miss Sarah. Ye startled me. I'd a thought ye'd be downstairs amongst the happy throng." Like some newly arrived phantom Sarah rocked Wee Joseph. Where had she come from? Had she used the back stairs?

"Someone needed to stay with the bairns." The terse reply seemed foreign coming from the lass.

"Pardon, miss, is there a problem?"

"Perhaps you think it satisfactory to leave two defenseless babies alone where they can get hurt, but I certainly don't."

Shannon staggered back at the verbal blow.

"Miss Sarah, yer welcome to take this position anytime ye want it."

⬥

SARAH KNEW SHE HAD GONE TOO FAR BUT DIDN'T KNOW how to make things right. She wasn't angry at Shannon, merely worried and scared and desperate to find Joseph. Yet anger seeped out of her words like acid, no matter what she said. The acid burned the wrong people, though. How did she keep Shannon from leaving?

All the same, the young widow packed her bag.

"Where will you go?"

"I've still got me cottage. It were Sean's parents' home, and now it will be mine and Samuel's."

A new fear settled in Sarah's heart. Wee Joseph needed Shannon. No matter how she tried, she couldn't give him everything he needed. And Joseph would be angry. Tanté Louise would be too. She'd let her rage get the better of her again, and now look at the mess.

"Widow O'Connor… Shannon, please. What about Wee Joseph? He needs you."

Shannon stopped packing and remained still with her back to Sarah. Hope filled her heart. Maybe she wouldn't leave.

"Ye can do it. I've known babes younger to be weaned to the cup. It won't be easy at first, but ye can do it, Miss Sarah." She resumed her packing.

This morning all she wanted was to run away. Now it seemed as if God would make her keep her promise one way or another.

⬥

SHANNON SCOOPED UP SAMUEL IN HER RIGHT ARM AND then tried to grab her two bags with her left. They were heavier than she expected. She put Samuel back down. "Ye'll have to hang onto Mama's skirt, love." Her voice sounded unnatural. Pride had gained an upper hand. But it was too late to back down now. Besides, this appeared to become a dangerous place to be in the next few days. The Combers had never bothered the Catholics in the past, so she and Samuel might be safer in their own home.

But there were still the stairs to negotiate. How could she do that with her two bags and Samuel hanging to her skirt?

"I'll need to leave Samuel here long enough to take me bags down the stairs. Will ye watch him?" It took every ounce of strength she possessed to ask for help from Miss Sarah. A part of her knew if she just waited and talked with the girl, things would be back to normal. But that would call for swallowing more pride than she could stomach.

Sarah nodded but didn't speak. Shannon nodded back her thanks, hefted the two bags, and headed for the front door.

Placing them out of the way of incoming traffic, she hurried back to the nursery, tucked Samuel on her hip and took the stairs again. She sat him down, admonished him to hold tight to her skirt, grabbed the bags and was out the door.

Just getting out of her carriage, Mistress de Grillet gave Shannon a wondering gaze. Now there'd be questions.

"Widow O'Connor, what is the problem?"

She hadn't expected anything so direct, or so fast.

Mistress de Grillet hurried over to her. "Is there a problem? Where are you going?"

"I'm going to me home." Yet as she spoke the words, she realized it was no longer home.

"Oh, ma petite, it is very dangerous. It won't be long until sunset. Then you must be here inside. This is where we can help one another."

Master de Grillet unloaded the bags and took the carriage to the barn. But Alain-Robert stood with his mother, a silent support against Shannon.

"No, I need to go. Tis important, I canna wait." Shannon tasted resentment reminiscent of a thwarted child.

"But you can't take the baby. Leave him with me." Mimi scooped up Samuel. "I will watch him, and Alain-Robert can accompany you to take care of your business and bring you safely back." Shannon had little choice. Her son now a hostage assuring her return. And a willing hostage at that as he laughed and wrapped his arms about the woman's neck. "I'll keep him safe for you, Widow O'Connor. Just hurry back after you finish your business."

Tis here my business is finished or will be as soon as ye give back me baby. That is what she wanted to shout but thought better of it. Instead she tried a softer approach. "I'm not sure how long I'll be. It might be best to keep Samuel with me."

But Madame de Grillet was no longer listening. Instead she played with the little traitor in her arms as she walked through the very door Shannon left open.

"Widow O'Connor, allow me to put my parents' bags inside, and I will go with you." Alain-Robert didn't wait for an answer but grabbed up the luggage his father had left and followed his mother through the door.

Shannon stared back at her own bags. Now what?

Chapter Fifteen

Something wasn't right, and Cullen O'Keefe knew it. Business had never been this slow. Even the de Grillet lad didn't show. Was it even worth staying open?

"Michael laddie, looks like there won't be much to do today. Go see what yer friends are doin'. Tis time ye had some fun."

The rail-thin youth dropped the rag he used to wipe shelves badly in need of dusting, his freckled face breaking into a toothy grin. "Aye, Uncle." Out the door in a flash, he quickly popped his head back in. "Thank ye, Uncle." And then he was gone.

Cullen chuckled under his breath. His sister's boy had been a joy to him. He and his missus never had any children of their own. Michael filled that void as good and kind as any loving son. Cullen picked up the rag the lad dropped in his rush and took over the boring job. Hot and perspiring, he longed to join his nephew, but for now, daydreams must suffice.

Behind him the door creaked open. He called over his shoulder, "What'll it be?"

"Information."

"Wha—?" Cullen spun around.

"O'Keefe, I'm thinkin' ye've got a big mouth. Now, who've ye been runnin' it off to?" Kevin O'Rourke and Seamus Flaherty leaned on the makeshift bar, reminding him of jackals toying with their prey.

Sweat poured down Cullen's head. "I, I dinnae know what ye mean." He wiped his face with the dirty rag, but the sweat only continued, pooling at his neck.

"Maybe we need to be helpin' him remember, aye, Kev?" Seamus's eyes gleamed.

O'Rourke nodded and Flaherty landed a rock-hard punch in Cullen's middle. All breath escaped. He doubled over. Cullen's lungs screamed for air, but he'd lost the ability to take it in. Gasping, he stared at the men's sinister grins. Their laughter rang with foreboding.

"D'ye think he remembers now, Seamus?"

"I'm not sure, Kevin." Flaherty grabbed at the wisps of fine hair on the back of Cullen's head and yanked hard, viciously pulling Cullen's face directly under his.

Cullen's knees buckled. His hands reached to free himself, to clutch something as a weapon.

O'Rourke grabbed his arms, twisting his left one behind him. "Who'd ye talk to, and what'd ye say?"

"Master Crockett just wanted to know if I saw anything. I told 'm I didn't." Cullen didn't recognize his own voice, or rather rasp. He'd barely again started breathing.

"Then where'd he get the information?" Seamus hissed in his face.

"I don't know, I tell ye."

O'Rourke pushed Flaherty aside and pulled Cullen to his feet. "Where did he go when he left here?"

The truth slapped Cullen as surely as if Seamus Flaherty has issued the blow. Kevin O'Rourke killed Christopher Dougherty. Someone knew it.

O'Rourke dropped Cullen's arm, grabbed him by the throat and slammed him against the wall. Kevin's teeth gnashed. His eyes became thin slits. "Where?"

Cullen moved his lips, but no sound came. O'Rourke loosened his grip allowing a whisper. "De Grillet."

Kevin dropped him.

He slid down the wall in a trembling heap. Cullen held his breath. He was about to die. The dull glint of O'Rourke's metal-toed boot flashed before it struck Cullen in the side of the head. Then all went black.

SHANNON DIDN'T BOTHER TO WAIT FOR ALAIN-ROBERT. Instead she swiped her bags and started walking. It was about three miles, but if she kept up her pace she could be there in thirty minutes.

"Widow O'Connor, wait." Alain-Robert ran to catch up.

She didn't even look back, though she felt a twinge of guilt remembering his face when she'd hurt her ankle. He hadn't been around since. From what she could tell, neither of them had much of a life.

But she didn't have time for niceties. She needed to leave off her things so she could get back to Samuel. With her hands free, she could hang on to him and get out without impediment. Out of their house, out of their lives. Away from James's presence.

"Widow O'Connor, here. Let me take that." Alain-Robert reached for her bags. Instinctively, she pulled back. They'd already grabbed her son from her. In fact, nearly everything she had had been pulled away in some sort or fashion. Sean, her parents, the ability to make her way in the world, her son and now her possessions.

"No. I'll carry them."

He appeared startled. And why not, he had offered to do something kind, and she'd just snapped at him. She shook her head, thinking she needed someone to shake some sense into her. "Fine, you take one, and I'll take the other." She offered the heavier one, feeling guilty for doing so.

He took the bag and matched her stride. She knew he wouldn't start a conversation with her and didn't feel like starting one herself. But the silence only added to her feelings of having mistreated him. Almost like she'd kicked a puppy.

"I appreciate your help. The bags were getting heavy."

He stared at her as if he'd just seen a snake, and then back at the road ahead. "My pleasure."

Succinct, with manners. It looked to be one very quiet hike home.

⁂

"They've got a lot o' bodies there at that Crockett house. We're gonna need more 'n just you an' me." Kevin O'Rourke quickly made plans, good plans. He liked the excitement and the power of surprise. He also knew his gang respected him for that ability. They could be called on a minute's notice.

"How'd ye think they found out?" Seamus wasn't much on brains, but what he lacked, he made up for in brawn. In any trouble, Kevin wanted Seamus on his side.

"We'll know soon enough. I… Well, lookie here." O'Rourke pointed. "I think I've figured it out, Seamus."

"What? Who is that?" Seamus stared at the couple Kevin pointed out.

"It's that lad what sits back in the corner at O'Keefe's every night. I didn't notice'm when I got back. He could've seen somethin'. They haven't spotted us. Get over here." Kevin pulled his partner behind some trees at the side of the road. There they could stay out of sight, but still keep an eye on the dark-haired lad.

"Who's that with'm?"

Kevin motioned for Seamus to be quiet, then whispered, "I'm thinkin' it's Sean O'Connor's widow. But why would she… Now I know who that is. He's that de Grillet kid. His family is friendly with the Crocketts. That's where O'Keefe said Crockett was headed, to see de Grillet." Kevin knew he'd figured it out. And now he could do something about it. This current situation with the law left him more than unhappy. But this might fix a thing or two. He might even have some fun in the process. "You go get the lads. Hurry. Gather'm up quick an' I'll meet ye in the orchard by the Crockett house. I've got a score to settle here first."

ALAIN-ROBERT COULD NOT WAIT TO GET DONE AND BACK to the Crocketts'. Shannon O'Connor, though definitely lovely, was also a woman. And that made him uncomfortable. He did not understand women. He did not understand himself when he was around women. And he was never a big talker, but the fairer sex had a way of tying his tongue into one giant knot.

He had tried hard to converse with Shannon that day he'd seen her out, harder than he'd ever tried before to speak with a female. But once James was around, it was no use. Odd man out, that's what he was.

Alain-Robert sneaked a glance at her and noticed the determined jut of her chin, the purposeful step after step. A woman with a mission. He only hoped it would not keep him in her company for long. But she was nice to look at; he had to admit that much.

A rustle among the trees at his right caught his attention. He turned his head. A body flew at him. It pushed him to the ground, knocking the breath from him, and landed on top. Alain-Robert raised his eyes. A rock came straight at his head. A sudden spray of lights.

Then only blackness.

"WHERE'S THE WIDOW?" JAMES HOPED HE SOUNDED

calmer than he felt. Ever since she welcomed him home, he'd longed to talk with her. All alone. He'd finally slipped away from his sisters. But Mimi de Grillet, not Shannon, played on the floor with Samuel.

"She wanted to take some things to her house. I told her I'd watch Samuel while she was gone."

"You let her go alone?" The force of his words stunned him even more than the look on Tanté Mimi's face. At that moment he realized more fear for Shannon than he had experienced for himself over the last twenty-four hours.

"No, no. Alain-Robert went with her."

"Is he armed?"

"Oui, he has a pistol. She is safe, James. Do not worry. They will be back before dark and—"

James didn't wait for her to finish. He tore down the stairs. "Joseph, Robert." He ran through the rooms yelling. Both came running.

"Shannon is out there. She decided to walk home."

"What?"

"I'm going for her."

"I'll go with you." Joseph spoke first, checking his boot dirk.

"I'll stay here then and let the others know." Robert handed the pistol in his belt to James. "Go."

James and Joseph ran out of the house.

SHANNON SCREAMED. THE WILD MAN BROUGHT THE BLOW down on Alain-Robert's forehead. Then he faced her.

Kevin O'Rourke.

She again screamed and swung her bag at him. He merely laughed and grabbed it. The force threw her to the ground, against the rocks. Her leg hurt, but she continued to scramble backwards out of his grasp.

"Yer not goin' anywhere, Widow." His laughter chilled her.

Grasping leaves, dirt, whatever she could, she threw it. She hit his eyes.

He roared, rising tall. He swiped his eyes clear. In two strides he caught her. Grabbing her by her hair, he lifted her. "I can have you anytime I want Missus Shannon O'Connor." His breath burned her ear. "Anytime."

She spit in his face.

He threw her back to the ground, wiping his palm over his nose and cheek.

Shannon knew now her leg wouldn't hold her. She rolled over and started crawling. A swift kick in her ribs landed her on her back. Fire burned in her lungs.

"So yer still a brave lass. I'll teach ye to remember yer place." He reached into his coat pocket. What he brought out appeared so innocuous. A simple tool used by sheep farmers everywhere. But when the Combers used it, it was a weapon of fear. She trembled.

Using her good leg, she scooted backward on her bottom. Something blocked her escape. A tree. Wild with fear, she gaped at her attacker.

Kevin O'Rourke's eyes gleamed.

Her heart beat hard enough to burst from her chest. She opened her mouth to scream, but her voice refused to work.

Slowly, he brought the wool card toward her cheek, letting each razor-sharp point graze her skin.

She pulled her head back as far as possible.

He teased her fear.

She knew it.

His eyes narrowed, and his hand raised the comb.

"GONE? WHAT DO YOU MEAN SHE'S GONE?" THOMAS STOOD in his daughter's bedroom, his gaze searching as if Sarah played one of her childhood games with poor timing.

"Just that, Thomas. Sarah's not here." Meg wrung her hands. "I came in to see if she felt any better, and here Bridget lay in Sarah's bed, in Sarah's clothing."

"Up. Get up."

Bridget cowered before him. Stupid girl. She stood, eyes watching the floor.

"Thomas, you know Bridget didn't do anything of her own volition. Sarah is behind it. You cannot blame Bridget."

"I can blame whomever I wish." He stepped closer and she cowered more. Grabbing at his hair, he turned away from the terrified maid. "But yer right. I know it, and ye know it. Sarah has a mind of her own. Just tell me where she went, lass. Tell me so I can bring her safely back."

Bridget slowly raised her face. She didn't trust him but right now his daughter's safety was the important thing. "She's away to Edenmore, sir." She curtsied.

"Edenmore? I should have known she'd head right into the thick of things." He strode to the door. "I'll take six guards with me. Meg, you must keep everyone else here. Do not let another out or in this house until I return." He turned back to Bridget. "Is that understood?"

"Aye, sir." Bridget's answer echoed after him down the stairs.

"Mount up." Thomas bellowed as he headed for his stables. "All of ye." He pointed to six private guards of Balleylawn tower house who did as ordered. With the front two holding aloft torches, they cantered as one to the end of the laneway, then broke into a gallop, Thomas Stewart leading. *I will find a way to keep her safe if it is the last thing I do.* With a grim reminder, he prayed she'd be safe until he could find her and keep his vow.

⚜

ALAIN-ROBERT'S HEAD RANG WITH NOISE. HIS LEADED EYES fought opening. Light burned. He couldn't focus.

Scrambled sounds came from near the trees as it all came

rushing back. He felt at his belt. Yes, he still had his pistol. Pulling it out, he forced himself to a sitting position and pulled back the hammer. He couldn't see. Swiping his face, he cleared his eyes. It was still too blurry. Alain-Robert blinked, squinted, and aimed as best he could. *God help me.* A breath and he pulled the trigger.

❧

"DID YOU HEAR THAT?" JAMES DIDN'T WAIT FOR AN ANSWER. He ran faster toward the sound. Blood charged through his veins sending him flying down the road. He couldn't imagine what he'd find, but prayed it would be Shannon, unhurt.

❧

THE EXPLOSION CAME FROM NOWHERE. SHANNON, BLOOD pounding in her brain, longed to scream, but couldn't get enough air.

Kevin's eyes grew wide. He dropped to his knees and fell. On top of her.

Someone whimpered. The noise came from her. She hadn't even the strength to push her assailant away. Her chest hurt too much to take in a deep breath. Pinned against the tree, under his body, she couldn't move a muscle. *Oh, God, if Ye've ever heard me, hear me now. Help me.*

Chapter Sixteen

"Where did they think they were going? Why would Shannon be out of the house?" Antoine could not understand how things were already so out of control.

Robert had found him speaking with the other two out in the barn when he delivered the message. "I explained, Father. James told Joseph and me that the Widow left for her house and he was going after her. Joseph agreed to go, so I gave my pistol to James. I said I'd let you know." Robert held his palms out. "That's all the story I have."

Though it frustrated him, Antoine could see Robert had given all the information he knew. Turning on his heel, he announced over his shoulder. "I'll talk to whoever is with the babies. Maybe then we'll discover the rest of the story."

He led Albert, Michael and Robert back into the house, all four traipsing to the nursery together.

The staircase could have been just one more mountain to be scaled today. Over and over Antoine's emotions took a frightening ride. Just when he thought he had his loved ones protected, one more mountain loomed. He prayed this would be an easier climb.

The nursery door stood wide open. Mimi and Lucy sat on the floor playing with Samuel. Sarah Beth stood at the dresser, changing Wee Joseph's diaper. Mary Frances and Sarah Stewart sat on the edge of the bed in conversation. All glanced up when the men entered.

"What do you know about the Widow O'Connor leaving for her house?"

"I told her I'd watch her Samuel while she was gone." Mimi volunteered, her smile showing a hint of worry. "I do not think she planned to be gone long, though. Alain-Robert went with her."

"How long ago did they leave?" Antoine felt somewhat better knowing the lass had not left alone. So why did James run after her?

"Not long. Maybe thirty minutes ago?"

Thirty minutes, not enough time to get there and back. But more than enough time for trouble to find them.

❧

THE GRISLY SITE APPEARED MORE LIKE A BATTLEFIELD THAN a familiar country path. Heart pounding in his ears, James spotted Alain-Robert first, lying silent on the road, his pistol still in his hand. Then he saw the body by the tree. "Where is she? Shannon. Answer me. Where are you?"

"Here." Her voice was feeble, but he heard her. Following the sound, James found her beneath O'Rourke's body. Her left eye was puffy, nearly swollen closed, while her left cheek showed faint scratches running from her ear to her nose.

James pulled the body off Shannon. Dropping to his knee, he felt for a pulse. O'Rourke had none. James pushed the corpse farther from her, then tried to pull Shannon to her feet.

"Ah-h-h."

He let go, stooping next to her, brushing soft blonde strands from her face. "Where are you hurt?"

"Something…wrong…my chest. Hurts…to breathe. Right leg. Won't hold me." The skin around her mouth had taken on a pale bluish cast, and the notch at her neck deepened with each breath.

James glanced over his shoulder to find Joseph bent over Alain-Robert. "Joseph, she needs help."

"So does he. He's still breathing, but his head is in bad shape. He's unconscious."

"She's in no condition to walk. What do you want to do?" James's brain refused to work. He hadn't planned beyond finding Shannon—safe and unharmed.

"I don't know. Let me think." If anyone could come up with a quick plan, James knew his brother would. He hoped.

The sun sank lower by the second and he now understood, more than ever, this was not the night to be out after dark.

⁂

"WHAT ABOUT THESE BAGS? WHERE'D THEY COME FROM?" Joseph grabbed up the one near Alain-Robert without waiting an answer.

"She says they're hers." James didn't even turn but called out over his shoulder.

Joseph dumped the bag, picking up toddler-sized gowns, toys, personal items, ribbons and small blankets. He grabbed the other bag and dumped its contents as well. Here he found a woolen cloak, a couple dresses, and some female-type under-garments.

He stared at the contents. "I think I have an idea. Go find two long limbs, at least as long as you are. Longer is better. Bring them back."

James didn't move.

"Go! Now. Or else we're all stuck out here and she won't get any help." His brother only paused a second longer to look at Shannon. She gave a small nod and he was off.

Joseph began tearing a baby blanket into strips. "I'm sorry to have to do this with your clothes, Widow O'Connor. I'm afraid I'll owe you some new things before we're done. Right now, I need to bandage Alain-Robert's head." He used a second baby blanket to gently wipe away as much blood as he could from the man's forehead before placing a thick pad of the torn blanket over the wound and wrapping the strips about to hold the pad in place. He wished for water to cleanse the wound. It would be a sticky mess before they got home.

Could he even get them home? No time to think about that now.

Next he picked up her two dresses, tugged on the skirts of each and settled for the chambray work frock. Stretching it out on the ground, he then placed the woolen cloak on top of it, studied it a moment, and then put the cloak to the side. Afterward he tore her muslin chemise into long strips. Taking two of the strips, he twisted them tight into a makeshift rope, tying knots at both ends. He repeated the method until he had four pieces of rope. They weren't long but he hoped they'd be long enough.

James came out of the woods about then, dragging two long, dead branches behind. "What are you doing?"

"We need something for hauling him." Joseph picked up one of the branches and worked it inside the dress, from the skirt to the bodice, making sure the narrower end came out the neck. He did the same with the other branch and tied the two ends together with one of his ropes. He spread the bottoms of the branches to the outer sides of the skirt.

Without an offer to help, James wandered back over by Shannon.

Taking two of his ropes, Joseph tied them together at the ends and placed the knot at the neckline. From there he slid part of the rope through each sleeve, letting the endings hang out the cuffs. He again spread the woolen cloak over the dress contraption. "James, come here. You need to help me move him over on this."

James came and picked up Alain-Robert's feet while Joseph lifted from under his shoulders. "What about Shannon? How are we going to get her help? I've tried the pick her up, but I think she's got some broken ribs. I'd better not carry her."

"I've been thinking about that. While I get Alain-Robert secured on this, you get the widow's things put back in her bags. Then, we'll both help her to a standing—"

"She can't walk. She's either broken her leg or ankle or something."

Joseph didn't feel patient but knew his brother wasn't thinking clearly. "I know about her leg. You already told me. We can't let them stay out here all night, and we can't separate and go for help. So, we'll help her to stand on her good leg. She'll use us as crutches. If you are on one side and I on the other, we should be able to head for home."

"But it's over a mile. She'll never make it."

"Do you have a better idea? I know we'll have to go slow. I also know we have to head for home since wherever we stop is going to be where they will stay to heal. Where do you want her getting care?" He had to make James understand, and he had no clue what else he could do. His brother's attention entirely focused on the widow, but Alain-Robert appeared in greater need of help.

Joseph began to loop the sleeves with ropes inside under Alain-Robert's arms, over the injured man's shoulders, and tying them together beneath his head at his neck. The last rope he used to loosely bind the injured man's hands at the wrist so they wouldn't drag on the journey.

Instead of arguing, James picked up the nearest bag and started stuffing Shannon's things inside. Once the widow's strewn belongings were packed, he walked over and leaned down, quietly talking to Shannon.

Joseph checked to make sure Alain-Robert lay secure. The

man had not regained consciousness in spite of the jostling to carry him to the drag, and that concerned Joseph all the more. Plus, his head wound continued to bleed, seeping through the linen baby-blanket bandage. It would be a long walk home and sunset was closing in. Could they make it home with everyone still alive? Would they even be able to make it at all?

Robert kept watch from the upstairs window. The location of the apple orchard made this west side of the house the most vulnerable. All the other sides were far clearer, giving a better opportunity to see an enemy's approach. But the area outside his window lent an attacker more cover and a defender less time for defense.

The sun sinking low behind the trees, gave off an amber glow both beautiful and somewhat blinding. Robert would need to pay very close attention to every tiny movement.

Earlier, his father passed out guns to the other men, positioning them at various posts throughout the house. His mother also kept watch from another window. All awaited the signal to arms, and the responsibility weighed on him.

What a time to be wishing for less attention. Robert strained his eyes harder, looking for any movement out of the ordinary.

But what if the movement turned out to be James and Joseph returning instead of a hidden enemy? *Lord, keep my eyes sharp and my brothers safe.*

He rubbed his tired eyes and stared again at the edge of the trees. Was that a movement he saw? He blinked and willed his eyes to see in the darkening twilight.

Wisps of smoke wandered into view. "Fire. The barn." Robert sounded the alarm, staring out the window before charging from the room and down the stairs. "Fire." He sprinted for the back door. Grabbed by the arm, he spun to face his father.

"Wait here, Robert. Two of us will go and two stay. This is most likely a diversion. Tell your mother. Help her get the women and children to the cellar." And he was out the door.

Robert spun on his heel. Going back to the stairs, he found Sarah and his mother on the landing. Mimi, holding the babies, stood at the top of the stairs. "Take them to the cellar. I'll get the girls." He tore past without looking to see if they obeyed.

"Mistress O'Toole is in the girls' room." Good that his mother reminded him.

Without acknowledging, Robert threw open the door to his sisters' room. "Get downstairs to the cellar." He didn't wait but ran to the nursery. "Lucy, Sarah Beth, Mary Frances, go to the cellar now." Robert reached in to grab Mary Frances's arm, making her move faster.

Shooing like a mother hen, he chased them down the stairs. Sarah, holding Wee Joseph, guided all the others past her, before passing the baby off to Lucy.

Mother had an arm around Grand-mère Josephine, helping her hurry. Two other servant girls followed.

Once Robert had them to the door, he grabbed his mother's elbow. "Get them all down the stairs. Bolt the door after and keep everyone silent." She nodded and closed the door. He listened to be sure she obeyed his instructions, then ran to check the rest of the house.

He rounded the corner of the dining room just as Michael and his son entered, from another door. "I sent the women and children to the cellar."

"Good. Then you take the front of the house. We'll take the back. Pray your father and Albert can put out the fire before it spreads any further."

Robert was already praying.

Chapter Seventeen

Stars broke through the night sky, millions of tiny holes revealing light in a black velvet curtain. A fingernail of a moon hung in the corner offering little light. A dark, unnerving night, and they were still far from home.

Joseph refused to dwell on that fact. Light, dark, day, night, none of that mattered. They *had* to reach home.

Shannon gasped, her toe catching on a stone in the road. Joseph held on to her, and to the drag he pulled behind. He slowed his pace.

There had been no sound from the drag, and Joseph worried. Should they have stayed and waited for help? But who knows when that would have arrived?

No, they did the right thing.

He hoped.

Shannon had difficulty getting enough breath. Her breathing remained shallow, so there'd been little conversation. It was a wonder she hadn't fainted. Maybe she had, and they were unaware.

Joseph started to pray but changed his mind. If God wouldn't help Kathleen, why would He help Alain-Robert or

Shannon? Or, perhaps it was only the prayers of Joseph Louis Crockett the Almighty refused to answer.

Joseph Louis Crockett, Sr., he reminded himself. There were now two with that name.

Distant thundering from the road behind interrupted his revelry.

"We need to move over." It was the first thing James had uttered since they started walking.

"Shhh. This way." Joseph led them to the side of the road and helped Shannon lean against a hawthorn tree for support. He then made sure Alain-Robert's drag had no part on the roadway.

"Whoever they are, they're on horseback. Do we stay hidden or see if they can help?"

Why did James want him to make all the decisions? "I don't know. What do you think?"

James remained quiet for a second. "I say let them pass. We don't want to risk anymore."

Finally, his brother had an opinion. So why did it unsettle Joseph?

"I'm not sure."

"What do you mean you're not sure? A minute ago, you didn't know what to do and needed my help. Now that I tell you, you want to do just the opposite?"

Joseph could barely make out James's outline in this light, but he knew from the sound of the whisper, his brother neared a breaking point.

"They must be carrying torches. I can see light coming toward us."

James grabbed his arm. "Then stay hidden. The Combers could carry torches to set the thatch on fire when they attack."

"Wait to see if their faces are covered. If they're not, we should know who they are, and if it is safe to come out."

James didn't answer but let go of his arm. They stepped

behind the hawthorn tree with Shannon. He could hear her breathing becoming more labored.

The horsemen drew closer. Would he step out? Would he make a mistake? If Joseph made a mistake either way, it could end up deadly.

The horsemen rounded the bend. Their faces were uncovered, but they rode so fast, if they didn't see him, he would be trampled.

Joseph made up his mind. He felt James's hand reach for him, but he ran out anyway.

"Whoa. Help us. Please. Whoa."

The horses skidded to a stop, nearly colliding into each other. The leader dismounted. Pulling a dirk from his side, he strode to Joseph, grabbed his shirt and pointed the tip at Joseph's throat.

"Where is my daughter?"

❦

"La la loo, little one. La la loo." Sarah patted the baby's bottom while he perched against her shoulder. She kissed his cheek and continued her circular walk in the cellar, whispering in his ear, trying to keep him still. He squirmed more by the second, and she knew it wouldn't be long before he let out with a cry, giving away their hiding place.

Samuel slept on Mistress de Grillet's lap. She'd found an old crate and turned it into a seat so she could hold the toddler.

If only Wee Joseph would sleep. She still wouldn't be able to relax, but it would be one less worry.

No sound came from overhead. Sarah didn't know if that was good or bad. In the meantime, though, the air seemed cool enough, it just didn't move. And the musty smell didn't help.

"Mary O'Toole, would you help me here?" Though Tanté Louise whispered, urgency came through her voice.

"Aye."

Sarah followed Mary to where Louise knelt next to Josephine LeSuere. Louise held one small candle. Dim though the light, Sarah saw too clearly.

Josephine, seated on another crate, leaned heavy against Louise, her eyes closed. She gripped her left arm firm against her chest. Her breath came in ragged gasps.

Sarah's heart leapt to her throat.

"Tanté, what do we do?"

❧

"I don't know, sir." Joseph fleetingly thought he'd said that phrase quite often of late. There was much he didn't know, like if Alain-Robert still lived or if any of them would survive the night. But the look in Thomas Stewart's eyes, as much as the knife held at his throat, kept him focused on the present. Alain-Robert and Shannon needed immediate help. "I have two injured people here. We need to get them to Edenmore. Can you give assistance?"

"Calhoun, MacDonald, see to it." Two men dismounted. One took a torch and they strode to where James stood between Shannon and Alain-Robert."

"Sir, there are three people, two injured. One is a woman."

Stewart lifted Joseph's chin slightly with the tip of his blade, his eyes narrowing.

Joseph stood his ground, staring back. Didn't the man have an ounce of compassion? Alain-Robert and Shannon would die if they didn't soon receive aid.

The guard returned. "Sir, the woman is not your daughter. She says she is Widow Shannon O'Connor. One male is unconscious. They say he is Alain-Robert de Grillet."

"What happened, Joseph?" Stewart slowly returned the knife to its sheath.

Though momentarily relieved, Joseph's gaze never faltered. He swiped a knuckle under his jaw, past the area now free of the knifepoint. "We learned the Widow and Alain-Robert left the house. We followed and found them hurt and Kevin O'Rourke dead. We've been trying to return to Edenmore ever since." Joseph swallowed his pride. "Sir, they need immediate help. Will you assist?"

"Where is Sarah? Did you see her at Edenmore?"

"No, sir, I have not seen her. I believed her safe at Balleylawn." A cold chill ran up Joseph's spine. She wasn't at Balleylawn. So focused had he been on getting Alain-Robert and Shannon help, he'd missed an important part.

Was Sarah in danger?

"Get the animals out." Antoine ran to the stable. The horses snorted and pawed the earthen floor. He opened their stalls, shooing the horses to the pasture. Returning to see if Albert needed help, he rushed to the barn. His friend pulled a terrified heifer to safety.

"The hay is ablaze, and the thatch has caught. Get back." Albert pulled him away from the growing inferno. "Get back. The animals are out."

Antoine stopped in his tracks. Staring, he helplessly watched as the flames inside grew. Soon they'd bust through the thatch, sending a volcano of sparks hundreds of feet in the air. *God, let the other roofs be damp enough not to catch.*

Grabbing a bucket, he ran for the well.

"Sir, leave men here with James to help. I'll ride with you." Joseph felt each second ticking away as he waited for Stewart to agree.

"Fitzhugh." A rider came closer. "Leave your mount and

remain here with Calhoun and MacDonald. Help Crockett to stabilize and—"

"Fire! Sir. Over there." Fitzhugh pointed in the direction of Edenmore.

Joseph pulled the man from his horse taking the mount from him. Thomas Stewart started at a gallop. Joseph immediately joined him, followed by three more of Ballylawn's guards.

His son was at Edenmore. That he knew. Could Sarah be there too? He spurred his mount to run faster. Everyone he loved, everything he held dear, his whole heart lay at Edenmore Manor. His one and only thought left no room for compromise. He had to get there in time.

He had to.

⚜

Antoine swiftly filled another bucket. Handing it to Albert, he prayed and dipped again.

"Look out."

Antoine spun to the sound. Albert's bucket flew past. It hit a figure, a man, in the face. A yell. The figure dropped.

Blood pounding in his ears, Antoine pulled his pistol from his belt. Michael O'Toole advanced from the house, gun poised.

The man slowly rose.

Antoine held steady.

Tossing the bucket aside, the figure swore and ran at Antoine.

One shot.

An owl cried overhead.

The figure ran no more.

Antoine lowered his weapon, switched hands, and reached for his dirk. Caution guarded each step, closer and closer.

Albert and Michael met him at the body. Antoine pushed with his toe, turning it over. The firelight revealed. "Seamus Flaherty."

Michael lowered his pistol. "Make a search around the outside?"

Antoine shook his head. "No. Let them come to us." No need of Robert or young O'Toole firing on their fathers.

A shot rang out.

"The front."

Antoine led the men though the backdoor, into the house.

"Robert?"

"Father, in the dining room. Look there, out by the old elm." His pistol remained trained on the spot. "Don't think I hit anything."

SQUEAK.

Military preparation took over. A quick count of persons told Antoine all were accounted for. No one remained at the back of the house. Pulling his dirk from its sheath, he caught Albert's glance and nodded to the stairs. He motioned for Michael to go down the hall. Robert and Liam were to stay at the front.

Antoine silently mounted the steps, staying to the wall side. At the landing he pointed to Albert to take the right hall. He started down the left . Senses heightened, he stepped into the first bedroom, his daughters'. Glow from the barn fire illumined the room with an eerie red light, and smoke seeped in through an open window. The thatch on this roof most likely wouldn't catch fire. But a spark flying in could cause the house to burn. Best to close the window.

He stopped.

Draperies could well hide someone. Using his dirk, he moved the fabric. No one. He pulled the sash closed. On to the next room. What would he find there?

WHAT WAS THAT? SARAH FROZE IN HER TRACKS. SO DID THE other women. All eyes gazed at each other.

There it was again. Someone trying to open the cellar door.

Sarah realized she held her breath. Wee Joseph squirmed. She held him too tightly. She loosened her hold and put her lips to his tiny ear.

"Hush, sweet darlin' boy. Shh. There, there's a good boy." *Oh Father, put a guard over his sweet mouth. And bring us an angel of mercy for Miss Josephine too.*

There'd been no change for the poor woman. In the candlelight she appeared as pale as the moon. Sarah hoped the light only played tricks with her eyes.

The baby shoved a fist in his mouth and began sucking loudly.

A tear dripped down Sarah's cheek. "Oh, darlin' I'm so sorry. Your Shannon isn't here, and I can't feed you." She kissed his head. *Lord, please send help soon.*

❧

A SHOT.

Antoine ran out the bedroom door.

A shout.

Albert nearly ran into him at the landing.

"It came from the dining room." Antoine held up a hand, put a finger to his lips, and started slowly down the staircase. One boot over another, one step at a time.

Once at the newel post, Antoine motioned Albert closer. He pointed to himself and to the front door leading to the dining room. Then he pointed to Albert and to the pantry door.

Albert nodded and moved off. He would know to use the pantry door to the dining room.

Antoine reached the front dining room entrance. With a measured breath, he wiped his hand on his pant leg before little by little easing open the door.

Deep shadows filled the room. One shadow near the window moved. Something flashed.

Antoine stood still. Someone with a knife held Liam O'Toole. The blade rested at the boy's throat. Liam's eyes glowed round with fear.

"Lemme outta 'ere, an' I'll let the boy go."

Antoine slowly raised his hands, but his mind raced, searching for a plan. Though the light was dim, he hoped the person could see him. "You may go. Just don't harm the boy."

"Git outa me way. I'm goin' out the front." He pushed the terrified lad along in front of him.

Antoine stepped back to let the pair pass. As they came close, the man with the knife turned to keep Liam between them.

Antoine knew he had one chance. Let him get to the door.

There'd been no sign of Robert. Albert had gone in through the other door and so must still remain in the dining room. No help.

"Get yer filthy hands off me boy."

The voice made Antoine jump in his skin.

Something thudded against the wall. Antoine yanked Liam out of the way. He could make out two forms wrestling, but not clearly enough to see who was who.

Another thud.

A cry of pain.

A clatter.

One figure jumped up, scrambling toward the door.

Antoine grabbed him.

"Let me go."

Though he fought like a wildcat, Antoine tackled him to the floor.

"Robert, Albert, bring light. Look to Michael and then see who this hooligan is."

JOSEPH DREW UP IN FRONT OF THE MANOR, LEAPING TO THE ground before the horse had even stopped. Running to the house, he heard a shout and shot behind him. He whirled around to see a guard lowering his pistol.

"He had a knife, sir."

Joseph didn't wait. Turning back to the door, it suddenly opened. His father stood with dirk brandished.

"Father."

"Joseph?"

Joseph ran up the steps.

"Where is your brother?"

"He is well, with Alain-Robert and the Widow." Pushing past into the house, he nearly tripped over the others in the doorway.

Danger. There'd been danger. "Where is Wee Joseph? Where is Sarah?"

"They are safe, Joseph." Robert tried to take his arm. Joseph shook him free.

"Where?"

Crash.

A scream resonated from the root cellar.

"Sarah." Joseph ran to the kitchen.

A dark figure raced toward the back door.

With a burst of speed, Joseph dove on top of the escapee. They clattered to the floor. Joseph pulled back his fist and beat the man's head. Again. And again.

Hands grabbed him from behind, pulling him from the miscreant. Joseph shook them away. Grabbing the back of his head, he stepped back and took a breath. He could still feel the fury, beating like his heart, thundering in his brain. It made his body quake. "Who is it? Is he alive?"

His father knelt beside the unconscious man. "Bring light."

A baby wailed.

Joseph whirled. Running for the cellar door, he yanked with all his might. "Sarah. Mother. Somebody. Open this door."

A scraping sound.

"Joseph? Joseph, is it you?"

The door burst open. "Oh, Joseph. Joseph."

He grabbed Sarah to him. She held his son who wailed loudly. Hungrily Joseph kissed her soft hair, her wet eyes, her damp cheek. Lifting his face, he closed his eyes and breathed her in, like a scent. Sarah. His Sarah. With eyes wide open, he lowered his mouth to hers. This is what he'd needed to do his entire life.

Sarah pushed him away.

Grabbing his hand, she nearly dragged him down the stairs. The women all gathered about Josephine who slept against his mother. A candle flickered nearby, casting a soft glow around their corner of the cellar.

He stepped nearer, and his mother raised her head. Tears glistened in her eyes. Her hand stroked Josephine's gray hair. Peace radiated from the old woman's face. But she didn't move.

Not even to breathe.

Samuel, an arm wrapped around Tantè Mimi, watched with big eyes. Mary O'Toole, eyes rimmed in red, sat at Josephine's feet and held her hand.

Sarah released him. She snuggled Wee Joseph to her, softly weeping.

Chapter Eighteen

Lightening flashed, ripping the curtain of sky from top to bottom. James winced, waiting for the thunder's roar. How could it go from clear and starry one minute to imminent rain the next? He could see Edenmore up ahead, lit from behind by an eerie glow. The smoke already met them. He prayed it wouldn't cause Shannon to cough.

But if the smoke didn't to that, getting drenched out here in the cool night air certainly would.

He feared for her more than ever.

Thunder cried in the distance. At least the lightning struck away from where they were.

Plop. A droplet of rain splashed on his ear. "Stop. We need to shield her with something."

Up ahead the guards halted. One—James couldn't tell if it was Calhoun or MacDonald—took a wool blanket from his saddle and draped it over Shannon's head. The other guard on horseback placed something over Alain-Robert. When both guards were back in their saddles, they moved again in tandem, pulling the drag between.

Fitzhugh and James walked with Shannon in the middle. Ten more minutes should get them home, just ten minutes more. Home, to where his mother could care for Shannon, help restore her to health. Get her ready to marry him.

The idea no longer shocked him. He knew she belonged with him and he with her. He loved her fierceness, her strength, her tenacity to endure through hardship.

Yes, he loved her.

He loved her and would see her home, see her well, see her…

"Ja—" Shannon's arm slid from his neck, and she slithered down his body.

"Shannon." He caught her. "Shannon, hold on, lass, just a bit more. I can see Edenmore from here." Gripping her hand, he willed his strength to infuse her body. "Just a bit more, lass. You're almost home."

"Almost." Her eyelids fluttered. "Get…me…home…James."

"Aye, Shannon, I'll get you there." He gently helped her to her good foot, put her arms back in place, and kept her moving homeward.

❧

"Rain. Blessed, blessed, rain. Thank You, Lord." An answer to prayer, but it seemed heaven cried with him. Antoine sat alone on the stone front steps, letting the water bathe his senses. Daylight would reveal the worst of the damage. But barns could be rebuilt.

He waited for James. Joseph had explained. Now Antoine prayed for the Widow, for Alain-Robert, for all of them.

Life had changed. Nothing would be the same.

Josephine, faithful friend, and second mother to both Antoine and Louise, was gone. The only grand-mère his children ever knew. Josephine had been there for the birth of each one. Now she rested in her room while Louise and his daughters prepared her body.

Other bodies awaited preparation, but their families would

need to handle that undertaking. Three men, men he'd hoped would be reached somehow through the work of the committee. But that wasn't to be. Jacob Sullivan, Donovan Cummins, and Seamus Flaherty all let their souls be bought. And for what?

Maybe Patrick Flanagan could explain his choosing to throw in with O'Rouke's Combers. Let him explain to his father, Paddy Flanagan, how he'd caused the death of his father's best friend. Let him explain how he held a knife to the throat of a twelve-year-old boy. And when he's through, maybe he could explain to Mary O'Toole why she was now a widow. It was all such a waste. A pain-filled waste.

Antoine squeezed his eyes tight, pinching the bridge of his nose against the pain in his head. Too much had happened this evening.

Donovan Cummins still lay unconscious in the parlor, a guard on him at all times. Dead, wounded, prisoners—all the stuffs of war. Hadn't he left that life? Now here it had established itself again, in his own home.

The rage Antoine fought to control threatened to overtake him. Angry tears crashed to the ground as he pondered the senselessness. "Why, Lord? I don't understand." Dread for what the new day might bring rose in this gut. "Hang on to us, Lord. I feel so broken, a soft breeze could blow me to pieces."

Up ahead, a light he hadn't noticed before gleamed bright. A tiny flame of hope reignited. He stood to get a better look.

And he knew.

"Albert, Joseph, Robert, come with me. It's James." Without waiting for the others, Antoine leapt from the steps and ran with renewed strength.

"Father, I can't pick her up to carry her. It's her ribs."

"You're home now, son. Let's just get her inside." He guided James up the three front steps, gently helping Shannon's feet over them and the threshold.

"Widow, do you think it would be better to lie flat or sit upright?" She appeared much too pale and exhausted.

"Sit."

Antoine could see in her face there wasn't enough breath for niceties. He helped James and the guard put her in a straight-backed chair.

"Where shall we put this one?" Two guards stood at the door. When Antoine glanced up, they parted to reveal the drag bearing Alain-Robert.

"The dining room. Put him on the table." Antoine led the way. "Robert, go get your mother and Tanté Mimi. *Vite, vite.*"

Albert pulled the blanket from his son's face. Antoine side-embraced his friend, feeling his muscles tense. Thomas Stewart squeezed Albert's shoulder before turning to one of his guards. "Ride for the doctor. Drag him out of bed, if need be. Take three men with you."

Mimi and Louise rushed into the room. Albert shielded Mimi from the grisly site. The makeshift bandages around Alain-Robert's head were saturated with blood. His hair lay matted and sticky while long red tracks ran down his face, pooling at his collarbone and clothing.

"No, my love, don't." Albert wrapped her up in his arms. Though she fought, he still held her.

Antoine guided Louise away to where Shannon sat rigidly straight in the foyer. James knelt beside her. Shannon's lips appeared blue in the candlelight.

"Might I…have…a table…to lean…on?"

"Of course." James brought over a side table that stood a bit taller than most. Shannon leaned forward slightly from the hips, without bending, and rested her arms.

Louise brought her a cushion and put it on top of the table. Shannon weakly smiled , leaned her head against it, and closed her eyes. Louise brushed hair from Shannon's forehead, letting her palm linger a moment. She stepped behind the girl and shook her head, letting Antoine know Shannon's temperature wasn't right. "Perhaps I should get you a blanket." Louise hurried upstairs.

"May I get you anything, my dear?" Antoine felt helpless, but the Widow needed attention.

Shannon shook her head, so Antoine returned to the dining room, leaving her with James.

Mimi sat next to Alain-Robert, holding his hand. Albert stood behind, his hand resting on her shoulder. When Antoine entered, Albert locked gazes. Eyes full of pain, he came to Antoine.

"I'd forgotten how strong she is. Always so gentle and kind, but she was doing this when I met her, holding a dying man's hand. And now it is our son." Albert broke.

Antoine held his friend, crying with him.

SARAH ROCKED WEE JOSEPH. IN THE END, IT WAS THE ONLY thing she could do. The cow slept in the field, and Shannon couldn't nurse in her condition. With Lucy's help she had cooked a small amount of oats. They'd then mashed it up fine, thinning it to a runny porridge. A tiny amount of sweet from the sugar loaf made it palatable for the hungry baby. He'd worn as much as he'd taken in, but at least he had something in his belly. Now he drifted between slumber and waking, fighting to not give in to the sleep he needed.

Rocking him gave Sarah time to think. Especially about that kiss. That was no kiss between friends. Maybe Joseph really loved her.

Would he still love her if he knew why Shannon was out on that road? The guilt weighed heavy on her shoulders.

If she'd apologized to Shannon.

If she'd not let her temper get the best of her.

If she'd just stayed home.

The *what if* would drive her mad. She couldn't undo what had been done. Could she live with the shame of knowing she put so many lives in danger? Could she live that lie and still claim Joseph? Truth could set her free, but would she be free without Joseph's love?

Tonight, when she needed it most, no small voice whispered back. She'd never felt so all alone in her life.

❧

THE TOUCH OF HER HAIR, HER LIPS SO SOFT, HER EYES damp with tears… *Stop it.* Joseph shook his head and continued to help carry the body of Jacob Sullivan into a back room.

"Are you well?" MacDonald, one of Thomas Stewart's guards, carried the other end of the body. He eyed Joseph.

"Aye." He lied. How could he be well? People died here tonight. Even people he knew and cared about. The only grandmother he'd ever known died hiding in the root cellar. Except she really wasn't his grandmother. But still, he loved her as if she had been.

They placed the body next to his confederate, Seamus Flaherty.

Yet his mind continued to stray to the auburn-haired beauty in the upstairs nursery. Thinking about her now, with so much pain and heartbreak going on, was calloused, insane, wrong.

He left the guard in the kitchen and wandered toward Josephine's room. In reality, he longed to go upstairs but knew better.

Joseph had acted inappropriately, without thinking. He reacted. Kissing Sarah had been the craziest thing he'd ever done in his entire life. And it felt so good, so right.

What was the matter with him? Had he no feelings? No compassion? These people in this house stood by him when he lost Kathleen, and now all he could do was dream of another woman.

He betrayed his wife and everyone who loved him. What kind of a monster had he become?

He knocked at Josephine's door. Sarah Beth answered and

immediately wrapped her young arms about his waist, her head buried in his chest. Mary Frances and Lucy had finished washing and dressing their grand-mère in her favorite blue gown. Her hands crossed neatly on her chest. Coins held her eyelids closed.

Seeing her this way broke something inside Joseph. Before, in the cellar, she'd only seemed asleep. Now the truth could not be denied. Mary Frances glanced up and their eyes met. She joined Sarah Beth in wrapping her arms about her big brother. Tenderhearted lass, she came to comfort rather than be comforted.

And he so needed that comfort. As tears rained on his sisters' heads, he grabbed them closer. Lucy now joined the embrace and he kissed the top of each head. His sisters, how he loved them. His grand-mère Josephine, how he loved her.

Memories now flooded back. He could smell her roasted chicken, taste the apple tarts sweet with honey. Her voice floated back, filled with kindness and French endearments. She had fought learning English. A barbarian tongue, she'd said. He'd been the only one to teach her a few phrases, probably because he was her namesake. He knew she understood more than she let on.

Joseph released his sisters, kissed each one again, and left the room.

This made no sense. His parents, his sisters, Josephine all honored God. They had dedicated their lives to living as He led. How could God do this to them? Where was the justice, the righteousness about which he heard so much?

Going outside, the cool air cleared his mind of all else but his anger. Joseph tipped his head back and let the night mist wash over him. His mind heard only one word, a word that his heart beat over and over. Raising a fist to the sky, the word burst from his soul.

"Why?" He pounded at the doors of heaven. "Why? I want to know why You let this happen. Why You didn't help?"

He listened but heard nothing. Nothing but the sizzle of the dying fire. Nothing but the wind in the orchard. Nothing but the door of his heart slamming closed. He had one last question for the Almighty.

"Now tell me, why should I trust You to take care of my own?"

The silence followed him all the way back to the house.

Chapter Nineteen

"We need to get her out of these wet clothes. And she needs to lie down and let her chest be still." Louise blew out a breath while thinking aloud.

No one argued, yet there were few available to help. Mary O'Toole and Liam sat with Michael. Mimi and Albert sat with Alain-Robert. Her daughters sat with Josephine and Sarah had the babies in the nursery. One guard kept the unconscious and conscious prisoners in hand and three searched for the doctor with Robert. Antoine and Thomas were planning for morning, so that left two guards and two sons with services to enlist.

Another time it might have been sweet to see how James never left Shannon's side. Now, when it concerned the lass's very life Louise counted on her son's help for ideas to make Shannon secure.

"Could she lean back in the chair? And then we could carry her chair and all up the stairs. If Wee Joseph and Samuel are asleep, Sarah might be able to help me get her into dry things."

"Perhaps. Shannon, what do you think?" He refused to make a move that might hurt her.

Poor thing. He was so smitten.

Shannon never opened her eyes.

James listened, then nodded. "She said, 'aye'."

"Good then, we can have those two guards carry the chair…"

James stood, protectively moving closer to the Widow. "I can carry it."

"I'm sure you can, son, but let them carry her. I think Shannon would feel more comfortable knowing you can make sure she is handling the move."

James nodded and knelt back by Shannon.

Louise garnered Fitzhugh and Calhoun into assisting. "First, Shannon, you will need to sit back in the chair. James, help her… ouí. Now, move that table back out of the way there." She pointed her directions, and Calhoun removed the table. "Now, gentlemen, please lift the chair…gently, gently." Louise walked up the first two steps backwards. "Turn the chair around, ouí, so she is looking back at James, and lean her back. There you have it. Up we go now."

She didn't feel encouraging, but her time to mourn would come later. Right now, too many wounded bodies and hearts needed her. No longer the innocent she had been when she first met Josephine a quarter century ago; raising a family and living life had taught her much.

So had Josephine.

Louise bit her lip, blinked back the tears that threatened and focused on Shannon.

Still walking backwards, she led the men to a small guest room normally reserved for the Reverend Fontaine. The firm bed would better support Shannon's back and offer less wiggles to the injured ribs.

"Thank you, gentlemen. You may set her down in this room. Shannon, dear heart, I'm going to send James to get Sarah, and then we'll get you changed."

James left the room. For the first time, Louise noticed a tear glisten in Shannon's eyes.

Louise took the girl's hand and knelt next to her. "Oh, dear,

I am so sorry this is hurting. I'm afraid it will hurt more before we're through."

"Not…that." Shannon stopped for breath. "No…more…clothes."

"No more clothes? No, don't worry about it right now."

James returned with Sarah behind him.

"James, she says she has no more clothes. I have a gown for her for tonight, but where are her things? What does she mean?"

"She means, we used her clothing to make bandages for her and for Alain-Robert."

Louise knew there was more to the story, but that could wait until later. While Sarah and James stayed with the wounded girl, she ran to her own room and found a chemise of soft linen with embroidered Celtic knots around the hem. She would also need long strips to bind around the injured ribs. Locating those, where Josephine had laid them only yesterday, she hurried back to Shannon.

Louise stopped outside the door, took a deep breath and put on a smile before entering. "Now James, I'm going to have to send you out. Sarah and I will take good care of Shannon. Go downstairs and make sure your sisters are doing well."

"I'll wait just outside the door."

"No." She needed to be firm on this. He didn't need to listen through the door. "Your sisters have been keeping watch by themselves for some time now. I need you to make sure they are managing." She cupped her hand to his cheek. "I'll send for you, I promise."

James stood to his full height, towering over her. For a moment she thought he would refuse to obey, but he turned to Shannon.

"I'll be right downstairs. I can be back here faster than you can blink." She gave a half-hearted smile and blinked at him. He smiled back and left, closing the door after.

"Ladies, we need to get you, Shannon, standing." Together Louise and Sarah helped Shannon to her feet. She couldn't put any weight on her right leg, but she could balance with the women's help. They began by unbinding her, then slipping off the wet clothes. The bruise on Shannon's ribcage spanned the size of Louise's palm, but it had already turned a deep purple. Louise's heart squeezed even tighter and she bit her lip. She glanced at Sarah.

The girl's eyes filled with tears.

Louise gathered the chemise together and dropped it over Shannon's head. Once it was in place, arms in the sleeves and her hair pulled free, it was time to rebind her ribs.

"When the binding is in place, you must try to breathe as deeply as you can. The binding must be tight, and it will make it hard, but please believe me, it is essential that you breathe as deeply as you can. Do you understand?"

Shannon nodded. She seemed so pale. Louise didn't know how much more she could take.

Picking up the binding strips, Louise set to wrapping them around Shannon's ribs while Sarah held her arms up. Just like Aaron and Hur did for Moses. *Oh, Lord bring us victory in all of this.*

Once bound, the worst part still lay ahead—getting Shannon onto the bed.

Turning her so the girl's back was to the bed, Louise stood on one side and Sarah the other, facing the bed. Shannon rested her upper arms on their shoulders. They guided while she hopped closer to the bed's edge, each hop bringing a soft cry of pain. At the edge, Louise and Sarah lowered her to a sitting position. Then Louise deftly turned and lowered Shannon's back to the mattress of the box bed, keeping a hand on the girl's back to keep it straight. Sarah lifted the legs and finally, Shannon lay flat.

Now Louise could see to her leg.

Carefully undoing the makeshift brace, she noticed one of the stays had been rubbing on Shannon's calf, causing a sore.

"I'll be right back. I neglected to bring in a couple supplies."

Shannon reached up and grabbed Louise's hand.

"I'll be right back."

Shannon nodded and released her.

Louise opened the bedroom door, stepped into the hall and closed the door again. Leaning against the jam, the pent-up tears threatened. Not now. There was a time to weep and a time to do. Now she must do. *Lord, give me the wisdom and strength.*

Wiping her wrist across her eyes, she took a deep breath and went in search of what she needed.

❧

Seeing Shannon's suffering up close, Sarah's guilt nearly overwhelmed her. The words she needed to say lay caught in her throat.

Kneeling by the bed, she took Shannon's hand. Sarah bent her head, squeezed her eyes shut, and prayed for strength. Once more, she opened her eyes to see the wounded young woman.

"Shannon, this is all my fault. I am so sorry, so truly sorry."

Shannon pulled her hand back.

Sarah's heart broke further.

Then the Widow cupped Sarah's cheek. "You…didn't do… this. Kevin…O'Rourke…did."

Sarah started to speak but Shannon's fingers touched her lips.

"I chose…to leave…because…of my…pride." She paused. "Not…your…fault."

Blinded by tears, Sarah stroked Shannon's hair. "Can you ever forgive me?"

"Nothing…to forgive."

But Sarah knew better. She'd asked forgiveness of God and of Shannon. Yet the burden still weighed heavy on her heart.

Somehow Shannon found and grasped Sarah's hand again. "Tis well…between…us."

It may be well between them, but something wasn't right.

Sarah was grateful, though, for the girl's forgiveness. She kissed Shannon's hand that grasped her own. "Thank you."

And they remained like that; Sarah holding the back of Shannon's hand to her cheek with one hand and stroking Shannon's hair back from her forehead with the other.

The young widow appeared so weak, so frail, yet even now, with her body broken, she held more depth of spirit, more sustaining strength than Sarah could imagine. More earnestly than ever, Sarah prayed for Shannon O'Connor.

❧

JAMES STOMPED OUT ANOTHER GLOWING EMBER. ONE MORE step closer to returning to Shannon's side. He raked a new clump of ash free and imagined her well and whole.

And in his arms.

"All the horses are stabled at my barn. The cow is milked and out in the pasture. Do you want me here or elsewhere?" Joseph stood at the entrance of what had been his father's barn.

Morning, like the doctor, had come and gone, as did the constable who arranged for the families to collect their dead after taking Donovan Cummings and Patrick Flanagan to jail.

As soon as light allowed, Father had them all working. James silently stuck with the arduous task of raking out the debris from between the stone walls and stomping live coals ready to burst into flame.

Joseph had volunteered to find the horses, check for injuries, and milk the cow.

That was fine with James. Anything allowing him to remain alone in his thoughts. He moved to another area further from the rest.

"This is the biggest job. Find a rake and join us." Father's focus was on the job. He missed the emotional turmoil roiling right in front of him. But James wasn't ready to discuss it anyway. He glanced up at the man. Smudged with soot, Father appeared older today, as though the fire aged him overnight. This barn that he built by hand, stone upon stone, appeared more like a Celtic giant of old, yawning, with is mouth full of blackened granite teeth and charred rubble. So, perhaps he understood. James returned to his task.

A shift in the atmosphere caused him to glance up.

Father leaned on his rake, staring at him.

"James, I'm thinking we need Gabriel." He met his father's gaze.

"I'm not going. I'm not leaving here while Shannon is unable to move."

"Your mother is caring for the Widow. There's nothing you can do here. But you can help—"

"I'm not going. Send Joseph or Robert." James moved to another area and returned to raking, closing the subject.

"I'll go." Robert sounded almost eager.

"Good. Go clean up and leave immediately. I do not believe we have time to spare."

James took the last comment as a commentary on his refusal. He didn't care. The woman lying in the room upstairs needed him. Whether she knew it or not, they needed each other. He wasn't going to leave her to go racing off to Glasgow.

Robert propped his rake against the stone wall and headed for the well. James longed to join him there and clean up so he could go upstairs. Instead he drew his rake through the ashes again, finding yet another live ember. So like the tiny ember of fear beginning to glow in his mind.

He stomped them both out.

"Robert, ask Mary Frances or Sarah Beth to bring out something to eat, and we'll take a break."

"Aye."

The men continued working several more minutes until Father laid aside his rake. "Come lads, rinse off and rest a bit. You have worked hard and well. I am proud of you."

James shrugged his father's hand from his shoulder, propping his rake against the wall. "I'm getting a drink."

He strode to the well and pulled up a bucket. The first cup cooled his palate. He dumped the second cup on his head to cool his temper.

It partially worked.

Chapter Twenty

"Och, wee one. The brochan goes in yer mouth, not out." Sarah dabbed at Wee Joseph's chin.

Lucy giggled. "He's enjoying himself, that's for sure."

Wee Joseph's tiny fists beat the air with baby enthusiasm and drool-tainted gruel flew all around.

"But he is taking something in, and for that, I am grateful. How are ye doing with wee Samuel, there?"

"He's done about all he's going to do, I believe. Should I clean him and see about taking him to visit his mother?"

Though Lucy should have been in charge in her own home, she seemed to look to Sarah for all the answers.

Only Sarah had no answers. She prayed and guessed and did her best, praying again that it was the correct thing to do. The babies needed substance; an easily discernible fact. But beyond moment-to-moment care of the little ones, she knew she was lost.

"Aye, he needs to see her, and she needs to see him. Let me clean this imp, and we can go together."

Lucy nodded agreement. They wiped little faces and hands

before taking the babies upstairs where they bathed and dressed them.

"If you stay with the bairns, I'll go see if the Widow is of the mind to see them."

"Aye." Lucy started a game of peek-a-boo on the floor with the boys, not even looking up when Sarah left.

Down the hall in the guest room, Louise sat by Shannon's bed, reading to her.

Sarah knocked at the open door.

"Widow O'Connor, would ye be up to some wee visitors?"

Shannon's pale face brightened like a lit candle.

"Help me…please. I need…to be…up."

Louise patted the girl's hand and pulled back the bedclothes. Once again, Sarah moved Shannon's legs while Louise supported and raised the Widow's back. Though Shannon's face blanched, and her eyes squeezed tight, she bit her bottom lip and never uttered a cry. When she sat upright on the edge of the bed, both Sarah and Louise lifted from under her arms and guided her to the straight-backed chair Louise had vacated.

Shannon picked at her chemise, arranging the folds, before giving a brief nod.

Sarah returned to the nursery, collected Samuel and signaled for Lucy to bring along Wee Joseph.

Shannon smiled at her boy, though she didn't appear to breathe. Louise had placed pillows against the girl's ribs and on her lap.

"Here's yer mama, sweet boy, here's yer mama." Sarah knelt next to Shannon's chair, still holding the child. "Gently, Samuel, gently. Mama's hurting."

The toddler seemed to understand. He lifted his hand to his mother's cheek and softly patted. "Mama owie."

Tears started down Shannon's cheek. "Samuel…me…darlin' boy."

Samuel tried to climb up onto his mother's lap, but Sarah

held on, allowing no weight or movement to touch Shannon's torso.

Wee Joseph squirmed against Lucy, straining toward Shannon. His nurse glanced up just as her milk released, drenching the front of the borrowed gown. Shannon's eyes grew wide, but Louise chuckled. Picking up her grandson, she brought him closer. "Do not worry, dear heart. Of course, you let down. You haven't been able to feed him for hours, and your body cannot forget the babe at your breast."

"Nor…can me…heart. Aye…Wee Joseph…aye."

"Sarah, maybe you and Lucy should return the babes to the nursery. Then you can help me get Shannon into a dry chemise."

"Aye." Sarah pulled the toddler back from his mother and he cried out. "Och. Samuel, we'll be back, we will. Let's let yer mama rest, now, darlin'." She rubbed his back, but the little one's plaintive cry broke her heart.

After helping Lucy bring the babies to the nursery, Sarah returned to Shannon's room.

Louise lowered the top of the chemise and bathed Shannon's breasts in cool water. "I am sorry, dear heart, I didn't think about this discomfort before. I've been concerned for your ribs and leg, and now you are so engorged. I think we must do something about this before infection sets in. It will be easier from the chair. Do you think you can do it?"

Shannon nodded, tears still flowing down her face.

"Sarah, we will need warm water, two bowls, and towels. Do you know where to find it all?"

The plan suddenly became clear to Sarah. She nodded and turned to leave.

"Sarah, if you can, please make at least one towel warm."

"I'll bring up the warm towel first."

As quickly as possible, Sarah heated the towel in a copper kettle over the fire in the kitchen, returned with it and then left to gather the rest of the supplies. The reason behind the need for this remedy wasn't lost on her. She knew once again this stemmed from her selfish pride. If she hadn't argued with Shannon, the girl wouldn't have been injured, Wee Joseph wouldn't be hungry, Samuel would have been able to climb on his mother's lap, and Shannon wouldn't be engorged and fighting infection.

And Alain-Robert would still be alive.

All due to selfishness and pride; *her* selfishness and pride.

She didn't deserve Joseph's love.

The weight of the truth nearly tripped her on the stairs. Hot water sloshed from the pitcher, burning her hand, and she gasped in physical and emotional pain.

She set the pitcher on the next step before it dropped from her trembling fingers. Shaking her hand first, she blew on the burn. The pain, she realized came more from her heart than her skin.

She wiped her hand across her skirt, picked up the pitcher and returned to the bedroom.

❦

Sarah returned the bowls to the kitchen and stretched. There'd been no sleep the night before and no time to nap today. Surprisingly, her father said nothing about her staying. He hugged her before he left for home, saying he'd return in the afternoon.

"Sarah, have you seen Mary Frances or Sarah Beth?" Robert stood damp and soot-streaked in the kitchen doorway.

It was the first thing she'd seen worth a smile in a very long time. "No, I'm sorry, Robert. I'm just down from the nursery myself. Can I help with anything?"

"I'm off to clean up. Father wants me to ride for Glasgow, bring Gabriel home. He also requests something for him and James and Joseph to eat. That's why I'm looking for Mary Frances or Sarah Beth."

"I'll get the food. You get clean. I will leave you something on the sideboard."

Taking a quick look through the larder, Sarah found some bread, cheese, and smoked salmon. Large crockery bowls filled with vegetables and fruit sat in the pantry. A few carrots and pears and her basket was complete.

Out the back door and to the barn, she saw no one. All the rakes lay propped up against stone walls.

"What do you have there?"

"Oh." She nearly jumped out of her skin. Spinning around, she bumped into Joseph and dropped the basket, spilling the contents.

"Here, let me help." He reached for the same chunk of bread as she did, his hand brushing her fingers and sending a shock up her arm.

Streaked in soot, his hair was coming loose from his ribbon. His shirt neckline lay open and his sleeves were rolled halfway up his forearms. Strong and masculine, he quietly assisted her.

Her voice fled. Biting her lip, she picked up the other things.

Joseph gently took her arm, helping her to her feet.

Her body began to tremble. Finally looking up, she found his gaze; a deep, sad gaze. Her heart broke.

"Oh, Joseph." She dropped the basket and threw her arms around his neck. His arms pulled her close. She gazed at his face. Pulling his head to her, she kissed him as she had always wanted.

His arms wrapped tighter, and he kissed her the way she'd imagined he would. The way he had last night.

"Sarah, oh, Sarah."

Her name. He said her name, not Kathleen's. She pulled back and leaned her forehead against his chin. His kiss lingered on top of her head.

"Sarah, I... I need to speak with you. Not here." His voice tickled her ear.

She pulled back to see his face. "Where? When?"

"In an hour. In the nursery." His palm caressed her cheek.

Stooping, he refilled her basket and handed it back before leaning in to brush a kiss across her lips. "One hour."

"One hour."

But Sarah's heart would beat through her chest before the hour was up.

Chapter Twenty-One

Tap, tap.

Shannon's eyes flew open.

She'd dosed off after Louise helped ease her problem. A quick bath from the pitcher, and she needed a nap. But the slightest noise roused her.

The chair next to her was empty. Louise had gone.

Tap.

Someone knocked at the door.

Could she answer? Taking the largest breath she could, she squeaked, "Come."

The door inched open, and James peeked his head around the corner.

Her heart fluttered.

"I can come back."

Shannon shook her head and motioned him to the chair.

"Are you feeling any better?"

Shannon nodded. She lied, he appeared so pitiful.

It worked. James relaxed into the chair. "So, what are you reading?" He picked up the book from the small nightstand and glanced at the title. "*Revelations of Divine Love* by Julian of Norwich? Sounds like something my mother would choose."

Shannon smiled at his attempt at humor. She noticed his hair was damp, pulled back smooth, and tied with a ribbon. He smelled of smoke, and his clothes were streaked with soot. "What…ye've…been…doing?"

"What? Oh, I…a…Joseph, Robert, and I have been helping father with the barn. I would have changed clothes, but we're only taking a break. Still much to do, but I wanted to see you."

"See…me?"

"Of course." He took her hand. She felt his strength flow up her arm, straight to her heart.

"Do you want me to read more to you?" He obviously wanted to do something. If only he knew what his presence did for her.

She shook her head. "Talk…to me."

"What do you want to hear? Sarah and Lucy are taking care of the babies. Mother has been here with you, but you already knew that." He grinned and paused. "I caught Joseph kissing Sarah. About time, I say." He chuckled.

Shannon nodded, smiling in agreement. His laugh gave her hope. How could things be so much better just because James Crockett smiled and held her hand? It made no sense.

He brought her fingers to his lips. The tingle of his gentle kiss surprised and delighted her.

"I peeked in at Samuel and Wee Joseph. They are both asleep or I might have tried to bring Samuel with me."

Thoughtful. But he'd had proven that when he rescued her. "He…came…earlier."

"Good, good." Leaning forward, he brushed strands of hair from her forehead, his fingertips warm to the touch, as soft as a caress. Shannon closed her eyes, allowing the sensation to stoke her soul. His fingers bussed across her brow and past her ear, sending shivers to her toes. A long-lost feeling, one she thought gone forever. It reminded her she still lived.

And could still love.

So comfortable and exciting, all at the same time. If she could have sighed, she would have.

"What can I do for you? Do you need anything?" James's handsome face reflected worry with tiny lines showing near those clear blue eyes.

You, all I want is you, was what she wanted to say, but instead she smiled and shook her head. It was a dream beyond reality's reach.

But, for now, she would enjoy the illusion.

⚜

"YOU'RE PACING LIKE ONE OF THOSE CAGED TIGERS AT Versailles my mother told me about."

Heat crept up Sarah's neck. Could Lucy see how nervous and excited she felt?

"With both bairns asleep, I'm not certain what to do." She took off her apron and sat in the rocker, brushing a piece of lint from her skirt. Joseph would be here any time now. Should Lucy stay? What could she say to send the girl away? Did she want her to go away?

Aye.

No.

Hopping from the chair, she stifled a frustrated scream. Och, she had no idea what she wanted.

"Lucy, would you let me speak privately with Sarah?" Joseph. Clean-shaven and in fresh clothes. He entered the room.

Aye, she knew what she wanted, what her heart had wanted her whole life.

"I'll spell Mary Frances downstairs. You keep this door open, though." Lucy tempered her warning with a sisterly hug. He tweaked her hair before kissing the top of her head.

"Thank you, Lucy."

"Just behave yourself." Lucy scooted out the door.

And then Joseph turned her way.

JOSEPH KNEW BETTER THAN TO BE HERE WITH SARAH. THE physical labor had allowed action in the face of great vulnerability. Yet, working alongside the men, even in silence, only heightened Joseph's feelings of anger and guilt at his own betraying attitude and callous behavior. Could she see it in his eyes?

She fidgeted with her hands and avoided his gaze.

He had avoided her all day since that first kiss. But when she brought the basket of food out, he knew he needed her, to touch her, to hear her voice. He couldn't stay away.

It was time to tell her the truth. If she forgave him, then he would do all he could to make things right. If she didn't... He wouldn't think of that now.

"Sarah, I..." Where should he begin? He guided her to the rocker. "Sit, please." He hunched down on one knee in front. "I need to explain something to you. After, if you no longer want to see me, I will understand."

"Joseph." She reached for his hand.

He wanted to hold that hand, he wanted to hold her. In his arms. But instead, he stood and paced.

"I love you, Sarah. I think I always have. You know me and still you care."

"I love you, Joseph."

He racked his fingers through the hair dropping over his brow. "I know. That's why you must know the truth." Joseph peeked a glance at her. She sat with her hands folded in her lap. Her eyes glistened with fear and he hated to be the cause.

He glanced away. Why couldn't he just love her and forget the rest? Or why couldn't he just walk away? No, that option vanished the second he kissed her.

"When I came home from school, I asked your father for your hand. I wanted to do things with honor. You deserved that. You still do."

"I know, he told you no."

That was not what he expected to hear. He met her gaze.

"Joseph, I only learned of it yesterday. I didn't know when you asked me to marry you."

Nodding, Joseph turned back and continued. "You were gone when Kathleen arrived at Balleylawn."

"To Fort Stewart. My aunt was ill and needed help."

"Aye, I remember. I was asked to escort Kathleen to the garden party your parents threw in her honor. That's when we met. At one point her necklace broke, and I put it in my pocket. Late afternoon, I walked her to the house. I didn't follow her in, and to this day I don't know why, but after I left, she wandered out for a walk. I think she just wanted to be alone after all the people at the party. It hadn't been that long since her father had died. But on the way home I realized I still had her necklace in my pocket. Since I was closer to Balleylawn than Edenmore, I decided to return it rather than wait."

Joseph closed his eyes as long-repressed memories surfaced. "When I knocked at the door, your father answered demanding to know where Kathleen was." He shook his head. "I explained what happened and offered to help look."

Joseph's emotions churned and pounded in his brain. Gripping his head, he relived what happened next.

"She couldn't be found anywhere in the house, so we took to the grounds, each in different directions. I found her. She had twisted her ankle and walking greatly hurt her. I carried her back, arriving as several of our prominent neighbors were leaving to continue the search. No one thought to mention I had been there earlier helping in the hunt. Rather, I was pulled aside and told I would need to marry the lass or ruin her reputation."

"Oh, Joseph, did my father—"

"Don't ask, Sarah. I am telling you my part, only my part. I won't point fingers at anyone else." Her father had his own guilt to carry, but he wouldn't burden Sarah too. Stewart probably wouldn't see it that way, though. Palm to palm, Joseph tapped his fingertips to his lips, living the past as if it were the present.

"Your father, being Kathleen's legal guardian, agreed to allow me to propose. You need to understand, Sarah, I knew I couldn't be with you. Our fathers were such good friends, I was stunned. I could have fought harder, should have fought harder. But I didn't see how to do it then. I knew I'd never marry since I could not marry you.

"But you know…knew Kathleen. She had no guile. Sweet, kind, honest, none of this was her doing. I couldn't let her receive that type of reputation for something she didn't do. She loved me generously and was a good wife. She would have been a good mother. All she ever wanted from me was my heart."

Kneeling before Sarah, he scooped up her hands. "Sarah, I grew to love Kathleen. I did…do. How could I not? But she didn't have my heart. She couldn't. She wasn't you. And no matter what happens, my heart belongs to you."

Sarah pulled her hands free and lifted his fingers to her lips. "I love you, Joseph. I always have. I always will. Nothing has changed that. Nothing ever will." Her gentle palms cupped his face.

She still loved him. She didn't see him as a fraud or a betrayer of Kathleen's memory. He closed his eyes, drinking in her touch.

Yet all wasn't as it should be. He pulled his hands from her.

"Sarah, I still need to speak with your father."

"Aye, tis about time ye remembered that bit of importance." The voice from the doorway growled.

Joseph jumped to his feet. "Sir."

Thomas Stewart stood tall, formidable, scowling. "Me answer's still the same. Ye will not marry me daughter."

Chapter Twenty-Two

Sarah rose from the rocker. "Da, no."

"We will not discuss it, daughter."

Her temper boiled at her father's resolute posture. "Ye can't stop us. I will marry Joseph. I love him."

"No, Sarah, not without his blessing."

A slap from Joseph would not have stunned her more. She stared at him in disbelief, willing him to fight for her.

"No, you wouldn't want me that way. Sarah, how could you respect me?"

Samuel woke, crying at the sharp voices. His cry woke Wee Joseph.

Sarah walked away and picked up the toddler. Rubbing his back, she went to Wee Joseph, but Joseph had his son. "Now we've waked the bairns." She closed her eyes, took a breath and held it while she counted to ten. A bit of calm touched her heart, and an idea finally dawned. "Joseph, would ye please ask Lucy to help me?"

Joseph grabbed her shoulder. "Sarah, it's not over. But we must do this honorably."

"Just get Lucy for me, please." *Please, Joseph, hear me with yer heart and let me speak to my father.*

Joseph slowly nodded and left, holding Wee Joseph.

When Samuel had calmed, she placed him on the floor with his wooden blocks and turned her attention back to her father.

"Why, Da? Why won't ye let me marry Joseph?" Her fingers curled into fists at her sides while the words stripped away her veil of calm.

He strode to her, trying to pull her close. "Sarah, ye must trust me."

Her body shook as she pushed him away. "Why? Tell me why, Da? Why is Joseph good enough for Kathleen, but not me?"

"Sarah."

"No. Tell me. Yer destroying every dream I hold. I deserve to know why. Tell me."

"Remember who ye be. Yer a Stewart. Ye share the blood of High Stewarts and Scottish kings. Ye are my daughter. Ye will not marry beneath ye."

"Beneath me? Joseph's father was a marquis before he left France. He served King William so well he received the rank of brigadier and Edenmore. Louise is cousin to Louis XIV. Joseph has always shown noble intent. Even now, insisting upon yer blessing. What more do ye want?"

"Sarah, ye have fire in ye, a passion that flows through ye from yer ancestors, the same as their blood. Joseph is content to stay and farm. *Content.* And he will never inherit Edenmore. If Gabriel stays in Glasgow, James will inherit. Joseph has no inheritance. Do ye want yer husband to work for his brother the rest of yer life?"

"So that's it."

Sarah spun to the voice.

Joseph stood, white faced, in the doorway. He handed Wee Joseph to Lucy, who slipped past him over to Samuel on the floor.

"Aye, that is it." Her father stood as resolute as before.

But now Joseph stood tall, unwavering. His blue eyes glinted of steel. "Then, sir, I suggest we step outside."

"Joseph." Sarah's hands flew to her mouth.

"Yer calling me out?"

"No, sir. I am saying you and I need to take this conversation away from my son and Wee Samuel."

"Very well."

Joseph stepped aside, allowing her father to leave first.

She followed.

Joseph grasped her arm. "No, Sarah. Stay here. It is my turn, now that I understand." His hand stroked her cheek. "I will speak to him. Alone." Determination shown in his eyes.

Her heart pounded. Joseph would fight for her. Maybe not with violence, but he would fight.

For her.

For Sarah.

❧

ONCE DOWNSTAIRS, JOSEPH LED THE LAIRD TO HIS FATHER'S study. A quick knock confirmed the room was unoccupied. Opening the door, he held it for the older man before entering and bolting the door.

"So, let me clarify; you do not think I am worthy of your daughter because I am lazy."

A tinge of pink colored Stewart's cheeks. "No, I do not think yer lazy."

"But, I haven't enough ambition to suit you?"

"No, ye haven't enough ambition for me daughter."

Joseph didn't think in terms of ambition. He worked with his hands, he knew the land, his animals. He could see the possibilities in his head before they came about. What he did know was that he wasn't worthy of Sarah. On that they were agreed.

But he wanted to be. With every fiber of his being, he

longed to be worthy of Sarah. "What would be ambitious enough for Sarah?"

"Don't toy with this, lad. You speak of me daughter. I won't frivolously bandy about on this subject."

"Sir, I am serious. I love your daughter. I want to know how to be worthy of her. What do I need to do?"

Thomas grew silent. His gaze searched Joseph's face. With a sigh, he sat in Antoine's chair. "Lad, I know yer a good man. I have watched ye grow, and I know yer parents raised ye well. I find no fault in ye as a man." Stewart clasped his hands, leaning forward on the desk. "Yer a good man and ye love my daughter true. I don't know, perhaps it was a mistake to push ye into marrying Kathleen. But I didn't believe ye should be with Sarah. I hoped if ye were married, I could give Sarah's hand to a man who could support her as I have with land and servants and comforts to which she has become accustomed."

A sick feeling built in Joseph's stomach. He'd thought all along that the reason Stewart didn't stand up for him about Kathleen was to keep him from Sarah. Had he said anything, though, he'd have deeply hurt Kathleen. Not for the world would he have done that to her. But inside, he knew. He knew why Stewart let the others think those thoughts of him and of Kathleen. Still, it was a shock to hear him admit the truth.

"She loves ye. I know that. And ye love her. Show me. Show me ye love her enough to work toward keeping her comfortable. If ye do that, I will give me blessing."

Something in Joseph heard but couldn't believe. "You will… you will give your blessing?"

"Aye, *if* ye can show me Sarah will be well cared for."

Blood rushed to Joseph's brain. He didn't know what to say.

"Joseph, I saw ye struggle to help the Widow O'Connor and young de Grillet. You raced to protect Sarah at the house. I have no doubt ye'll keep her safe. I want to know ye'll keep her happy and comfortable."

"Aye, I understand. I will, sir, I will. Thank you, sir." Now all he needed to do was figure out how.

⁂

"How long have they been gone?"

Sarah paced the nursery. No need to hide the problem from Lucy now. Let her think she resembled a caged tiger. She had given up on her dreams so many times believing Joseph didn't return her love.

But he did love her. He loved her and wanted to marry her. And her father wants to keep them apart. Never had she been so close to what she wanted, needed, and yet so far away.

"Two minutes longer than the last time you asked." Lucy didn't even look up.

But Sarah caught the smile. "It's not funny."

"No, of course not." She made no attempt to hide the chuckle.

"This is serious, Lucy. Me father is trying to keep us apart. I don't know what Joseph is saying and I've no idea what me father will do."

"But you know what you are willing to do to have Joseph. And you have always found a way to bring your father around. He has never denied you a thing."

The words made her feel like a manipulative Jane-of-apes. Not a pretty picture. "Am I really so spoiled?" She wasn't sure she wanted to hear the answer.

Lucy stood. "If I were Mary Frances, I'd probably be hugging you and saying, 'of course not.' But I'm not Mary Frances. I'm the plain speaker. Sarah, you have a kind heart and you aren't afraid to work. But you do tend to want things your way. And you are not afraid to manipulate your father if it gets you what you want."

Sarah might as well be naked. This lass clearly saw her flaws.

"Sarah, I've known you my whole life. You're my friend and you love my brother. You're just not perfect. None of us are."

Tears threatened. She turned away and sniffed. She didn't want to cry, not now.

At the touch on her shoulder, she turned. Lucy hugged her.

"Mary Frances isn't the only tender-hearted Crockett lass." Sarah giggled, and Lucy joined her. "Joseph had better change my father's mind. I need ye for a sister."

Lucy squeezed her tighter before breaking off the hug. "I think you would make a fine sister. However, I already have two. Do I really need another?"

Sarah gave a playful tug on Lucy's hair, like she'd seen Joseph do earlier.

"Aye, you and Joseph make a pair." Lucy chuckled and sat on the floor to play with the little ones.

Sarah joined the group and helped Wee Joseph to stack blocks. The baby had more interest in pounding the floor, a cube in each hand.

A shadow passed over the toys, moving to her side. The hair at her nape grew taut and the skin on her arms prickled. Slowly she turned to gaze up, up the lean body to the handsome face she loved.

Joseph stooped beside her, clasping her hands. His eyes, what did his eyes tell her? "He didn't say aye, but he is allowing a chance."

"A chance? What does that mean?"

He kissed her fingertips. "It means, dear heart, I have some things to accomplish. If I can, I may call you mine."

"Things? What things? I can help, I will help you, Joseph."

He held her hands tighter now. "No, Sarah, you cannot help with this. But I love you for wanting to. I can do this, I will do this, for you, for us. Can you wait? Will you?"

"Aye, aye I will wait for ye. Oh, Joseph, I will wait as long as it takes."

As long as it takes.

Chapter Twenty-Three

The tickle started at the back of her throat. Never before had Shannon feared the sensation. *God please don't let me cough.*

She tried gently clearing her throat and breathing through her nose. A cup of water sat on the stand next to her bed. If she could reach it… Wrapping her fingers over the rim, she touched the tepid liquid. Not too full. Maybe if she were careful, she might get it to her lips.

Slowly, carefully she brought the cup to her mouth. All she needed was a sip.

The cough erupted just as the water passed beyond her teeth, spewing droplets all over her and the bedclothes.

Worse, though, was the knife stabbing her chest from the inside. She couldn't breathe. And she was afraid to.

Her lungs screamed for air. Shannon gasped only to cough again.

The mistress burst through the door. "Ma petite." She helped Shannon sit, gently rubbing her back until the sensation passed. "You are all wet."

"Water…spill."

Mistress Crockett helped her to the chair. "I will return."

It only made sense that she occasionally left. Shannon had been here in this room for four days now. There was much to do in running a household, besides the wake and funeral for Josephine. But now, with the cough, came the fear of something worse, something Shannon prayed she could avoid. Being alone only added to her fear.

The mistress breezed in, arms full of dry bedclothes and another clean chemise. Miss Mary Frances followed with fresh water. Together they changed the bed and Shannon into dry clothes, making her as comfortable as possible.

In truth, there was little comfort to be had. Aside from the pain of the ribs and leg, her back ached from the hours of lying in bed, and her head fought a dull throb. At times she thought she might be gaining health, but at other times, like when the coughing started, she feared she might lose the battle.

Mistress Crockett gathered the damp laundry, taking it out and leaving Miss Mary Frances to stay with Shannon.

"Would you like me to brush your hair?"

Shannon nodded and the girl undid the braid.

"Your hair is lovely, Widow O'Connor. I wish mine were this color."

Shannon smiled, thinking she'd rather have the lass's raven mane. Those blue-black curls, tied back with the satin ribbon were easy to envy.

Miss Mary Frances's strokes, gentle as the girl herself, eased some of the headache's tension.

The tickle returned. Shannon stiffened, breathing through her nose.

"Is everything all right? I am not hurting you, am I?"

The cough would not be stopped. Yet Shannon couldn't get enough breath to force it all the way out. She wrapped her hands around the binding, desperately trying to hold the stabbing pain at bay. *Oh, God, make it stop.*

She heard a clatter and the young miss calling for her

mother. Soon Mistress Crockett eased her forward, rubbing her back until the spell finished.

"She will be well, Mary Frances. You did well to call. I can take it from here, dear heart." The mistress squeezed her daughter's hand and sent her back downstairs. Then she picked up the brush from the floor and kissed the top of Shannon's head before continuing to brush.

Shannon carefully cleared her throat. "Why?"

"Why what, Shannon?"

"Why…you…so…kind," she cleared her throat again. "to…me?"

"Why shouldn't I be kind?"

She thought until she could form her message with the least amount of words.

"You…me…not alike."

The mistress put the brush down and began the braid. "In some ways we are different and, in some ways,, we are very much the same."

"I…Catholic."

Mistress Crockett knelt in front of her. "Do you believe Jesus is the Son of God?"

Shannon nodded.

"Have you asked Him to come into your heart?"

"I…pray."

"Yes, but is Jesus your Savior? Do you know Him?"

This was confusing. What was the mistress asking? "When I…was…baby…priest…baptize me." Shannon closed her eyes, calmed her breathing. "I go…to…mass. I…pray. I…do what… priest…tell…me. Be…good. Believe."

"Dear heart, I did the same thing. I tried to be good, the best I knew how. But I couldn't figure out what was good enough. I thought the bad things that happened to me were due to my not being good enough."

"What…you…do?"

"I finally learned I cannot be good enough. It isn't possible.

If it were possible, I wouldn't need a savior and Jesus wouldn't have needed to die on the cross."

"I…go…to mass…all…my life." Shannon paused. Something was missing; something vital she needed, perhaps urgently needed. "What…I…need…t'do?"

"You only need to realize your need for a savior and ask Jesus to take away the guilt you carry for not being good enough. Then ask Him to be your Savior and Lord of your life."

"Will…I…still…be a…Catholic?"

"If you choose. My dearest friend, Madame de Grillet, is Catholic, but has a deep and close relationship with our Lord Jesus. The true difference is not between Catholics and Protestants. It is between those who know and love Jesus as Lord and Savior and those who don't." She cupped her palm to Shannon's cheek.

The loving touch spoke volumes. This woman treated her as one of her own, the closest thing to a mother Shannon had known in many years.

"Would you like to pray together now?"

Shannon nodded, a tear rolling slowly down her cheek.

"I'll say the words for you, and you can nod if you agree. Jesus understands."

Shannon blinked and nodded.

Mistress Crockett took Shannon's hands and bowed her head.

Shannon followed her example.

"Lord Jesus, Your Word reminds us we cannot be good enough, no matter how hard we try. But You have provided for us and paid the price for our sins when You died on the cross. Shannon asks that You forgive her sins and wash her clean with Your precious blood. Come into her heart and life and be her Lord and Savior that she may know Your promise of eternity with You. Thank You, Lord, for what You have done, what You are doing, and what You are about to do. We love You, Lord. Amen."

The mistress gently hugged her. "Now you are my sister in Christ." She smiled. "And you will call me Louise from now on."

Shannon blushed. "Aye."

"Shall I help you to bed or would you rather sit here?"

"Sit."

"Would you like to see Samuel for a few moments?"

She started to nod but felt the tickle again. Trying to clear her throat, she knew what was coming. *Jesus, I need You. Help me.*

The cough erupted ,and the knife stabbed inside. But the fear was gone.

Louise rushed to her side. "Dear heart, are you all right?" She poured and offered Shannon a drink.

She caught her breath and nodded. And for the first time since that awful day, she knew she was all right.

No matter what happened, she would be all right.

❦

"Father I have an idea I want to discuss with you. Will you soon have time?" It had taken Joseph awhile to come up with a plan. Then he needed the confidence to present it to his very busy father. His insides quivered like a wagon on a bumpy road.

"I have time now. What is on your mind, son?"

Joseph closed the door to his father's study and took a chair. It occurred to him that those who controlled his life always seemed to sit on the other side of that desk.

"I want to get involved in the export part of the business."

"You've always preferred to work the farming portion. Is there a reason?" His father covered his hand with his own, his gaze giving him full attention.

"I need to do this. If you agree."

Father nodded, remaining thoughtful for a moment. "I believe it might be best if you learn directly from Reverend

Fontaine. I received a letter stating he will be here next week. Perhaps you and he can discuss this then?"

Next week. Nothing around here happened on his schedule. Next week it would be. Joseph would just have to learn that much faster.

🙙🙘

SHANNON WONDERED ABOUT HER COUGH AGAIN. THOUGH she had no more fear of it, she did have concerns about her Samuel.

Louise had taken to reading the Psalms to her.

"Sing to God, sing praises to His name; Lift up a song for Him who rides through the deserts, Whose name is the Lord, and exult before Him. A father of the fatherless and a judge for the widows, is God in His holy habitation. God makes a home for the lonely; He leads out the prisoners in prosperity, only the rebellious dwell in a parched land."

A father of the fatherless? If something should happen to her, her sweet Samuel would not only be fatherless but motherless as well. She felt lonely far too often and longed for a home. And right now, she literally was a prisoner of her own body. Did God have prosperity for her also?

Louise didn't seem to notice that Shannon's mind roamed. Paying attention again, she heard, "Blessed be the Lord, who daily bears our burden, The God who is our salvation. Selah. God is to us a God of deliverances; And to God the Lord belong escapes from death."

Would she escape death this time? Each day her cough grew. When Shannon lay still, she could hear the crackling sounds starting in her chest. Breathing got harder and harder. She spent more time sleeping now than awake. Death didn't frighten her like before. In truth, death would be a comfort, but leaving her Samuel behind, without a father or mother, broke her heart.

Tap, tap.

James peeked his face around the door. "I think Shannon is ready for me to sit with her now." He winked. "Right, Shannon?"

She smiled with her whole heart, though she knew it appeared weak.

"Well, then, I will go and see how things are coming along in the kitchen." Louise gave her son a quick peck on the cheek before leaving.

James sat in the chair. Shannon could have sworn she saw Samuel sitting on his lap. She blinked only to realize he sat alone.

With a tender smile, James took her hand. "How are you feeling today?" His lips might be smiling, but his eyes gleamed with worry.

"Fine." Her voice croaked so she reached for the cup of water on the stand.

James grabbed it and lifted her head for the sip. "Thank you."

He sat back in the chair and again she saw her Samuel, bouncing on his knee, arms wrapped around James's neck.

A father to the fatherless.

"Do…ye…love…Samuel?"

"That's a strange question to ask." He brushed hair from her forehead. "Yes, I love Samuel. I love him like my own. Why do you ask?"

"Will…ye…be…his…father?"

James knelt by her bed and took her hand. "Shannon what are you getting at?"

"Marry…me. Be…father…to Samuel."

"Oh, Shannon, yes, I will marry you. I want to ask you. As soon as you are better. And then we will marry, when you are well again. I will adopt Samuel and be his father. And I will be your husband, and you will be my wife."

Shannon shook her head.

"You don't want to marry me?"

She closed her eyes, pulling all her strength to this moment. "I…want…to…marry ye…now." She grabbed his hand tightly. "It…must…be…now." Her chest wasn't giving her enough air, and she needed him to understand. "If…I…die…"

James jumped to stand over her. "You are not going to die."

He must understand and accept. Now. "But…if I…do…"

"No, I won't talk about it. Shannon, you cannot die."

Another cough erupted, stealing what little breath she had, cutting her from the inside out. She could hear James, yelling for his mother. Then his hands, sure and firm, helped raise her while droplets dripped down her face.

When she could again breathe, she realized James's tears mingled with her own.

"Shannon, I love you. I will marry you whenever you want. Just don't leave me. Stay with me, Shannon. I love you."

She leaned her head against his chest, her very shaky hand on top of his.

He gently lowered her back to the pillow, brushing her hair from her face. "Don't leave me, Shannon. Fight. You must live. You must."

"James." She traced his brow, his cheek.

He grabbed her hand and kissed it. Then, very slowly, he leaned in and kissed her lips. Soft as a breath, it whispered of the love she longed to share with him.

"I…love…ye…James."

If only I could live long enough to show ye.

Chapter Twenty-Four

A pall descended over the Laggan proving as thick and visceral as the burial garments entombing the mourned residents of the community. Though Robert had explained to him, Gabriel staggered at the change. Shrouded in grief, the greens of the meadows dulled, and the sun hid its face behind clouds full of tears. So many dead, so many in pain, he longed to run, tear open the veil that held everyone in its folds.

The brothers reined in their horses for a look. "It's almost as if someone took a somber grey to the whole world."

"Aye, a lot of sorrow and hurt needing the Lord's healing touch." Gabriel had to bring it back to God. He was the only hope.

No one ran to greet them when they pulled to a stop in front of Edenmore Manor. Robert dismounted and took the reins for both animals. "Go on in. I'll take the horses around back."

Gabriel nodded his thanks and, removing his hat, climbed the three steps to the door.

"Gabriel, if you have a minute."

"James, he just arrived. Might I have some time with my son?" His mother's good-natured smile didn't entirely hide her impatience with the brusque request, but James didn't care. At this point, manners were the least of his worries. Time was of the essence. Shannon needed his help.

"Aye, shall we talk in Father's study?" His brother caught the urgency.

James nodded.

Gabriel gave his mother a quick kiss on the cheek before leading the way.

Once the door securely closed, James began. "You can now perform marriages, correct?"

Gabriel didn't show surprise. "Aye, I've already performed a couple. Are you thinking of getting married?"

"Shannon, the Widow, and I would like to be married."

"James, I thought she was badly injured and would be needing time to heal. I won't be here that long."

Shaking his head, James felt the tightness in his throat. The tightness always came when he realized Shannon might not recover.

"She has a son, from her former marriage. Samuel. If she… if…" He shook his head again and spit out the hateful words. "If Shannon should die, she wants to know her son has a father."

"And you, do you want to marry her?"

"Aye, Gabriel, aye. I love her and want her for my wife. I want Samuel for my son. I don't want to lose her." At this admission James crumbled. His sobs racked through his body, and he sank into the nearest chair. For the first time he faced that Shannon might not recover. This wedding would be all he would have of her. Except for Samuel. He would still have her son. He would make Samuel his son. "Please, Gabriel. Marry us. Today. Right away."

Gabriel's eyes still didn't register surprise, but compassion. "James, there'd be no time to have the banns read. No time to meet with the counsel for permission. I couldn't legally marry you two today."

"Then illegally marry us."

"What?" Now there's the surprise.

"Marry us today. Shannon doesn't have to know. We can take care of the adoption later. She needs this. There may not be enough time."

"And what if she recovers? Would you then have to explain why you are living in sin with the woman?"

James stared at the floor, defeated. "It won't happen. I… know. She's dying, Gabriel. She slips away a little more each day. I need to give her this. She needs to know Samuel will be safe." Looking up, he pleaded with his whole heart. "Please."

All movement in the room ceased while Gabriel met his brother's look.

The air was being sucked out of James. He didn't even blink.

"Aye, I will do it. But you must remember it is not a legal nor binding marriage and cannot be consummated. And, you will have to legally adopt Samuel soon."

"And you won't tell Shannon it isn't legal? She must never know."

"I leave that job to you, dear brother. You will be the one to tell her when she recovers. But I will come back and marry you then, if she will still have you. And you give me enough time."

"Time is what Shannon doesn't have. But if God is gracious and lets her live, I will tell her and send for you. That is a promise."

Gabriel grasped James's forearm and pulled him into a hug.

James melted onto his big brother's shoulder. It didn't matter that James stood taller and weighed as much as a stone more, Gabriel was his big brother and would take care of him once again.

"We will need to tell the family. You know mother and the girls will want to help."

"I don't know if she will even be able to get out of bed at this point."

Gabriel, always practical, patted his cheek. "Little brother, women must have the accoutrements. Trust me, it is necessary. We can tell them to keep it simple for Shannon's sake."

James nodded and opened the door. But in his heart, he closed the door to any other path. This is the one he would walk, one way or another. With Shannon beside him in spirit or in health. The choice had been made.

This is the path he would take.

❦

Movement and swirling swishes filled Shannon's ears. Whispers, soft with importance floated around her. What was happening?

A touch.

Shannon's eyes flew open.

A hand stroked her cheek. Turning her head, she saw Louise kneeling next to the bed. "Shannon, would you like to be married today?"

She still dreamed, that was it. Reaching up, Shannon touched Louise's face. No, this time she was wide awake. "Married?"

"Ouí. James has asked Gabriel to marry the two of you today. Would you like that?"

Shannon nodded her head and a tear escaped down her cheek.

"My daughters brought flowers into the room. We will help you into something pretty and arrange your hair. Do you think you can sit in the chair?"

Shannon again nodded. She was about to be married. How did James do that? No, her Heavenly Father did it. He answered her prayer. Now Samuel would be safe.

As the weight of the burden lifted, Shannon found she could breathe a bit easier, as if her brain received more oxygen, her thoughts became clearer. She was about to become a Crockett, a true member of the family. The kindness of God overwhelmed her.

"Don't cry, dear heart. You don't want your eyes all red for your groom."

At that, Shannon smiled. Red eyes were the least of her beauty problems. But she would be a good wife, even if she couldn't be a pretty one. As good as God would allow. *Lord, please don't let me cough during the wedding. I won't ask to live and recover from my wounds, but please don't let me cough.*

A peace settled over Shannon. She was ready to face whatever lay ahead.

Louise and Lucy helped her sit and move to the chair. Today was her wedding day. Inside, Shannon laughed with glee. Who could have imagined?

⚜

THE FAMILY SQUEEZED INTO SHANNON'S TINY ROOM. Sarah, holding Samuel, stood to the back by the door. If he got too boisterous, she would quickly slip out.

Joseph stood at her side, holding Wee Joseph with the same plan.

When Sarah first learned of the immediate wedding, her thoughts held a twinge of jealousy. But watching now from the doorway, she felt a tremendous sadness. Daily Shannon slipped further away. Her waking moments were fewer and farther between. It must take tremendous will for Shannon to sit there as frail as she was.

Samuel squirmed.

"Look, lovey." She pointed. "Mama's getting married. You are going to be a Crockett." She kissed his head.

"Mama." Samuel surprised Sarah with his whisper, as if he

understood not to interrupt. She turned him around so he could better see, and he quietly watched.

It was strange to see the bride and groom's faces so clearly and only the minister's back. But the view allowed Sarah to see James's eyes full of love for his bride. Looking over at Joseph, she caught the same look on his face, staring back at her. It made Sarah wish all the more for their day.

"And now, our new Mistress Crockett, I congratulate you and welcome you to the family." Gabriel leaned over and kissed Shannon on the cheek while the family cheered.

"I have the shortbread." Sarah Beth pushed forward, holding the cake over Shannon's head.

"So, break it." Lucy shouted, as pieces of the shortbread tumbled down into Shannon's long braid and onto her lap.

Though the new Mistress Crockett couldn't laugh, Sarah was sure she heard her anyway. The bride-glow belied how truly ill the lass was, but Sarah noted weariness in Shannon's eyes.

Tanté Louise stepped forward. "Shannon, dear heart, I know this is supposed to come from your parents, but I hope you will accept it from us." She handed the girl a small bell. "I doubt if you will have need of it to have family help with an argument with James." Louise winked at her son and kissed the top of her new daughter-in-law's head. "But you may also use it to call us if you need anything. Anything at all."

"Thank…you."

Tanté Louise turned back to her family. "And now we need to go to the dining room for refreshment. I will send some up for the bride and groom and you may, one at a time, come and bring your gifts. But please make your visit short. Shannon needs her rest and James wants time with his bride."

Though the last part was said with a smile, Sarah knew it was all too true. She was afraid James would have very little time with his new bride.

Chapter Twenty-Five

I'm sorry." Joseph found James by himself, sitting under a tree by the river. He never expected to hear those words. He'd come to do his best to comfort his brother. Instead James apologized to him. "About what?"

"About not understanding what you were going through. I think I understand a little better." He plucked another shamrock, tearing it to bits and throwing it with other shreds onto the ground around him.

Joseph claimed a spot next to him and, grabbing a large shamrock, began to pull each heart-shaped leaf from the stem. "Now I know why everyone asked me if I was all right. It's hard to think of anything else to ask."

It had only been one week since they buried Shannon in the family plot on Edenmore. No sense in asking for problems with the church for wanting to bury a Catholic on Protestant soil. A stone reading "Shannon Crockett, Beloved Wife" had been ordered to mark her resting place.

"Does it ever stop hurting?" James didn't raise his head. Instead he found another shamrock victim.

Joseph closed his eyes to the fluffy clouds passing through the azure sky. The pain no longer stabbed, he realized, but it still hurt.

Somewhat. Yet no longer to the point of being debilitating. "I don't know. I know it changed me. And I'm ready to again know joy."

"With Sarah?"

"Aye, with Sarah."

James, forsaking the shamrocks, picked up a small stone and skipped it out onto the River Foyle. "I can't imagine ever loving anyone else."

"I wouldn't worry about it now. It's enough to get through the day."

"Aye." James raked his hand through his hair and leaned against the elm's trunk. "I think I need to hear you say it will get better."

"It will get better."

James turned his deep blue eyes on his brother.

Joseph nearly broke to see the tears waiting to spill down James's cheeks. He embraced the new widower, pulling him close. "It will get better, I promise."

❦

"Are you sure?" They stood by Antoine's barn, or what was still left. They had made much progress, yet this scar—like so much—would take time to heal. And now another blow. Antoine knew the answer even as he asked the question. Albert never did anything without thoroughly thinking it through.

"We are ready to go back." Albert scuffed his boot in the sod. "Mimi needs to be with her family. Of course, her father is gone now, but her mother and sisters all still live near Versailles, so that is where we will go." Albert didn't look him in the eye when he spoke their destination.

"We will miss you. I know Louise will miss Mimi. They are like sisters. What can we do to help?"

Albert finally met Antoine's gaze. "I feel like a traitor, a failure."

"You are neither of those things, my friend. When do you plan to leave?"

"We're not yet sure. It could be in a month or next week. It all depends on how soon I can gather the funds. I still have holdings in Versailles. Mimi's father had watched over it for me, and then her brother-in-law. We need to wait for God's timing. But we are going back."

Antoine wanted to hold on to his friend, beg him not to go. He wanted to but knew better. This wasn't an easy decision for Albert. But with Mimi's twin gone and Alain-Robert's passing and resting beside his aunt, the only reason to stay was their friendship.

Miles wouldn't change that. Albert was more than a friend. More like the only brother Antoine had ever known.

Antoine grasped Albert's arm. "Please, if you need anything…"

"Just your prayers. I don't know what we would have done without you and Louise these past few weeks. In the midst of all that chaos, I felt like I'd just gotten my son back. And then…" Albert shook his head.

"Of course, we will pray. You know Louise, it is the same as breathing for her."

Albert nodded.

"Come. We'll start planning what you need. You are welcome to anything I have."

Albert grabbed him into a bear-hold, very much like their old friend, Jean-Luc would have done. The bond was deep, the memories long.

"We need to break the news to Louise."

"We?" Albert asked.

Antoine arched an eyebrow. "We've been through a lot together. Why stop now?"

Albert chuckled. "I like to think I am a brave man, a man of intelligence. But telling your wife that I am taking her best friend back to France is more than I can do. You must to do that on your own, my friend."

Though Antoine laughed along, he still didn't relish the task before him. Louise had yet to fully mourn Josephine's death before Shannon, who had come to be like another daughter, passed away. Louise may be the prayer warrior of the family, but she was wounded and in need of prayer.

❧

"Father, Reverend Fontaine is here." Sarah Beth nearly sang in her excitement as she burst into his office.

Antoine closed his journal. "Thank you, ma petite." Leaving the volume on his desk, he exited to greet his friend and business partner.

"Jacques. It is good to see you. How was your trip?" Antoine greeted the man with a kiss to each cheek and stepped back to get a good look. Though it had been awhile—since Kathleen's passing—Jacques Fontaine looked the same as he always had. Tall yet slight of build, his boyish eyes danced with excitement. Antoine could tell he had another enterprising idea in mind.

"Good Reverend, welcome. We're so glad you are here." Louise took his coat. "And you will have to tell us how your wife fares and the children." She guided the men to the parlor. "Come. Sit. Sarah Beth has gone to see about the tea."

"Thank you, Louise, Antoine. I keep telling my dear wife I need to bring her along to visit you. She so wants to meet you. Well, one of these days. The children are doing well. James and Aaron are back at home now. That is a story in itself."

Sarah Beth brought bannocks with the tea and poured for each.

Antoine smiled. "Well, it looks like we're ready for a story, Jacques so please tell us."

The Reverend Fontaine sat back on the seat and crossed his long legs. "Well, you know my sons had been in Amsterdam. I sent word to come home and made arrangements for the captain of a certain vessel to pick them up. The captain had cargo to go to London first, so I made plans for the boys to stay with my brother while there. The night after they left, I had a terrible dream. I saw both my sons struggling in the water among broken bits of cargo."

Sarah Beth's eyes were wide. "What did you do?"

"Well, Miss Sarah Beth, I wrote to my brother at once and said for him to keep my boys with him. Do not let them go with the captain, I implored. The dream returned off and on until I finally heard back from my brother."

"What happened?" Louise sat forward in her chair, eyes big.

"The captain called for my boys, but because of my letter, my brother refused to let them leave. The captain tried to create a fuss, but my brother and sons stood firm. After he left, my boys made plans to come home by overland. They arrived safe and sound, but that captain and crew, well, no one has heard from them since they left London."

"Oh, my." Louise and Sarah Beth were mirrored copies of each other, both with hands to their mouths.

"How gracious of God to give me that dream. His kindness is amazing." The Reverend uncrossed his legs and sat up straight. "And so, what has been going on here at Edenmore? Be sure to tell me everything, as my wife will undoubtedly ask hundreds of questions."

Louise glanced at Antoine, and Sarah Beth left the room.

"Did I say something wrong?"

"No, Jacques." Antoine patted his wife's hand. "We have experienced great changes. It seems the last time you were here, we expected it to be a joyous time with the birth of our first grandson. Instead we had to bid farewell to his mother. Now rather than joyous news again, we have sad tidings once more."

Louise stood and the men did as well. "Gentlemen, I will leave you to talk. If you are in need of anything, please let me know. If you will excuse me."

"Of course." Jacques sat as soon as Louise left the room. "Perhaps my timing is not the best?"

Antoine watched Louise's fleeting form. She'd never run from anything in her life. Turning back to Jacques, he replied, "Or perhaps your timing is His timing. You always have been good at comforting your flock." Antoine proceeded to explain what had transpired with the Combers, the deaths and damage to the peace he and the committee attempted to bring the community. "We lost a good man in Michael O'Toole, and Paddy Flannigan is a shell of a man since they hung his son and Donovan Cummins. Albert and Mimi are moving back to France soon, so that only leaves Cameron McHugh, Thomas Stewart, and myself on the committee. The desire to reach all the people is still alive, but with only Protestants in our group, we are no longer trusted."

"Then I am afraid I have even more ill news. The British have now made the export of our wool and linen fabrics illegal."

"No. Who is to buy if we cannot export?"

"Exactly. That is why I have a plan."

Antoine laughed. "I could tell by your eyes you had something stewing in that brain of yours. Tell the plan."

"Well, I don't know if you heard, but I gave up my congregation right after I returned from my last trip to Edenmore. It may have been a bit hasty, but there's no going back to change it now. A member of the congregation was grossly breaking one of the commandments. I won't say which one, but I swear I didn't know about it. I happened to be in the middle of a sermon series on the commandments and the Sunday after he'd been caught, I preached on the very one with which he had difficulty."

Nodding, Antoine couldn't help but visualize exactly what happened.

"Well, the poor offender just knew I'd preached that sermon for him and yelled for the elders. I told them I had no foreknowledge of the situation. But the man wasn't satisfied until he'd slandered me to the whole congregation. I finally released my post to concentrate on the weaving business. But now that we can't export…"

"Out with it, Jacques. It's not like you to make me drag a story from you."

"We are moving. To Bantry Bay. To become fishers of fish."

"What?"

Jacques laughed and slapped his knees. "I knew that would catch you. I have found two backers in London, and we have a three-year plan. The first year will be getting things all together; the salt house, the press, the ships and a place to live. I want you to come along. Join me in this. It would be like having another kinsman with me." The reverend stood and held out his hand. "Antoine, let us do this together. Shall we?"

Antoine stood. "I'll take your hand anytime my friend, but you must first let me pray over this decision. I believe God is in it, as you wouldn't make such a change without His guidance. But I need to know if this is for me, for my family."

"Of course." The men shook hands.

"Now, I'm sure Louise wants you to make yourself comfortable in your room upstairs. It will give you time to rest before dinner."

"An excellent idea. It isn't an easy trip to the Laggan, or maybe I'm just getting too old."

"Do not say that, good sir, in the presence of your elders." Though Antoine joked, he knew Jacques to be about twelve years younger. However, that had never mattered, as the reverend had always offered sound spiritual guidance to Antoine and Louise since their first meeting in Bordeaux.

"Oh, and I nearly forgot. Joseph is interested in speaking with you about the business. But now that the business has changed, he may not be as interested. Just the same, I know he will want to speak with you on his own."

"Good. We can talk after dinner."

Chapter Twenty-Six

So, you see, Reverend, I believe I have much to offer. Would you be…" The man in the mirror shook his head. No matter how he tried to phrase things, it never sounded right. Joseph knew he would sound like the fool he was and no one, not even the good Reverend Fontaine, would be willing to help him learn to be a success.

He tied his hair back and took one more look. Good grooming couldn't fix what he lacked. But if he didn't come up with something, he would lose Sarah.

For her, he would try.

For her.

The Reverend Fontaine agreed to meet with him after the noon meal. Joseph excused himself early to come back and…and what?

What would he say to the Reverend given the chance?

Chance. That was the word. All he wanted was a chance. A chance to try, to prove to Thomas Stewart he could provide for his daughter. But even with that chance, Joseph wasn't sure but what he might end up flat on his face.

Down the stairs, Joseph tried to keep his focus on his goal. Sarah. *You can do this, for her.*

The reverend waited for him in his father's office. Once again, Joseph sat in the chair opposite the desk. Once again, the person behind controlled his life.

"Sir, I understand my father spoke with you concerning my interest. I have helped manage the farming aspect of our product for several years now. With Gabriel in the ministry, James will be the one to inherit Edenmore. I would therefore like to learn about the export side of the industry. My father thought you would be the better one to teach me."

The Reverend Fontaine listened, his hands on the desk. "Joseph, there is a problem with the business."

Of course there was. Why shouldn't there be, now that he wanted to be involved in the export portion? He leaned back in the chair, ready for whatever blow was about to come.

"The British Government has declared it unlawful to export woolen textiles."

The blow left his mind reeling. He couldn't think beyond *unlawful to export.*

"Your father and I have discussed this. I have a plan and have asked your father to join me. He is praying about it. But I make the same offer to you. I am moving to Bantry Bay where I will begin a fishing export business. There is a great call for the fish in Spain. My business partners in London have a winery outside Madrid. We would unload the fish and pick up the wine. Send the wine to Barbados and pick up molasses there. The molasses goes to Virginia where we exchange it for tobacco and then return. The business should be quite lucrative, and we have a three-year contract with the gentlemen in London. What do you think?"

Joseph leaned forward. "How soon would you need me?"

"Would you be able to leave with me in two days?"

Two days.

"I would need to build a house there and make plans to return to be married. Would that be agreeable?"

Jacques Fontaine's face broke into a wide grin. "Married, you say? And who is the young lady? Do I know her?"

"I believe you do, sir. Miss Sarah Stewart."

"Thomas Stewart's daughter? Ouí. I remember when she was a little girl. But of course, you must build your house and come back for that lovely young woman. I hope you will let me be the one to marry the two of you. Oh, but you will have Gabriel here, too. And someone will have to look after things while you are gone. Oh the plans, the plans we can make."

An explosion of fireworks went off in Joseph's brain. He would be able to do this. He would be able to marry Sarah. Finally, something good was about to happen. He fell back in the chair. "I can't believe it."

The reverend laughed. "Perhaps you need to believe it, because we will be leaving Edenmore in two days, whether you believe it or not."

⚜

"Two days?" Sarah couldn't believe it. "Why only two days? Why can't ye stay here and handle the business?"

Joseph pulled her close as they stood in the nursery, but it didn't help. How could she stand being so far from him?

"Sarah, I know, I know, but the sooner I leave, the sooner I can come back for you. The sooner I can ask your father for your hand. The sooner we can be married and be a real family. You will still wait for me?"

"Oh, Joseph, ye know I will. Hold me tight. I don't want to forget the feel of yer arms." Sarah buried her face into his shoulder. Though she tried to stop them, tears still welled.

"And you won't let my son forget about me, will you?"

Sarah shook her head against his woolen waistcoat. "I'll tell him about his handsome, brave, and strong father every day."

"Tell him his father loves him, and that his father loves a certain red-haired lass who is getting his shirt all wet."

Sarah batted at his chest. "Oh, Joseph, did ye think I would not cry?"

"No, my tender-hearted love, I knew you would." He ran his fingers gently across her cheek, catching a tear. Sarah closed her eyes, memorizing the touch of his kisses lightly placed on her eyelids. Her knees grew weak. She knew if she didn't step back, she'd have no control whatsoever.

"Go, go make yerself ready for this trip."

Joseph's eyes shimmered with the silent question.

"I will be here, waiting. Do what you must. Ye know where to find me, love."

He caressed her face, then walked out the door.

Leaving her behind.

❧

"WE'RE GETTING OLD, MY LOVE."

Antoine pulled Louise close as they snuggled in their bed. He caressed her cheek. "You are still as lovely as the day we met." She shook her head, but he continued. "Your hair soft about your face, and then you look at me with those eyes. I'd never seen such eyes. And to think I may gaze on them every day." He tilted her chin and kissed her.

Louise melded to him, her cheek against his shoulder. "Thirty years and seven children will age one. We've seen much. You have worked hard to make Edenmore a legacy for our family. As much as I want to leave our recent sorrows, I believe it is here God has planted us and given us root."

Antoine scooted up against the pillows. "I had not—How did you know?"

She rolled, leaning on his chest. "It was not so hard to guess. I could see the gleam in Jacques's eyes. Where would he have us go?"

Drawing her back into his arms, Antoine shared the reverend's offer. "So, if we went, it would be back to Bantry Bay.

We have memories of there. Two of our sons were born there. I told Jacques I needed to pray about it. So far, I believe we are to stay."

"I said it before and say it now, wither thou goest, my love, wither thou goest."

Lovely, disarming, with eyes that peered to the very bottom of his soul; that was his wife. How blessed beyond measure to have known her love and gentle spirit. But that gentle spirit had greatly suffered of recent, and with no time to grieve, she continued to see to others' welfare.

"You worry too much."

Antoine ran his fingers through her hair, already coming loose from her braid. She too easily read his mind. "Why do you say that?"

"I say that because it is true. You worry for me, now. I have mourned our great loss. God has heard my cries over and over. But can we only accept blessing and not suffering from our Lord? Both Josephine and Shannon knew Him. They were ready. Mary O'Toole has allowed me into her home, and we have spoken many times. And while Master O'Keefe slowly improves, his nephew has taken over their establishment. Not that I condone that type of place knowing what it does to you men." She gave him a playful pinch.

"Ow. You men, is it? When was the last time you saw me go imbibe at the Stray Dog?" He began to tickle her. "Perhaps you think I am so old I need to sit in my corner and regale others with my tales of conquests?" He rolled, looming over her. "Or perhaps I have conquests yet to make?"

"No, sir. This battle you have won before you start."

And with a chuckle, he kissed her.

ROBERT BROUGHT THE HORSES TO THE FRONT OF THE house.

Standing on the front steps, Sarah watched as first the Reverend Fontaine and then her heart walked out the door. She held Wee Joseph on her hip and Bridget, ever still her shadow, held Samuel by the hand.

Joseph placed his portmanteau in back of his saddle.

Sarah had slipped a hasty note inside so that when he unpacked, he would think of her and know she would wait.

Though they spent every moment possible together, she had yet to confess her part in the attack. She hadn't even told him of her promise that seemed ages ago. If he knew those things, would he still love her? Or worse, would he ever trust her again?

No, she had Joseph's love. She would not risk it all with a confession of what God and Shannon had already forgiven.

Joseph stared at her. Could he see inside? Could he tell how selfish and manipulative she was?

Smiling, he guided her around the corner of the house.

"Joseph…"

He put his fingers to her lips. "This is what I want to see when I close my eyes. You, holding our son. I'll make a home for you, Sarah. We'll make a life together."

"Aye. Oh, Joseph." She embraced his neck with her one free arm and held on. If she let go, she was afraid she would drown in her tears.

Joseph loosened her grip. Tipping her chin, he peered into her soul. "Sarah, I love you. I will come back. I promise." He kissed her, melting her like snow under spring sunshine.

She returned it with her whole heart.

"A-hem."

Joseph released her.

His father stood there, a familiar smile on his face. Yes, there was something about those Crockett men and their lopsided grins. She knew her face was turning redder than the scarlet of her best tartan.

"Son, it is time." Antoine returned to the front of the manor.

Joseph grasped her hand. She let him lead her back to the family.

He gave her hand a squeeze before letting go and hugging each sister in turn. An embrace from his father, a kiss from his mother, and playful punches from his brother before he mounted the horse.

Reins in hand, Reverend Fontaine turned to Joseph. "Ready?"

Joseph stared at Sarah, looking straight into her heart. He nodded. "Ready."

As they left, Sarah hugged Wee Joseph tighter. Somehow, she knew, whatever happened, she would be ready too.

Chapter Twenty-Seven

Mistress Fontaine called out to him. "Letters. Joseph, you have two of them."

Standing, he stretched his back, put his hammer into the loop at his side, and lowered himself from the roof.

Taking the sealed notes from her hand, he noted her curiosity. "Thank you, Mistress."

"She has a lovely script."

"Who does?"

"Why, your mother, of course." But her smile told him different.

Joseph laughed, knowing that later she'd want all the pertinent details. She seemed to look on him as a fresh font of information. Perhaps she worried her husband's trough of knowledge might run dry? No, he shook his head. She just had an insatiable thirst to know what went on in the world.

Finding a barrel over by the new salt house, Joseph sat and debated which one to open first. He wanted to read Sarah's, but he'd never get to his mother's if he did. With a chuckle, he broke the wax seal.

Dearest Son,

Life here at home remains much the same, only there is a hole where you should be.

I know Sarah is writing, too, so I will let her regale you with tales of my amazing grandson. Suffice it to say, he is brilliant, adorable and growing very fast. He looks more and more like you every day.

I am thinking we may have some more weddings on the horizon. Master McHugh's eldest son, Daniel, has asked permission to call on Lucy. She greatly pinks whenever anyone speaks of it and rushes to care for something in the kitchen. I think the two of us will talk later this evening.

I also learned Sarah Beth and Ian Mackenzie, Gabriel's friend, have been corresponding. I should have guessed but was preoccupied with other things. Master Mackenzie wrote to your father to say he'd like to come for a visit, so we will see what transpires.

And since I mentioned your father, I should tell you he is doing well. He is very proud of you, as we all are.

Sarah visits every day and spends much time with Wee Joseph. They are bonded as any mother and son. Young Samuel joins in the fun, and I think Sarah would keep him, too, if James would let her.

James moved into your cottage and is slowly healing. He either works very hard for your father or spends his time with Samuel. I miss his smile and ready laugh but know God will return those in due season.

We love you and miss you.

Sending you love and prayers,

Mother

News from home always felt bittersweet, but now he could spend his time with Sarah.

My dearest love,

As I write, I am watching your son take his nap, and can't help but see you in him. I miss your touch and your voice. I miss you with all my heart.

You would have been so proud of Wee Joseph yesterday, though I was scared to bits. He woke from his nap and someone had left the nursery door ajar. He toddled out of the room and headed for the stairs. When I found him, he had turned around and was crawling down the steps backwards, quite carefully mind you, and was half-way down. For fear I'd startle him, I bit my lip and watched him negotiate the rest of the way, whereupon I raced to the bottom and scooped him up. He is a brave and determined lad. Something more he gets from his father.

I have begun sewing my wedding dress. It makes me feel like you will be home soon, and we will then be a true family. I will not tell you about it, but Bridget gives her approval.

Come home soon, my love. Each night I fall asleep, thinking I cannot miss you more, and then I awaken to find that isn't true. But my heart is. I love you and cannot wait to see you again.

I must close now and post this note to you. May God keep you safe and bring you home to me soon.

Your loving Sarah

Soon. Joseph gazed at all the work still in need of completion. He shook his head. Soon might as well be a million years from now. The Fontaines hadn't even started on their own home but were living in the salt house for the moment. And Sarah's father would not give his blessing without her having a proper home.

He folded the letters and put them in his pocket. A quick scan of the area located the reverend by the wagon, helping unload the new press. Joseph ran the short distance, joining in the work.

"Reverend, might I speak with you when this is unloaded?"

Jacques Fontaine grunted, gave another lift, and the press came free of the wagon. The men lowered it to the ground, and the reverend pulled out a cloth to wipe his face.

"She's a beauty. Now, Joseph, what were you saying?"

Joseph ran his sleeve across his brow and smiled. "I asked if I might speak with you after the press was unloaded."

"Of course, Joseph, of course. Let us get some water and we can talk."

How should he explain the need to build a house, not a cottage, when there is still so much to be done?

Sarah. Remain focused on Sarah. Reverend Fontaine will understand.

Please let him understand.

"Wee Joseph, I have a letter from your da." Sarah picked up the toddler and swung him around. "A letter from your da. Shall we read it?"

Wee Joseph nodded most seriously. Sarah sat him on her lap and opened the letter. His baby hands kept reaching for it, so she finally sat him on the floor and began to read.

My lovely Sarah,

I didn't think the day would come when I could write this, but finally I can say, you have a house of your own in Bantry Bay. It is not as big as Edenmore Manor, nor as imposing as Ballylawn, but it is more than a cottage. The first floor has a parlor, study, dining room, pantry and kitchen. The second floor contains four bedrooms so there is room to bring Bridget with you (though I am sure your father would send her if you didn't bring her yourself). There is a small bit a thatching yet to finish and I will let you plan how you want your rooms to look.

The reverend has gone to London to meet with the sponsors. When he arrives back, I will be coming for you, Sarah. You and our son. Make ready, my love, for I am soon to be there. I love you and long to hold you in my arms once again.

Hug our son for me and let him know his da mightily loves him.

Do you still wait for me, Sarah? Have I taken too long? I will be there soon, I promise. I love you with all my heart.

Ever your Joseph

"Wee Joseph, your da is coming home."

Home

Yet…

What if he changes his mind when he arrives? What if he learned about her promise? Might he think she wanted to marry him out of duty? What if he ended up preferring Kathleen to her?

No, Joseph would come home to her and they would live together happily just like his parents and her parents. That is what happens when two people in love marry, correct?

It had to be.

Her heart depended on it.

❧

SARAH BURST THROUGH THE DOOR AT BALLYLAWN AND dashed up the stairs. "Mother. Da." She waved the letter from Joseph in her fist. "Mother."

"Sarah. Whatever is the matter?" Her mother stood at the landing.

"I have a letter from Joseph. He's coming home." Sarah grabbed her mother's hands and twirled her.

"Whoa. Stop, before we tumble down the steps."

Sarah obeyed and plopped down on the top step, hugging her knees. "He's coming home to me and soon."

"So tell me when, what does he say?" Meg sat next to her.

"He says he built me a house. A house of me own. It's not as big as Edenmore Manor, but he writes about all the rooms and says I may decorate however I choose. It is definitely not a cottage, but a proper house. Da has to say 'aye' to this."

"Da has to say aye to what?"

Sarah's father rounded the landing.

"And why do I find me wife and daughter sitting on the staircase when we have lovely chairs both above and below?"

Sarah waved her letter under his nose. "Joseph is coming home. He has built me a proper house. He's coming home to me."

"I haven't said 'aye', yet, daughter."

"But ye will."

Da leaned his foot on a step. "And how do ye know I will?"

"Because ye are a man of yer word, and I am yer only daughter, and ye love me too much to deny me this."

"That sounds a bit saucy, lass."

Sarah entwined herself about his neck. "But it's true and well ye know it. Joseph is a good man, Da. He has done what ye asked of him. I know he is a good man. I've learned to recognize good men because of me father's example."

He kissed her on the forehead. "All right. I will speak with the young man when he comes home. And, provided he has done what ye say, I will give me blessing."

"He has, Da, I know he has." Sarah hugged him again.

"He well better have, for I won't give me blessing otherwise."

One look in her father's eyes told Sarah he spoke the truth.

Chapter Twenty-Eight

S arah, I think I see Joseph coming up the road." Lucy beckoned from the nursery doorway. "Come look."

Jumping to her feet, Sarah swiped Wee Joseph into her arms, and followed Lucy to her bedroom.

"Look there." Lucy pulled a drapery aside and pointed. "Doesn't that look like Joseph riding?"

Sarah didn't wait to answer. Setting the toddler on the floor with his aunt, she tore down the stairs and out the door. Running across the wide drive and out to the road, she knew who rode that dark horse in the distance. She'd seen him ride enough times to recognize the gait.

The rider could now see her and began to gallop. She ran with all her might, faster than when she raced the Crockett boys. Arms pumping, knees rising, feet pounding, keeping her skirts out of the way. Her hair flew out behind her, the wind cooling her face as she ran.

The horseman pulled to a stop, not but a stone's throw ahead and jumped to the ground, running toward her.

"Sarah."

And then she was wrapped in his embrace.

He held her as she buried her face in his shoulder, the rough feel of his beard tickling her cheek.

"Joseph, don't let go, never let go."

He laughed, squeezing her before loosing his hold. "I want to look at you, and I must let go for that."

She brushed the hair from her face, gazing into his eyes. "I look the same—"

But then his lips met hers. His kiss warmed all the way to her toes. Her whole being woke from a deep sleep.

"Sarah, I've come home for you, if you still want me." His clear blue eyes demanded reassurance.

She stroked his stubbly cheek. "Aye, I want ye, Joseph. Now and always."

His hands cupped the back of her head, fingers threading through her hair. Leaning in, he kissed her deeply.

She pulled him to her, holding him ever closer.

And she knew. Joseph had come home. Everything else melted away like the winter's frost. He stole her breath. Thinking came at a price. She would have to release him. She licked her lips, still savoring the taste of his kiss as she pulled back. "We need to, um, we need to let the others know yer home."

Slowly, Joseph nodded his head. He mounted his horse and reached for her. Without a pause, she put her hand in his, and a foot in the stirrup, letting him lift her into his arms. Sarah leaned against him and sighed.

She'd come home too.

"Aye, it seems yer back again, Joseph."

"Yes, sir, I am." *And I'm here to claim your daughter.* No, Joseph couldn't jump to it like that. This man, sitting behind yet another desk, controlled him like a marionette. Every move Joseph had made over the past eight months had been determined by this man.

Keep your mind on Sarah. It will not always be this way.

Joseph massaged his knuckles and sat straighter.

"The Reverend Fontaine is teaching me his new enterprise. I helped negotiate with the London affiliates. And, while setting things up in Bantry Bay, I built a home. Not as big as Edenmore Manor, nor your home here at Ballylawn but far more than a cottage with room to build on as needed. I have papers here from the reverend attesting to all this." Joseph reached into his pocket, withdrawing a sealed letter addressed to Laird Thomas Stewart of Ballylawn. He held it out to Sarah's father.

The Laird made no attempt to take the letter. "I believe ye, lad."

Joseph set the letter on the desk and wiped his hands along his pant legs. "Sir, I believe I have kept my part of our bargain. I would ask for Sarah's hand in marriage." He watched Stewart's face for some sign of an answer.

Instead, Thomas rested his elbows on his desk, his chin on his fists. "I knew ye would come back, lad. I could see it in yer eyes. Ye may not believe it, but I love my daughter. I want what is best for her. She is my only child and the delight of my heart. I would not hesitate to walk through the fires of perdition to keep her from harm. I want no less of the man she marries. Ye love her deeply, I know, but would ye lay down yer life for her? Could ye walk away if it meant her protection? Do ye love her that much?"

Joseph took the time to find the answer within himself. Standing tall, he faced the older man. "Yes, sir. I believe I love her that much." Then he leaned forward on the desk. "But I am not putting her in danger. I have provided her a safe home. Unless you know something I don't, there is no reason to walk away for her protection."

Stewart leaned back in his chair, his fingertips tapping together. "Ye are a brave lad, strong and clever. I respect your parents. I know they reared ye in a godly home. Me daughter loves ye. I canna think of a reason to withhold me blessing."

Thomas stood and held out his hand. "Aye, ye may marry me Sarah.

Joseph straightened. He heard the word, saw the outstretched hand. The sun came from behind a cloud bringing streams of light into the study. Bubbling up from his core, a laugh erupted, and he clasped the laird's hand with both of his.

"Thank you, I, ah…thank you." Tears started down his cheeks. He wiped them away with his sleeve only to look up and see Thomas Stewart, Laird of Ballylawn, with glistening eyes.

"Promise me ye will always care for her, Joseph. Promise this old man ye will care for his daughter."

"I promise."

Not just you, sir, but God above. I promise I will take care of Sarah.

With or without Your help.

⁂

"Mistress Sarah, why are ye up here in yer room?" Bridget picked up a strewn dress that was sliding to the floor from the bed.

"I'd be too tempted to eavesdrop if I were downstairs." Sarah began to pick up after herself so as not to leave Bridget with all the mess. She wanted to wear the perfect dress for Joseph, but nothing seemed right. Everything she tried on seemed old and drab. Everything but her wedding dress and veil.

Her fingers ran along the delicate lace, itching to put it on her head.

"Och, no ye don't. I won't be the reason for ye having bad luck all because I let ye try on yer veil."

"That is just superstition, Bridget, just an auld wives' tale." How she longed to try it on, just for a moment.

"And how do ye think they get to be auld wives? Aye, they pay attention to the lessons of their elders."

Perhaps, with Joseph downstairs speaking with her father,

she shouldn't tempt the fates. How long did it take for men to strike a bargain?

But then, she hoped she meant more than just some commerce.

"Bridget, I grow weary of waiting. If I don't soon receive news, I think I will run downstairs and demand to settle this meself."

"No, Mistress, ye know that's not the way of things. Would ye care to sit? I'll rub yer shoulders for ye. Or I can brush yer hair?"

"No." Sarah tapped her chin. "Well, perhaps ye can brush me hair. I want it to look the best for Joseph." She sat on the stool and Bridget picked up the brush. The long strokes soothed, and Sarah's body began to calm. She closed her eyes and let her mind wander.

"Bridget, have ye ever been in love?"

The young maid giggled. "No, Mistress, though, don't tell me mum, but I do fancy a certain lad. He's a good and honest one and maybe one day, perhaps. But I've enough to think about here. If ye marry Master Joseph, ye'll be moving to Bantry Bay. If yer wanting help, perhaps yer father will send me with ye. And if that be the case, tis best I keep me heart to meself."

Sarah laughed. "Bridget, yer wise beyond yer years."

"Aye" The voice sounded serious. Sarah had to look up. The twinkle in Bridget's eyes told the truth, and both girls fell into giggles.

"Sarah?" Her mother tapped at the bedroom door before entering the room.

At once she was back to the present. She searched her mother's face for some sign. "Is there a decision?" Fear gave birth in her belly.

"Come and see." Her mother pulled her from the chair. Looped arm in arm, she patted Sarah's hand and led her to the stairs.

The steps had somehow multiplied; the first floor seemed

miles away. Finally, at the foot, she spotted Joseph and her father coming out of the study.

Joseph came to her, dropping to one knee. He took her hand in his. "Sarah, I love you with all my heart. I promise before God and your parents, I will cherish you as long as I live. Would you do me the honor of becoming my wife?"

It seemed impossible to laugh and cry at the same time, but Sarah could not stop doing either. Shaking all over, she put her hands to her mouth, furiously nodding, unable to speak. Finally, she pushed a squeak past her lips. "Oh, aye."

Joseph laughed, but she could see moisture in his eyes. Standing, he took out a Luckenbooth brooch and timidly reached to pin it to her kirtle. Sarah could feel his hands shake while he struggled to latch it. The beautiful silver brooch of entwined hearts hosted her birthstone in the middle.

"Ahem."

Joseph stepped aside, and Sarah spotted her father.

Running to his arms, she hugged him and planted a kiss on his cheek. "Thank ye, Da. Thank ye." She kissed him again.

Her father hugged her back and then pulled her to his side, his arm sheltering her. "I have two small requests."

Fear reared again, but she pushed it aside. Joseph was hers. They would be married. She could grant her father any request.

"I would like for ye to be married at Rath Mullin, where yer mother and I were married."

Sarah peered at Joseph. He nodded, so she turned back to her father.

"My other request is to ye, Joseph. I have no son to carry on me name. The name of Stewart in my line dies with me. Would ye do me the honor of wearing me *Feileadh Mo*r at the wedding?"

Sarah studied her father's face, then Joseph's, and back again. Suddenly, her heart hurt for her da. A part of her wished she could be a boy to carry on his legacy. Yet she was a woman, a woman deeply in love with a man she hoped would say "aye."

She turned back to Joseph.

He stared at her. Nodding he gave his answer. "Aye, I will wear your belted kilt."

Sarah flew to Joseph's arms. This man, so caring and willing to put others before him would now be her husband.

And she would be a Crockett.

Chapter Twenty-Nine

The wind whipped across the barge and through Sarah's hair, tiny fingers tugging and pulling strands free of the braid Bridget so carefully plaited this morning.

This morning. The morning of her wedding. She awoke to birds singing and knew instantly this day bode well. Sarah held out her arms, her fists keeping tight to her plaid, as if the wind might transport her faster across Lough Swilly.

Across to Rath Mullin.

Across to Joseph and her new life with him.

Her father came near. Standing behind her, he placed his hands on her shoulders and she drew her arms in about her.

"*Virescit vulnere virtus.* Courage grows strong at the wound. Ye are a true Stewart, lass. I know ye have been wounded more than once in yer love for the lad. But ye have stood strong. Yer courage has grown and will see ye through when things are not as ye dream."

Sarah turned to study her father's face.

"Ye think I didn't know how ye pined for the lad all these years? Aye, but I knew ye'd n'er be happy to live a quiet life in a cottage. Ye have an adventurous heart, lass, but it can be broken. And when it is, remember ye are still a Stewart. Virescit vulnere virtus. Let yer courage help ye to forgive, to relentlessly hang onto yer God, and to keep yer heart true."

"I will, Da." She smoothed her hand across his cheek before standing on tiptoe and planting a kiss.

"And that's all I'll say on the matter. Just ye remember, lass." He hugged her, and then left her to her thoughts.

Her father deserved a son, she should have been a son to carry on his name. Had she disappointed him? She shook her head. No, she didn't think she'd been a disappointment.

The shoreline flowed past with her thoughts. The man deserved a namesake. She would speak to Joseph. If he agreed, and heaven too, she would give her father that namesake. Thomas Stewart Crockett. The best of both families.

She laughed at herself. Here she was on her way to her wedding, already planning her family with Joseph.

Joseph.

She hugged herself then flung her arms and twirled. "Oh wind. Carry me to Rath Mullin. Carry me to the arms of my love."

❧❦☙

"James, how do I wrap this thing?" The cloistered room at Rath Mullin only added to his nerves.

James laughed at the sight. The first good laugh Joseph had heard from him in nearly a year.

"What do you think you're doing?"

"I'm trying to wrap this contraption about me. Sarah made my liene and her father wants me to wear this. I had no idea what I agreed to."

James shook his head and took the long plaid from him. "Sarah did nice work on the embroidery, but do you think she got a little zealous with the fabric?"

Joseph played with the length of linen material flowing about his feet. The wedding shirt, decorated with an intricate design of hearts, hands and crowns, had room for a man twice his height. Though enormous, the detail of the purple embroidery down the sleeves and around the neck impressed him. He'd never thought of Sarah being so nimble with a needle.

"What do I do?"

James studied the cloths. "I think if you blouse it to where you want it, I'll dress you in the plaid. We can tuck a little more after. Maybe once the plaid's end is over your shoulder and pinned, the liene won't look so…"

"Vast?"

"That's the word."

The men chuckled, and Joseph bloused the shirt up to a normal length.

"How tall does she think you are anyway?" James waggled his eyebrows. "I believe she spent too much time dreaming while you were away."

"Just get it around me."

James eyed the back of Joseph's legs.

"What are you doing?"

"Just getting an idea for the length. You have nice legs."

Joseph swatted at him. "Get on with it."

Nimbly, James folded a section over and then gathered the pleats, one after the other, with his right hand while holding the finished ones secure with his left. He shook the material, smoothed the creases and brought it to Joseph's back waist, short half in.

"Where's your belt?"

"On the bed."

"You'll have to get it. I can't let go."

"But what about the shirt?"

"We can fix that in a minute. Just put the belt on."

Joseph let go of the liene and grabbed his belt, threading it between the folds of tartan with James help. After buckling it, he again bloused up the long shirt. The he watched, amazed, as his brother adjusted the aprons on each side and brought the ends securely in front. "How did you learn to do this?"

"When I attended school in Glasgow, I met a Highlander who taught me a thing or two." James stood in front and picked up the corners from the long ends now hanging to the floor in front. Twisting the tips several times, he tucked them back into Joseph's belt and brought the center of the fabric from the back over Joseph's shoulder. Holding it in place, he felt around the table and bed.

"What are you looking for?"

"The brooch."

Joseph clenched his jaw, sucking a breath in through his teeth. "I don't have one. Now what do I do?"

"Hold this and don't move. I'll be back."

His brother exited behind him, and Joseph stood perfectly still, afraid to shift position. James had left him in front of the mirror. The stranger looking back appeared as lost as he felt. The only truth he knew in all this was his love for Sarah. But did she really want him or the man her father wanted him to be? The temptation to rip the plaid off and wear a comfortable pair of trews, which would have given the same tartan effect and been less complicated, grew with each frustrating moment.

Finally, the door opened.

"I have an idea, or rather Father has one."

In the mirror Joseph could see his father had joined James.

"Son, I have the brooch for you, if you will wear it?" His father opened his hand to reveal a pin shaped into an open four-petal lily forming a cross. A Huguenot cross. Fleur-de-lis in each corner touched the petals, forming hearts. He'd heard many times how this symbolized loyalty and how his parents' friend, Matthew Maury, had given it to his father when he accepted Jesus as his Savior.

As angry as Joseph felt at God, could he honestly wear it?

James took the brooch from his father's hand and worked it into the plaid's fabric. When in place, he stepped back to admire his handiwork. "A right proper Highlander, ye are, lad." He gave Joseph a playful punch to the arm. "But now I need to make myself beautiful." With a wink he left the room.

Father sat on the cot. "Son, I want you to know Thomas Stewart is a good man. We have been friends for a very long time. But I am not blind to his faults. He wants what he wants, often thinking his way is best. Perhaps I am like that myself. You are my son and I would like some of our heritage to be remembered as well. It is selfish of me, no?"

Joseph joined his father. "No, it is not selfish and for you, I am glad to show our Huguenot heritage where the world can see. I always thought Gabriel would be the one to wear your pin."

His father patted Joseph's bare knee. "He is a Presbyterian minister. I am proud of him for that. Though very close, it is not the same as Huguenot. Perhaps one day you will pass this cross on to Wee Joseph."

Joseph nodded his head.

His father slapped his thighs and stood. "I will see if your mother is yet ready." At the door he turned. "Joseph, I am very proud of you. I always have been whether you farmed or built a thriving business. You are a good man. I am proud you are my son."

Dazed, Joseph watched his father leave. He wiped the sleeve of his new liene across his eyes.

⚜

THE KNOX FAMILY, OWNERS OF RATH MULLEN ABBEY, greeted Sarah and showed her where she could change into her gown. The small room with walls of great grey stone stood off the sanctuary and hosted a high window but very little light, even in the middle of the day. Fortunately, candles glowed from the chandelier.

A dockhand brought in Sarah's trunk, and Bridget opened it.

The wedding dress lay wrapped in fabric to keep it from being crushed.

"Let's make ye ready before I bring out yer gown." Loosening the lacings on Sarah's dress, Bridget helped her step from it and put it over the open trunk's lid. She pulled the new chemise from beneath the gown, took the one Sarah shimmied out of and handed over the fresh linen in exchange.

Sarah's skin tingled as the soft folds dropped down over her head. Plunging her arms through the sleeves, she sighed, giddy at the touch.

Her mother brought her a bench.

Seated, she rolled her stockings down and off, wiggling bare toes on the stone floor.

Bridget handed her the new pair and placed the new wedding shoes on the floor in front of her.

Sarah pulled each stocking up and slipped her foot into the first shoe.

There was a knock at the door. Bridget answered it, revealing Lucy.

"Is Joseph here?" Sarah needed to hear he was close. Her family had made sure they'd kept the two away from each other all day to ensure their luck.

Lucy grasped both of Sarah's hands in her own. "He's with Gabriel and Father in the sanctuary. I wanted to see what I could do to help."

"I think I'm ready for the gown." She put on the other shoe and fairly danced with anticipation.

As Bridget lifted it out of the trunk, Sarah took one more look at it. Of deep blue velvet, with sapphires down the wide sleeve, embroidery danced around each stone forming flowers. Lined in a lighter blue, the sleeves fell open almost to the floor. Bridget shook the gown, chasing away any rogue creases. The sapphires gleamed in the candlelight.

Sarah held the gown in front of her. "Do ye think Joseph will like it?"

"If I know my brother, I doubt he'll even notice your gown. His eyes will only see you."

Sarah laughed. "Then forget the dress. I am ready to go."

"Nay, daughter." Her mother knew she jested, but poor Bridget's eyes appeared about to pop out of her head.

"Have no fear, Bridget. I have waited too long to wear this gown. I'll not throw away the opportunity now." Gathering the skirt, she raised it over her head and let the folds fall soft and warm. Her mother and Lucy helped her get the sleeves of her chemise into the gown's sleeves while Bridget adjusted the waist and skirt. The train of the gown dragged elegantly behind. In the hand mirror she could see how the white of her chemise shown in bright contrast to the dark blue at the neckline. Her mother pinned the Luckenbooth brooch to a strip of matching velvet and tied it at Sarah's neck.

"Sit and let Bridget brush your hair. I'll get your veil." Lucy lifted the delicate lace from the trunk and shook the wrinkles free.

Sarah turned her head to look, but Bridget made her turn back the way she'd been. "My mother needs to put it on me. She's been happily married and needs to bless me."

Lucy handed the veil to Mother and glanced about. "Where are the flowers?"

"They're… No. Where are they?" Sarah jumped up, but Bridget pushed her down again.

"Sit still Mistress Sarah so I can finish yer hair. The flowers are just outside the door. I saw them as I came in."

Sarah did as she was told, her hands smoothing her skirt. "Are you yet finished?"

"Done." Bridgett stepped back. "Mistress, if ye will put the veil on yer daughter, I'll fetch the flowers."

Without a word, her mother draped the veil over her head, the filmy lace flowing down onto her face, her arms and back.

Bridget returned with the wreath of heather.

Sarah took it from her and held the tiny pink and white

flowers to her face. Even through the veil she could still smell the honeyed fragrance. "Mother, will ye do it?" Her hands trembled as she handed over the wreath. She was nearly ready. Her heart thumped in anticipation.

Mother kissed her head before placing the wreath of heather on her crown.

Sarah stood.

Lucy straightened the train of the gown. Bridget handed her the bouquet of heather and myrtle. Her mother reached under the veil to wipe away a tear.

Someone knocked at the door and Bridget opened it.

Tanté Louise stepped in. "Dear heart, how very lovely you are. My son believes you are the most beautiful woman in the world, but he has yet to see just how beautiful. Are you ready?"

Sarah's heart pounded so hard. She placed a hand to her chest to keep it from pounding its way out. Nodding, she let the women out before her to find their places.

Bridget hurried back. "Mistress, your horseshoe." She dug it out of the bottom of the trunk and handed it to Sarah, ends up.

Her father met her at the door, draping her arm through his.

Stepping into the sanctuary, she first saw the rays of light filtered through the stained-glass windows on either side of the room. Gabriel stood at the front, dressed in his pastoral vestiges. He smiled and nodded.

And then the man next to him turned.

Joseph stood at the altar, regal in the Stewart plaid. The look on his face drew her forward. Her father's hand held her in check.

At the altar, Father put her hand in Joseph's, kissed her cheek and sat with Mother. Gabriel spoke. They spoke. But all she knew were Joseph's eyes. Their hands were looped with Gabriel's stole. Vows were made. But she only knew Joseph's eyes.

Then he lifted her veil.

And she knew his kiss.

Chapter Thirty

Mistress Crockett. I want to welcome you to Bantry Bay and bring you some of my fresh bannocks."

Sarah held the door wider. "Come in, come in. You must be Mistress Fontaine. How nice to finally meet you."

Taking the basket of oat cakes, Sarah led her first visitor to the parlor. "I am still trying to decorate, but we should be able to sit and talk in here. Make yourself at home, and I'll see to the tea."

Sarah tried hard to walk from the room with grace, but as soon as she entered the hall, she rushed to the kitchen. "Bridget, I have company. She called me Mistress Crockett."

Bridget laughed. "Aye, and that ye are, Mistress Crockett. What should she call ye?"

Sarah's fingers fluttered by her mouth. "I know. I need to get used to hearing it, though I do confess I love hearing it too much to just get used to it. Mistress Crockett."

"Well, Mistress Crockett, ye might be wanting to return to yer guest before she thinks ye have no manners."

Such a thought! She flew back to the parlor, pausing only long enough to pat her hair and take a calming breath before entering.

"Mistress Fontaine, I am so glad we can have this chat." Sarah sat across from her guest on a straight-backed chair, a gift from her mother.

"And I also." Mistress Fontaine's lips curved into a smile as if she knew something no one else did.

And then it dawned. "The tea." Sarah hopped up. "Och." She nearly crashed into Bridget, entering with a tray of tea and bannocks.

"Your tea, mistress." Bridget set the tray on the table, curtsied and surreptitiously winked at Sarah before leaving.

"My dear, please relax. You are doing a fine job." Again, the smile returned.

The whole thing must seem terribly funny. Laughing at herself, she was glad to see her guest join in.

She poured the tea and leaned back in her chair. "Please, as much as I enjoy hearing Mistress Crockett, I think we will be dear friends, especially after this. Would you please call me Sarah?"

"Oui, if you will call me Anne. I am so glad to have another woman here on Bere Haven. The whole of Bantry Bay is covered with pockets of people who mostly keep to themselves. Jacques and I have reached out to the community in Christian charity, but it will be good to have someone who understands." Anne Fontaine appeared to be close to her mother's age though her hair now gleamed mostly grey. But the twinkle in her eyes gave away her truer, timeless age.

"Have you been here long?" Sarah took a polite sip, setting the cup back on the saucer in her hand. Nothing seemed to taste good this week. But she had too much to do to allow herself to get sick.

"We've passed about a year here. My hope is to move from the cottage into a proper home before the year is out."

Sarah's face warmed. Would Anne think her spoiled as well?

"Dear, don't worry. We were all aware you were coming as a bride. We wanted you to have a nice house to begin your married life. My dear husband and I have been through so much together, I know that sometimes we will live in a cottage and sometimes we will live quite well. I have learned to live a contented life like St. Paul. We left everything behind in France to escape to freedom. And it took time before we had enough put aside to marry. My Jacques is not just a great thinker but highly practical as well. It is as it should be for you to be in this house."

"You are very gracious, Anne." Sarah's eyes stung. She was becoming more emotional of late.

"And why shouldn't I be? My Heavenly Father knows my needs and has never ceased to care for me." Anne took a sip from her cup. "How is Wee Joseph adjusting to the move? Joseph has spoken constantly of you and his son."

"He's napping now. He seems to be enjoying his new room, though I still have much to do before it is finished."

"No doubt you will have things in hand quite soon. Please let me know what I can do to help. I would enjoy doing what I can."

"Thank you."

Anne put her teacup on the table and stood. "Now, dear girl, I will take my leave."

Sarah walked her guest to the door, wishing she would stay a while longer. Anne brought cheer and hope, and it would be nice to talk with a woman who had so much more experience with married life. Bridget, though good and kind, just didn't ken. "You must come again, or perhaps I can stop by with Wee Joseph and meet your children one day."

"That would be wonderful. Oh, my." Anne slapped her palm to her forehead. "I nearly forgot. You have a rather large package waiting. I didn't want it to become damaged, so I had Jacques bring it to our home. I think it may be a surprise from your groom." She smiled that I-know-something smile and kissed Sarah on the cheek. "I'll tell Joseph, if I see him on the way home. Thank you again for the tea, dear."

"Thank you for the bannocks, Anne."

Sarah closed the door and leaned against it. What could be in the package? A large package, from Joseph? He had given her Luckenbooth earrings to match her brooch for a wedding gift.

She walked into the parlor, picked up the tea tray and carried it to the kitchen. One thing for sure, she'd have a headache if she kept worrying about this mysterious gift until Joseph returned home.

"Bridget, I think I hear Wee Joseph. I'll check on him, and then we can see what our next project will be."

⁂

"Gentlemen, I've decided to go in through the front door as I don't want to risk taking it up the back stairs." Joseph pulled the wagon to a stop in front of his house. Jumping down from the seat, he motioned for the three men with him to follow and went to the wagon bed. A large wooden box about the length and width of a small coffin, lay ready to take inside.

"Please, with care, it is breakable."

The men grunted. Joseph wondered at the wisdom in asking these hardened fishermen to carry something so fragile. But he had no choice. He couldn't have moved it by himself.

They all got into position, picking up loops of rope Joseph had attached to the box. "On the count of three. One, two, three."

"Oww. It didn't seem this heavy when we put it in here."

Joseph said nothing but had to agree. Sarah had better like his gift.

At the front door, they rested the box across the step edges while Joseph opened the latch.

"Wife of the house. I am bringing men up to our bedroom. You will need to make clear our way."

The fisherman across from Joseph turned to the others. "They're newly married." All three chuckled.

"Husband of the house, welcome home and welcome to our guests." Sarah appeared in the hall, coming from the kitchen area. "Oh my. What is this? Oh." She nearly tripped squeezing past Joseph on the stairs. "Where are you going?"

"To the bedroom. These gentlemen will help me deliver your package there, and then I will handsomely pay them for their trouble while you open your gift."

"But…but…"

"But you don't want your gift? Gentlemen, I don't think she wants it. We must take it back."

"Wait." The flustering only made her lovelier. Her eyes sparkled greener than the Emerald Isle itself. "Gentleman, Husband, I would be honored to lead the way to the bedroom." With a swish of her skirts, Sarah turned and guided up the stairs.

"You heard my wife, let us go to the bedroom." Joseph laughed, and the men just shook their heads, one muttering "Newly wedded, tis true."

The box lay delivered across the bed. He'd have to retighten the bed ropes once this was over.

"Thank you, gentlemen." Joseph opened his purse and put two silver coins in each man's outstretched hand. "I'll escort you out."

"Wha…we don't get to see 'er open it? Where's the sport, man?"

"No, that fun I save for myself." Joseph laughed and pushed the men from the room.

"Thank ye, sir." The fishermen all tipped their caps and left.

Joseph closed the door behind them before returning to Sarah, taking the stairs two at a time.

"So, dear husband, how do I open it?" Sarah sat next to the box, tugging on a rope.

Withdrawing his boot dirk, Joseph held it up for Sarah's inspection. "Allow me, dear wife." A swift slice, and the ropes quickly fell away. He then pried the lid free and set it on the floor.

Sarah reached in, pushing sawdust and fine wood chips to the sides. "Perhaps we should have done this downstairs?"

"I didn't want to risk breaking it without the box's protection. I'll help you clean. Just find the gift. I want to watch your face." Joseph stepped back, crossed his arms and laughed at her expression.

"Fine, then, if you won't help me…" Sarah pushed more wood chips to the side. "This had better… Oh. Joseph."

She found it. Now it was time to help. He brushed additional debris away and pulled the stand from the box, more sawdust sprinkling everywhere. Setting the stand on the floor, he turned it to allow Sarah to see her reflection in the full-length tilting mirror.

Her hands covered her mouth and her eyes grew round as saucers. "Joseph this had to have cost much too much money." She didn't take her eyes off it as she spoke.

She liked it.

"Sarah, I lived in a cottage but that didn't mean I was penniless. I am not as poor as your father believes. We haven't enough to waste on lavish living, but we will not want."

"Did you make this?" Her left hand stayed at her lips, but her right hand reached out to trace the lifelike carvings along the oval top.

"I carved the base and frame and had the mirror put in while in London. Grinling Gibbons was commissioned to add the design. He agreed when he heard our story. Do you know, dear wife, he has a cravat he carved from wood that is so lifelike, a friend of his mistook it for the real thing? He showed it to me while I was there. A very talented man he is."

Suddenly Sarah embraced him. "I had faith in our love, but I should have had more faith in you. I love you, Joseph."

He ran his hands lightly up and down her back. "It is not a problem, my love. Do not cry. You don't want the mirror to see your tears." He pulled his hand into the sleeve of his shirt and dabbed her eyes.

"I can't help it. I don't think I can stop crying."

"Oh, Sarah love, what is the matter?" He took her in his arms and stroked her hair.

"I don't know. I've been like this all day. And even some yesterday. Mistress Fontaine came by today, and I even wanted to cry when she was here."

"Sh, don't worry. This move hasn't been easy for you, I know." He released her. "Here, let me remove the box and help you." He hoisted the case, briefly wishing he'd let the men stay long enough to take the box back, and set it on the floor. Grabbing the bedcover by the edge, he shook it free of sawdust and then folded it back before lifting Sarah and reclining her on the bed, propped by pillows.

She wiped her eyes with the corner of a blanket. "Wee Joseph is down in the kitchen with Bridget. Perhaps he'll want to cuddle with me."

"I will see about that. And I'll have Bridget fix you a cuppa." He leaned over and kissed her forehead. "I won't be but a minute."

"Joseph?"

He stopped, hand on the door. "What, my love?"

"I love your gift, but I love you more."

Joseph blew her a kiss and went to find Bridget.

TEA WAS NOT WHAT SARAH WANTED, BUT THEN NOTHING tasted good. And she had too much to do to be lying about in bed or crying like a baby because her husband loves her and buys her expensive gifts.

She and Joseph had only been married little more than a month, well, closer to two months.

Two months. Could time have passed that fast?

They spent a lovely week in Derry. The heat rose in her cheeks as she thought of the nights as a new wife. Joseph treated her with tenderness and patience and she, in turned, loved him with a passion she hadn't known she possessed.

When they came back to Edenmore, Wee Joseph had grown so tall. Tanté Louise had packed his things, sending most of them on to Balleylawn where her mother had packed Sarah's belongings as well. The families shipped all the crates to Bantry Bay to be waiting for them on their arrival.

Joseph suggested they take their time, not rush the trip to their new home. And he'd been right. Resting next to him each night, loving and being loved by such a…

Her eyes flew open. That was it. Every night he'd held her in his arms. Every night he proved his love.

And not once had her monthly visitor made its presence known.

She grabbed the pillow and wrapped her arms about it, burying her face into its softness to muffle her laugh. She had a gift to give back to her loving husband.

She would make him a father once again.

Chapter Thirty-One

W ee Joseph, do you want a brother or a sister?" The woman blooming in Sarah's mirror turned to the side, roving her hands over her enormous belly in the same manner her hands caressed her own unborn child.

The toddler playing on the floor stood and ran to her, wrapping his arms about her knees. "Mama."

She leaned over. "Mama's got ye, son. My, yer getting heavy." Pulling him onto her hip, or what was left of it, she kissed his head and tightly hugged him.

Though Joseph encouraged her, she had held off referring to herself as "Mama" to Wee Joseph. He belonged to her heart, but she needed that last bit of permission from Kathleen before she could make the total claim.

Then one day he woke from his nap and called her "mama" on his own. The last obstacle melted away and from then on, it had been no problem to say, "I am yer mama, and ye are me son."

"Look, Wee Joseph. Who is that handsome lad in the mirror?" She pointed, and he mimicked, pointing to his mama instead of the laddie she held.

Wee Joseph began to swing his legs. "Down."

"Then down ye shall go." She lowered him to the floor and immediately grabbed her back. "Ow." The heaviness grew and pressed. She reached for the bedpost and hung on, breathing out in a soft whistle. The sensation passed and she was able to stand up straight again.

Wiping the back of her hand across her forehead, she waddled through the doorway to the hall. "Bridget, could ye come up here, please?" Sarah waited at the doorpost, ready to grab hold if the pressure returned. But nothing else happened. Maybe her imagination was playing tricks on her. By her calculations, she still had not quite a week before the baby's due date.

"Mistress Sarah, do ye need something?" Bridget's head and body rose up the stairs.

Sarah shook her head. "Nay, my imagination seems to be getting the best of me."

Bridget wrapped her arm over Sarah's back and guided her into the room. "Would ye like for me to go get the master?" The young maid's eyes registered concern.

"I'm such a bother. Don't worry about me. I—" The heaviness returned, making her abdomen grow tight. She forced through another breath and the pressure slowly eased.

"I'm going to put ye to bed, and then I'll go get the master."

She allowed the lass to help her into bed and then grabbed her hand. "Go to Mistress Fontaine first. When she is on her way here, ye can go get Joseph. I think I'm needing Mistress Fontaine more right now." She smiled though she felt her lips trembled.

"Aye, mistress, I won't be but a stitch."

Bridget started to leave but turned back. "What about Wee Joseph?"

"He'll be fine until you return. But please hurry. We probably have a week's worth of time, but I would feel better knowing Mistress Fontaine were here."

Bridget nodded and left, her rapid descent sounding on the stairs before the door slammed.

Sarah closed her eyes and leaned back into the pillows. "Well, Wee Joseph. It seems yer about to learn if ye will have a brother or sister."

And I'm about to give birth. Father, hold us all. I am suddenly very afraid.

Joseph gazed over the shoulder of Captain McFain. The man didn't want to keep his end of the bargain. Though things had been explained quite plainly, the man still insisted he was due more before setting sail.

Wasn't that Bridget running toward the Fontaine home? What could she need going so fast? What could she need indeed? His wife was heavy with child, and due to give birth at any time.

"Captain McFain, I'm afraid you will have to either trust us on this or take it up with the reverend. I'm needed elsewhere."

Joseph called Jacques's son, Peter, and instructed him to guide the good captain to his father. Shoving the paperwork at the lad, he called over his shoulder, "And tell your father Sarah's about to have the baby," and took off at a run for the house.

He pulled open the front door. "Sarah, I'm here, love."

"Joseph?" She was upstairs.

Racing up the staircase, he found her in their bed. Wee Joseph sat next to her, holding her hand, looking quite serious. "Baby come."

"Yes, son, the baby is coming."

Joseph started to scoop the lad off the bed, but Sarah shook her head. "He's a comfort to me."

Walking around to the other side of the bed, he pulled up a creepie. Joseph sat on the stool and held his wife's other hand. "When did it start?"

"Just a bit ago. We most likely have a long night or more

ahead. I let my imagination carry me away and sent Bridget for Anne and you."

He kissed her fingertips. "There's nowhere else I'd rather be."

"Would ye read to me? I'd like to just listen to yer voice awhile."

Joseph chuckled. Standing, he kissed her. "What would you like me to read?"

"Psalms."

He nodded, the lump in his chest that always appeared when the subject of God was broached making itself known.

Her Bible lay on the nightstand, looking more used than his own. Returning to the stool, he flipped through the pages. "Any particular one?"

"Eighty-four." She waited until he found the page, then grabbed his hand.

> "How lovely are Thy dwelling places. O Lord of
>   hosts.
> My soul longed and even yearned for the courts
>   of the Lord;
> My heart and flesh sing for joy to the living God,
> The bird also has found a house,
> And the swallow a nest for herself, where she
>   may lay her young,
> Even Thine altars, O Lord of hosts,
> My King and my God
> How blessed are those who dwell in Thy house.
> They are ever praising Thee.
> Selah."

Sarah's grip tightened. He read faster.

> "Behold How blessed is the man whose strength
>   is in Thee;
> In whose heart are the highways to Zion.

Passing through the valley of Baca, they make it a
    spring,
The early rain also covers it with blessings.
They go from strength to strength,
Every one of them appears before God in Zion.
O Lord God of hosts, hear my prayer;
Give ear, O God of Jacob. Selah."

Joseph set the Bible down and brushed the hair from her forehead with his free hand.

"Don't stop. Please read on."

He nodded and began again.

"Behold our shield, O God,
    And look upon the face of Thine anointed."

Mistress Fontaine and Bridget hustled into the room. Joseph glanced up for only a moment and continued.

"For a day in Thy courts is better than a
    thousand outside."

Anne began to recite with him.

"I would rather stand at the threshold of the
    house of my God,
Than dwell in the tents of wickedness.
For the Lord God is a sun and shield;
The Lord gives grace and glory;
No good thing does He withhold from those
    who walk uprightly.
O Lord of hosts,
How blessed is the man who trusts in Thee."

"Amen. Now, Joseph, I need to see how your wife fares, and you need to go out."

Sarah squeezed his hand and nodded.

He closed the Bible, putting it back where he got it, and kissed his wife. "I will be right outside if you need me."

"Don't be afraid for me. I will be all right." Had she only pretended not to see his fear this past year?

"I know." He caressed her cheek and kissed her one last time before scooping up Wee Joseph and moving to the hall. Bridget closed the door while the words echoed in his brain.

O Lord of hosts, how blessed is the man who trusts in Thee.

But that man in the verse was not same man who sat in this hall. This man had no one to trust but himself and, at the moment, there was nothing he could do.

IT SEEMED LIKE HOURS SINCE THE FIRST PAIN, BUT ANNE told her she was actually moving very fast.

"It is important not to push before the time, ma petite. You will only prolong things if you do. I know what you are feeling, having done this six times myself. And I have lost count of how many little ones I've helped the Almighty bring into this world."

Bridget wiped Sarah's forehead and held her hand when the pressure grew.

"How much longer do ye think? Will I hold me babe tonight?"

"God willing, ye will. I will check again when the pain returns. Your waters have not yet broken, but I have known that to happen early or right before the child is delivered." Anne patted her free hand. "You are doing a good job, Sarah. You are strong. Rest easy now. When the next pain starts, tell me."

There wasn't long to wait. Sarah could feel the pressure start to build before Anne had finished speaking. The urge to bear down early won, but she pressed her free hand into the bed and forced herself to breathe in and out. The heaviness pressed down more than before. Sarah felt a small pop and the bedclothes suddenly became wet.

The fear she had fought with Scripture rose with new force. "What happened? Why is the bed wet? Am I bleeding?"

"Shh-shh, ma petite." Anne stroked her cheek. "I will look, but I doubt you are bleeding. I believe your waters have broken. This is good. Your baby is wanting to come to his mother." She walked around the bed and handed Bridget a leather-bound stick. "When the pains return, I want you bite down on this. And you must do exactly as I say."

Sarah nodded. Suddenly the pressure began to build again. She opened her mouth and Bridget put the stick between her teeth. The pressure built to pain. Coming faster, with more intensity. Her breath was snatched away. She had no control to keep from pushing and giving in to the urge was a relief.

Anne checked for the baby's head. "I can see dark curls. I think this next time will bring him or her to us. But don't push when I say to stop."

Sarah nodded again, catching her breath. How did she stop a push once it has started?

The pressure mounted again, and she bit hard on the stick. A scream filled her ears, a wounded animal cry that resonated in her mind.

"Stop. Don't push."

But there was no stop. Her body writhed wanting to push and trying not to.

"Sarah, stop."

The scream came again, and she knew it came from her.

Don't push. Don't push. I can't stop. O God, help me.

SARAH'S SCREAM TORE AT JOSEPH'S SOUL. *GOD, SPARE HER. Please. Do not take her too.* He scooped up Wee Joseph and held him tightly, pacing back and forth in front of the door. He could hear muffled voices but didn't understand them. *Spare her God, and I will never put her in danger again.*

The door opened a crack and Bridget peeked out. "Master Joseph, go get the reverend."

She began to shut the door, but he pushed it open. "Is she alive? Tell me."

"Aye, she lives. Please go get the reverend."

Again she tried to close the door, but he pushed his way in.

Sarah's eyes were closed, her face drenched in sweat. "Sarah? Sarah, love, are you all right?" He knelt by her side, but she turned her head away. "Sarah?"

"I'm sorry Joseph. The Almighty wanted your son to return to Him." Anne squeezed his shoulder. Her words began to sink into his mind, and he knew what he hadn't heard.

A baby's cry.

Chapter Thirty-Two

The clawing fingers pulled at Sarah, dragging her deeper and deeper into the pit. She hated the fingers, the clawing, but the pit surrounded her and kept other things from touching, hurting.

She opened her eyes. Once more she had reached for her baby, for tiny Thomas Stewart Crockett. But he no longer lived inside her. He was never allowed to live in this world.

Shannon's face floated through her mind. For one brief minute she wanted to cry out how sorry she felt. Sorry that Shannon had to stop nursing Wee Joseph. Now she understood that discomfort as well. Though Anne taught Bridget how to help alleviate the discomfort, it only reminded Sarah that her arms were empty.

She had failed Joseph. The shame overwhelmed her to the point she could hardly look him in the eye. Did he blame her?

Yet he came to her, over and over, trying to hold her. She didn't deserve his love.

Sarah dragged herself out of bed. Pouring from the pitcher on her nightstand, she made a cursory attempt at a toilet.

Bridget left a dress out for her. Slipping it on, she tied an apron over it. Turning, she caught her reflection in the mirror.

Her hands went to her deflated belly and her heart shattered all over. Racing from the image, she slammed the door and ran to Wee Joseph's room.

He played on the floor near his bed, already fully dressed. How late had she slept? Peering up from his blocks, he grinned. "Mama." He ran to her and she embraced him. Maybe if she could hold him forever her heart might begin to heal.

He nuzzled his head into her neck, stroking her cheek. She put his small baby hand to her lips and sobbed. "I'm sorry, Wee Joseph. I'm so sorry."

"Joseph, I am truly sorry for your loss."

The gentle words were meant well but did nothing to relieve Joseph's misery. He worried day and night over Sarah, feeling guilty he didn't mourn more for his tiny son.

Not that he didn't mourn for Thomas. He did. He mourned for what could have been, for the love of a son he never got to know. But Thomas hadn't had the chance to become as real for Joseph as he had for Sarah.

She felt his moves and kicks every day. Their hearts had been entwined from the first flutter of life. And now she moved about as if in some kind of shell.

Joseph sighed. "I know you are, and I thank you for all you and Anne have done."

"What have we done but what the Almighty asks? When our Aaron went to his reward last spring, I wanted to rail at God. But Aaron begged us to release him into the Almighty's hand. We have been blessed beyond measure in this life. How could I not accept this suffering without trusting my Lord to bring me through."

Joseph pushed back from the table. "If we are finished here, I need to go home to Sarah."

The reverend's blue eyes filled with compassion. "Go home to your wife. My boys will help me finish."

Joseph nodded his thanks, grateful to be gone.

The wind off the bay tempered his frustration. He hadn't called on the Almighty in years. But for the one time, a month ago. Ironically, his prayer had been answered to the letter. Sarah had been spared. He never thought to pray for his child.

Would it have made a difference? Had God already planned this out before he bothered to pray? And if that were the case, why bother? Did his prayers truly move God's heart, or did they even reach His ear? Perhaps God sat behind His desk, watching to see how He could manipulate Joseph's life.

Bridget would have the noon meal ready by now. He came in through the back, taking the rear stairs up to the room he shared with Sarah. Would she be awake?

Slowly opening the door, he noticed the bed, though empty, was unmade. Until Thomas' birth, or rather death, Sarah would have immediately made the bed. Other things were amiss in the room, so he knew Sarah hadn't been up long enough for Bridget to tidy.

He poured clean water into the basin, washed his face and hands, and dried them on a towel tossed carelessly on the bed.

His next step would be to locate Sarah. Heading down the hall, he looked in on Wee Joseph's room.

Sarah sat in the middle of the floor, baby blankets, gowns and caps so carefully embroidered lay scattered over her lap. Her hair hung in her eyes and she gripped baby clothes to her face. Her body shook.

It was the first time since the night Thomas died that he'd known her to weep. Usually she moved in a numbed stupor. Though it broke his heart, Joseph wondered if this might be the beginning of her healing process.

He knelt on the floor and she threw herself into his arms with loud racking cries. Holding her tight, his tears drenched her hair. "Sarah, my Sarah. Oh, my love." He kissed her temple and smoothed back the hair from her face.

"I'm so sorry, Joseph. I'm so sorry. Forgive me, I beg you. I am so sorry."

He stroked her hair. "Sorry for what? You have done nothing wrong."

"I failed you. I failed you and Thomas and Wee Joseph and my father. I have failed you all. We should be holding our son and dressing him in these things and rocking him, and he is gone.

Joseph pulled her onto his lap and rocked her back and forth. "He isn't gone forever. He's just waiting for us." The thought came unbidden and out his mouth before he realized it.

"Do you believe that?" She nestled into him and didn't look at his face.

Did he believe it? He wanted to, for her sake if not for his own. "Yes, beloved, I do believe it." Maybe.

Sarah relaxed in his arms. He rocked her until he heard the even breathing that told him she slept. The first peaceful sleep she'd had in a month. And the first time he had held her in his arms in as long.

Perhaps the healing really had begun.

He held her and rocked, not worrying about the time.

Yet all the while, a small voice questioned in his heart. Though he strove to ignore it, the question persisted. He tried to close out the voice, but to no avail.

And when will you let the healing begin in you?

The echo clanged in his soul.

Joseph had no answer.

❧

THE DIFFERENCE IN SARAH'S DEMEANOR OVER THE NEXT few days convinced Joseph that the healing had indeed begun. Her hair shone healthy, she took care in her dress, and most importantly, she revealed an occasional smile. She also cried sometimes, but not the heart-rending sobs from before. His Sarah had returned, and for that he was thankful.

Thankful and determined she would never again hurt so deeply.

Walking past Wee Joseph's room one evening, he spotted the tender scene of mother and son readying for bed. Leaning in the doorway, he enjoyed how Sarah dressed the growing lad for the night and sat with him in the rocker. Her crooning lullabies were the sweetest music he could imagine. He let her song transport him away from trouble and pain to a place where all could be made right when rocked in the arms of love.

"Aye, Wee Joseph. Close yer eyes. Dream of lovely fields and flowers, of ponies with swift feet, of yer mama and da. Aye, sweet lad, maybe dream of a brother or sister. Maybe yer da and I can work on that for ye too."

She wanted to try again.

A cold vise twisted his heart. She wanted to try again.

He should have known. What would he do? What could he do?

He pushed off from the doorframe and strode to his room. His and Sarah's room.

I'll not ask for Your help. No. Did You protect Kathleen? Or Wee Thomas? I cannot trust You. Blessed is the man who trusts you? Ha. Foolish is the man who trusts You, and I won't be foolish with Sarah or my family any longer. I will protect them no matter what I have to do.

An image of Sarah from their wedding night floated through his memory. Sweet, innocent, full of love and passion.

He sat on the edge of the bed, his head in his hands. Was he so selfish as to put his own urges before her health? Was he a man, or a dog wanting only to satisfy himself?

No, he was a man, made of flesh and blood, but a man of responsibilities and self-control. Sarah's welfare came first. His love for her was not dependent on fleshly passions. He could love her and care for her and deny himself, especially if it kept her safe.

"Joseph? Have ye pain in yer head?" Sarah stood before him. So deep in his resolve, he'd not noticed her entry. Now that she was near, his resolve began to evaporate.

"No, love. Just a pain in my heart."

She knelt down before him, taking his hands in hers. "Dear Joseph, I am so sorry. I would do anything to keep ye from hurt."

"As I would you, love." He needed to tell her, to let her know. How? How did he say he could not share that intimacy with her again? How did he prove his love yet withdraw that part of himself?

"You have been so patient with me, Joseph. I love you all the more for that." She held his hands. "I want you to know, I am ready to again try. I want to carry your child, have another baby." He pulled his hands away. "We can do this. I know God will grant us another child."

He stood looking down at her. "How? How do you know God will grant us anything? How do you know He won't decide to take the next baby or you or both? How many mothers must Wee Joseph lose?"

She gasped, staring as if he were a stranger.

It was a hurtful thing to say. He knew it and regretted it the second the words left his lips.

He reached out to her, but she pushed his hand away and stood on her own. "What are ye saying then? Am I to never again know ye? Do ye plan to withhold yer love from me?" Her eyes blazed with fire, and the candlelight's glow reflected in her hair.

"Angry though you are, you are alive. You are able to stand here, and feel, and think, and cry because you are alive. What guarantee do you have from God Almighty that this will continue if we have another baby? The loss of Wee Thomas nearly destroyed you." He grabbed her hands and, though she tried to pull them back, he hung on. "I love you, Sarah. More than myself, more than any passion, more than life itself. If I lost you with our babe, I might as well have walked into the bay and never come back. I will do what I have to do to keep you safe."

She tore her hands from his grasp. Reaching behind her she grabbed a pillow from the bed and threw it at him. "Then get out. Go. Keep me safe, then, but get out of this room."

He had never seen her so angry. Her arms locked at her sides, fists trembling with tension. And her eyes, blazing, but full of pain. Pain he had caused.

"Sarah…"

She pointed to the door. "Get out."

He did.

Chapter Thirty-Three

"Wee Joseph is asleep." Sarah stood in the doorway of the study. Her fingers played with the ribbons at her neckline.

Joseph continued to focus on his ledgers.

It had been weeks since he had touched her, ever since he moved into the guest room. Though polite, and even sounding concerned at times, the passion between them seemed to have died with Wee Thomas.

She stepped closer, watching his careful notations with the quill. He never even acknowledged her. She longed to run her hand through his thick mane, pull him close, force him to see her. She would be happy just to have his fingers touch hers once more.

But that hadn't happened in so long. It almost felt like it had only been her imagination that it had ever happened at all. Not even in the time after Kathleen's death had she ached for him as much.

Tonight, though, tonight she would make the first move. She would reach out to him. Her hair was carefully brushed, gleaming over her shoulders the way he liked. Her new chemise, embroidered at the slightly lower neckline. She'd added a small dab of perfume to entice.

"Joseph, we're alone."

Still not a pause. Could he so completely shut his passions down? Did he not realize what he did to her by withholding himself?

She touched his shoulder.

His muscles tensed beneath his shirt.

"Joseph, come to bed."

He continued to work as if she wasn't there. If not for his muscles betraying him, she would have believed he didn't know she existed.

How could he sit there and just keep writing? She couldn't have been more blatant. He had to know. Must she humiliate herself?

But as he continued to scratch out the perfectly formed notations, she knew he wouldn't acknowledge her invitation.

He didn't even care enough to look.

Her fist clenched at her side. She longed to take the hated ledger and throw it into the fire.

A single tear dripped onto his sleeve before she brushed the others away. She wouldn't cry, wouldn't beg. She had her pride. Instead she would do as she had done.

Wordlessly, she climbed the stairs to her room.

One more lonely night.

Why did she bother?

HE COULDN'T DO IT. IF HE HAD TO SPEND ONE MORE NIGHT with her so close, he would either give in to his passions or go insane.

Had Sarah no idea of her effect on him?

Joseph dropped his quill leaving an inky splotch on the ledger. Raking his hands through his hair, he wanted to scream.

Her perfume still lingered in the room and only the memory of their baby son's still form kept him from taking the steps two at a time and breaking down her door.

Shoving back his chair, he left his study and strode through the kitchen, rushing outside to the cool night air.

A breeze blew off the bay. He turned his face to the wind, longing for the air to blow the storm in his heart far out to sea.

Maybe the answer lay out there, out beyond Bantry Bay. If he could just sail away from his troubles…

No, his heart would never leave Sarah.

But perhaps his body could. Perhaps he could help with the negotiations in London. He'd done it before. He knew they needed new backing what with all the expansion. Perhaps Jacques would agree. And Sarah would be safe enough. Bridget would be there at the house, and the Fontaines now had a large tower house on the bluff. They would gladly offer her help, should it be necessary.

Tomorrow he would talk to Jacques, tell him he was interested in becoming more involved in dealing with the London partners. The idea gave him a way out, and the agitation in his mind settled. He sighed and returned to the house.

To his bedroom.

Alone.

❧

Sarah sat on the floor inside her bedroom. There was no desire to feel the extra space left in her bed. Listening, she heard the back door close and the measured tread of her husband on the stair.

Let him stop at the door. Let him want me as I want him.

The footsteps sounded closer. She held her breath, listening for them to slow.

Instead they moved faster past her door. Seconds later she heard his door open and close.

Or was that the door to her heart slamming tight?

She couldn't say.

JOSEPH WOULD HAVE RATHER LAID ON THE BED AND TAKEN a nap. Instead he placed his portmanteau on it and proceeded to fill the case with clothing. His eyes felt bleary and, no wonder, since he had tossed and turned the whole night. Jacques didn't argue. In fact, he was happy to have Joseph relieve him of some of the traveling burden and wanted him ready to sail with the noon's tide.

He still needed to tell Sarah. After last night, there was no telling what she would think.

"You're leaving?" She stood in the doorway.

He'd not heard her approach. It was a surprise he heard anything as tired as he was.

"Sarah…"

But she was gone.

He finished packing and went downstairs to the kitchen. Bridget baked shepherd pie for the noon meal while Wee Joseph played with some pans on the floor. There was no sign of Sarah.

Picking up Wee Joseph, he squeezed him close. "Take care of your mother, son. I will be back before you know it."

Bridget didn't raise her head. Did she know? How could she not, living under the same roof? She must think…He didn't know what she thought.

He put his son back on the floor. "Bridget, please tell Sarah I will be back as soon as the business in London is completed."

"Aye, sir." She never turned around.

"And Bridget, please tell her… tell her…"

Now she turned and arched an eyebrow at him. Bridget most definitely knew. "Perhaps that is a message ye should deliver yerself?"

He nodded. "Perhaps you are right."

The idea that had seemed so wonderful last night only appeared to make matters worse in the daylight.

Joseph shook his head, kissed Wee Joseph, and left.

SARAH CLIMBED THE BLUFF OVERLOOKING THE HARBOR. She could easily see each ship docked. Unless he planned to leave by horse, this is the way he would go.

She stood tall, daring him to spot her, hand to her forehead to block the sun's rays.

Soon he came into view, stopping to speak with a man. Most likely the captain. He pulled out a paper and handed it over. The captain handed it back and gave him a clap on the shoulder. Joseph nodded and went below deck.

It was all so simple, fast. Over and done.

She turned and wandered back to the house.

JOSEPH PUT HIS CASE BELOW DECK AND RETURNED TO watch as they pulled from the harbor.

He could see someone on the bluff to the west. Studying the walk, he knew it had been Sarah. Was it her way of seeing him off?

Or of saying goodbye?

Chapter Thirty-Four

I can't get her to come out of her room, Mistress Fontaine. She doesn't answer my knock, and I don't think she's even taken nourishment in a couple days."

Sarah could hear the conversation outside her door. She hadn't meant to worry anyone. She just hadn't felt like eating. Or doing anything, for that matter.

"You did the right thing to send for me. I will speak with her."

Someone went down the steps, presumably Bridget. She didn't want to talk with Anne or Bridget or the Queen if she blessed the bay with a visit. She might talk with her mother. But then, her mother was not anywhere around here.

Sarah continued to stare out her window. It looked over the bay and she could see the sea gulls soaring overhead. Did the males fly away and leave the females behind, all alone on their nest?

At once she wanted to throw something at the gulls. How dare they leave their females alone. Searching for anything that might make a hefty projectile, she turned too quickly. The room spun about her. "Ho." The lightheadedness caught her by surprise. She steadied herself against her dresser.

There, that was something. Bridget's vase of daffodils. What did she want with daffodils? She picked it up and lost her balance. The vase tumbled from her hands. She fell back against the tilted mirror, knocking it over.

The beautiful, one-of-a-kind gift from Joseph lay shattered in a thousand pieces. The cracked base poked up at her like an accusing finger. "Oh no! Oh no!" She scrambled on hands and knees grabbing shards, trying to fit them back into the frame.

A large piece of the glass still clung to the top part of the oval. The woman in the reflection stared back. A complete stranger. Her hair hung unkempt, her sallow skin accentuated the sunken, red-rimmed eyes.

The woman began to cry, and Sarah cried with her.

"No wonder Joseph left. Who would want me?" She raised her hand to wipe her tears but saw red dripping down. Holding her arm in front of her, she watched as blood ran from her palm, to her wrist and forearm. It reminded her of a stained-glass window she'd seen as a child, one depicting the crucifixion.

Inside she heard the small voice again.

I want you, Sarah. I bled for you and died for you. And I will hold on to you. Don't let go, Sarah. Courage grows strong at the wound.

Arms wrapped around her and pulled her to her feet. She took a couple steps to the bed and the arms turned her around.

"Take courage, Sarah. The Almighty is your champion. He will prevail."

Sarah nodded to Anne and sat on the bed.

"Let me see your hand."

Sarah obeyed.

Anne examined her palm. "It doesn't appear to have any glass in it. Bridget, bring bandages as well."

Sarah closed her eyes. She could feel pressure being applied to her hand. Maybe that was the courage growing strong. She fell back on the bed.

"I feel so foolish." Sarah shook her head, staring at her bandaged hand. "Forgive me for causing you worry." She had no idea how long she had slept, but vaguely remembered being fed some broth and having her face wiped with a wet cloth.

Today her head felt clearer, her body stronger.

Anne plumped another pillow and propped it behind Sarah's head. "I don't worry. Well, perhaps I do a little, but when I recognize it, I turn it over to my Heavenly Father who is much more capable and will work it out for His glory and my good."

"Where does your faith come from, Anne? I read my Bible, I listen to my minister, but I still doubt and feel afraid. Where do you find that kind of faith?"

Anne sat on the edge of the bed, holding Sarah's uninjured hand. "I have had many years of leaning into His grace. I believe what Paul has to say—nothing can separate me from the love of God, which is in Christ Jesus. Nothing. So, what is there to fear? Pain? I won't suffer like He did for me. Death? It is but gain. Being alone? I'm never alone. The Holy Spirit resides in me and is my Comfort. I have perfect peace."

Sarah picked at the bedclothes. "What if Jacques left you?"

"He will one day, or I will leave him to go on to our reward. It will hurt. We have been together for many years now, and he is a good husband. A good man of God. But I still have the peace of Christ."

"I mean, what if he rode away one day and chose to not come back?" Watching the woman's eyes, she wondered if she'd said too much.

"Do you think your Joseph has gone for good? Is that what all this is about?"

She nodded meekly. She was ashamed to admit even that much to Anne.

"First, let me tell you Joseph loves you. I know. And second, he is on a business trip to London for the company. He will be back as soon as the business is concluded. Didn't you ask him?"

"We haven't been…communicating very well…for some time now." Sarah thought she was past tears, but the hot liquid burned in her eyes just the same. "I don't think he wants me anymore."

"Then let us pray about it." Kneeling down next to the bed, Anne placed a hand on Sarah's head and closed her eyes. "Oh, Almighty God, Thou art God over all things great and small. Thou deliverest Daniel and the Hebrew children yet allowed Paul and Peter to die for Thee. We do not understand Thy ways but know Thou workest for our eternal good in all Thou doest. I bring my young sister to Thy throne of mercy. Thou knowest the depth of her pain and suffering, and Thou knowest the outcome. We pray for Thy Holy Spirit to fill her with the faith she needs to trust in Thee to bring her dear husband back. Not only back to Bere Haven, but back to her arms and Thy will. Do whatever needs to be done to accomplish Thy will in this matter, we implore Thee. We leave this worry at the foot of the Holy Cross of Thy Son, Jesus, in Whose Name we pray. Amen."

"Amen"

Nothing more needed to be said.

STRENGTH RETURNED A LITTLE MORE EACH DAY. AND WITH it came a new hunger, a desire to spend time reading the Bible and praying about what she read.

Often Anne would come by, or Sarah would take Wee Joseph and spend the afternoon at the Fontaine's house, or rather, fortress. Rumors flew quite regularly of French corsairs making trouble for Protestant villages along the Southern Irish coast, but none had been spotted near Bere Haven.

This beautiful morning, Sarah planned to go with Anne to visit the sick and poor in the neighborhood, bringing food and doing good as St. Paul instructed. Her window was open and the sea air invigorated. Leaning out over the sill, she took in a deep breath and heard a cry. Holding the air inside, she closed her eyes and listened.

She heard it again. Letting the breath out, she realized it couldn't be her imagination. The cry sounded too young for Wee Joseph. And weak.

She ran down the stairs and to the back door. As she opened it, there sat a basket on the step.

The cry came from inside.

Peeling back blankets, she saw the angriest face she'd ever seen on a baby. Scooping him up in her arms, she patted his back and paced in the kitchen.

That didn't seem to be what he wanted. Or was it a *her*?

Bridget came into the room, tying on her apron. "Whatever is making such a racket on this bright new day?"

"It is more like who is making such a racket, and I don't know the wee one's name. Or gender, for that matter. There, there, little one. From whence came ye?"

Feeling around in the basket, Bridget held up only the covering. "There's no note and I do not recognize the basket or blanket. Could she be hungry?"

"Aye, she could, or he could or he or she may want a clean nappy. I think there are still some up in Wee Joseph's room." Sarah headed for the stairs and Bridget followed.

Wee Joseph woke as the women entered. His eyes grew at the sight of the baby and he covered his ears.

"Tis but a babe crying, Wee Joseph, just like ye used to do when ye were little. I think we need to change the nappy."

Wee Joseph climbed off his bed and toddled to his mother, wrapping an arm about her leg and popping a thumb in his mouth.

"Would ye like to help me, son?"

Wee Joseph nodded and reached toward the baby. Sarah

stooped so he could see. "Look at the tiny feet and hands, love. They look just like yers, only smaller."

"I found the nappies. Would ye like to change him or her?"

"I think I remember how." Sarah tweaked Wee Joseph's nose and stood. Taking the baby to the dresser she made a soft place for him—or her—and unbundled the soiled nappy.

This was definitely a boy, and she remembered just in time what little boys can do when feeling exposed. "Bridget, would you bring that basin here. I think we should bathe this little one before putting him in clean clothes."

She removed his gown and noted he couldn't be but a day old by the look of his navel. Taking care around the stump of cord, she washed his little body and his fine blond hair, of which there was little on his nearly bald head. Bridget held out a towel, and Sarah carefully wrapped him up. "Now to put you in a fresh nappy and gown. What is your name, little lad? We can't very well keep calling you babe or laddie, now can we?"

Someone knocked at the door downstairs, so Bridget left to answer it.

By the time Bridget came back with Anne Fontaine, Sarah had the baby dressed and wrapped in a clean blanket. She sat in the rocker with him on one side and Wee Joseph on her other.

"What shall we name him, Wee Joseph? He needs a name, don't you think?"

Wee Joseph gently touched the baby's cheek. "John."

Sarah gazed at her son, "John? You think that is a good name for him?"

Wee Joseph nodded.

"Why John?"

"Jesus loves him."

Sarah's glance caught Anne's. Wee Joseph remembered the Bible story she'd told him before bed about John, the disciple Jesus loved.

She stroked the baby's downy head, watching his face. "What do you think, wee one? Do you like the name John?"

The baby shoved a fist in his mouth and began to suck furiously.

Anne leaned over to get a better look. "I don't think he is concerned with what you call him. I think he is more in want of something to eat."

Sarah glanced up at Anne. "I know. Do you have any ideas?"

"I do. Bridget, I'll be needing a clean horn, an old but clean leather glove, and some boiled goat's milk."

Bridget left to gather the articles, and Anne sat down on the edge of Wee Joseph's bed.

"Do you know from where he came?"

"Heaven, as far as I'm concerned. We found no note in his basket and I don't recognize the blanket. It's on the floor by the dresser if you want to look."

Anne picked the blanket up between her thumb and finger and held it out. "Actually, I believe it is one of mine. An old one I gave away some time ago." She grabbed her chin and squinted her eyes. Then, with a shake of her head, she tossed the blanket back on the floor. "I'm not able to recall. Sarah, ma petite, I can see you are becoming attached."

She couldn't deny it and nodded her head. "He's so helpless and needs me almost as much as I need him, I think."

Anne put her hand on Sarah's shoulder. "Will you give me time to check the villages? There is a mother somewhere without her baby."

What kind of mother willingly gave away her baby? But in the end, Sarah agreed. She had to. If someone had her Wee Thomas, she would want to know.

They spent the rest of the morning trying to get John fed. The cow's horn had been hollowed and the point cut off. A finger from the glove slipped over the narrow end of the horn, forming a nipple, and the palm of the glove was strapped over the wider end after the goat's milk had cooled and been poured in.

It took some practice keeping a finger over the nipple end

while tying the other end off with a leather strip. Neither Bridget nor Sarah could do it alone, so the old cradle had been brought down into the kitchen to hold John while they worked together.

Anne left to do the visiting without Sarah. That evening, she returned to see how things progressed.

Sitting on creepies in the kitchen, Sarah and Bridget shared about their adventurous day of feeding baby John—not Johnny. Wee Joseph insisted. Anne laughed until she had to wipe her eyes free of tears.

"Bless me, I think no child ever had such determined and entertaining nannies." She slapped her thighs. "And I should now tell you what I learned today about the child's parentage."

Sarah's heart grew tight. She knew Anne would search for the information while out but hadn't expected her to learn anything so soon.

Leaning forward, Anne folded her hands and rested her elbows on her knees. "I learned of John's mother. She was a young slip of a girl still in need of a mother herself. It seems she had kept her secret about carrying the child until she delivered, all alone. A friend found her, cared for her until she died. This friend found clothes for the infant. No one in the mother's family would care for the child, and the lass I spoke to was afraid of what might happen if they ever got their hands on him."

Sarah wiped a tear from her cheek. "What of her friend? Is she safe? Can we help her?"

"Not much we can do at the moment, at least not more than I am doing. Young girls can be prey without loving parents. But you can always pray God will keep her from the same fate." Anne cupped her hand to John's soft cheek. "So, it looks like he is yours. What do you plan to tell Joseph when he comes home?"

"He's been gone so long now. I don't even know when to expect him back. I thought…prayed he would send a letter, but I have yet to receive one. I don't know what to do." Not long ago, she would have broken in pieces to say such a thing. Now, she spoke the truth knowing she would give it to God in prayer before she went to bed.

Anne stood. "Courage, dear Sarah. The battle isn't over yet."

"Courage rises from the wound."

"What was that, dear?"

"Something my father told me. Courage rises from the wound." Sarah smiled. "And it does."

Chapter Thirty-Five

By five in the morning, as the sun glistened over the bay, Sarah laid little John back into the cradle and stretched. Her body felt like it had spent the night in the rocker, and that was very close to the truth. The laddie housed a great appetite.

Fortunately, Bridget had the presence of mind to create several horn feeders. And due to Anne's prolific love of reading, they knew to boil the horns after each use to rid them of the tiny things one could see under a microscope. Fascinated with the work of Robert Hooke and Anton van Leeuwenhoek, Hooke's *Microscopia* had captured Anne's imagination. The wonder that God created things so small the human eye alone could not see them, only gave her more praise to sing.

Even still, after each boiling, the leather nipples and bases had to be made pliable with butter, which also acted as a proofing to keep the liquid from passing through. And that called for poking tiny holes in the tip of each nipple so Wee John could drink.

Then there was the matter of boiling the goat's milk, to keep it easier on Wee John's digestion, according to Anne. Boil the milk. Cool the milk. Make ready the feeder. And all the time the wain waited quite impatiently.

And it had only been one night.

Yet when he lay sleeping in her arms, Sarah could think of nothing more lovely, like a piece of herself had returned to its place.

She woke to the hungry cries of an insistent young lad. Rolling to her side, she noted the sun higher in the sky. She must have lain on the bed after putting John into his cradle.

Stretching again, Sarah rose, still fully dressed, and lifted Wee John to her. "Shh wee one. I know, I know. We will change yer nappy and see about some more milk."

She carried him to Wee Joseph's room and changed his clothes, all of which were very damp. Wee Joseph rubbed his eyes and watched.

"Why John cry, Mama?"

"That's how wee ones tell us they have a need. He needs his nappy and clothes changed, and he's most likely hungry too. Are ye hungry?"

"Aye" He climbed out of bed and held her skirt as they went down the stairs.

"Mama, will John be me brodder?"

"I'm praying about that, Wee Joseph."

"Will Da love him?"

"I'm praying about that too."

Bridget's eyes appeared tired, but she was already at work in her kitchen fixing Wee Joseph's breakfast and Wee John's milk. "What might I fix for ye, Mistress Sarah?"

When Sarah shook her head, suggesting a bannock left over from yesterday, Bridget overruled. "I'm not about to let ye get sick again now that yer nearly back to yer auld self. Ye will have some of the brochan I prepared for Wee Joseph, and there's tea for while ye wait."

Wee Joseph perched on a high stool at the preparation table.

While she waited, Sarah paced, John nestled in her neck sucking on his fist. She knew Wee Joseph watched closely.

"I don't want a brodder."

Turning to face her son, Sarah studied his face. "Why, Wee Joseph? Why don't ye want a new brother?"

"Him cries too much. I wanna sisser."

Sarah leaned against the wall and bit her lip to keep in the laughter. A glance at Bridget showed her back shaking, though she, at least, kept quiet. "Son, I am very sorry to tell ye this, but sisters cry too. Babes are noisy creatures. They can't talk so instead they cry."

Wee Joseph squinted his eyes and puckered his lips, thinking quite seriously. Finally, he nodded. "Den I teach him, so he don't cry so much."

Bridget lost control. She snorted, bent over double, an arm about her middle while she held the table for support.

Wee Joseph's eyes widened. "What's wrong? Is Bridget sick?"

Sarah chuckled and cupped her son's chin in her hand. "Yer an amazing young lad, that ye are, son. I think ye should teach John to talk, but ye'll want to be patient. He's learning so very much all the time, just like ye did when ye were his age. And do not worry about our Bridget. I believe she's feeling better already."

Bridget caught her breath and straightened. "Aye." Her stoic agreement couldn't hide how her eyes danced with laughter.

A knock sounded at the front door. Sarah motioned she would answer so Bridget could continue her preparations.

Little Elizabeth Fontaine stood on the top step, a miniature of her mother. Without a word, she held out a sealed packet.

Sarah accepted it. "Thank you, Elizabeth. Would ye like to come in and sit a spell?"

Elizabeth shook her curls and ran back toward her house.

"And a good morning to ye, too, lassie." Sarah smiled as she watched the child race to her father who glanced up and waved. Sarah waved back and closed the door.

Adjusting the baby in the crook of her arm, she headed back to the kitchen, turning the letter over in her hand. The handwriting made her heart skip a beat.

She handed John to a surprised Bridget. "I need to read this. Please. I will return as quickly as I can." Racing up the steps, she ran to her bedroom and closed the door.

Joseph's unique penmanship burned against her skin. Suddenly she feared opening it.

Trust Me, Sarah. Let your courage rise. Nothing can separate you from My love.

"Courage. Aye." She took a deep breath and sat down on the edge of the bed, sliding a fingernail beneath the edge of the seal. Opening the pages, she nearly cried that he had written so much.

My dearest Sarah,

I know I should have written you long before this, and in truth, I have started many letters to you. None conveyed my heart, though, so I make my poor attempt once again.

First let me say I love you. I have always loved you and will never stop loving you. You may call me a coward and perhaps rightly so, but to tell you that in person and not be able to take you in my arms is more than I can bear. Now that I am miles and miles from you, I can tell you, though, I still long to hold you near.

Yet, what kind of a man would I be, what kind of a loving husband, if I pursued my own passions to your detriment? I tell you true, lass, you greatly move me. I am only human. You are the most beautiful woman in the world to me, and I would lay down my life for you in an instant.

And that, in a way, is what I am attempting to do. I have never wanted to hurt you. I long for us to have a peaceable home.

So, dearest Sarah, I ask you, I plead with you to please, please let me keep you safe. This has nothing to do with your desirability. I desire no one else.

Please understand. I saw Kathleen die. I helplessly watched while you suffered at Wee Thomas' death. We have a wonderful son in Wee Joseph. If we never have more children, if we never try to have more children, we remove a risk to your very life. And there is no point to life if it means going on without you.

I will be home very soon after you receive this post. Dealing with the new backers has been disappointing, to say the least.

I pray you will understand what I so vainly attempt to explain. We can speak of it more thoroughly when I am there. Until then, please remember I love you. I have never stopped loving you. I will never stop loving you and will protect you until my last breath.

Joseph

No matter how many times Sarah read it, she couldn't stop thrilling at his words. He loved her. He still loved her.

She still wanted to be held and loved as a wife should be, but this was a step. Though misguided, his heart still belonged to her. And he would be home soon.

Soon.

And he didn't know anything about Wee John. Would he accept the babe? Would he give him his name? "Oh Father, Ye showed me one answer only for me to bring Ye one more problem. I am learning this is not too much for Ye. I will take courage in Yer love for me and trust in Ye for the answers. One answer at a time, if necessary."

She stared at the letter again. "And, Father, thank Ye."

THE WALK FROM THE DOCK HAD NEVER SEEMED SO LONG. Joseph dreaded to learn how Sarah received his letter. Would she be agreeable? Would she leave him or demand he leave? He had no idea what to expect.

The midday sun beat on his tired shoulders. Dragging his

feet to the back door, he opened it only to hear a baby's cry. He stopped to check his surroundings. "Do I have the correct house?"

Sarah came running, but stopped short, more than an arm's reach away. "Joseph. Yer home." She picked at her apron.

"It appears that way." He smiled. "I wasn't sure at first. Who is crying?"

"Da." Wee Joseph ran to him.

Joseph dropped his bag and picked his boy up over his head, swinging him around. The child laughed with glee. Lowering him back to the floor, Wee Joseph grabbed his father's hand. "Da. Come see. Come see Wee John."

"Wee John?" Joseph peered at Sarah for understanding as his son pulled him up the stairs.

Sarah followed behind while Wee Joseph mounted each step, never letting go of Joseph's hand. "Him is a babe and I want him. I want him to be my brodder."

Did he hear that right? Sarah wouldn't use Wee Joseph to press her side, would she? Who was this baby? Where had he come from?

"Show me your friend, Wee Joseph."

The lad reached the top of the steps and stared back as if his father were quite dense. "Him's not my friend. I want him for my *brodder*." And then he continued to pull Joseph down the hall.

The room had been altered in his absence to look more like a nursery. The cradle lay at the foot of his son's bed, and Bridget rocked a small baby while holding a horn of some kind to his mouth.

"Him's Wee John. Can we keep him, Da?"

Chapter Thirty-Six

Joseph stared into Wee Joseph's pleading eyes searching for something logical to say. "Son, I need to speak with your mother about this. Would you help Bridget while we go talk?"

Wee Joseph took on a serious expression and nodded.

Joseph held the door for Sarah and followed her into the hall.

Now he faced a quandary. Did they go to her room? Could he even again enter it? He surely couldn't take her to his room. She might see it as if he'd changed his mind.

"Shall we go downstairs to yer study?" Sarah felt his discomfort. Just as always. His heart clenched at her beauty, and he forced himself to not reach for her hand.

"Aye. After you." He directed toward the front stairs.

She led the way. Stepping further into the room, she seemed intent on keeping space between them, for which he was grateful.

"I'm supposing ye want an explanation." She tucked her hands behind her back and rocked onto her toes.

He sat on the edge of his desk. "That might help. Do you want me to ask questions or do you just want to tell me?"

"I'll just tell ye." She took the chair behind the desk.

The hair on the back of his head tingled, but he ignored it. This was Sarah. He would listen to what she had to say. He changed his seat to the other chair.

"I found the wain on our doorstep. Anne investigated while Bridget and I cared for him. Oh, Joseph, he couldn't have been more than a day old. And so hungry and angry. Anne taught us how to make the feeder horn and later found his mother."

Was that a tear in her eye? She took a breath and blinked quickly. "Wee John's mother was an abused young lass. If it had been discovered she was with child, there's no telling what would have happened. A friend helped her…"

"You mean no one even knew she carried a child? No one cared for her?" He could not fathom such apathy and neglect. Yet, hadn't he neglected his family by leaving? No, he protected his wife.

"Aye. She had a friend who did what she could though the mother died. The friend placed the babe in a basket on our step, hoping we might raise her son as one of our own."

"And you said 'aye' without consulting me?" The irritation grew. This was his study. Why again did someone control him from behind a desk—his own desk?

"Nay, Joseph. Of course, I would not do that. I told Wee Joseph we would need to pray about it and ask ye first."

"You didn't tell him this was his brother and to ask me if you could keep him?"

"Joseph." The hurt in her eyes stabbed him. She didn't lie.

"I'm sorry. I should never have accused." He started to reach out but remembered and pulled his hand back. "Why John? Who chose his name?"

Sarah smiled. "Our son. I had been telling him Bible stories before bed. He remembered about John the Beloved and decided Jesus loved the babe so he must be named John. Oh, and do not try to call him Johnny. Wee Joseph will correct you. However, you may call him Wee John since our sons carry that title." Her smile faltered, but she quickly recovered. "Do you have any other questions?"

Carefully watching her face, he realized she was still as beautiful as ever. Yet she glowed with something he'd missed for some time. "Are you sure?"

"Aye, that I am. If yer sure. God supplies my needs. Even to again filling my arms." She crossed her arms and leaned forward, resting them on the desk. "Joseph, I ken how ye believe. I don't agree, but if ye won't…" Her cheeks grew pink and she averted her eyes.

He waited. Perhaps she was right. Maybe God was supplying the family she wanted. As the idea took shape, he smiled. Yes, this could be a blessing in disguise.

"Would ye be willing to give him yer name?"

That came as a shock. Her eyes, those enticing emerald orbs, seemed to beg him. He'd denied her enough. Perhaps he could consider it.

"Might I think on it, Sarah?"

"Aye, of course." She relaxed, even chuckled slightly.

"Then shall we go back? I'd like to officially meet Wee John."

He stood and held the door for her, following her back up the stairs to Wee Joseph's room.

His son had crawled up on Bridget's lap. Letting the baby hold onto his finger, he sang the lullaby Sarah often sang to him.

Joseph's heart caught in his throat.

How could he deny this to his family? And this babe would obviously receive more love here than anywhere else.

He reached out to take Wee John from Bridget. "Let me see this laddie."

"Be careful, Da. Him's little."

After adjusting the baby in the crook of his arm, he ruffled Wee Joseph's dark curls. "I will, son." He caught Sarah's gaze and nodded. Her smile said everything he'd hoped.

This could be an answer to his prayer.

If he had prayed.

"Why must ye again leave? Ye've only been home a few weeks." Sarah stood in the doorway and watched Joseph pack his bag. At least this time he explained first.

"Now that Jacques is a justice of the peace, he cannot leave as easily as before. He's too busy sending the pirate spies to Dublin. I need to do the traveling for our business. It will not be as long as the last trip." He never glanced up but kept putting things into his bag.

The trips were a convenient escape. She knew it as sure as she knew her name. He didn't trust himself with her for long. And that was a good sign. Maybe.

Wee John slept in her arms, finally resting after she'd paced the floor a good hour. She still swayed from side to side, hoping the motion kept him asleep. "Do ye need me to fetch anything for ye?

"No. Thank you. It looks like your hands are full." He peeked up at that and smiled.

It stabbed her heart.

How could he believe everything would be fixed because they adopted a baby? Aye, God had filled a part of her that had been empty. But a baby didn't replace a missing husband.

"Why are ye running away again? I've done as ye asked." Why did she say that? She didn't want to argue, and she didn't want him to leave on an angry note.

She didn't want him to leave at all.

"I am not running away. I've explained. Sarah, please understand."

Her temper was getting the best of her, and she felt too tired to fight it. She flipped back a loose tendril with her wrist. "And why is it that I am the one who must always understand? When are ye going to ken I need a husband?"

Hot tears started down her cheeks. She swiped her arm across her face, disturbing Wee John who began to howl.

"Och. I am tired and hurting and angry and not wanting this conversation right now. Ye promised in yer letter we would talk when ye came home, but ye have yet to keep yer promise." She put Wee John to her shoulder. "Unlike ye, this babe needs me." She turned on her heel. Storming into the nursery, she plopped into the rocker.

"Shh, wee one, shh."

She funneled her temper in rocking, but Wee John would not be pacified.

Putting him in the crook of her arm, she kissed his head. "Then cry, love. Cry for both of us.

He should have seen that coming. And Sarah was right. He hadn't kept his promise to talk about things when he came home. But now with the baby, Joseph had hoped they wouldn't need to talk.

There had been little time to have such a discussion. Wee John claimed Sarah's attention all through the day and night.

Buckling his portmanteau closed, Joseph decided he would write her from Dublin. He could tell her things in writing that his voice wouldn't say. Couldn't say.

But he didn't want to leave without good-bye. Tiptoeing to the boys' room, he watched as she rocked and crooned. The poor little one seemed to be wearing himself out.

Sarah raised her gaze. He could see she still cried. Why did he have to hurt her like that?

"Ye can go. God will keep us safe."

Joseph could feel the angry response start to rise. She baited him, and he wanted to snap back.

Her eyes, boring into his heart, stopped the ugly retort. She had told him the truth. She was tired and hurt. It would do no good to hurt her more.

He swallowed his pride. "God be with you then."

And he left.

❦

AT DAWN, A FEW DAYS LATER, SARAH STOOD IN HER kitchen heating Wee John's milk and bouncing him on her hip when someone pounded at her back door.

She hesitated, not knowing whether to open it or not. Leaning to the side of the door, she called out, "Who is it? I have a pistol and I'm not afraid to shoot." She inspected her empty hands and hoped God would forgive her ruse.

"It's James Fontaine. My father sent me to bring you and the children to our house."

Sarah unlatched the door and swung it open. He closed it, quickly re-latching it.

"French corsairs have just pulled into the harbor, and my father has a bad feeling about it. You will be safer with us."

James, a skinny young man of twenty years, appeared to be a younger version of his father. His brown hair was windblown, and his brown eyes shone in earnest.

She didn't take the time to thoroughly question him. An urgency in her heart spurred her on.

Bridget, possibly from hearing the noise, came into the kitchen area, tying on an apron and sporting a wide yawn.

"Take Wee John for me, please, Bridget. His milk should be about ready. I will go wake Wee Joseph and dress him. What should we take with us?"

"Where are we going, Mistress Sarah?"

"To our house," James said. "And bring only what is most necessary for now."

"Aye, then. Come with me." Sarah motioned for him to follow her. She led him to her sons' room. "I will take the rocker and the cradle. And we will need nappies for Wee John. Do ye know how long I should plan for?"

Young master Fontaine shook his head. "There is no way to

know. It looks to be retaliation for my father sending the spies off to Dublin."

She took a moment to think.

I will supply your needs, Sarah.

She nodded and bent over to wake Wee Joseph. "Son, we're going to go visit Elizabeth, yer friend. Shall we get dressed?"

He nodded his sleepy head, rubbing his fists at his eyes.

"Faster, now, son." She helped him into his clothes and sent him down to Bridget.

James picked up the rocker, and Sarah put the nappies and changes of clothes in a bag and added it to the cradle before hoisting it to her hip.

"Wait." Sarah thought of something and thanked God for reminding her. Setting the cradle down, she ran to Joseph's room.

She felt guilty entering without his invitation, but she knew he would want her to do this. It was nestled in a box on his table. Leaving the box, she grabbed the Huguenot cross pin from his father and sped to her room. There she took her Bible from its place and carried both back to where James waited. Sarah pinned the cross to the blanket lying in the cradle and added her Bible to the bag. "Now I am ready."

She followed him down the steps.

Chapter Thirty-Seven

S arah locked her house, carrying the cradle full of
necessary items. They trudged to the Fontaine fortress,
like gypsy refugees Sarah thought. James led the way,
carrying the rocker and holding a pistol Sarah hadn't noticed
until they stepped out her door. Bridget followed, holding Wee
John in one arm and Wee Joseph's hand with her free one. Sarah
brought up the rear.

They made good time up the bluff where the sturdy stone
house with slate roofing stood proud over the harbor. The
French privateer could easily be seen from that vantage point.

They arrived minutes before Jacques, who had mustered
neighbors into helping with a ruse. He returned, and after Anne
found refreshment for his men, he briefly told her and Sarah
what had happened.

"I knew that ship could not stay where she was and our
house withstand the cannonade. Only twenty men were available, so I handed out the muskets, and we pretended to hide
ourselves so they would see us but think we didn't want notice.
Once we reached the top of the bluff directly over the cove, I
placed the men behind that large rock there and stood alone on
top of it, knowing they could see me. Then I had the men peek

out from one side and made a pretense of being angry at their showing themselves. When I turned my head, the men peeked out the other side and I did the same thing. I hoped our enemy would think we had twice the number of supporters as are truly here." Jacques rubbed his hands together and chuckled. "And it worked dear wife, praise God. We truly hid ourselves well on the way back as soon as we saw them move their ship. They are still out there, but in not so dangerous a position."

He scrutinized the windows. "We'll need to shore up the openings and make sure we have our high ground well manned."

While Jacques set about placing his men, of which only seven of the original remained, Anne and Sarah began pulling beds apart and filling in the exposed areas with mattresses. Bridget took Wee Joseph and John along with Anne's Elizabeth and Moses to the study, away from the outer walls of the house.

Sarah watched Jacques climb to one of the towers over the door. He called down. "The lieutenant is advancing with several of his men. Their pistols are drawn." The reverberation of the blunderbuss followed by a pistol's shot made her jump. "The lieutenant is down. He tried to shoot at me, but God's hand protected. I need another firearm."

The lieutenant's men removed his body while Jacques searched for another ready weapon. The quiet ended all too quickly, though, as another band of men were dispatched from the ships, and two small cannons began firing from the north.

Sarah heard the small children scream, and her own terror grew with each burst of powder.

Jacques's voice rang. "Courage my dear children, their cannon balls have no more effect on our stone walls than if they were so many apples."

Very noisy apples, but somehow that eased her fear. Some.

One of the men, John McLiney, fired from his window over-looking the cannon on the shore. "I tell ye, I'm not hitting a thing." He reloaded, adding a double charge of powder into his musket and fired. "There. Ye'll not be doing that again." The death of the one who manned that cannon caused the enemy to move the big guns to a more sheltered spot. It also made the cannon less able to do as much harm.

One more prayer answered. God continued to provide.

Another one of Jacques's men, Paul Roussier, constructed a type of rampart of sheep's fleeces. He was a soldier by trade and had one of his young officers keeping his muskets loaded, though it was obvious to Sarah the young officer had as much experience in battle as she had. She helped Ann distribute more powder and ammunition to the rooms. Overhead, the recruit cried out to Anne, "Alas. My dear lady, we are undone. It would be the height of folly to attempt to resist any longer when our arms are in bad order; here are no less than three useless muskets."

But Anne's response was clear. "We are in the hands of the Almighty, and nothing can befall us without His permission. I trust He will not suffer us to fall into the hands of these wicked men. We must not lose our courage but try if we cannot repair what is defective."

Once she left the room, Anne pulled Sarah aside. "Please continue to see that the men have what they need. I will report the malfunction to my husband and return shortly."

Sarah continued on and a while later overheard Jacque laugh from Roussier's room. "There is no problem which cannot be quickly remedied. This one is in want of a flint. This contains some dirt in the touch hole and this third has two cartridges in it, one on top of the other with a ball below both next to the touch hole. I will make these right immediately. You continue to help Monsieur Roussier." Jacques brought the three muskets out with him and asked Anne for a sewing needle to help with the repairs.

Anne went straight for her kit near an open window.

Sarah's heart jumped to her throat. "Get down, Anne!"

Anne immediately stooped, turning back with a silly grin. "God has protected so well, I did not think to get low."

She took the needle to her husband before going to check on the children. Sarah followed her to the study. Bridget sat on the floor in the corner, Wee John held tightly in her arms. The other children crowded around her, their faces buried in her skirts.

Sarah moved to comfort the children, but Anne restrained her. "It is the noise from the slates that frightens them. In here, they only experience the noise." She turned to the children. "Courage my children, we are in the hands of God. And it is not fear that will ensure our safety; on the contrary, God will bless our courage. Drive away all fear if you can and leave the care of your persons to God."

Sarah shook her head. The words were too high for the little ones. But when she looked again, they all began to sit tall.

Little Moses peered at his mother. "God is our helper and shield."

Anne nodded.

"He takes care of us," quiet Elizabeth added.

Her mother agreed.

"Jesus loves us." Sarah had never been so proud of Wee Joseph.

The battle continued for many hours, the sounds of the cannonade never letting up. Anne and Sarah still passed out the powder and ammunition.

About three-thirty in the afternoon, Anne pulled her aside. "We began with twelve pounds of powder. That seemed like so much at the time, but now we are getting lower into the barrel. Sarah, we must pray for God's intervention, for I don't think this powder will last more than three hours at this rate, and if the men slow in their firing, the enemy may guess we are low on supply. Pray with me now."

Sarah clasped hands with Anne. "Almighty God, we have seen Thy hand of protection many times today in the midst of this battle. We give Thee our praise for Thy generosity and loving kindness. Thou knowest the state of our ammunition and stores. We pray Thee multiply it as Thou didst with the widow's oil. Or if Thou wilt not, then remove our enemy from us as Thou didst for King Hezekiah. Thou knowest the plans Thou hast for us, to prosper us and to do good for us. We beseech Thee to be our shield and defense, our high tower, our Holy Provider once again. We bring this petition to Thy throne of grace in the name of Thy Son, Jesus Christ. Amen."

Anne squeezed Sarah's hands and she squeezed back. They continued making their rounds. They had only been to two rooms when she heard Jacques. "They retreat. Running for their ship. Praise God."

Claude Bonnet, at the window of the room where she stopped to leave more supplies, leaned out and took aim. Someone fired from outside. The ricochet hit against the house before Monsieur Bonnet slumped to the floor. She cried out for Anne and rushed to him.

Bonnet struggled to sit and held his upper arm, blood dripping between his fingers.

"Let me look." She pulled his hand away from the wound and used the end of her skirt to halt the flow.

Anne rushed in. "Is he…"

"The lead hit the fleshy part. There doesn't seem to be any damage to the bone. But it is profusely bleeding."

"James, Peter, come help." Anne's sons ran immediately to her. "Help carry Monsieur Bonnet to your room. You still have a mattress on your bed?"

"Yes, Mother."

As the two women and two young men lifted the soldier, he protested.

Anne cut him off. "Monsieur, if you become faint, it would be harder to get you there. Please allow us to carry you."

The man relented, and they put him in the bedroom across the hall.

"Peter, bring two bottles of wine from downstairs. James, please bring me my sewing basket. Monsieur, we will have you repaired in no time."

James brought the wine and Anne gave one bottle to Bonnet. He drank it down quickly and, since none had eaten in many hours, the alcohol promptly helped him sleep.

Anne poured the second bottle of wine all over the wound as well as her needle and thread.

Sarah assisted as best she could, mainly doing as Anne directed. When done, the women cleaned up their makeshift surgery and left Bonnet to his dreams.

Downstairs, Jacques informed them that the corsair had weighed anchor and set sail. Everyone gathered around while Jacques led them in a prayer of thanksgiving after which Sarah and Anne fixed a quick meal.

By the time Sarah's head hit the pillow that night, she had more for which to be thankful. Closing her eyes, she could still hear Jacques rushing in with the news.

"Sarah, praise God. We went to see what damage we incurred and perhaps get a better idea what we inflicted on the enemy." He grabbed her by the shoulders. "Your house, Sarah, the whole of it. It is destroyed. Cannon shelling fell through the roof and knocked in walls. If God hadn't warned me to bring you and the children here, I don't know what would have happened." Jacques pulled her into a fatherly embrace. "Praise God you were here. Praise God you and your children are safe."

Curling up with Wee John in her arms, Sarah felt a blanket of peace settle over her. "Father, I do praise Ye and thank Ye for Yer loving kindness and protection. Yer teaching me more each day how Ye can protect against whatever happens. Yer my shield and defender, *in Thee I put my trust.*"

Kissing the baby's head, she closed her eyes and drifted off to sleep.

Chapter Thirty-Eight

ir, might I interest ye in a paper? Only a ha'penny, sir.
And all the news for the past weeks even from London
and Derry."

The waif appeared dirty and in need of a good meal. Joseph
flipped him a sovereign and took the pages from the boy's hand.

"Thank ye, sir. God bless ye, sir."

Joseph merely nodded his head and walked down the street,
all the news in the land tucked under his arm.

"Good afternoon, Master Crockett. A lovely day now,
isn't it?"

He nodded to the woman sweeping the steps in front of the
house where he'd rented a room. "Good afternoon, Mistress
Doyle."

Taking the steps two at a time, he unlocked his door and
tossed the paper on the bed. He removed his jacket and waistcoat before pulling off his boots. It had been a long, dismal day,
no matter what Mistress Doyle thought. It could have been
raining Noah's flood, and she still would have thought it a
grand day.

He stretched out on his bed and picked up the paper. It
seemed Charles XII of Sweden hadn't been satisfied to defeat the

Russian army. He now had toppled Augustus of Poland from his throne.

Dublin's high society read very much the same as London's. Change a name or two, and the very same things went on.

He turned the page and his heart stopped cold.

Bravery of Bantry Bay Minister Sends Pirates out to Sea

Jacques's name prominently displayed in the lead paragraph left little to the imagination. Pirates had attacked Bere Haven while he was gone.

He jumped out of bed and stepped on one of his boots. "Ow." Hopping on the other foot, he found his waistcoat and jacket and threw them on. Then he leaned against the bed's edge and pulled on his boots. In less than five minutes he had gathered all his belongings, paid Mrs. Doyle, and run out the door. Finding the first ship leaving toward Bantry Bay, he booked passage and climbed aboard.

The ship, the *Maeve*, would set sail in under an hour. If wishes would have moved her, he would've had the ship immediately to sea. He leaned against the rail and remembered the newspaper, now crumpled in his portmanteau. He dug it out and checked for the date.

According to the information, the attack happened eight days earlier.

Eight days.

He couldn't help it. The words flowed from his heart. "Lord, keep my family safe."

JOSEPH LEAPT TO THE DOCK THE INSTANT THE SHIP moored. As it pulled into the harbor, he'd tried to see their house, but it was still too dark this early in the morning.

Running with every ounce of strength he had, he rounded the bend to home and pulled up short.

There was nothing left. Only rubble and splinters lay about

where the house once stood, like some giant fist came down from the sky and smashed it as easily as a house of cards.

His mind gone blank, he stood frozen, rooted to the spot, staring at the rubble. Then one thought fought its way to his consciousness.

Sarah. He must find Sarah. He must find his family. Were they even alive?

No, his thoughts mustn't drift that way. Where would she go? Sarah and the boys were his whole life. He had to find her.

He had to.

The tower house. In the blink of an eye, he was pounding and pounding at the Fontaine's door. Jacques, in his nightshirt, opened.

Joseph pushed his way past. "Are they here? Where's Sarah?"

Anne, still in her nightcap and gown, reassured. "She is safe, Joseph. They all are safe."

Joseph's whole body shook. He gaped at Jacques, silently pleading, afraid to speak.

"Yes, Joseph, they are here."

He heard a rustle and turned.

A vision of Sarah, holding a candle, floated down the stairs toward him. Her lovely auburn hair tumbled loose and free. A wrapper tied about her slender waist. She set the candle down on the newel post and called his name.

"Joseph, we're safe. We're safe."

He cut her off from speaking more as he pulled her into his arms, weeping, holding her tight, never wanting to let her go. He was a starving man, she was his nourishment. The whole trip from Dublin, he'd worried that he'd lost her. And when he saw the house, he feared the worst.

"Good night, dear boy." Jacques patted his back and ushered Anne from the room.

Ever so slowly, Joseph allowed his hold on Sarah to relax. He stood in a fog of emotion. Her tears soaked into his shirt, raining on his heart. If he let go of her, he would be lost forever.

She turned in his arms and reached for the candle. He released all but her hand and let her lead him up the stairs. The touch of her fingers entwined in his generated an electric charge through his very being. She turned to look at him over her shoulder. Her smile melted his fear.

Once in the hall, she whispered in his ear, pointing to the door at the end of the hall. "Bridget sleeps in there with Wee Joseph and Anne's Elizabeth." They stopped before a different door. "Wee John is in here with me." She led him into a bedroom. Wee John slept in the cradle in the corner.

She closed the door and set the candle on the bed stand. But he refused to let go even then. Her other hand gently cupped his cheek, and he turned his head to kiss her open palm.

His desire for her outweighed his fear. Her wrapper hung loose now. His shaky fingers tenderly traced the curve of her face, remembering by touch the warmth of her skin. Wiping a tear from her cheek, he saw her for the first time in a very long while. He kissed her damp eyelids, her cheeks, her jawline, hearing the music of her moan. Weaving his fingers through her hair, he brought his mouth to hers.

The passion she returned left him without breath.

He closed his eyes and drank in her scent, her skin delectable, intoxicating, her hair, soft against his face.

When he opened his eyes, her fingers loosen the string at her neck. Her chemise softly slipped to the floor, forming a milky pool at her feet. As she trembled before him, he reached for her, wanting only her.

Scooping her into his arms, he laid her on the bed and blew out the candle.

❦

THE MORNING LIGHT BROUGHT WITH IT THE responsibilities and fears Joseph had endured their whole married life. Only now they were heightened.

He watched Sarah sleeping next to him. Her hair splayed against the pillows, her face relaxed and at peace.

And once again, terror gripped his heart in its vise. What had he done? What if she became pregnant and he lost her? *O God, please don't let her become pregnant. I don't want to live without her. I begged You on the ship to keep my family safe and You did. Now I plead, Lord, please. Don't take her from me. Don't let her be pregnant. Please, Lord, let her live.*

Her closeness brought more emotion than he could bear. He silently dressed. Wee John, in blissful slumber, lay curled in the cradle. Softly, he touched a kiss to his son's hand before he slipped away.

Once outside the house, he felt more control—more like his old self. He took in a deep breath, and the scene of where their home once stood returned to him. Praying it would be less daunting in daylight, he strode in the direction of the burned-out rubble.

SARAH SMILED BEFORE SHE WAS EVEN FULLY AWAKE. JOSEPH had returned home—her Joseph. Not the stranger she had been living with, or rather without. God answered another prayer. Joseph returned to Bere Haven and to her arms. Joseph, who loved her and found her desirable, Joseph who had made love to her like when they were first married. Her Joseph.

She rolled over to reach for him but found his side of the bed empty. Undaunted, Sarah breathed in his scent from the bedclothes, hugging his pillow. Yes, he really had come home. With her eyes closed, she remembered the look of love in his eyes, the feel of his touch.

Joseph had come home.

Joseph stood before his home, or what was left of it, wondering what to do. What could he do? If he rebuilt, there would be the same dangers. Shaking his head, he remembered all that had gone into building this home for Sarah and Wee Joseph. How Jacques and his sons, men from the village, and even many of the sailors, had all joined in to build her a proper house, not a cottage.

Jacques's uneven tread came up behind him, but Joseph didn't turn around.

"Shall we gather the men and start to work?"

"Not on this, I don't think, Jacques. Not on this. The pirates will only come again. I can't keep my family here."

Jacques gave a fatherly embrace and stood at Joseph's side. "I understand. Where do you plan to go?"

"I wish I knew." All he could do was stare at the ruins he once called home. "Will you buy me out of the business?"

"If that is what you wish. Have you prayed about this, Joseph?"

He shook his head. "I prayed, truly prayed for the first time in years when I sailed here. I prayed God would protect Sarah and the boys. I haven't let Him do the protecting. I haven't been happy about His way of doing things. But that was all I could do, Jacques. Every day just beg God to keep her and the boys safe. I don't know if I'm ready to ask for more at the moment."

The friend became the minister. "I will pray for you. Come. Let's walk away from this disaster. I believe my good wife has a hearty meal to break our fast, prepared and waiting."

He let his friend guide him to the house. More than a meal waited for him there, and he longed to run to her as much as he knew he should run in the other direction.

Delicious aromas greeted them as they arrived back at the house. He held the door for Jacques, putting off the moment a little longer.

The dining table sat ready for the family. Bridget carried a platter of hot cakes and Sarah followed with a bowl of butter in hand and Wee John in her other arm.

"Would ye hold him for me? I need to help Anne in the kitchen." She smiled, and handed the babe to him, letting her fingers linger in their touch. The sensation sent electricity through him, adding to his guilt.

Sarah returned to the other room while he adjusted the baby's blanket. Something hard was wrapped in the bunching. Straightening out the folds revealed his father's Huguenot Cross.

How?

"I got it out of yer room before we came here." Sarah stood by his side, another dish in her hand. "I'd forgotten I pinned it to that blanket. I don't think Wee John has even used that blanket the whole time we've been here. It's always been a different one. I must have forgotten."

He hadn't thought beyond their safety. To have lost this pin would have hurt since he valued it more than any of his other possessions. "Thank you. I'd just assumed it was lost."

He studied the pin again, and then he knew where they needed to go.

They would go to France.

Chapter Thirty-Nine

Think of what you are saying, Joseph." Jacques paced his office as if not content to sit behind the desk. "You are like a son to me. I know what it is like for Protestants there. Do you want to subject your family to that kind of prejudice?"

Joseph shook his head. "How many years ago was that, Jacques? The pirates are only a band of renegades, anyway. My father still has friends there, Jean-Luc de Turenne continues to correspond with him. And Albert de Grillet is back near Versailles." He grasped for ideas to back up his choice. "The export business would be less stressful under the French flag, and my family would be protected away from the corsairs."

"Is that what you think? The pirates are nothing compared to the dragoons. I have experienced them firsthand." Joseph had seen Jacques's fire and passion before, but never had it turn toward him. They had been friends and partners. This was not the way he wanted it to end.

"Jacques, you told me yourself you would pray that I would know where to go. Now I know, your prayer was answered. Will you buy me out?"

"I cannot change your mind?"

Joseph shook his head.

"Very well, I will buy you out, but let Sarah and the children stay with us until you have found them a home."

"Agreed. That would be better." He came around and hugged his friend. "Jacques, don't worry. God is working this out. You said so yourself." And perhaps he might start to believe it. God had protected Sarah and the children. Now if only she did not have to suffer for his weakness.

He closed his eyes and sent up one more prayer. "Now I need to tell Sarah."

❧

"You are leaving again? I dunna ken. Why Joseph? Why are you running away again?" Sarah had been so sure. Joseph had wanted her, and maybe that was the problem. "Ye do not trust yerself do ye? Ye've said all along ye didn't trust God, but really ye don't trust yerself."

Joseph opened his mouth as if to speak and stopped. Turning away, he grabbed his portmanteau from the corner of their room. It had yet to be unpacked. "Sarah, we cannot stay at Bere Haven. I am only searching for a place for us to live. Jacques and Anne will let you stay here until I return."

She grabbed his hand. "Ye did return, Joseph. But yer running again. I won't give up, though. God has not deserted me, and I know He'll bring my husband back."

He pulled his hand away and strode to the door. Pausing, he turned back, his eyes full of pain. "Sarah, I want to believe enough to trust. I do. But I don't yet. Do pray. Keep praying. I'll be back."

❧

So much for God's protection.

Joseph sat back on the old creepie and stared at the manacle around his ankle. Dirty, achy, and flea-bitten from the old rag they called a blanket, he doubted he would ever get out, let alone see Sarah or his sons again.

"Hey Crockett, you have a visitor." The guard brought another man to his cell, a man he'd never seen before.

Approximately his father's age, this man at one time stood much taller. Now time and life had rounded his shoulders and stooped his back.

But it had done nothing to his vocal cords. "Crockett? No, you mean Crocketagné. I knew his father. Almost as handsome as moi."

The guard opened the door and let the stranger in. The man swept off his hat with great flair and bowed. "Jean-Luc de Turenne, at your service."

"So, you are the famous Jean-Luc of whom my father speaks. I am Joseph Louis Crockett, and yes, it is Crockett. Father changed it when we moved." Joseph wiped his hand on his pants and held it out to the man.

"Nonsense." Jean-Luc pushed the hand away and wrapped him in a strong hug. "Whew, you stink, boy. Let us get you away from here." Turning, he called over his shoulder, "Guard."

The little sentry returned and unlocked the cell for Jean-Luc. The big man paused, his hand on a bar. "I will return. Do not go anywhere." He shuffled on his way.

Funny man. But if Jean-Luc could get him out, Joseph would laugh all day at his humorous quips.

True to his word, though, Jean-Luc returned less than an hour later, an hour that had dragged as slowly as thirty years. The same little guard escorted him to Joseph's cell and unlocked the door. "Are you coming?"

Joseph glanced at Jean-Luc and then at his ankle.

"Oh, but of course. How stupid of me. Monsieur, see to his manacle."

And the guard did.

Joseph rubbed his leg and walked out, looking over his

shoulder for someone to shove him back in and say it was all a joke.

Jean-Luc draped his meaty arm over Joseph's shoulders and leaned in. "You just have to know how to talk to people." He clapped Joseph on the back. Joseph thought he felt every one of the bones in his spine crack. "First we get you out of here and to a bath." As they walked into the sun's light he added, "Maybe clean clothes too, no? Then we can go for a ride."

"A ride?" Was he being kidnapped?

"You are here, so close to where your father and Albert and I had our famous exploits. You would not want to leave without seeing that, now would you?" Jean-Luc's laughter made him question what was humor and what was to be taken seriously.

But the idea of bathing and clean clothes helped him to be more agreeable. After all, the man had just gotten him released from a French jail after five months of being forgotten. The least he could do would be to see what Jean-Luc had in mind.

❧

"So, how did you know where to find me?" While soaking in the bathtub, Joseph had thought of many questions. Now, more comfortable in clean clothes, he was ready for some answers as they sat eating at a table in the corner of the local pub.

At the beginning of his incarceration, he had tried to get word to someone who might help. After so long without a word, he had given up on any message getting through.

"I happen to have a great appetite." Jean-Luc behaved as if that explained everything.

Joseph gave him the look his father used to give him when he only had half the story.

Jean-Luc roared with laughter. "That, that is the look of your father. You are his son. I would know that look anywhere."

"But that isn't all of the story. I would like to know how you found me."

"True. But it is the beginning. When I was younger, women and wine soothed my appetite. Now that I am more mature, food has taken over the care of my passion. So, I was enjoying a lovely meal when I happened to overhear a conversation. The guards at your jail are not as discreet as their employer might think." Jean-Luc leaned in to whisper. "You apparently wrote some notes looking for help? Well, they intercepted them, hoping to expand their fortunes. Little did they know, I sat at the next table and overheard every word. So, I finished my meal and sought you out. And that is the whole of my story."

Joseph took a bite of his dinner, struggling with the coincidence. He didn't want to believe God helped him when it had taken so long.

"And now, it is my turn." Jean-Luc cut into his meat and stabbed a large piece. Plopping it into his mouth, he spoke around the food. "Wha ig oo do?"

"Pardon?"

The big man swallowed. "What did you do? You know, to be stuck in such lovely accommodations."

"Oh." He still wondered about that himself. "I arrived aboard a ship and got off at Calais where I purchased a horse. I spent the night in the town with plans to leave the next day. But guards broke into my room before dawn. They dragged me to the cell. I wasn't even given a trial. When I asked about it, I was ignored. At least I know why I was allowed paper and quill at first."

Jean-Luc wiped his sleeve across his mouth. "So that is their game. I wondered. You, my friend, purchased a stolen horse. But not really stolen. The owner sells it to you and then reports it stolen. You are arrested and allowed to contact help by note. They use the information in the note to get money for your release." He slapped the table as if his hand were a gavel. "But they didn't count on me. And they didn't count on my connections to those in authority over them. Their days of this little game are numbered, I'm afraid. But someone else will find another game, so do not let down your guard."

Jean-Luc threw a few francs on the table and stood. Joseph followed suit. The men went upstairs to the room Jean-Luc had rented.

With only one bed, Jean-Luc tossed Joseph a blanket from his pack and then took the bed for himself. "Get some rest for tomorrow we ride."

He put the blanket on the floor and stretched out. Though not as good as a bed, it was much better than the cell. "Where are we going?"

"Joseph, my boy, how can you ask? We ride to Versailles."

THREE DAYS LATER, JOSEPH RODE UP BEHIND JEAN-LUC TO a country house near Versailles.

"Wait here." The big man dismounted, shuffled up to the door and pounded. "Open up, I've brought a guest."

The door swung open. "Oh, you great oaf, come in, come—"

Joseph spotted his mother's best friend, Mimi de Grillet.

She ran from the house to where he still obediently sat on his horse. "Joseph Louis Crockett. Come in. Oh, Jean-Luc, you made him sit out here."

He dismounted and Tanté Mimi immediately hugged him. He kissed her cheek and walked with her into the parlor.

"Oh my, I cannot believe you are here. Tell me, how is Sarah? And Wee Joseph? Please I want to hear all."

No, not everything. But he did tell her about Wee John and Wee Thomas. She squeezed his hand, and a tear rolled down her cheek. When he told about the pirates and how everyone was safely with the Fontaines, he could see the excitement in her eyes. "And so, I had thought to move us to France."

"Oh, my. I am surprised. I did not expect to hear that."

Jean-Luc remained with them. He cocked an eyebrow once or twice while Joseph talked, but never once said a word.

"When will Albert return?"

"I expect him anytime. He has gone to look at a new horse."

Jean-Luc stood. "I think I will wait for him outside." The older man shuffled out the door.

"He is such a contrast. His voice booms, and he seems full of laughter and joking. But he moves like an old man who is tired of life. I don't understand him."

"His friends all married and had families. In fact with you, his friend's son has a family. Jean-Luc flirted and loved all the ladies. Oh, he was so charming in those days. His life was full of adventure and risk, but he missed out on the one adventure he really wanted. You will find he has a heart of gold. I do not know how he was a soldier with so tender a heart." Mimi stood. "We've been talking all this time, and I never offered you tea. May I get you some?"

"Yes, I would like that." He followed her to the kitchen while she prepared a tray.

"I am so glad you are here, Joseph. I have wanted to tell you something for a long time, but the opportunity never presented itself."

"What did you want to tell me?"

"Besides how proud I am of you and the wonderful man you have turned out to be?" She tweaked his chin. "I want to thank you for all you tried to do for our Alain-Robert. Your mother learned from Shannon what you did, and how hard you worked to save my son. Thank you. You are a good man, Joseph." Though her lashes were damp, she didn't cry. Rather she gave him a motherly kiss on the cheek before she picked up the tray of tea and scones.

He took it from her, carrying it back to the parlor.

They had just poured when Albert and Jean-Luc entered.

He stood and Albert rushed to him, hugging him the same

as Jean-Luc. "Joseph, you do not know how glad I am to see you. And I know Our Father in Heaven arranged this."

"You do?"

"Oui. Sit, sit. I will tell you how I know. I received a letter today, *today* from your mother. They are worried because no one has heard from you. Sarah wrote to them that you had come to France but had heard nothing more. They asked if I could find information."

"Perhaps, then, you are right. Maybe God has orchestrated my release." Joseph still didn't want to admit it to himself, though.

"Wait, that is not all. Joseph, I have news that is hard. Your father is not well. They have asked that if I find you, to see you get home to Edenmore without delay."

"My father? He hasn't been sick in his whole life. Are you sure?" Though he knew Albert wouldn't have told him if it weren't true, he hoped for something, anything to show it was a mistake.

"I am sorry, Joseph, and I know you have not had much time to rest…"

"No, no, that's not it. I…I need to leave." He stood. "Tanté Mimi, thank you, Jean-Luc, I don't think I can thank you enough. *Oncle* Albert—" Joseph drew Albert into a hug. "I must go."

"Wait, we are taking care of that. My new horse, it is swift and strong. Jean-Luc and I will ride with you to Calais and get you aboard ship. If we can just get you to Dublin, you can go overland from there."

Joseph paused. In the heat of planning, an important point was missed. "I have no money. My bag, my purse, everything was taken when I was arrested."

"Arrested?" Mimi's question reminded him he hadn't shared that bit of information.

Albert shook his head. "I will tell you all after we have him on the ship, my love, but for now, that problem is nothing."

Jean-Luc must have explained everything to Oncle Albert before they came in. Albert went to another room and returned with a purse, putting it into Joseph's hand. "This should get you home to Edenmore and to Bantry Bay after."

"I can't accept this." Joseph tried to hand the purse back.

"You cannot refuse. Joseph, I owe you more than I can pay for all you did for my son. Please, allow me to help the son of the best man I ever knew."

He is the best man I ever knew. And he may be dying. "Thank you." He could hardly get the words out for the catch in his throat.

If only he could make it there in time.

Chapter Forty

The house appeared deserted. Fear clenched Joseph's heart as he rode up to Edenmore Manor. Leaving his horse out front, he mounted the steps and hesitated. Did he knock? Just go in?

The door pulled from his hand, and Lucy flew into his arms. "Joseph you are here. Thank God. We didn't know what happened to you." She dragged him through the doorway.

He gazed about, taking in the timelessness of home. "Is Father…"

"He's upstairs in his room." She started up the staircase and he followed. "No one knows why, but he's still alive. Mother thinks he's been holding on for you."

When they arrived at the door, Lucy opened it and stepped back for Joseph to enter.

He wasn't prepared for what he saw. His father, always a virile man, appeared old and frail on the bed. His eyes were closed, but his chest rose and fell with a rhythm that proved breathing. Joseph blinked the moisture.

His mother sat on a creepie next to the bed. When he walked in, she glanced up. The joy in her face brought more tears to his eyes. "Joseph, you are home. Thank God." She stood, a bit slowly, and embraced him, kissing his cheek.

"How is he?" Joseph hoped to hear something other than what he could see.

"Why do you not ask me?" His father's eyes opened, and a slow smile came to his face.

Joseph sat on the creepie his mother had vacated and grasped his father's hand. "Then tell me, Father, how do you fare?"

"Better, son. Your mother has been worried about you, and you know how that bothers me."

The corner of Joseph mouth twitched at his father's humor. "I heard you felt neglected and wanted some attention."

"Oui, son, but I'm sure there are better ways of getting attention than dying."

The smile faded. "Father, don't talk that way."

"Son, we all know it. Everyone must at some time leave this life for the next. I have lived a remarkable life with a remarkable woman. I have been blessed beyond what most people could ever imagine." His father's grip strengthened. "I hope I have left you all a legacy in what I believed. Joseph, there came a night when I needed to make a choice, a choice for my family, a choice for the future. There would be no going back, whatever I chose. As I wrestled with it, I opened my Bible. This is what God showed me." Antoine closed his eyes. "A wicked man shows a bold face but as for the upright, he makes his way sure. There is no wisdom and no understanding and no counsel against the Lord. The horse is prepared for the day of battle, but victory belongs to the Lord."

He had heard that Scripture many times, and the story behind it. But this time it was different. It was a baton his father passed, a battle cry of the spirit.

"So, my son, make sure you are right, then go ahead. How do you make sure? You rely on the counsel of the Lord. Trust him, Joseph. Trust God." Antoine's voice faded, and the grip on Joseph's hand slackened.

His mother touched his shoulder. "Go rest from your trip, son. I am glad you are home. We will talk again later."

He stood, allowing her the stool once more.

Lucy waited in the hall. "Daniel put your horse in the stable and brought your bag up. I've put you in your old room."

He nodded, suddenly very tired. He tried to stifle a yawn, but Lucy caught him.

She gave him a playful elbow in the ribs. "Don't worry about it. Go rest. I'll wake you for dinner."

He gave her a hug and noticed something. Holding her away from him, he stared at her abdomen, which appeared a tad fuller.

"Lucy?"

"Yes, big brother?"

"Are you…?"

"Am I what? Gaining weight?" She slugged his arm. "Am I expecting a baby? Is that what you are trying to ask?"

The heat rose in his cheeks.

"You are so adorable, Joseph. Yes, Daniel and I are expecting our second baby in about four more months. You will be an uncle again."

"Again? How old is your other one? A boy? Girl?" He should know this. Why hadn't Sarah told him? Because he avoided her, giving her no time to share anything.

Lucy gave him a funny look. "Daniel and I have a little girl. She is a year old as of last month. Her name is Rebecca Louise."

"May I ask you something?"

"Of course."

"Does it ever frighten you? Or Daniel, does it ever frighten him?

"What do you mean?"

"Giving birth, all the possibilities…"

Lucy wrapped her arm about his waist. "No. Well, since Daniel doesn't have to do it, I'd say no for him. Maybe, for me, a little bit, before Rebecca was born, but no. Life is a gift, Joseph.

I have to trust the Gift Giver since He is the One who knows it all. I don't pretend to know. But as long as He does, I will trust Him."

Joseph gave her a squeeze and planted a kiss on top of her head. "Wake me up in time for dinner, please."

"I said I would." She started to close the door.

"And, Lucy, thank you."

She blew him a kiss and closed the door.

He laid down on his bed and fell asleep.

TRUE TO HER WORD, LUCY WOKE HIM IN TIME TO EAT WITH the family. Everyone was there but his father, whose chair remained empty. Gabriel was home with his new bride, Agnes. Sarah Beth and Ian MacKenzie sat near them. Lucy and Daniel were seated on Joseph's left, and Robert and his fiancée, Rachel Watkins, were to Joseph's right. Mary Frances, who still lived at home, was seated between Robert and Joseph. James and his wife, Martha, sat directly across from him, and his mother took her seat at the end of the table opposite her husband's chair.

The family had grown. And this didn't even include all of the nieces and nephews.

Or Sarah.

By all rights Sarah should have been there at his side. As much as he loved his little sister, Mary Frances made a poor substitute for a wife.

Mary O'Toole had taken the job of housekeeper for the family. Her son Liam helped out on the estate and they lived in Joseph's old cottage.

So many changes. How could it be the same and yet so different?

Mistress O'Toole turned out to be an outstanding cook. The meal, excellent. When it was over, his mother touched his shoulder as she left the table. "I know James wants to speak with you, so when you are through, please come find me. It will be my turn." She patted his cheek and left the room. He knew he'd find her with his father.

James came around the table and held out his hand. "Welcome home, Joseph. I have missed you more than you know."

Joseph pulled him into an embrace.

"Come, let's talk." James led the way to their father's study.

Joseph hesitated, though he couldn't say why.

James entered first, walking around to Antoine's chair. He sat, leaning his elbow on the desk.

"Get up."

"What? What is the matter?" James squinted his eyes, bewildered.

"Get up. That's father's chair. Get up." Joseph shook. Try as he might, he couldn't tolerate James in the chair. Yet he couldn't say why.

James stood, hands in surrender. "What is the matter with you? I just want to talk to you about something."

"I don't know… no, I do know. James, I fight for control of my life, of the lives of my family and everywhere I turn, someone is on that side of the desk telling me what to do."

"You can sit there, and I'll sit across from you." James came out from behind the desk, but Joseph knew that wasn't the real problem.

"No, I can't sit there, either. I have tried, but I can't do it. I think I make the best decision for everyone, and no matter how hard I try it all comes apart."

James came to him, concern pulling worry lines together on his forehead, and grasped Joseph by the shoulders. "I don't understand. Tell me how to help you."

"Father says to make sure you are right, then go ahead. How do you make sure? How do you hear God's counsel? And how do you trust God after all He's done?" He leaned back against the wall.

James dropped his grip. "That's what I want to talk to you about. This is hard, Joseph and I'm hoping you can help me."

Other people had problems too. It was time to stop thinking he was the only one. Joseph nodded and sat.

James perched on the edge of the desk rather than sit in their father's chair. "Robert and I have been talking, doing some planning. We think we can get around some of the export problems by starting a business in the colonies. There's a group of Huguenots ready to leave for New Rochelle in two months. That would give you time to return home, pack up and return with plenty of time."

"But why me? You and Robert can't do this?"

"Robert loves to travel and would be good for the exporting portion, but no one knows the sheep or the growing of flax like you do. If we sent over the basics and grew the products over there, we could export them to all of Europe and not have to worry about it. You would be able to run the operation there. What do you think?"

"What of the colony? Would there be Indian raids? How hard are the conditions?"

"Robert went over a few months ago. He came back more excited than I'd ever seen. There are cities going up there, Joseph. It is becoming civilized." James brought out a map of New Amsterdam. "If you are worried about your family's welfare, don't. There's wilderness aplenty, but the area we are looking at has a large community of Huguenot believers. The trip is about three weeks over, and you have been aboard ship before. You know those conditions."

"Five months ago, I wouldn't have even listened. Today, I think it might work." A weight lifted from his shoulders. "This just might work."

"Then I will purchase the passages for your family along with Robert and Rachel's fare, and we will start the planning."

Joseph stood to leave.

"There is one more thing, and you cannot tell anyone else. Sarah, yes, but no one else."

He returned to the chair. "What is it?"

"Martha, my wife. You don't know her, Joseph, but she's a very loving lady. She is good and kind and loves our son." James stood and began to pace. "But that's the problem. When we first were married, she was a kind mother to Samuel, and he loved her back. But then we had Adam. And she changed. Oh, not that she was ever mean to Samuel, but even he noticed the change. She finally told me since Samuel isn't my blood relation, she will insist our Adam inherits Edenmore as firstborn. I tried to tell her I'm not even the firstborn, and only God knows how things will go. But she is insistent. Will you take my Samuel with you to the colonies?"

Joseph wasn't sure he correctly heard. "The boy is what...seven now? He needs his parents."

"I agree, but if he stays here it will get worse. I know he will discover what's going on. Please. Have him sign for land there; they'll let him if you sign with him. Sarah was always good to Samuel; she'd be the mother he needs. I promised Shannon I'd take care of him, but if he stays, I don't think that will happen."

"What will you tell him?"

"That he is old enough to be part of the family business and that he will be helping us. He's a strong lad, and clever. And he has a kind heart, just like Shannon."

"Does he know about Shannon?"

"He knows that I married her and adopted him."

"Did you ever make the adoption legal?"

'No, and that's what Martha holds over me. Please, Joseph. Will you help me?"

Joseph closed his eyes, trying to make sure. "Yes."

James relaxed again, sitting back on the edge of the desk.

"What does Robert know?"

"Nothing yet. But I will tell him before you leave."

Joseph stood and embraced his brother. Other people

certainly had problems. It was time he stopped making more of his than necessary.

⚜

Tapping lightly at the door, Joseph peeked in to see if his mother sat with his father. Of course, he knew that was where she would be. And she was. Still seated on the creepie, holding her husband's hand.

"Mother?"

She peered at him and smiled. Joseph came to her rather than make her stand again, draping his arm lightly across her shoulders. Her hair shone silver in the candlelight and her skin had a soft parchment appearance. She leaned her brow against his side, and he kissed her head.

"We have been together more than thirty years, Joseph. I don't know what I will do."

More than anything, Joseph wanted to speak a comforting word, but he didn't know any. Any Scripture he might quote, his mother already knew by heart.

So he stood with his arm about her shoulder, letting her lean on him all that she needed.

⚜

Joseph didn't sleep well. There were things to settle in his soul, but he didn't want to open that door. Not right now when his father's death lay imminent.

Rising before dawn, he pulled on his breeches and stockings, leaving the tails of his shirt loose. He tiptoed to his parents' room, pushing the door ajar. His mother still sat on the creepie, only now her head rested on the bed, over his father's hand. He walked softly to her, not wanting to suddenly wake her. Perhaps he could encourage her to rest on his bed and he could keep vigil with his father.

Softly he placed his hand on her back, but immediately pulled away.

He brought the low candle over near her face. The flame never flickered. With mounting grief, he moved the light to examine his father. The rise and falling rhythm of yesterday's breathing had vanished in the night, taking his mother's breath with it.

He returned the candle to the table.

THE HORSE PICKED HIS WAY UP THE PATH TO THE HOUSE. Joseph felt a rush of excitement mixed with dread as the Fontaines' home loomed before him.

He had practiced all he wanted to say, how he loved her and if she would trust him again, he would try to trust God to care for them. Maybe they could have a normal marriage. He was willing to think about it if she could be patient with him. He still felt terrified, but seeing his parents together that fateful morning—together in life, together in death—made him want to have that closeness, that depth of relationship with Sarah.

They must pack and be ready to move. Not that there was much to pack. But they had less time to do it in than originally planned. Joseph had stayed for the funeral and then the reading of his father's will. Gabriel had been named the executor, but James inherited Edenmore, just as everyone expected. But his father had been generous with his money to all his children, so Joseph had means once again to care for his family.

Delicious aromas of the evening meal's preparation wafted on the breeze as he pulled to a stop. Dismounting, he chose to walk the rest of the way.

Three children, two boys and a girl, sat on the stop step throwing small stones toward the edge of the bluff. It took a strong arm to even come close, but one little boy in particular tried very hard on his turn.

"Well done, Wee Joseph. Well done."

The little boy with dark curls and a missing front tooth glanced up. Recognition flooded his features and he jumped from the step. "Da." Running, he jumped into Joseph's outstretched arms and clung with five-year-old might to his father's neck.

Joseph held him close, savoring the feel of his son's embrace.

"Da, I'm so glad yer home."

"So am I, son."

Wee Joseph wiggled down and ran for the house. "Mama. Da's home. Da's home." He tore through the door and out of sight, though his voice still reverberated. "Da's home."

Joseph walked up the three steps to the door. Wee Joseph came running back, dragging the most beautiful woman in the world with him. Pulling her hand to Joseph's, he stepped back, giving his father the full view.

Joseph dropped the clasp and stared.

Sarah was with child.

Chapter Forty-One

Wee Joseph, would ye go outside with Elizabeth and Moses, please?" Sarah's gaze never left Joseph's face.

"But Da's home. I want to stay here."

"Do as I say, son. Ye'll soon have time with yer father."

Wee Joseph scuffed the toe of his shoe at the floor before grudgingly doing as he was told.

"I'm glad yer home, Joseph. We've missed ye."

He continued to stare, not saying a word.

"Perhaps we should go to the parlor?" Sarah reached for his hand to lead him, but he pulled back. "Joseph, we can talk in private." She turned and hoped he would follow. When he did, she raised a quick prayer of thanks.

She'd known this would be a shock. If he had come straight home from France the way he had said, she could have better prepared him. But without even knowing where he was for more than five months, and then with his parents' deaths, she couldn't just mention it in a letter.

Gratefully, he'd sent her one, enclosed in one from Albert explaining what had happened. Then she received the post from Lucy about Antoine and Louise.

Perhaps it wasn't fair. She'd been privy, though after the fact, of what transpired for him, yet he had no way of knowing what waited for him in Bere Haven.

Sarah sat on the settee, allowing space for Joseph. He chose a chair.

Finally, he found his voice. "You are with child."

Sarah nodded. "Aye."

She could see him wanting to ask, and not wanting to ask. "Joseph, aye, this is yer babe, There is no other."

He put his head in his hands. "I know. I'm sorry to even have thought that. I know, Sarah. I do not doubt."

"Lucy tells me we are to soon leave for the colonies."

"We were. Now we cannot."

"Why?"

His head shot up. "Why, indeed. I cannot take you across this island and to a ship where you will live for three weeks when you are so close to your confinement."

"I am not in my confinement yet, and if we leave soon, I will be confined aboard the ship anyway." She smiled, hoping he'd see the humor.

He didn't. "Who would be there to help you?"

"Ye, of course. Joseph, ye'd not be the first man to deliver a babe, nor the last, I'm thinking. I will be at home wherever you are. I don't want to wait behind again. In fact, I cannot. Anne and Jacques are considering leaving Bere Haven themselves. They've had quite enough and are considering a move to Dublin to open a school."

Joseph stood, his back turned to her, his forehead resting on his palm.

Again, she sent up a silent prayer and hoped this last would not be too much for her husband to handle.

Again, You force. I plead for help to trust You, and You

bring me the impossible. How can I take Sarah across the Atlantic in her condition? How?

He turned to see her, serene and at peace. And more beautiful than ever. "Sarah, how can I take you on a ship while you are with child? If you have a problem, there is no help. I know what to do with sheep—just watch. I wouldn't know what to do to help you. How do I keep you safe?"

"Joseph, Who has kept me safe thus far? He is still there whether I am aboard ship or left behind without ye. I just don't want to again be left behind without ye." Tears stood in her eyes, but she wiped them away.

"I will take you to Edenmore. You can stay with James and Martha until things are settled and I will come back for you."

"No! Please Joseph, ye cannot leave me again. I don't think I could bear it."

He shook his head and left the house. Walking to the docks, he found Jacques at the little office they'd built together.

"You are leaving Bere Haven?" Joseph didn't even give the man time to stand. "What am I to do? What about Sarah?"

"Joseph, welcome home. Sit"

Joseph did, and for once, the desk in between didn't bother him. "What am I to do, Jacques? How can I take Sarah on a voyage over the Atlantic when she carries a child? How?"

"Is that what you are supposed to do?"

Is it? He wasn't even sure about that now.

Wasn't sure. His father's words echoed. *Make sure you are right, son, then go ahead. Rely on the counsel of the Lord. Trust God.* How?

His gaze fell on the old worn Bible on Jacques's desk. "May I borrow that?" He nodded at the book.

Jacques picked it up and handed it to him. "Of course."

"I think I'll go for a walk." He didn't even turn to say goodbye. Rather he was thumbing through the pages before he crossed the threshold.

With a mind of their own, his feet took him up the path to

where his house once stood. The home he had built for Sarah. He sat beneath a tree and let the Bible fall open. The story of Abram and Sarai stared back. Beginning with chapter twelve, he began to read. Eventually his eyes grew tired and he closed them, letting the book rest open on his chest.

He could still hear the story in his mind, but as he listened, he saw his Sarah instead of Sarai, and himself instead of Abram. And instead of walking through a desert, they climbed aboard a ship with their nephew, Samuel.

> Go forth from your country, and from your
>> father's house, to the land which I will show
>> you; And I will make you a great nation, and
>> I will bless you, and make your name great;
>> And so you will be a blessing; and I will bless
>> those who bless you and the one who curses
>> you I will curse. And in you all the families
>> of the earth shall be blessed. So Abram went
>> forth as the Lord had spoken…And Abram
>> took Sarai his wife and Lot his nephew, and
>> all their possessions which they had
>> accumulated, and the persons which they
>> had acquired in Haran, and they set out for
>> the land of Canaan: thus they came to the
>> land of Canaan… And the Lord appeared to
>> Abram and said, "To your descendants I will
>> give this land." So, he built an altar there to
>> the Lord who had appeared to him.

The wind blew the pages of the book, losing his place, but bringing a refreshing touch to his face.

Plop. He opened his eyes as a drop of rain splashed on his forehead. A clap of thunder sounded, so Joseph closed the Bible and ran for the Fontaine house.

All through the evening meal, the words of the Scripture

floated through his brain. Sarah had to ask him twice to pass the butter dish.

The more he thought about it, the crazier he felt, but then, how else was he to learn the counsel of the Lord?

When it was time to retire, Sarah showed him to their room. As he prepared to make a pallet on the floor, she laughed. "Ye've been so worried that I would be with child again that ye withheld yerself. But now that I am with child, what is there to fear?"

What indeed?

He joined in her laughter and took her in his arms. His soul felt at peace and his body, alive.

Oh, how he had missed his Sarah.

THEY LAY CUDDLED TOGETHER IN THE EARLY-MORNING light. She rested her head on his arm, hoping he was home to stay. "Joseph?"

"Mm?"

"Have ye decided about the ship?"

"I'm as sure as I know how to be." His finger traced the edge of her jaw.

"And what is yer decision?" Sarah closed her eyes and held her breath.

"We will go as a family."

She hugged him close.

"I don't know if I can trust God, but I am trying so hard. I want to, but I'm doing it a step at a time. I know He has orchestrated this. Too much has happened for me not to have seen His hand. But trusting Him is a different matter. I believe He has called us to go together. But my fear is not gone."

She nodded into his shoulder. If needed, she would trust God for both of them.

By the time they were back at Edenmore, Joseph faced the onslaught of every adult family member. The one thing they agreed on—he was out of his mind. He couldn't argue, he wondered if he'd gone mad too. How could he allow Sarah to go? All he could do was remember the Scripture. It was his confirmation and he would trust to the best of his ability.

James pointed out that none of the passages would be refunded (though an extra had been added for Bridget to accompany the group) and another ship wouldn't try the crossing for several months. This was the moment, and everything rested with them now making this venture work. Somehow that stopped the arguing.

Riding with them to Derry, James used the time to be with Samuel.

"I'm fine, Da. You don't have to worry about me." Standing taller than most seven-year-olds, Samuel had a presence greater than his years.

"I know you are, son. I think it is my problem. I'm not ready to see you go off. You've grown up so big and strong. I know I can trust you…" James pulled his son into his arms. "Samuel, you are my son and I love you. Always remember that."

Samuel nodded, blinking hard.

Joseph, watching the exchange, was heartbroken for his brother. Pulling James into an embrace he whispered, "Don't worry. I will take care of him. It will be well."

James pulled back, took from his pocket a gold coin and gave it to Samuel. "Hold onto it, son. This is your money for the land. I know you will do well." He hugged the boy once more and left, pushing through the crowd and out of sight.

Samuel stared after his father's back.

Joseph pulled the boy to his side. "Put that in a safe place, Samuel. You don't want to be letting others see it."

Glad to see Samuel obey, Joseph grasped Wee Joseph by his hand and guided the boys along. Bridget carried Wee John as she walked beside Sarah up the gangplank. Robert met them at the top and showed them where they would all travel together.

It helped to see how Sarah and Rachel, Robert's new bride, quickly bonded. Raven-haired Rachel's grandmother was Joseph's father's sister. She and her second husband had also escaped from France for the same reasons but had settled in London. At Antoine's urging, Robert had looked up the family on one of his trips and immediately fell in love with Rachel.

The voyage also gave Joseph back what he had lost in time with Sarah. He enjoyed walking the deck in the afternoon, arm in arm, before she went to rest below.

"Joseph, I've something to tell you I never thought I would." They were on the port side, just after a short rainfall.

"What's that, love?"

"I made a promise that I had to keep."

"To whom?" He only half listened. Her hair sparkled from the sunlight's glints, and he simply enjoyed hearing her voice.

"To Kathleen."

Something in the way she said "Kathleen" gave him pause. "Tell me."

And she did. She told him everything, including how she had been afraid if he knew, he wouldn't trust her love for him.

"But that was the one thing I could trust, Sarah. You were always honest with me."

"Not exactly. I didn't tell you my part in Shannon and Alain-Robert's deaths."

He didn't know what that could be. He'd never known Sarah to even hurt a fly, in spite of her infamous temper. A temper in which he found a perverse joy, as long as it wasn't directed at him. Her eyes flashed like emeralds and her posture quite nicely showed off her curves.

"Ye aren't listening, Joseph, and this is important."

"I'm sorry, I am listening, though I can't imagine you having done anything hurtful."

But he could tell she felt like she had. When she had finished, she asked him to forgive her.

Joseph drew her close, feeling the baby kick between them. "I forgive you for you ask me to, but I don't think there is anything to forgive."

"Shannon said that, too, but I know what I did. I asked her forgiveness, and God's as well. But I knew I had to ask yours, Joseph."

The baby kicked again.

Sarah held his arm tighter.

"Are you all right?" In spite of daily putting his trust in God, Joseph's fear rose each time he knew Sarah felt a pang or twinge.

"Joseph, please trust Him. He has made our way clear. He holds us in His hand, and nothing can separate us from His love."

"Dear heart, I am trying. I want to trust. But trusting with the baby and you and this ship and…I want to trust."

Sarah turned, reaching to embrace him, but stopped. "Joseph. Turn around. Look." She pointed over his shoulder.

He moved, following her finger's direction. There on the horizon shone a double rainbow. The most bright and clear rainbow he'd ever seen. Its beauty beyond his description.

"Oh, Joseph. See. See how God keeps His promises. Hold tight to your faith, Joseph. Hold tight to your trust in God. Let go of all else. Fall into His hand, Joseph."

Moving behind her, he wrapped his arms about her, feeling the baby's movement. She leaned into him, and he whispered in her ear. "Pray for me, Sarah. I am doing my best."

IT CAME AS NO SURPRISE FOR SARAH WHEN SHE LEARNED OF the possible storm on the horizon. She could feel the difference with the way the baby moved. She rested on their berth in the passenger hold.

"Me mother used to say that storms brought the labor, but the pain brought the sun." Wee John lay on Bridget's lap fighting a nap.

"I wouldn't be surprised to find she's correct about that, Bridget." Sarah rubbed her hands over her swollen belly. It felt as if the baby pressed down, and she knew there was more room between her breasts and her abdomen. "I think I need to walk about some."

"Shall I go with ye?" Bridget stood, plopping the baby on her hip.

"No, stay here with the wee ones. Perhaps I'll see if Rachel is available. Joseph is out on deck, but I think she just finished washing the clothes."

"Methinks that is what brought the storm." Bridget winked at Sarah, laughing at her own joke.

Sarah smiled, but in truth, she was concerned at how the pressure was building inside her. They were only a few days from land.

As she waddled to the stairs, she held her stomach. "Could ye not wait two more days, child?" The kick she received in her ribs answered her question.

Rachel was nowhere in sight, but Joseph waved in her direction. As he walked to her, she suddenly felt the pressure increase. She grabbed at a post for support as a warmth trickled down her legs.

He rushed to her side. "Sarah, what is it? Is it the baby?"

She nodded, and when he leaned in, she whispered, "I've broke me waters."

He scooped her up in his arms and carried her below to her bunk. "Bridget, find Rachel for me. Tell her to come now."

Samuel came over, tiny worry lines forming between his brows. He reminded her of James in that moment. "Tanté Sarah, are you all right?"

She tried to nod, but her first real pain came, and she cried out. Joseph gripped her hand, and she squeezed.

Samuel nervously fiddled with something in his fingers and backed away. Joseph turned to see him. "Put that away before you lose it. Go keep watch over Wee Joseph."

As the pain eased, Sarah caught her breath. "Joseph, don't be so hard on the boy. He's scared."

"He isn't the only one scared." He put her fingers to his lips. "I am ready to do whatever you need me to do, love."

The roll of the ship increased, and a sudden swell loudly splashed overhead. They could feel the ship rise up to the wave's crest and then all at once drop.

Bridget, holding Wee John, returned with Rachel, who drew a curtain around the bunk before raising Sarah's skirt.

"Do you know what you are doing, Rachel?" Joseph's free hand combed through his hair while his eyes darted from Sarah to Rachel.

"I helped my mother when she gave birth to twins in a storm." She spoke while checking Sarah's condition. "We couldn't get anyone to the house, so I was all my mother had. I was only fourteen. Made me not want to have children for quite some time." Rachel laughed.

Sarah knew she was trying to put her at ease. However, Joseph's grip tightened. *Oh Lord, help him put his trust in You.*

Rachel touched Joseph's shoulder. "Joseph, I think I might have more room if you stepped outside the curtain."

"No, I'll just move a bit for you." Joseph scooted next to Sarah's head, never letting go of her hand.

Another wave of pain came, just as another swell lifted the ship and dropped it. Rain began to pelt harder overhead, and a sudden crack of thunder sounded ominous.

The tightness about her belly relaxed. She could hear footsteps rumbling down the steps and running to their area.

Robert called from the other side of the curtain. "Joseph, the captain's called for all able men up on top. You need to come."

"No! I can't leave her. She needs me here."

"Joseph, we need you up there."

"No!"

"Joseph…" Robert stammered. Sarah could hear he didn't want to say something. "Joseph, if we don't get enough help, we will lose this ship."

"Go, Joseph. I'll be fine. Trust God. I do. Go, my love."

"Sarah?"

She squeezed his hand. "Go, Joseph. Do what God needs ye to do."

Unbending to his full height, he took a step back. His gaze traveled to their hands.

Sarah pulled his hand to her face, rubbing her cheek against it for an instant.

Then she let him go.

◌◌◌

JOSEPH HAD NO IDEA HOW HE GOT ON DECK, HIS MIND TOO much on Sarah and his anger at God for putting him in this position. He blocked out all else. However, once on deck, slippery dangers grabbed his attention.

A ship's mate shoved several rope coils at him and told him to start making thing's secure. He pointed to a cache of barrels before sliding to do something else. Joseph wiped water from his face and slipped one rope from his shoulder. Just as he got the rope around the cache, a wave splashed over, pushing a barrel free. It slid across the slick boards and smashed into Joseph's fingers.

With an intake of breath, he shook them. He rose to his feet and shouted over the crashing waves to the sky. "Why? Why, when I am starting to trust, do You remove every reason to trust? Why? Couldn't the baby have waited until we were safely at port? And this storm, why tonight? Why can I not be at Sarah's side? Why? Where is Your answer God?"

The thunder's low rumble grew in intensity. Lightning split the sky in half.

In the flash of light, Joseph saw Samuel step out onto the deck. The thunder rumbled again. The boy jumped. The next flash illuminated the glow of something shiny bouncing onto the flooded deck.

Save him.

Joseph didn't know where the words came from, but as if pushed from behind, the boy fell and started sliding helplessly toward the edge.

Rope.

Without understanding, Joseph tossed the end of the rope to Samuel. Somehow he saw it and grabbed for it, latching on just as a wave washed him over.

"Samuel!" Joseph clung to his end, coiling the rope over his arm. There still was weight to it. He knew Samuel held on.

Robert came from starboard, holding the rail. He'd tied a rope about his waist and attached it to the rail. "Pull, Joseph."

The rope remained taut as Joseph worked his way closer to the side.

Robert reached over and grabbed Samuel by the breeches, pulling him back on deck.

Joseph grabbed the child into his arms, holding him secure.

Samuel, coughing and sputtering, held on.

The wind's fury died out, and the rain softened to a light drizzle. Joseph chuckled.

Samuel pulled back and stared at him, and then at Robert, who shrugged. Then back to Joseph who now broke into a full roar.

Joseph laughed harder, bewildered stares on Samuel and Robert's faces. "God is good. And He answers prayers. I asked Him why I had to be on deck and away from Sarah. He lit up the sky and showed me you, Samuel. You." Joseph pulled the boy to him. "I don't know why you were up here, but God kept you safe."

Samuel raised his head. "I heard them ask for all able-bodied men to come help."

Joseph exchanged a look with Robert before he put a finger under Samuel's chin, staring him in the eye. "You are as able-bodied as anyone, Samuel, and you are being trusted with a man's job, but please, next time, ask."

Samuel buried his face in his uncle's chest and nodded.

Already the sky had lightened. The captain came around and motioned for them to go below.

Joseph's fingers curled about the handle that opened the hatch to the stairs, but hesitated. What would he find?

Trust Me.

He closed his eyes, breathed in deeply, and pulled open the hatch.

A baby's cry filled the air.

Jumping to the bottom of the stairs, he ran to Sarah's side. An angry bundle with red hair waved a fist at him.

"Sarah?"

"Joseph, would ye like to meet yer son? I don't think he liked the weather's reception."

He kissed the newborn, then leaned over and received a proper kiss from the lad's mother.

Epilogue

The ship moored two days later at New Rochelle. Sunshine glinted off the Hudson River, reflecting tiny rainbows in the puddles along the rail. Simple reminders.

Sarah, growing stronger, held their newest Crockett—William—while she sat on a trunk. Bridget carried Wee John and Samuel held Wee Joseph's hand. The baggage sat on the deck. All the family needed was the opportunity to disembark.

Joseph, having received all needed information from the captain, surveyed his family in wonderment. What had his father called life?

Remarkable.

That was the word, remarkable. And, like Abram and Sarai of old, he and Sarah were here to start a new life, in a new land.

With a new dependence on the God of Abraham. The God of his father. His God in Whom he placed his trust.

Sarah motioned to him.

He came to her side.

"Are we ready?" Her eyes shone with the gentleness of a new mother, yet he knew the fire in her heart lay ready for this New World.

"Yes, my love, we are ready." He took the now sleeping William from her and helped her to her feet.

She placed her hand at the crook of his elbow, and together they walked down the gangplank to their new home.

Cast of Characters

Bold denotes a mentioned historical figure. Italics denotes fictional characters.

- 1. **Joseph Louis Crockett, Sr.**
- 2. **Antione Crockett**
- 3. **Louise Crockett**
- 4. **the Reverend Jacques Fontaine**
- 5. **Joseph Louis Crockett, Jr. (Wee Joseph)**
- 6. **Sarah Stewart**
- 7. **Robert Crockett**
- 8. **Thomas Stewart**
- 9. **Gabriel Crockett**
- 10. **James Crockett**
- 11. **Sarah Elizabeth Crockett (Sarah Beth)**
- 12. **Louise DuSaix Crockett (Lucy)**
- 13. **Mary Frances Crockett**
- 14. **Samuel Crockett**
- 15. **Albert de Grillet**
- 16. **Alain-Robert de Grillet**
- 17. **Anne Fontaine**
- 18. **The Knox family**

- **19. Grinling Gibbons**
- **20. Thomas Stewart Crockett**
- **21. John Crockett**
- **22. Elizabeth Fontaine**
- **23. James Fontaine**
- **24. Moses Fontaine**
- **25. John McLiney**
- **26. Paul Roussier**
- **27. Claude Bonnet**
- **28. Rachel Watkins**
- **29. Martha Crockett**
- *30. Kathleen Crockett*
- *31. Mimi Roché de Grillet*
- *32. Josephine LeSuere*
- *33. Cullen O'Keefe*
- *34. Christopher Dougherty*
- *35. Margaret (Meg) Stewart*
- *36. Ian MacKenzie*
- *37. The Widow Shannon O'Connor*
- *38. Bridget*
- *39. Paddy Flanagan*
- *40. Michael O'Toole*
- *41. Cameron McHugh*
- *42. Kevin O'Rourke*
- *43. Seamus Flaherty*
- *44. The sheriff*
- *45. Matthew (O'Keefe nephew)*
- *46. Gwendolyn Stewart (aunt)*
- *47. Aaron Murphy*
- *48. Liam O'Toole*
- *49. Mary O'Toole*
- *50. Jacob Sullivan*
- *51. Donovan Cummins*
- *52. Patrick Flanagan*
- *53. Calhoun (guard)*

- *54. MacDonald (guard)*
- *55. Fitzhugh (guard)*
- *56. Captain McFain*
- *57. Mistress Doyle*
- *58. Jean-Luc de Turenne*
- *59. Daniel McHugh*
- *60. Agnes Crockett*
- *61. Adam Crockett*

Afterword

Thank you for continuing this journey. This is another story that has been on my heart for a long time. I first traveled to Ireland back in March 2005. I stood in the ruins of Rath Mullin, where Joseph and Sarah were married. I wandered what was left of Balleylawn, finding parts of the tower house that dated back to when Sarah lived there. I even met a "long-lost" cousin, Robert Crockett, who had named his youngest son Davy.

So, once again, many of the characters in this book really lived and are set in the correct time and place. The rest is my imagination, still running amok. One thing to note, among those historical figures, there were several with the same or similar names. It can get confusing, so I gave out nicknames (Lucy, Sarah Beth, etc.). I've often wondered what they really did back then when so many had the same name? Hope my nicknames helped you keep them straight in your mind!

Jacques and Anne de Fontaine's experiences with the French corsairs and that dream story about his sons are taken from his memoirs. When possible, I used their own words to share what was happening. Their non-wavering faith didn't need a lot of embellishment from me. Again, I thank them. You can find these and other firsthand stories at http://garnet.acns.fsu.edu/~rbr3325/fontainemaury-home.html.

Please note that the character of Kathleen is totally fictitious. As far as I know, Sarah is the one who gave birth to "Wee Joseph." And as for Wee Thomas, it depends where you look. Since I first started this story, ancestry research has boomed. There are so many places that list multiple outcomes, so I went with what I first found: that he had died at birth. Also, Sarah's mother's name has been debated on the ancestry sites, so I went with one I liked. Because of that, I'm putting her under the fictional characters on the list, not because Sarah didn't have a mother, but because I basically made her up, name, personality, and all. And, of course, I have no proof that Wee John was a foundling nor any that says Samuel wasn't James's son. All that is fictitious as well.

Please keep in mind, this story is fiction *loosely* based on history. In the end, it is not for a history class or even for charting out ancestry. It is merely one over-imaginative story-teller's possible version with a lot of license.

And so, thank you once more for reading *The Sojourners*. Until we meet again, this time on the pages of *The Prodigal*…

Abundant blessings,

Jenny

If you enjoyed this book, please leave a review. Reviews can be as simple as "I couldn't put it down. I can't wait for the next one" and help raise the author's visibility and lets other readers find her.

Acknowledgments

Again, I thank You, Lord, first and always. I am still amazed that my fingers type what they do and I know it is because of You, the best Storyteller ever. You are still faithful to a thousand generations.

To my friend and mentor, Esther Bailey—thank you for believing in me, encouraging me and editing me. You are the true meaning of a Godsend.

To Debbie Atkinson, Wanda Chiles, Kimberly Alexander, and Donna Miller who continued to ask for another book —thank you!

To North Hills Book Club—thank you for reading and responding. You helped shape this story.

To Liz Tolzma—thank you for your friendship and wonderful editing.

To "my friend Jen," Jennifer Crosswhite—I couldn't do this without you. I still think you are amazing!

To Jacques de Fountaine—again I say thank you for your forethought and for passing the torch. Here you are in my second book!

To my family, I love you all!

To my sweet husband who has taught me the meaning of trust, I love you.

And to my EB—I still miss you.

Reader's Guide

1. After reading *The Patriarch*, did you wonder about
   how the Crockett family made it to the colonies?
   What about their journey surprised you in *The
   Sojourners*?
2. What previous knowledge do you have of the
   Huguenot settlements in Ireland and in the colonies?
   Has this had an effect on the story as you read?
   How? In what way?
3. What previous knowledge do you have of
   seventeenth century Ireland? How has this effected
   the story for you as you read? What if anything has
   changed since this time period as far as political
   relations go?
4. Joseph took drastic measures to ensure Sarah's safety.
   Would you call him selfish or selfless or foolish?
   Why?
5. Sarah had been given all the comforts her father's
   position could afford. Do you think she was
   manipulative? Spoiled? Or Clueless? Have you

known someone like her? What seemed to get through to him/her?

6. There are many who have not only researched their background but have done DNA testing to find out more about their ethnicity. Have you? Why or why not? If you have, have you ever visited a place where your ancestors lived? How did it feel?

7. Pirates and corsairs were common during this time. Movies and media have romanticized this. Jacques Fontaine's version isn't so romantic. Did it change your perspective to know that part of the story was actually a firsthand account?

8. British laws on Ireland's commerce and inheritance caused a large exodus over the years. Comparing this to the persecution of the Huguenots from France, what are some of the same results? What is different?

9. What is the one thing you hope to find out about in the next book, *The Prodigal*?

10. What part of the story would you have changed? What was your favorite part?

About the Author

Jennifer Lynn Cary is a direct descendent of Davy Crockett making Antoine and Louise her ancestors as well. A retired elementary teacher, she resides in Arizona with her husband where they enjoy family time with two more generations in the Crockett linage.

You can find her at www.jenniferlynncary.com

facebook.com/authorjenniferlynncary

Sneak Peek of The Prodigal: The Crockett Chronicles Book 3

Beaufort, North Carolina ~ 1730

"Willie!" The voice called from behind.

William increased his pace. Not now, please, not now.

"Willie! Mama says you are to help me!" Five minutes, he only needed five minutes.

The voice now panted. He really should stop, but William strode faster toward the summit.

"Willie, please wait for me!"

His conscience poked him, but his goal was in sight. He could not hold back. He needed this moment, the briefest of solitudes to take in what is soul craved.

Finally, at the top of the bluff, the panorama of the shore opened. The ocean's breeze smacked him in the face, and he smiled from the inside out. This is what he needed, what he'd missed. The scents, the atmosphere, it all fed him as he closed his eyes and stretched out his arms, embracing everything. He could feel the currents, ride the waves, soar the blue while the wind caressed his cheeks. In all his almost twenty years, this was the one thing that calmed the storms raging inside him. He inhaled one last breath of freedom when he felt the tug on his breeches.

"Willie, why didn't you wait? Didn't you hear me?"

William opened one eye and glanced down.

His youngest sister held on to him while gasping for breath. "Oh, Willie, I'm going to tell Mama!"

He scooped her up in his arms, though she was getting too big for him to do that anymore. "Aw, Janie, you don't want to tell Mama. See!" He pointed to the bay. "See all the ships? All the goods coming in? I'll bet Mama has something special for us before the day is out. That will make her happy. You wouldn't want to spoil that, would you?"

Sarah Jane's forehead squished into thinking wrinkles. She shook her head. "I guess not. But why wouldn't you wait for me?"

William hugged her and set her back on her feet. "I needed an alone moment, Janie. That's all." He couldn't help the sigh that followed his admission.

She seemed to accept his explanation because she dropped the subject and grabbed his hand. "So, will you help me with my sums, then?" Her earnest face reminded him how much he had missed this little pest.

He stole one more glance at his ocean before swinging her hand. "Sure."

Leading her to a sweet gum tree, standing tall in a lonely spot near the cliff's edge, they sat beneath its shade and cracked open the book Sarah Jane had lugged along. "Where are you having trouble?"

"Mama says I need to practice carrying over. She says I forget to add that in." She squinched up her mouth and gave him a sideways glance.

Now he understood why she was sent to him instead of one of his other many siblings—that was a lesson his mother managed to get him to understand when he was the same age as Janie—seven. Truth be told, he still imagined Mama's voice in his head when he tallied up sums. Willie, don't forget to include what you already have. He set the book aside and grabbed a twig from the ground, scratching number problems in the dirt. "Try this one, Janie. Talk it out so I can hear what you are thinking."

She took the twig from him, using it like a pointer. "Seven hundred and fifty-six—"

"Don't say the 'and,' Janie. It means something different if you say 'and'."

"Seven hundred FIFTY-six plus three hundred an..." she glanced at him, "I mean sixty-nine. I need to add the nine and six first."

He smiled and nodded, trying to stay focused, but hearing the call of the ocean's waves.

"That's fifteen so I write my five and put the one over the top of the five in the next column. Then I add five and six, oh, and the one. That's the same as six plus six, so I know that is twelve."

Now she smiled, acting pretty sure of herself. "I write the one and put the two up on top of the seven...?"

He wasn't sure if she made the mistake to see if he would catch her or if she really thought that. His instinct told him she knew what she was doing, so he kept his mouth shut, curious what she would do.

"What do you think, Willie?"

"You can figure it out. Give it a try."

She sighed and fixed the placement for the parts of the twelve. "Like this, the two goes into the answer and the one goes over the seven."

He smiled and nodded again. She was a manipulator with more than numbers. But she was tenderhearted to a fault. He pointed to the final column. "Finish it."

She did. "Seven plus three plus the one I carried over comes to... eleven." She added that to her answer. "So, seven hundred fifty-six plus three hundred sixty-nine equals one thousand, one hundred twenty-five, right?"

"Right you are, Janie." He gave her a wink. "Ready for another?"

Just as she nodded another voice called. "Sarah Jane, William. Mother wants you! Now!"

Fourteen-year-old brother Jason crowned the hill. He stopped before coming any closer than necessary. Fear of catching the infirmity that kept William forever in trouble with his parents was most likely what held him back. Oh, well. No need of Janie catching his disease. "You go on. I'll be along soon." He helped her. "You don't want to get in trouble along with me, Janie." He winked at her and sent her off with Jason.

As he turned, he spotted the arithmetic book still on the ground. "Oh, Janie girl, you are going to end up a black sheep like me." He bent to retrieve it when a small chunk of bark landed on the cover. He glanced up in the tree.

A rustle having nothing to do with the wind cut the leaves brought a smile, and he shook his head. Little sister Martha must have finished her studies early and scrambled up the tree so not to get roped into more chores. Still the tomboy at age ten, Martha preferred running and climbing to about anything else. His eight-year-old sister Mary, on the other hand, would be too prissy to climb, but Martha didn't know the definition of prissy. "Time to come down, now, Martha. I'll walk you home."

No answer. No movement. She would make this difficult.

"Come down, lass, before I must come after you."

"Ye wouldn't!"

That wasn't Martha's voice.

But it was a lovely voice. An intriguing voice. "So, you are not Martha. Who are you?"

"It be none of yer business who I am, so away with ye. Leave me be."

Rather than intimidate William, the voice sent funny little tingles through his soul. "I don't think I can do that."

"And why, pray tell? Do you mean me harm?"

Harm her? He wouldn't hurt a fly! "Oh! You cut me to the

quick, miss... whatever your name might be. I do not mean you harm. It's just that you have aroused my curiosity. It would delight me to make your acquaintance." He paused, searching for the best idea. "Shall I come up and join you on a branch or would you prefer to come down?"

Rather than a reply, the leaves again rustled. She made her decision. Soon shoes and legs dangled overhead and then a full person appeared, dropping to the ground at his feet. She rose to her full height, standing no taller than his breastbone, her raven hair slipping in soft wisps from beneath her mob cap. Her back skirts were pinned at her waist from where she had pulled them between her legs, so she untucked them. She smoothed out her clothes, transforming herself into a proper young lady of sixteen or seventeen years of age.

William held out his hand. "I am William Crockett, Willie to my sisters and brothers. With whom have I made the acquaintance?"

She placed her hand in his and made a small curtsy. "My— BEE!" In one motion she pulled her hand from his and flipped her apron over her head.

William couldn't stop the laugh that burst from him. "Maybe? Your name is Maybe?"

Indignation seeped through her linen apron, dripping chagrin all over him, even before she pulled the cloth from her face.

He stopped laughing.

"Is it gone?"

"Is what gone?"

"The bee! Oh, they terrify me! Please tell me it's gone!"

He glanced about. So that's what scared her. "I'm sorry. Yes, it's gone. I didn't realize. Shall we start again?" He bowed. "I am William the Oaf Crockett, and you are?"

"My name is Elizabeth Boulay." She curtsied again and paused, then snickered. "You thought my name was Maybe?"

William snorted, and they laughed together. "I didn't know

what to think. Elizabeth is a pretty name, Miss Boulay, but I must confess, I prefer Maybe."

҉

Sarah continued to pump the treadle of her spinning wheel, tugging the wool into a thin, tight string. If Da could see her now. She shook her head, wondering what he might think of the fine lady he had wanted her to be. She wouldn't trade her life, this amazing life she'd spent with Joseph and their children, for all the emeralds in the world. But a house full of children in a settlement situated between the wilderness and the deep blue sea meant she worked hard. The whole family did. They needed to pull together.

Why didn't William see that?

Oh, her Willie boy. Now he was a young man and should be finishing up his studies at William and Mary. Joseph worked hard to get him into the university. But it was William's job to stay there until they graduated him. Not that it was easy for him, but it was necessary. He needed an education.

Instead, he pops in here last evening saying he was done with schooling. It was not for him. Oh, the look on Joseph's face!

"Mama, you will pump your spinning wheel to death!"

Sarah glanced into the concerned eyes of her daughter, Mary. "I'm sorry, darlin' girl. Had me head in the clouds, I reckon." She chuckled, slowing the wheel as she did. "Now I know where your sister gets it." She leaned over and tweaked the child's chin.

"More like where Willie gets it. He always seems to be wondering about something out there somewhere." Mary wrinkled her nose as though "out there" was not a pleasant place.

She chuckled and found a stopping spot before going to the fireplace. Using the tongs she pulled the kettle hanging from the hook out where she might stir and check for doneness. "Yer father will be home soon, with yer brother. Ye need to be helping set the table for dinner."

"Yes, Mama. Shall I set places for Joseph Louis and Jeanne?"

Sarah shook her head just as William burst through the door. "I dinna think it took that long to follow yer brother and sister home."

He brushed a kiss on her cheek. "I'm a grown man now, Mama. Sometimes I need to be about manly things."

"You are a man when you show us you can behave as one and not go gallivanting around when you should be working with your father." She sounded sterner than she meant to, but if she could smooth things before Joseph came home, it would be so much better.

His sigh didn't escape her notice. "Mama, all I wanted was a day or so to just breathe in freedom before getting tied down to responsibility all over again. Is that too much to ask?"

"That depends. Have you gotten yer breath of freedom now so ye can start working with yer father in the morning?"

He stared at the floor. She'd seen this before, when he felt blocked. "Yes, Mama."

She caressed his face. "It isn't a bad thing to be a responsible adult, ye know. Now, go get washed for dinner."

He turned and left, tossing a towel over his shoulder as he exited. Her miracle baby, born during a storm at sea. Something about the ocean called to him, louder than all the love and guidance she and Joseph could give.

When God blessed her with baby William, Sarah had promised God that she would be the best mother she could be. The red-faced, bellowing snippet of a thing with a down of strawberry hair captured her heart. Since that moment there were days where living with Willie amounted to living with a hurricane, but inside that storm beat a tender, loving heart that craved acceptance.

The sound of boots scraping caught Sarah's attention. She rehung the ladle just as Joseph entered, hanging the towel back by the door, followed by John and William. "Go call the others," she directed at Mary before greeting her husband with a warm embrace. "Dinner is ready to dip. I'm glad yer home."

Joseph returned her squeeze and placed a kiss on her cheek before getting out of her way. They knew each other's every move, and she knew that he knew that feeding their sizable, crazy family took maneuvering. In groups of two and three the rest of her children, those still living at home, found their way to the table—the large, family table Joseph had made for her when the family began to grow at a rapid rate. They had six sons, one she left in a grave in Ireland and another was still at William and Mary, where her William should be. The eldest, Joseph Louis was a married man so, though she longed to see all her children around the table, there was always someone missing. The bittersweetness of that thought made it difficult to be too upset with William when he filled his chair at mealtime.

Everyone stood until Joseph asked the blessing. Both William and Jason grabbed at her chair, vying for the honor of holding it for her. William won the skirmish. Jason pouted. She'd have to speak with him after dinner.

Once she was seated, the girls brought the food to the table and dinner was underway.

"Tell us about your day." Sarah hoped her request of her husband might spark a desire in her son to help his father.

"Like any other day, I imagine. Between working the field and carving on the rocker for Jeanne, it was another day. Joseph Louis gave me some help with the steamer and John worked on an order from Master Pratt." He paused and gave John a smile. "Oh, and I got the sideboard to the docks to sail back to Ireland. Should bring a pretty penny."

"That is wonderful. We had a lovely day of lessons. I think Janie is getting better at her sums." She winked at the child. "Mary, Lettie and Martha are getting on so well with multiplying and dividing, I think they will need a better teacher soon enough. Beth and Jason, suppose you share with us what you've been reading."

Jason opened his mouth, but before he got out a word, his father cleared his throat. He pouted again, glaring at his food. "Ladies first, Beth."

Beth hoped Jason would go first, and take so much time that they'd forget her. Sarah could not comprehend the crippling shyness that attacked her daughter at every turn—Sarah had never had a shy day in her life—but she felt the pain. Even now, Beth's head dipped, her quiet words falling onto her plate. "I read—"

"Speak up, girl, we all want to hear." Joseph meant it kindly, and his tone was gentle, but the words still bruised.

Beth cleared her throat. "I read Shakespeare's The Merchant of Venice." Her eyes began to search her plate as if something else captured her interest.

"What did you think of the story, Beth?"

"It… it made me cry." Again, her voice was soft. But as she raised her head, she began to quote from the play. "'The quality of mercy is not strained. It droppeth as the gentle rain from heaven upon the place beneath. It is twice blessed: It blesseth him that gives and him that takes. 'Tis mightiest in the mightiest. It becomes the thronèd monarch better than his crown. His scepter shows the force of temporal power, the attribute to awe and majesty wherein doth sit the dread and fear of kings, but mercy is above this sceptered sway. It is enthronèd in the hearts of kings. It is an attribute to God himself. And earthly power doth then show likest God's when mercy seasons justice.'"

"'Therefore, Jew, though justice be thy plea, consider this— that in the course of justice none of us should see salvation. We do pray for mercy, and that same prayer doth teach us all to render the deeds of mercy.'" William gave her a slow smile as he added to her monologue. "You did well, Beth."

"So did you, son. I am glad you remember that from your mother's lessons." Joseph smiled and Sarah's heart swelled a mite.

She spotted the silent nods between William and his father. Whatever happens, it will work out.

After dinner, Jason fetched water to heat for dish washing while the girls cleared the table. John hung the chairs up out of the way and pushed the table against the wall while Beth swept the floor. Joseph still marveled at how well Sarah got the children to help. They all knew what to do, no one begged off, and quicker than he ever imagined they set the room in order. He had an inkling she had learned this from Anne Fontaine over in Bantry Bay. That was a forever ago. Yet her eyes still flashed like emeralds when their gazes locked, just as they had back then. She still stood tall and lithe and her auburn mane still thrilled him when she let it down to brush. He longed to watch her brush it all day. Even after all these years. Even after all their children.

Joseph found his heart mellowing with his thoughts. He wouldn't be as strict as he should with William.

He wondered why the boy was home. James was still there, or at least he was according to Willie. What made him leave his younger brother and come home? He had an idea. Should he demand to know? Should he send him back straightaway? Should he let William find his own path? If he ever needed wisdom, it was now.

"Willie, let's go for a walk." Hopefully that wouldn't make the boy too defensive. He didn't want to ignite that short fuse.

"Sure, Da." William stood, and Joseph was taken with how tall he'd grown. Even more since being away. He held the door open for his father.

Joseph nodded, grabbing his hat from the peg by the door as he passed. William followed, pulling the door shut.

They walked, Joseph waiting for his son to say the first word. Back home in Ireland they would have walked to the River Foyle. Here, it was safer not to venture too far into the wilderness. The docks were a busy place with the recent arrivals, so he headed in the direction of the center of Beaufort.

Once at the Commons, he found a tree with a good-sized

rock near its base. He could sit on that and lean back, still waiting for William to speak.

Finally, after kicking at stones and scuffing his toes in the sod, the boy found his voice. "I suppose you'd be wanting to know why I came home."

Joseph nodded. "That might be the place to start."

William sighed and began to pace. "I'm just no good at this school stuff. I thought Mama had taught me enough to make it, but it is like they speak a strange language."

"You are not stupid. What seems to be the problem?" He was in no hurry to push the boy. If he could hold his tongue, William just might use his to explain it all.

"Well, I feel stupid. And it is so boring! All anyone does there is study. Read. Read. Read. No one takes a break, to see the town, or just live. I felt so... confined." He stopped pacing, meeting his father's gaze. "Da, I'm not cut out for classes or classics or antiquated philosophies. I've got to move and breathe and experience things. Da, I want to travel, to see places, not just hear about them. I get excited when ships pull in, imagining where they've been. I want to go to sea."

"You do not understand what you are asking, son." The words were out before he could stop them. The look on William's face told him he should have tried harder. "Son," He reached for him.

William pulled away. "You don't understand! I'm trapped here." He raised his hands, palms out, as is to push back any arguments. Turning on his heel, he left in the bluff's direction.

The place called to his son. He'd seen him up there, allowing the sea breeze to pour over him. It was better to let him go. At least he wasn't heading for the docks. Yet his heart told him Willie would head in that direction soon enough.

❧

William had promised himself he wouldn't lose his temper. And he knew his father tried to listen. What an ignoramus he was! He didn't give his father a chance. His father, who worked so hard to pay for him and James to attend William and Mary College. His father, who took care of his family, loving each of his children. His father, the man he admired and wanted to emulate.

"I am so daft!" He shouted to the wind. Of course, his father didn't understand. He was solid, strong. The protector. Craving freedom wasn't in his father's blood. Perhaps the storm that brought him from his mother's womb left him bewitched, for if ever there was a person to embody a mix of thunder, lightning and wind, that person was he. And right now, the storm within raged beyond his control.

⁂

Elizabeth slipped in the back door, snatching a leftover biscuit on her way past the larder. To sleep outside wasn't a safe idea. As far from the center of town as they were, an Indian kidnapping or worse was still a possibility. If she chose closer to town, there were sailors to consider.

Yet, none of that was more dangerous than what she faced in her own home.

Or rather, her stepfather's home, as he often corrected.

She made sure the house remained clean, that he had food, and worked to accomplish those things while he slept or went out. Other than that, she gave him a wide berth. If he'd been to the tavern, there was no telling the condition he'd be on his return. He might stagger in and collapse into a deep slumber for enough hours to give Elizabeth time to sleep. Or he might come back angry that someone bested him at cards. Then he was more likely to take out his anger on her—with his fists or a leather strop. And then there were the times he claimed he was lonely, now that her mother had gone. Elizabeth reminded herself that her mother hadn't abandoned her to this. She had died. Unexpectedly. Her leaving seemed to unlock a door for her husband, a door that led to Elizabeth's bedroom.

After waking to find him standing over her one night, Elizabeth had added a bolt. Still, she never felt safe.

"Lizzy? Dat you girl?"

A chill slithered up Elizabeth's spine. "What do ye want?"

"C'mere, girl. I need yer 'elp."

Elizabeth took one, then two steps toward the front room.

"Get in 'ere, ya trollop."

She inhaled and stepped into the room.

He'd slid down the wall to land on the floor. It appeared he was part drunk and part pummeled senseless. His eyes were bruised, swollen. The right side of his mouth bulged. A trickle of blood ran from the corner, down his chin. When he parted his lips to call again, she spotted a new bloody gap where he once had teeth. "There ye be." His nose wrinkled, as if he were trying to squint his eyes but the swelling refused to cooperate. "Lizzie, need a drink."

She brought him a whiskey bottle, he snatched it with his left hand. She jumped back. That was when she noticed his right arm's strange angle.

He bit out the cork and spit it onto the floor before taking a giant slug.

"Yer arm, 'tis broken."

"Ye, dear girl, are a master of ob-ser-VA-shun, that ye are. Me arm's broke. Ye need to set it for me."

Had he lost his mind? What could he be thinking? "I know nothin' of settin' broken bones. I will get the bone-setter." She turned toward the front door, the one she noticed stood wide open.

"No!"

Freezing her step, she turned to him. "Ye need more help than I can give ye. I won't be long." Her heart tendered a smidge as she knew he suffered.

"No," He hung his head. "There's n'money ta pay. Nuthin'

left." He took a breath, raised his head, and tried to focus on her face. "Ye haveta do it, Lizzie." He tossed back another drink, his Adam's apple bobbing as he chugged.

She scanned the room for something sturdy for the setting. Perhaps a blown-off roof shingle courtesy of the last storm? Then she spotted it. Draped across the chipped basin in the corner. His strop. It would have to do—at least it wouldn't be used on her if it was holding his arm together. She added a stick from the fireplace that had yet to burn and found an old linen sheet of her mother's, and at last dumped her supplies on the table. A quick prayer might be in order, though it seemed hypocritical. Useless, although she thought *help me*!

She would have to get close enough to touch him. Goose pimples raced up her arms and her stomach twisted. But despite the bile at the back of her throat, she inched closer to look. "I need to be cuttin' away yer sleeve." She wouldn't call him Da, even now.

"Then be doinit." He slurred worse, except for the curses he muttered under his breath. Those were all too distinct.

"The knife be in the other room. One moment." She hopped up to get it.

"Lizzie, ye won't b'leavin'me lie this, will ya?" A tear made a track down his cheek to mingle in the blood pooled at his lip.

The thought had crossed her mind. Walk out the back door, never return. But who could do that? "I won't be but a stitch." She even offered a small smile, hoping he'd believe her.

The knife lay hidden at the back of the larder. Why leave an extra knife where he could get it? She pulled it from its hiding place and returned to the front room. "See, only an instant. Now, I'll check yer arm."

She cut the tattered cloth away as gently as she could.

He still moaned and finished the whiskey, letting the bottle fall to his side.

The bone was broken but had not punctured the skin. Her stepfather passed out before she could give him the stick to bite.

She tore off a section of the sheet and then tore that into strips, binding them about his arm, working the two parts of the bone together. The next thing to do was to wrap the strop about to give body and support, keeping the bones from pulling apart. She added the stick, since it wasn't between his teeth, at the base of his forearm between the cloth and the strop. Once done, she fashioned a sling from the leftover linen.

There was no moving the man. He was much taller than she and weighed at least fifteen stones. So, she got bedclothes from his room and tucked the pillow behind him. The motion caused a paper to fall from his pocket. She placed it into her apron waist and draped the cover over him. He was out for the night. If God were smiling, a good portion of tomorrow, too.

She closed and bolted the front door, gathered a candle, extinguish the others and made the back door secure before climbing the stairs to her room. The bolt slid into place, though she had little to fear tonight. She sat on the edge of her bed, stymied at the troubles her stepfather could find. The paper at her waist rustled, reminding her of its presence. Any bill needed to go through her, or it would most likely be lost or forgotten. She pulled the scrap free and unfolded the piece, reading the quill scratches. A bill of sale.

One girl, seventeen years of age, four and a half stones. Sold to Eleazar Ferguson in lieu of the thirty-pound debt. Delivery expected the twentieth of May in the year of our Lord Seventeen Thirty. Debt paid in full upon delivery of girl.

Sold to Eleazar Ferguson?

An icy wave poured over her. Elizabeth's hands shook. The paper fluttered to the floor.

Her stepfather had sold her.

To order *The Prodigal*, click here: https://www.amazon.com/dp/B0813W2GQL